CW00520328

A Schoolmaster's
Tale

ABOUT THE AUTHOR

Alun D. W. Owen spent his working life teaching English, first in a technical college, then a boys' grammar school, and finally as head of department in a large 11-18 comprehensive school, of which he later became the deputy headmaster.

Growing up in rural mid-Wales during the 1940s, his first language was Welsh, and moving on to an all-English boys' grammar school aged eleven proved a daunting experience. But thanks largely to an inspiring English master, he discovered the joy of writing; and when he began winning essay prizes and featuring prominently in the school's magazine, he thought that one day he might be an author! Indeed, throughout his teaching career, he always enjoyed putting pen to paper, and fully intended realising his childhood dream when time permitted.

In 2000 he published a memoir, *A Montgomeryshire Youth*; in 2004-5, he translated from Welsh to English a large tome of local history, *Llanbrynmair in the Twentieth Century*; and now, his life-long ambition, this novel. In *A Schoolmaster's Tale*, the author draws heavily on his rich and varied experience both in the classroom and in management, and although, as implied by the title, the setting and the characters are fictitious, he tries to capture the reality behind the façade.

A Schoolmaster's Tale

ALUN D. W. OWEN

British Library Cataloguing-in-Publication Data
A catalogue record for this book is available from The
British Library
ISBN: 9798761633179

Cover illustration and design by
James Gainham

ACKNOWLEDGEMENTS

I am immensely grateful to the following for their support and encouragement in writing this novel:

My wife, Pam.
My daughter, Wendy.
My grandsons, Harry and James.
My friend, Michelle Knight-Gregson.

For Pam
With Love

CONTENTS

Chapter One

It was a bright Monday morning in April 1977 when Miss Martha Wolf, the Senior Administrative Officer at Netherbridge High School, put her head round the Headmaster's door, and whispered, "Sorry to disturb you, Mr Nobbs, but there's a parent outside who wants to speak to you rather urgently."

"Who the f--- is it now?" groaned Nobbs, as he rose from his resplendent leather armchair, while cunningly slipping the staffroom copy of *Autocar* beneath a pile of unread mail. "Isn't there a deputy available?"

"It's... Mr Gentle," continued Martha, with an ironic glint in her eye, "his daughter set fire to the toilets during the Christmas disco, remember?"

Nobbs nodded mechanically as he edged nervously towards the sanctuary of the adjoining bathroom.

"Mr Gentle's come about his son now," insisted Martha, "he claims Mr Fairclough assaulted him last Friday afternoon."

"Look... I've... simply *got* to pop in here. Tell him... tell him... oh, I'm sure you'll think of something, Martha," said Nobbs with his customary wink. Indeed, if truth be told, Martha Wolf did a great deal of Nobbs's thinking.

She paused briefly before returning slowly to her irate visitor in the foyer. "I'm sorry to have kept you, Mr Gentle, but unfortunately the Headmaster has just this minute been called away. If you would care to take a seat, I'll go and see if one of the deputy heads is free. Would you like a cup of tea or coffee while you're waiting?"

"Look, Miss whatever-your-name is!" exploded Gentle, "I didn't come here for tea and sympathy. If I can't see the Big Chief, what about this Fairclough then? Or 'as he buggered off too?"

Standing there, ram-rod straight in his ex-army leather jerkin, John Gentle looked more like an off-duty Guards sergeant major than a long-distance lorry-driver: six feet four of lean, steely-eyed resolve and the self-assurance of someone unaccustomed to being thwarted.

"I'm afraid Mr Fairclough has a class at the moment," said Martha, determined to retain her composure, "but in about fifteen minutes it will be morning break, and I'll try and get him to see you then."

"F------ marvellous, in't it!" exclaimed the giant Gentle, frustrated as much by Martha's unruffled demeanour as by the situation itself, "I should be half-way to Birmingham by now, not pissing about here with you lot. I'm telling you, I hope Fairclough's got a good explanation. I won't have no f------ teacher man-handling a kid of mine."

"I'll go and tell Mr Fairclough that you're waiting,"

replied Martha, relieved to escape from his towering menace.

She walked unhurriedly along the deserted main corridor, her elegant black skirt hugging her shapely thighs. As far as anyone knew, she had never married, but even now in her fifties, she still attracted admiring glances from sixth-form boys.

Opposite the newly refurbished Music Suite, from which emanated the dulcet tones of the Junior School Choir rehearsing *The Sheep Shall Safely Graze* for the New Intake Open Evening, she turned sharply left and began the long climb up to the top floor of the new Science Block. After knocking twice on the main Physics laboratory door, she opened it gently and entered almost unnoticed.

Small groups of pupils were huddled around each workbench, absorbed in their respective experiments, and although it was now nearly break-time, an atmosphere of intense concentration filled the room. But there was no sign of Mr Fairclough, until someone pointed him out to her in the far corner, dwarfed by a couple of sixth-form girls.

FRANK FAIRCLOUGH'S lack of physical stature had always been attributed to some childhood accident, the exact nature of which remained a mystery. Some said that he had fallen off the pillion of his father's motorcycle on the Isle of Man; others that he had been butted in the back by the family nanny goat. But Frank himself, while never denying any of these theories, was signally reticent on the subject. The fact was that he had been born with a genetic defect, which had stunted his growth and caused one leg to be much shorter than the other, so that even a heavily built-up boot could not conceal a pronounced limp.

Now in his mid-forties, he had long come to terms with his disability, even to the point of sometimes making jokes about it; and although generally regarded as a confirmed bachelor, and everyone's favourite uncle, he had recently been spotted in the company of a tall, attractive young lady some fifteen years his junior, and, in fact, an ex-pupil of his, newly returned from two years' VSO on the island of Tonga. Naturally, this sudden and belated liaison gave rise to some robust leg-pulling, all of which he took in good part, if not secretly relished.

Nowadays, he divided most of his spare time between his two abiding passions: restoring vintage motorcycles, an interest inherited from his father, Tom Fairclough, who had raced motorcycles professionally in the 1920s; and crown green bowling, a game he had been encouraged to play as a child. For his sixteenth birthday, his father had bought him the Charles Atlas "Dynamic Tension" body-building programme, and on discovering that his body was amenable to acquiring heavy muscle, he had joined a local weight-training club, which over a period of four or five years had not only transformed his physique but endued him with phenomenal strength, and much-needed self-confidence.

By his mid-twenties, he was considered in his home-town of Leigh in Lancashire to be as strong as three ordinary men, a reputation actually put to the test late one summer's evening on his way home along the Bridgewater Canal after a weight-training session. Two drunken hoodlums, contemporaries of his at St Thomas primary school, had seen him approach, and lain in wait behind a derelict shed some half way between Mather Lane and Butts Bridge. As he drew level, they sprang out, one of them jeering, "Well, if it's not old 'Op-along! Is thee leg no better, then?"

Frank, of course, had long grown used to such insults, and he had also learned that it was generally best to ignore them. But this time he had a strange feeling that things might be different – a bout of lingering jealousy towards a grammar school boy, perhaps, or some other perceived old score to settle. Nevertheless, smiling benignly as usual, he walked on, until a sudden blow to his left shoulder stopped him in his tracks. Turning slowly round, he noticed in the half-light an empty beer-bottle coming to rest on the towpath, and the two grinning dolts striding towards him menacingly. Clearly, this was no time for smiling.

"Show us thee muscles then, 'Oppy," scoffed the taller of the two, encouraged by his chum's audacity, but soon wishing he had kept his counsel. With a sudden lunge, Frank grabbed his arm, which in his iron grip felt like a girl's.

Springing to his defence, the other closed in, brandishing what looked like a large jack-knife. "Does thee want some o' this?" he screeched manically, "because if thee does, thee can."

Frank kept a close eye on the knife-wielding arm, and with a sudden feint managed to distract his opponent sufficiently to seize his wrist. A little gentle squeeze saw the knife drop, with both assailants then completely at his mercy.

"What the hell do you think you two are playing at?" asked Frank, looking up at both in turn, but not quite sure how to deal with the situation from there on. Should he frog-march them to the police station? The offence was certainly serious enough, even though it had probably started as a silly, drunken prank; and characters like that, he felt, should be taught a lesson. He kicked the knife into the canal, and then made as if to do the same with his attackers. He forced them to the murky water's edge, but in the end was too kind-hearted to carry it through. After a moment's deliberation, he could think of nothing more original to say than, "Pick on someone your own size next time, eh!" And with a playful shove, he sent them sheepishly on their way.

From a safe distance, he heard one of them yell, "Thee better watch out, 'Oppy... we'll f------ get thee for this!"

AFTER a disappointing set of Higher School Certificate results in 1949, Frank had taken a job as a laboratory assistant at the Atomic Energy Research Establishment in nearby Risley, where he was encouraged to continue his studies towards the Higher National Certificate at Bolton Technical College. On realising that the routine work expected of him in the laboratory was well beneath his abilities, his manager suggested that he apply for a sponsorship to do a BSc degree at King's College, London. In 1955, the company's faith in him was handsomely rewarded, when he won the 'King's Prize for Physics', followed by an invitation to read for a higher degree with a study into the effects of light on crystals. He had completed writing up his thesis by the Christmas of 1956, and was awarded a 'starred' MSc the following summer. Although a suitable post had been kept open for him at Risley, he had become disillusioned with the idea of a career in atomic research, and in a moment of wild speculation answered an advertisement in the *Times Educational Supplement* for the post of Physics Master at Netherbridge Grammar School. As Frank never tired of relating, his interview took place in the Refreshments Room near Platform 12 at Euston Station, where he had been invited to meet the School's distinguished Headmaster, Dr George Davenport, who, he had been informed, would be readily identifiable by the red carnation in the buttonhole of his black overcoat. The great man was in London for the day on Headmasters' Conference business, and felt doubly pleased for also having filled the Physics vacancy between afternoon tea at the Strand Lyons Corner House and catching the 7.05 evening train back to Manchester.

FRANK'S IGNORANCE of educational theory notwithstanding, he took to as soon as he had gone ing as if bred in the bone. Perhaps, his own experience of "those two impostors, triumph and disaster" had made him more forbearing and compassionate than most of his colleagues. Certainly, his background in industry, viewed with some suspicion at first by some of the senior masters, had earned him enormous respect among his pupils, as had his Vincent Black Shadow motor-cycle, whose deep-throated growl as it entered the school gates in the morning soon became as recognizable a signal for the start of school as the ten-to-nine bell.

But perhaps his most loyal following came from the after-school Weight-training Club. Barely a month into his first term at the School, he had prevailed on the Headmaster to purchase some weight-training equipment, which, he argued, would not only provide an alternative outlet for boys with little aptitude for ball games, but also improve the strength and fitness of regular team players and athletes.

Indeed, within a remarkably short time, Frank Fairclough had been accepted, both at the school and in the town as a worthy member of that time-honoured fraternity – the Grammar School. "Many people thought I took a bit of a gamble with young Fairclough," Dr Davenport was overheard to remark over a pint of Walker's Best at Netherbridge Cricket Club, "and I must confess I did wonder at first if I'd been a bit impulsive, but in here (pointing to his heart) I was pretty sure I was on to a good thing." And then in the next breath he sought confirmation of what had evidently been an inspired decision by asking his friend, Tom Molesworth, the owner of Molesworth Motors, and Chairman of the Netherbridge Old Boys' Association. "What do *you* think, Tom? Do you think I did the right thing? Or should I have left it to the Governors?"

"Look, George, I don't know why you're asking me. I know a bit about cars, but I don't know owt about education. In my humble opinion, and speaking now as a boss, I think it would be better if *you* did all the appointing." But it is doubtful if such reassurance in any way assuaged his endless self-questioning.

YOUNG FRANK's relaxed and friendly manner with the boys had also raised eyebrows amongst the 'old brigade', but he soon proved to be a stickler for rigour and discipline, especially, as he put it, "the best kind of discipline – self-discipline". Since he worked and played very hard himself, he expected his pupils to do likewise; and with the passing of the years, he acquired a reputation as a fearsome disciplinarian. For this reason alone, many parents and colleagues had secretly hoped that when Dr Davenport eventually hung up his gloves and mortar-board, the governors would have offered Frank the headship.

Even now, and under a very different regime, miscreants were often sent to Frank to be disciplined, rather than Nobbs. Indeed, in one of the latter's many addresses to the Staff he famously declared: "Telling students off, in my view, is not the function of a headmaster. On the contrary, I see it as an intrusion on time more properly devoted to whole-school matters such as forward planning and... creative management. Imagine Monty," he added, as if speaking of an old comrade-in-arms, "being personally encumbered with cases of insubordination in the Western Desert! And besides, from my experience, if lessons are properly prepared and delivered, indiscipline should hardly ever arise". In reality, the teachers would never send unruly pupils to Nobbs anyway, because it was well-known that he recorded such matters in their personal files and vindictively referred to them when writing job references.

Be that as it may, even after NGS had been merged with Manchester Road Secondary Modern to form Netherbridge High School (usually referred to by the pupils as "The Comp"), the mere suggestion of "being sent to Mr Fairclough" was sufficient threat to quell even the most fractious individual, though not apparently young Darren Gentle from 4C on the Friday afternoon in question.

This particular pupil's normally miniscule attention span was sorely tested during what teachers sometimes dub the "graveyard slot' — the last lesson of the week into which only an inept or inconsiderate time-table writer would even contemplate placing the compulsory R.E. lesson. Gentle *fils* had already formed the opinion that education was not something he was in dire need of, and especially *religious* education. Accordingly, asking him to read aloud the verse from Matthew, Chapter five, "If someone slaps you on the right cheek, turn and offer him your left" was perhaps unfortunate, if not provocative. Shortly, an unpleasant altercation erupted between him and the tall, statuesque R.E. lady, Mrs Mary McCarthy, who, though generally sweet-natured and forgiving, when crossed, had a street fighter's sense of fair play, which may have accounted for her sobriquet, 'Bloody Mary'.

"Bollocks!" exclaimed young Gentle, with his trademark grin and cocky glance over both shoulders, "I'm not reading that crap! Me Dad always says to stand up to bullies."

Shocked gasps and half-stifled giggles rippled around the room in anticipation of Mrs McCarthy's next move.

"How dare you speak disrespectfully of Holy Scripture! And besides, if I tell you to read something, you jolly well *will* read it."

"Will I f---!" sniggered Gentle under his breath to the lad sitting next to him.

"I beg your pardon," replied Mrs McCarthy.

"Right, Miss, if I come up to you, yeah, and give you a slap on the face, like me Ol' Man sometimes gives me Mam ... that's okay, is it?"

"You listen to me, young man! I don't have to argue

with you. But since you ask, no, it's not 'okay', as you put it. What goes on between your parents in their own home is not my business, but what happens in this classroom *is*. Do you understand? And before I'm tempted to give you a bit more than a slap on the cheek, perhaps you had better apologise for this appalling outburst of bad manners, or else you will have to answer to Mr Fairclough."

"Why? *I'm* not apologising... I done nothing wrong?"

"All right, if that's how you want to play it..." The powerful lady from County Donegal took a good hold of young Gentle's right ear, and dragged him squealing out of his desk as far as the classroom door. Then, still holding firmly on to her prey, she turned to the class, and said calmly, "Now then, 4C, we've had enough fun and games for one afternoon. This shouldn't take long. While I'm out of the room, you may talk quietly amongst yourselves. But there's to be no nonsense, do you hear? Donna, there's the chalk... write the names of any troublemakers on the blackboard, as usual."

And off she swept along the middle floor corridor, her hapless victim firmly in tow, past the Humanities suite, the Rural Science labs, and finally arriving at the Physics laboratory door. After peering briefly in through a side window, she knocked gently and entered, dragging her crimson-faced culprit right up to Frank Fairclough's slightly elevated demonstration bench.

"Right then, 5A," said Frank, almost as astonished as they, "there's a nice little problem on that at the bottom of page 68. Have a good look at it, while I look at this little problem I seem to have here. Another live specimen for my menagerie, Mrs McCarthy?"

Ever since anyone could remember, the window sills and work-tops all round Frank's laboratory had been covered with cages containing lost or injured animals – mice, gerbils, white rats, rabbits, guinea-pigs and so forth, brought in from time to time by parents and sometimes the masters, and looked after in the main by Frank himself helped by a succession of interested and reliable pupils. Dr Davenport himself used to help out sometimes during the school holidays, when Frank was away. However, when Nobbs became Headmaster, he had asked Frank more than once to get rid of them "on health grounds". Apparently, an officious parent, who worked at the County Public Health Department, had written to complain. Or at least that was Nobbs's explanation.

"Barely alive, I would say, Mr Fairclough, considering the fuss he made on the way up!"

"Oh, dear, and has Mrs McCarthy not been nice to you?" asked Frank, much to 5A's delight, their little problem on page 68 utterly up-staged by this unexpected Friday afternoon diversion. "I wonder what you did to upset her."

"Nothing," replied the boy defiantly.

"Really?" said Frank stepping back with pretended surprise, and then after a slight pause, "What's your name, sonny?"

"Darren."

"Darren what?"

"Darren Gentle.

"Darren Gentle what?

"Darren Gentle… sir."

"Good. Now then, Gentle, perhaps you can tell me what your problem is."

"*I* haven't got a problem."

"Oh? So why have you come here, then?"

"Because *she* dragged me... sir."

Frank cast an exaggerated scowl at the one or two characters in the class who were highly amused at the boy's nerve.

"Look, Darren," intervened Mrs McCarthy, "we haven't got all day. Shall *I* tell Mr Fairclough, or will you?"

"I'm not bothered."

"This boy, Mr Fairclough, was very rude and disrespectful in my lesson this afternoon. He refused to read, and swore at me. He also refused to apologise, because, according to him, he couldn't see what he'd done wrong."

"Thank you, Mrs McCarthy; I think I get the picture. Leave him with me," interrupted Frank. And to the boy, "You'd better go and sit over there, where I can see you." Then, turning nonchalantly to face the class, who had thoroughly enjoyed their intermission, "Ah, I nearly forgot. It's Friday, isn't it? And nobody reminded me... Friday night is homework night, isn't it, Eccles? Tell you what... those of you who've managed to solve that problem on page 68 are all excused. The rest of you... I'll have it in on Monday... I can't say fairer than that, can I?"

And before anyone could demur, the end of school bell clanged as if on cue.

"When... we're... ab-so-lute-ly... quiet... 5A," insisted Frank firmly, and then after a few moments' silence, added, "Girls... please stand... and now, lead on." And as the last girl left the room, "Boys, you may now stand… and… lead on."

When the last boy had left the room, Frank got down from his high chair behind the demonstration bench, and limped towards the stool where young Gentle remained sitting. A faint, contemptuous smile passed over his face, which Frank could not help noticing.

"Stand up, Gentle!" commanded Frank quietly, but with a slight hint of severity in the voice. Comprehensive or no comprehensive, he had resolutely retained the grammar school custom of addressing boys by their surnames.

As the boy stood up haughtily, he found Frank's lack of inches at once both reassuring and disconcerting.

"Not many things upset me, Gentle, but there's one thing that gets up my nose. Do you know what that might be?

"No," grunted the boy with a shrug, adding "sir" reluctantly as an afterthought,

"Don't you, now?"

"Me bus goes in two minutes."

"Now, you listen to me, Sonny Jim… good... and hard."

"If I'm late home, me mam will kill me."

"And if you don't shut that little mouth of yours… I'll spare her the trouble. Now… this afternoon… you refused to read in Mrs McCarthy's lesson. Is that right?"

"Yep."

Frank looked him straight in the eye, until the boy added "sir".

"And why was that, might I ask?"

"Cos it was stupid, that's why... sir."

"What do you mean, 'stupid'? Mrs McCarthy

wouldn't ask you to read something stupid."

"Well...it said... if someone gives you a slap, you should let them do it again... or something. I wasn't going to read that, was I? Me mates would've laughed at me."

"As it happens, Gentle," replied Frank, "I am not all that fussed about religion myself, but the law says that every pupil must have one lesson of R.E. per week... right? And it's Mrs McCarthy's job to teach it... which reminds me..."

Frank paused for a moment to size up the situation. Would he, he wondered, be able to resolve this matter with words alone?

"Sh-t!" exclaimed the boy, staring out of the window, "I've missed the f------ bus now, haven't I?"

Frank's mind was made up for him, and he immediately took hold of Gentle's upper arm and squeezed until it really hurt.

"Gerroff, you!" screeched the boy.

Frank squeezed harder, and then said very slowly, "Now then, my friend, you listen to me. For your information, the one thing that gets up my nose is... rudeness... r-u-d-e-n-e-s-s... (And with each letter he gave an extra little squeeze to his arm.) any kind of rudeness, but especially rudeness to a lady. You're not too old to have your backside smacked. And that, I'm afraid, is what you're going to get. But first, I've got to wash that big mouth of yours out, haven't I?"

And with that he led the boy by the arm to the large Belfast sink at the back of the laboratory. Barely relinquishing the tight squeeze, he forced his head and shoulders down into the sink, and filled the sink with tepid water. He then took a piece of carbolic soap from the dish at the side, made a little lather in his right hand, and then forced his powerful fingers into the boy's spluttering mouth.

"Spit out… and shut up," snarled Frank. "And now for your second dose of medicine… bend over that desk."

Dumbfounded, the boy did exactly as he was told, and Frank brought his enormous right hand down three times with such force that the boy's eyes filled with tears.

Frank let a few moments elapse before saying, with genuine sympathy this time, "Now, I'm sorry I had to do that, Gentle, but you gave me no choice, really, did you?"

Being overwhelmed by both the humiliation and the physical pain of such sudden and unexpected chastisement, he, of course, was in no state to agree or disagree, but Frank did not press the matter.

Then after another slight pause, he added quietly, "Now, first thing Monday morning… I want you to go and see Mrs McCarthy for me… and say you're sorry. Can you do that?"

Utterly dismayed, and still heaving with intermittent sobs, the boy nodded.

And then, as if nothing had happened, Frank asked, "Ever been on the back of a Vincent?"

The boy's eyes lit up in spite of himself.

"Right, then... there's a spare helmet in that store room... meet me at the front door in five minutes, and let's see if we can get you home before the school bus... and stop that mother of yours committing murder!"

AT LAST, one of the two girls standing next to Frank drew his attention to Martha waiting patiently at the front of the room.

"I'm sorry, Miss Wolf, I didn't see you there. And what brings you all the way up here this fine morning?" asked Frank, as he made his way awkwardly past stools and benches towards her.

"I'm sorry to interrupt your lesson, Mr Fairclough," she whispered, "I've got a parent downstairs. Mr Nobbs is otherwise engaged, so he asked me to deal with it."

"And what might *it* be, Martha?" teased Frank, with his usual roguish grin whenever he suspected her of covering up for Nobbs.

"Well, it's a Mr Gentle... he's got a son, Darren, in 4C. Did you by any chance have dealings with him last Friday afternoon?"

"Yes, as a matter of fact, I did. Mrs McCarthy brought him to me, but everything was sorted out in the end," replied Frank. "I even had a chat with his mother afterwards. Nice woman. Anyway, let's see what the gentleman wants, shall we? Mustn't keep our punters waiting? Isn't that what Mr Nobbs is always telling us?" And then to the class, "Right, folks, I've been called away on urgent business. You can start clearing up now. We'll have another look at that on Wednesday. And make sure you finish that homework!"

With that, he left the sixth formers to their own devices, and laboriously accompanied Martha down the three flights of stairs to the ground floor, and then along the bottom corridor to meet the infamous John Gentle. Frank had yet to make the big man's acquaintance, but like everyone else at Netherbridge High, he was not unfamiliar with the legend. The seven-foot monster boasted a colourful *curriculum vitae*, including 'a dishonourable discharge' from the Irish Guards for sexually assaulting the CO's wife; eighteen months at Strangeways for inflicting GBH on two ex-servicemen outside a public house in Salford. Furthermore, he had celebrated his eventual release from gaol by jumping from Runcorn Bridge into the Manchester Ship Canal, because a cell-mate had told him that Vince Karalius, of Rugby League fame, had also accomplished this feat as a youngster. Of course, no one could actually verify any of these escapades, but the precision of the details did lend them a modicum of credibility.

The contrast between Frank and Martha Wolf as they made their way along the bottom corridor bordered on the bizarre – she, slim, upright, and with a measured gait, he, squat and ungainly, hobbling along behind, barely able to keep up with her on this most pressing of errands.

Meanwhile, Gentle, frustrated beyond endurance by the delay of officialdom, was at last relieved to hear the distant click, click of Martha's returning footfall, but she was obliged to pause at the bottom of the stairs for Frank to catch up. As the two entered the foyer more or less together, the giant drew himself up to his full height from the deep-piled leather sofa next to the magnificent, but alas near empty, trophy cabinet. A pained smirk played around his mouth as he looked down on this disparate pair and bethought himself of the misshapen Anthony Quinn and the voluptuous Gina Lollobrigida in the film of *The Hunchback of Notre Dame*.

"I'm sorry to have kept you, Mr Gentle," said Martha, "but I'm sure you'll find the wait was worthwhile, because Mr Fairclough himself has agreed to see you about your son. You are welcome to use my office."

"No, no, no, no... forget it!" chortled Gentle, adding

sotto voce, "If I'd known he was a f------ cripple, I wouldn't have bothered."

"Oh," said Frank, pretending not to have heard the insult, "does that mean you are quite happy to leave matters as they are then, Mr Gentle?

"Yeah... it's okay," replied Gentle, visibly embarrassed by this most unlikely of adversaries, and then, looking at his watch, added feebly, "Look, it's nearly ha' pas' ten... I mus' be off, or I'll be late wi' tha' delivery".

"Well, then," said Frank innocently, "if you're quite sure, let's shake on it, shall we, and forget the whole thing?"

Although a stranger to such niceties, Gentle perfunctorily took Frank's hand, thereby, no doubt, hoping to expedite his departure, but he reckoned without Quasimodo's strength. No sooner than the two hands were enjoined, the colossus shuddered briefly before crumbling and slowly falling in on itself like one of Fred Dibnah's chimneys. As he sank to his knees, his eyes now level with his impassive tormentor's, the mystique and the menace suddenly evaporated. Could this grovelling wretch be the ogre who moments earlier had carried the whole world before him? Grimacing with pain, he let out a series of high-pitched whimpers like an injured puppy, which brought Nobbs scuttling out of his office to investigate; and when there was no further risk to his personal safety, he made a great show of trying to take control of the situation by dispersing a small group of second year onlookers. Frank, however, waved him aside with his free arm, for he had unfinished business to attend to. Without releasing his relentless handgrip, he squatted down beside his prostrate victim, and spoke slowly and quietly into his ear, "Mr Gentle, now we know where your lad gets his foul mouth from, don't we? And I don't think it's from his mother. Now, are we perfectly sure we don't wish to make a formal complaint to the County Council, or anything?"

In great pain, and utterly confounded by this sudden and very public demise, nothing could be further from Gentle's thoughts. The most he could muster was a grimace and a feeble shake of the head.

"Well, then, if you really... don't want... to be late... with that delivery, Mr Gentle, perhaps you'd like to apologise to the Headmaster here for wasting his valuable time. And in future... perhaps you'd be advised... to leave the disciplining of your lad... in *our* hands during school hours?"

When Gentle nodded and mumbled something approximating an apology in Nobbs's direction, Frank hoisted him to his feet, and with the handgrip still intact, slowly escorted him to the front door. Then with a final bone-crushing squeeze and a hearty shake of the hand, he wished him good day and a safe journey. Needless to say, Gentle felt no urge to return the compliment, harbouring one thought only, how to escape to the safety of his cab as speedily and as inconspicuously as possible. Indeed, feeling mortified by this chastening experience at the hands of a "cripple", he could not even muster a valedictory V-sign, as he steered his growling sixteen-wheeler past rows of teachers' cars and out through the school gates.

When Frank turned round, Nobbs had disappeared.

"Thank you, Mr Fairclough, thank you very much for

that," said a much-relieved Martha.

"All in a day's work, Martha," replied Frank with a broad smile, and *somebody* has to do it!".

Chapter Two

Richard Charles Nobbs was not endowed with many of the qualities commonly looked for in a prospective headmaster of a large comprehensive school. He was, however, uncommonly blessed with some other qualities: not least a sublime unawareness of his own shortcomings, allied to an infinite capacity for doing unto others as he would *not* have them done to himself. For instance, he would sometimes arrange a 'Senior Management' meeting for 7 pm on a Friday even though one of his deputies, who lodged in Netherbridge during the week, had a 200-mile journey afterwards to get home for the weekend. Likewise, he was not averse to announcing suddenly that two subject departments should switch locations on the campus forthwith, "to prevent teachers from becoming too comfortable and stale in a particular environment". But it was generally believed that such decisions were prompted more by personal vindictiveness, such as punishing a hapless head of department for outsmarting him in a staff meeting; or more simply out of a constant need to assert his authority.

One memorable example of this kind of manoeuvre was induced by unadulterated envy. John Halliday, the unassuming and hard-working Head of Humanities, (and incidentally Dr Davenport's very last appointment, to teach Economics in the Sixth form) had been nominated by the local authority for a three weeks' teacher-exchange visit to Wisconsin, USA. This was planned for the last week of the Easter holidays and the first two weeks of the Summer term. Nobbs had done everything in his power to block the nomination including asking the Chairman of the Governors to write to County Hall, to explain that it would be less disruptive to send a junior member of staff, who might also be more open to new ideas. And failing that, of course, there was always the 'last resort' option of asking the Headmaster himself, who, as head of the institution, not only had no teaching commitment, but was also in a far better position to disseminate any new ideas on his return.

But in the event, the letter held little sway with the local authority and the original nomination prevailed, plunging poor Nobbs into one of his many profound and prolonged sulks. However, two days before the end of the Easter term, he called John Halliday to his office, to congratulate him, and to wish him well on his trip. No one, he felt sure, was more worthy of the honour, and he wanted him to know that both he and the governors had supported his nomination from the outset. He was also confident that, given his background in geography, he would find the venture both stimulating and enjoyable, and that it would also bring incalculable benefits to the

School. But – and there was always a 'but' when Nobbs sang your praises – to change the subject for a moment, although he appreciated that now might not be the ideal time to raise the matter, he wondered if John could possibly help him out with a tricky little logistical problem. When Miss McGregor, (a deputy head, currently on a term's sabbatical) returned after the Easter break, she would require a larger office; and, after much thought and consultation he had come to the conclusion that the current Humanities Office fitted the bill splendidly. Accordingly, he would be very much obliged if John could arrange for his Humanities team to exchange locations with the Languages Faculty before "crossing the pond". He had already "cleared it" with the Head of Languages, who had very kindly agreed to manage without a faculty office as such for the time being.

Before John Halliday could demur, Nobbs summoned his Administrative Officer, Martha Wolf, to his office on the intercom, which left John with little choice but to withdraw with as much grace as he could muster, and ponder on the stupidity of physically transporting the Humanities Faculty's entire stock of books and equipment to the Languages area during the remaining two days of term; and more immediately how to break the news to his colleagues in the staff-room at break time.

The habit of treating members of staff as so many chess pieces often spilled over into non-school time as well, such as when he rang Philip Evans, Head of the English Department, one evening inviting him over to his house to help put together a paper he had to give at the next Head Teachers' meeting on one of the burning issues of the day: "language across the curriculum". When the latter tried to explain politely that he had a pile of sixth form essays to mark by the following morning, his response was, "Never mind the f------ essays, Phil. It might be more in your interest to give me a hand with this paper." And so, fearful of incurring another of his boss's spiteful fits of pique, he drove over in some haste to his house, expecting to spend the next couple of hours discussing some of the points in the relevant chapter of *The Bullock Report*. But when he arrived, his wife explained that "his lordship" had rushed down to the builder's merchants before they closed, to get some fittings for the mirror he was putting up in his shower. When he eventually returned, he was surprised to find Phil already waiting for him.

The next couple of hours were spent quaffing Carling Black Label and gossiping about the staff at the School, until Phil ventured to mention *The Bullock Report*.

"Oh, bollocks to Bullock!" said Nobbs "actually, Phil, I have to be honest with you, when Martha checked my diary, that *language across the curriculum* thing isn't till next month, but since you're here, you could make yourself useful and give us a lift with this big mirror I've bought for the shower."

So, Bullock had to wait; and when Phil eventually got into his car, already nettled by the waste of two valuable hours, he was hardly amused by Nobbs's parting quip, "Hey, Phil, have you met our new Science technician yet? I wouldn't mind getting across *her* curriculum, ha, ha!"

CONTRARY to his much-vaunted field commission during the Burma Campaign (presented by General Bill

Slim himself, no less), Nobbs's war service had in fact comprised nothing more heroic than five tedious years as a corporal in the orderly room at the Donnington Ordnance Depot in Shropshire. At first, he had been pleased to land a safe posting within easy travelling distance of his native Oldham, but for most of his time in uniform he had nursed a bitter grudge against his military superiors for failing to discern his "indisputable gifts for organization and leadership". Accordingly, in February 1946, having resolved to do everything in his power after demobilisation to set matters right, he enrolled as a student at Swinehead Technical Institute under the Ministry of Education's Emergency Teachers' Training Scheme, emerging thirteen months later with a Certificate in Craft and Design, and a grossly inflated ego. Whilst not born great, and not having had greatness thrust upon him, Nobbs was determined to achieve it at whatever cost; and a teaching post at Netherbridge Grammar School, "founded in 1565 for the instruction of boys in the English, Latin and Greek tongues, and also in good manners", sounded like a good first step on the ladder.

In reality, he might not have reached the first step, were it not for a deceitful letter of application innocently composed on his behalf by a fellow student at Swinehead, who sadly was unable to finish the course himself owing to lingering combat stress reaction. In addition to the aforementioned bogus field commission, the letter referred to several of 'Lieutenant' Nobbs's other deeds of derring-do, all of which were endorsed by forged letters of commendation by two separate 'unit commanders'. These "valiant deeds beyond the call of duty" included "entering and re-entering a burning field hospital to rescue trapped amputees"; "single-handedly dismantling a land-mine"; and his proudest moment of all, when, "in February, 1944, he saved at least a dozen Allied lives by foiling a Japanese counter-attack with a judiciously timed piece of military intelligence".

It seems strange now, if not comical, that such details were not checked with the War Office. One can only presume that no one, least of all the Headmaster, Dr Davenport, would have deemed it pertinent to question the word of an officer and gentleman, especially one who had apparently served his King and Country so bravely and honourably, and who now, according to his letter of application was "seeking a career in which my invaluable experience could inspire the next generation of leaders and risk-takers".

EVER SINCE his own schooldays at Hulme Grammar School in Oldham, which he had attended as a fee-payer, having failed the entrance examination, Nobbs had always been an inveterate and resourceful dissembler, equipped with a sharp memory, a ready tongue and a conscience not over-burdened with moral niceties. Being taller and physically more advanced than his school contemporaries, and having a bullying disposition, he had always been surrounded by a coterie of smaller boys whom he exploited ruthlessly, often with menaces, false promises or bribes. Whilst most of his acquaintances dealt in sixpences and shillings, he sported a fine leather wallet stuffed with ten-shilling and pound notes — money, he claimed, his father, a successful fruit and vegetable merchant on the Tommyfield Market in Oldham, paid him for helping out on Saturdays.

However, this is not to say he was a *compulsive* liar, that is, one for whom the boundary between truth and falsehood is so blurred that a blatant untruth is sometimes preferred simply for being more decorous than the plain, unvarnished truth. Nor again could he be described as an *impulsive* liar, that is, one who tells lies 'from hand to mouth', and for that reason is all too often found out. On the contrary, the older he became, Nobbs's lying grew more calculated and purposeful, in order to secure the material or personal advantage he always craved. Not for him the brash denials of a cornered transgressor, although very occasionally even he was obliged to tell a spontaneous fib to save his skin. But his proper lying was invariably premeditated and well organized.

After entering the teaching profession, he had taken deception to a new level, regarding it more as an accomplishment than simply an expedient. The innumerable 'short courses' he claimed to have attended during the early 1960s generated a rash of 'certificates' and 'diplomas', framed copies of which graced the front wall of his woodwork room. While these 'qualifications', of course, enjoyed no credence with the *cognoscenti*, they massaged his ego, and created an illusion of professionalism for the less discerning on Parents' Evenings.

Since Nobbs had long concluded that chicanery was not something to be undertaken lightly, he abided by two underlying principles: the end result should always justify the means, and successful outcomes generally depend on detail, on the assumption that the more elaborate the untruth, the more credible it usually appears. Thus, he saw deception as both a science and an art, whose content and structure should be properly researched and thought through, and whose *modus operandi* should be fine-tuned with practice and rehearsal. For him, (to adapt Pope's *dicta*), "True ease in *lying* comes from art, not chance, / As those move easiest who have learn'd to dance." and again, "A little *lying* is a dang'rous thing; / Drink deep, or taste not the Pierian spring."

Latterly, his propensity for duplicity had served him extraordinarily well, not only to extricate himself from minor domestic impasses, but more importantly, to hoodwink those whose support he courted both to further his career and to improve his standing in the community. On his bedside cabinet sat a well-thumbed copy of *The Oxford Book of Quotations*, with whose contents his conversations and speeches were generously laced, one of his favourites being Hamlet's "There is nothing either good or bad, / but thinking makes it so." And by extension, presumably, there is nothing either true or false.

CLEARLY, therefore, a panel of "butchers and bakers" would not have held many terrors for Mr Nobbs at his interview for the post of Senior Crafts Master at Netherbridge Grammar School in May 1947. The event had taken place, as was customary for all governors' appointments, in the hallowed environs of the Senior School Library, adjacent to the Headmaster's study. Everyone recalled what a fine figure he had cut in his bespoke worsted suit, so unlike the 'demob suits' worn by most ex-servicemen at that time and the démodé attire of the masters and the governors.

Candidates for teaching posts at NGS were asked "to

report to the Headmaster's Secretary at least one hour before the scheduled start of the interview at 3 pm, in order to look around the School, and meet some of the masters. Nobbs, however, had travelled to Netherbridge the day before, and stayed overnight at *The Duke of Argyle*, a large Victorian establishment a stone's throw from the railway station. After a sumptuous dinner of roast beef and Yorkshire pudding, followed by apple pie and fresh cream, he had whiled away the evening supping half-pints of Walker's bitter, while posing as a young, entrepreneurial ex-serviceman looking for a suitable site to set up a small furniture factory on the outskirts of the town. Behind this disguise, he had succeeded in luring several of the regulars into his confidence, teasing out more telling truths about Netherbridge's illustrious school than a month of talking to the masters. Or as Nobbs might have put it, "By indirections find directions out."

Likewise, the following day, after an early lunch at *The Duke*, he had arrived at the School a good hour earlier than requested, and after reporting to Miss Wolf, wasted no time in familiarising himself with the lay-out of the buildings. He made a special point of looking into the Masters' Room, which at that moment happened to be empty except for one diminutive, gowned figure standing by the window, who clearly mistook him in his smart suit for a commercial traveller from one of the big publishing houses. Beating a hasty retreat, Nobbs continued his exploration before finally stumbling across what he firmly believed would soon be his very own domain. Through the partially glazed door, he caught his first glimpse of the renowned Taff Jenkins, clad in a plebeian-looking brown warehouse coat, as he shuffled amongst a class of thirteen-year-olds, two to a bench, each engrossed in drawing and making specimen woodworking joints – half-lap, half-lap dovetail, mortise and tenon, dog-tooth, dovetail, and so forth, ready for their School Certificate Woodwork Examination.

God, thought Nobbs presumptuously, there's going to be some changes round here... with modern glues, who the f--- needs joints? And an old fart in overalls with a pencil behind his ear is not my idea of a Crafts Master at a prestigious Grammar School.

However, having decided not to compromise his authority by introducing himself just yet, he began to retrace his steps to the Secretary's office. Miss Wolf showed him into a small anteroom off the library, which served as the School's museum, and when required, as a sick bay.

Being the first candidate to arrive, Nobbs amused himself looking at some of the *objets d'art* on display. All around the room hung many beautiful original oil paintings and limited-edition prints, most of which had been bequeathed or donated over the years by notable old boys or appreciative parents. Beneath the large, south-facing window, there was a long glass cabinet with a fine collection of British birds' eggs, and on the opposite side, other glass cabinets containing labelled items salvaged from the original grammar school building opposite the Parish Church. (This had been demolished in 1887, when the School moved to its present site, but someone had had the foresight to rescue the fine stone architrave and finials of the main door and re-use them to form the main entrance to the library in the new building).

Among the *memorabilia*, Nobbs noticed some rare

tomes, including early edition copies of Milton's *Paradise Lost* (1667), Pope's translation of the *Iliad* (1720) and Dr Johnson's *Dictionary* (1755). There was also a selection of educational heirlooms, such as a schoolmaster's desk, some quills and inkwells, all apparently dating from around 1600. Inside the desk, Nobbs found some pupils' exercise books, one belonging to a certain William Postlethwaite, "a scholar at the school, 1678", who must also have been something of a wag, for on the rear cover he had painstakingly drawn a creditable likeness of an exceedingly well-endowed boar mounting an equally well-endowed sow, with the inscription beneath, *Copulo, ergo sum.* Even though the ironic parody of Descartes's dictum may have been lost on Nobbs, even he could not but marvel at how a schoolboy's prank could span the centuries and metamorphose from a bawdy *graffito* into a historical curiosity. But more pertinently, although he had little knowledge or appreciation of fine art or furniture, Nobbs possessed a market trader's 'nose' for collectable antiques, and made a mental note of the items that might have had commercial potential.

It was in this room that candidates for teaching posts at Netherbridge Grammar School congregated, obliged by their situation to absorb something of the School's venerable traditions. It was here too that they made polite conversation, sized each other up and sought psychological advantage, until summoned in alphabetical order for their respective interviews. On that day, however, Nobbs was the sole candidate for the Craft and Design post, the other one having mysteriously withdrawn at the eleventh hour.

As the school clock struck three, he was called into the Library and escorted to his seat by a Mr Martin Shaw, a young local dentist and the most recent addition to the governing body. As was customary, two massive oak tables had been placed end to end to form one long conference table, with a massive high-backed armchair on one end for the Chairman, Mr William Ravenscroft, Esq., J.P., the avuncular proprietor of the Ravenscroft Cotton Mill on Vicarage Lane, a First World War veteran, and an old boy of the Grammar School. On the wall behind the Chairman hung an enormous slab of white marble inscribed with the names of the thirty-eight Old Netherbridgeians who had "sacrificed their lives for God, King and Country in the Great War, 1914-18". Beneath it, a small brass plate mounted on a piece of polished oak, proclaimed the six "Fallen in the 1939-45 War", including the Chairman's son, Lt. Jimmy Ravenscroft, R.N., who was drowned off the island of Crete in 1941, and barely two years earlier was the School's Head Prefect and Captain of Cricket.

Immediately to the Chairman's right sat the Headmaster, wearing a black suit and his trade-mark red carnation; and to his left his young and attractive secretary, Miss Martha Wolf, as always impeccably groomed, and today acting as Clerk to the governors. On the Chairman's left sat the multi-chinned and alarmingly breathless Reverend Canon Herbert Ramsbottom, M.A. (Oxon), Vicar of Netherbridge, who at six feet five and twenty-six stone, was perhaps the most visible clergyman in the Anglican Communion. The remainder sat in order of acknowledged seniority: next to Miss Wolf, Mr Jack Higginbottom, the landlord of the Boar's Head (popularly dubbed the 'Whore's Bed'), where the Netherbridge Rotary Club met on Tuesday evenings and some of the younger masters most evenings; then Mr Bob Phillips, the Manager of the Co-op; and next to him, Mr Fred Unsworth LL.B., Chief Clerk of Netherbridge Corporation. To the Vicar's left sat the medical contingent: Dr Kinloch, an elderly and alcoholic family doctor, now reliant on his good lady to chauffeur him on home visits in their large pre-War Daimler. Next to him, the dapper Dr John Winstanley, his junior partner and also a part-time general surgeon at the Netherbridge District Infirmary; and finally, the aforementioned Mr Martin Shaw, recently 'demobbed' from the R.A.D.C. and already a leading light of the Netherbridge Round Table. The chair directly opposite the Chairman's was left vacant, like Banquo's, for the interviewee.

"Thank you for your interest in the position, Mr Nobbs," began the Chairman genially, "I see you have an impressive war record, and I wondered, after all you've been through, how you would adjust to the more, shall we say, tranquil life here at Netherbridge Grammar School?"

"Well," replied Nobbs, smiling broadly, "if the War years taught me anything, it was to take each day as it comes, and to grab the challenges that each day brings. My dear old CSM used to say, 'Grasp the nettle with both hands, and then it will not sting'. And I'm sure Netherbridge will provide me with plenty of... challenges."

Everyone, bar Dr Davenport, seemed reasonably satisfied with this confident opening gambit, but then he rarely intervened in governors' appointments, unless his advice was sought.

"Now, you are probably aware that this post," continued Mr Ravenscroft, in no way discomfited by Nobbs's presumptuous tone, "is a new departure for Netherbridge, and, of course, as you will have noticed, with a substantial carrot attached. We are therefore looking for someone rather special, someone not only with the technical know-how but also the organisational abilities to develop the subject throughout the School. Perhaps you would be kind enough to explain to the Headmaster and the governors how you see your role in this post?"

"Well," replied Nobbs, "as you may have deduced from my *curriculum vitae*, I see myself very much as a 'doer'. Furthermore, I don't suffer fools gladly. If situations require decisive or even drastic actions, I don't let the grass grow under my feet. As they say, procrastination is the thief of time. So, if you're looking for someone to put this subject on the map, I'm your man."

Poor Dr Davenport could barely believe the fellow's swagger, and exchanged telling glances with Martha, thinking perhaps it might be as well to re-advertise the post there and then. He also wondered how in the short term such an appointment would go down with Taff Jenkins. But then he *was* the only candidate, and perhaps it was only right that he be given every opportunity to redeem (or hang) himself.

"Now, I'm sure one or two of the other governors," continued the Chairman, "have things to ask Mr Nobbs?"

However, there followed a long and embarrassing silence, broken eventually by the Vicar. "Mr Nobbs," he began breathlessly, as if addressing a ruri-decanal conference, "we have recently... brought together a team... of hard-working volunteers... to undertake the repair and enhancement of the oak choir stalls and pulpit... at our ancient and beautiful Parish Church, St Mary's. It is a long-term project... and one, God willing, that will continue long after my departure. You may be interested to know... that one of the most loyal members of the team is the School's very own Mr Jenkins, whose virtuosity with a carving gouge is the stuff of legend. Tell me, Mr Nobbs, given your practical skills, and indeed organisational abilities, could we also count on *your* support in this venture?"

Nobbs had learned about the restoration project in the Parish Church at the *Duke of Argyle* the previous evening, and had given it some thought before retiring to bed. There was always some mileage, he supposed, in being *seen* to be involved in the community, provided, of course, it was not inordinately distracting or time-consuming. However, this particular project was clearly very much Jenkins territory, with the very real risk of having one's limitations exposed working alongside 'the maestro'. Furthermore, as a freshly demobbed 'old soldier', he was conditioned never to *volunteer* for anything. However, since needs must, he resolved his dilemma with a fairly non-committal, "Well, what I always said when the padré came to me asking for volunteers, 'Men, as it says in the Good Book, let your light shine before men, that they may see your good works."

Dr Davenport gave the Vicar a knowing and appreciative wink for sheer opportunism, but more significantly, he felt the question had inadvertently shone a piercing shaft of light on the candidate's insincerity. As an agnostic, Dr Davenport only attended the Parish Church at Christmas, Easter, and ceremonial occasions connected with the School, but he was very fond of the old edifice, especially its fine acoustics, and was also very conscious of the close relationship the School and St Mary's had shared over the centuries. (Indeed, the very first Headmaster, the Rev. Maurice Peterson, MA, (Oxon) was also the Vicar at St Mary's).

"Well, if there are no more questions," declared the Chairman, "perhaps Mr Nobbs would care to...

"Excuse me, Mr Chairman," interrupted Mr Higginbottom of *The Boar's Head*. Everyone cringed in case Jack embarrassed them again with one of his unfortunate *double-entendres* or malapropisms.

"As someone who never had much of an education, let alone a grammar school education, but who has since studied long and hard at the University of Life, I'd like to ask the candidate one simple question. Mr Nobbs, as an army officer, the pips on your shoulders guaranteed you discipline and respect. Here at the Grammar School, as you probably appreciate, we also rate discipline and respect very highly. Now, discipline usually goes with the territory, but *respect*, well, of course, that's another matter. This, in my experience, has to be *earned*. Tell me, Mr Nobbs, how would you set about earning the respect of these gradely, but sometimes very lively, lads we have at our school?"

Far from embarrassing his colleagues, Jack's question was met with total silence, which suggested general approval, and it was something Nobbs had not been altogether ready for. However, never lost for words, his response was immediate.

"When you're hiding in a fox-hole with a bunch of terrified conscripts, hoping and praying the next shell or mortar won't blow you all to kingdom come, I assure you that you need something more than rank to win their respect. Of course, only time will tell if respect displayed in the jungle transfers to the schoolroom, but there's a good chance that it might, if we heed the Bard's advice, 'To thine own self be true/ And it must follow.../Thou canst not then be false to no man.'"

"*Any*," corrected Dr Davenport, *sotto voce*, "*any* man." But, apart from Miss Wolf and the Vicar, no one else understood.

After this final literary flourish, Nobbs was asked to retire to the ante-room while the Governors considered their verdict. Dr Davenport had nothing to say, but his unequivocal demeanour throughout the interview had not been lost on anyone, especially the Chairman. Nevertheless, the overwhelming tide of opinion was in Nobbs's favour.

"Perhaps he's just the ticket for these changing times," suggested the Vicar, always with an eye on another recruit for his beloved renovation project."

"He's certainly a fine looking fellow," added the lawyer, Fred Unsworth, "and with a ready tongue to match. He should have no difficulty controlling the boys. I'd say, all in all, he would be a very good advertisement for the School. Perhaps he'd also bring a breath of fresh air to the place."

"And he's got youth on his side," echoed old Dr Kinloch. "Many of the masters are like me, well, not as young as they used to be, and the School can only benefit from some new blood and new ideas."

Eager not to be overlooked at his very first governors' meeting, young Martin Shaw pointed out, "And let's not forget that despite his youth, he has enormous experience, gained in extreme circumstances... experience that would stand him in good stead when dealing with boys of different types and backgrounds."

"Thank you, gentlemen, thank you," declared Mr Ravenscroft, "if I can now draw some of these threads together... from what I hear, and observe, am I right in thinking that the candidate for the most part meets with your approval? Yes, he certainly is different... he's not your... traditional schoolmaster, and to a large extent we have to take his credentials and his ability to do the job on trust. But we have taken chances before. Now... is it your wish that we offer the position to Mr Nobbs?"

And so, with an *almost* unanimous show of hands, Nobbs's career at Netherbridge was launched, with duties to begin the following September, though his appointment created no more interest among the rest of the masters than that of a new caretaker – with one exception.

NOBBS'S NEAREST, though hardly closest, colleague on taking up his post would be one Dafydd ("Taff") Jenkins, a crusty, middle-aged South Walian who attributed his robust constitution to the life-enhancing properties of Capstan Full Strength, and an hourly mug of full strength Brooke Bond. After being invalided out of the *Machine Gun Corps* in August 1918 with severe shrapnel-wounds to the abdomen incurred in the second Battle of the Marne, he spent six months at the Lord

Derby War Hospital in Warrington where he met and eventually married the lovely Nurse Elizabeth Parker, a Netherbridge girl, who had looked after him throughout his convalescence.

After recovering sufficiently from his injuries, he eventually found part-time employment as an assistant caretaker and general handyman at Netherbridge Grammar School, supplementing his income extramurally as a jobbing joiner. But his exceptional skills, especially in wood-turning and carving, coupled with a natural flair for dealing with the boys, persuaded the old headmaster, Mr Harry Whitworth, to send him to Loughborough College on a six months' basic teaching course, in order "to deploy Mr Jenkins's practical and personal talents more efficiently in a teaching capacity". The decision, though strongly opposed at the time by some of the governors and nearly all the masters as demeaning to the profession, eventually proved to be one of the most popular and effective appointments of the Whitworthian era.

ONE OF Dr Davenport's long-term aims on becoming Headmaster of Netherbridge Grammar School was to raise the profile and status of practical subjects like woodwork and technical drawing. As this would have been seen by most as "jeopardising academic standards", he knew that he would have to bide his time and present very compelling arguments to persuade them otherwise. However, unexpectedly, on Friday, 9th October 1943, his intentions received an unequivocal, high-level endorsement.

On the day in question, he happened to be a guest at a

district Rotary dinner in London. The speaker was Mr R.A. Butler, the then President of the Board of Education, who explained how a recent tour of Merseyside and Tyneside had convinced him of the need for a national drive for improved technical education. He said, "It is the Government's full intention to proceed with the development of technical and adult education as soon as possible, and that this should take high precedence in authorities' programmes. We are convinced that this is necessary to meet the needs of industry and commerce, and to assist them in the tasks of readjustment and recovery. Opportunity must be taken after the war to furnish the new 'universities of industry' with the most up-to-date outfits."

Dr Davenport found himself in agreement with much of what Mr Butler had to say, and thought that if he began to explore possibilities at NGS right away, the School would be in a good position to take advantage of any extra Government funding for facilities and staffing that might be available.

When the Butler Education Act came into force after the Second World War with its emphasis on the technical as well as the academic, Dr Davenport felt thoroughly vindicated. He was very much aware that for the foreseeable future there would be an increased demand for high calibre engineers to help with the post-war reconstruction effort. More specifically, he also foresaw that if a high class Butler-type secondary "university of industry" were set up anywhere near Netherbridge, NGS could well lose some of its most talented pupils.

Accordingly, after much thought and consultation, he finally persuaded the Governors to enhance the status of

Craft, first, by investing in modern facilities and equipment, and secondly, by appointing a specialist to oversee and promote its development. Alternatively, in the first instance, they could hand the reins to Taff Jenkins and appoint a suitably qualified person to assist him.

However, much to his wife's annoyance, Taff categorically refused the newly created position of "Senior Crafts Master". "Too much pen-pushing for my liking with these new fancy jobs," avowed the blunt Celt, "give me a piece of Burma teak any day... I know where I am with Burma teak."

But it was not the paperwork that Taff dreaded so much as the social implications of such a promotion. He was very conscious that some of the old 'Oxbridge' brigade even resented his inclusion on the biennial staff photograph, always on the end of the back row and looking very self-conscious in a borrowed undergraduate gown; and despite more than twenty years as the accepted 'Woodwork Master', whose set-building services were considered indispensable for the annual school play or opera, he had never deigned to set foot inside the Masters' Room during school hours. He had always taken his breaks in the boiler room with Jim Nelson, the Groundsman, and Alf Newby, the Caretaker, because "he knew his place", and felt his presence in the "Officers' Mess" would not have been right.

But Nobbs, of course, was not burdened with such inhibitions. On the contrary, the moment the Chairman of the Governors shook his hand on that historic day, he had embarked on a long odyssey of self-promotion. At first there were simple, symbolic gestures, such as substituting the traditional workshop brown overall for a more 'scientific-looking', white lab-coat, which he wore unbuttoned over a dark suit like a duty doctor at the Infirmary. And then one day he ventured across the threshold of the Masters' Room, ostensibly to consult the yard-duty roster on the staff notice-board, but in reality, to establish a bridgehead before launching a full assault on this bastion of academic snobbery. For the occasion, he had deliberately left his white coat in the workshop, so that his dark suit would blend in more naturally with the surroundings. He repeated this stratagem several times over many weeks before finally presuming that his acceptance had been ratified by default.

When news of "these shenanigans" reached Taff, he could barely contain himself, and at break-time in the boiler room one morning he expounded his thoughts on the matter unequivocally.

"Who the bloody hell does he think he is, striding in there as if he owns the place? You know what, I never took to the bugger from day one, and I told the Gaffer so as well... but you know how he is."

"Look, Taff," replied Alf, "it's no use going on to us about him. You should have taken the job yourself when the Gaffer offered it to you."

But Taff ranted on regardless, "And I'll tell you summat else an' all... there's something shifty about him, have you noticed? He can't look you straight in the eye. But the worst thing is the bullsh-t. Bloody hell, that flashy car and all them fancy suits... I don't know. But there we are... it's spivs like him that get on in the world... no place for the likes of me and thee, Jim. Do you remember that old army saying, bullsh-t baffles brains? Well, I'll tell you one thing for nothing, it won't baffle this boyo... I may not have much of a brain, but I've got a bloody good nose, and I can smell bullsh-t at a thousand paces!"

"Hey, talking about the army," teased Jim, "I 'eard he were an officer... out in the Far East... with 'tChindits... not much room for bullsh-t there, Taff!"

"Who told you that? Because... you see," said Taff, touching his nose. "I heard different."

"What do you mean, different?" said Jim.

Taff went to the door to check that no one was eavesdropping.

"Well... a little bird told me he was never overseas at all... see... wangled a home posting... on compassionate grounds, or something."

"Get away! He couldn't have made all that up... the Governors would have sussed it out."

"Well, I wouldn't put it past the bugger... I'm telling you, lads, he's the ultimate shaizzenhausen."

Then, after a pregnant pause to light another Capstan, he added, "And I wouldn't mind so much if he was any good at his job. But do you know what, he can't even sharpen a chisel... honest! And last week I had to remind him to check the safety catch on that new electric plane... I ask you!"

"Well, Taff, I'm afraid you're stuck with him now," replied Alf, "at least he doesn't bother us over here! And you never know, if he's out for promotion, perhaps he'll be off soon, eh?"

"Huh!" retorted Taff, "more likely he'll end up running the place!

Chapter Three

In its heyday, Netherbridge Grammar School was a renowned 'direct grant' establishment comprising six hundred boys and fifty masters, where prowess on the games field was prized almost as highly as academic excellence. As a Cambridge 'Boxing Full Blue' and a 'Wrangler', its Headmaster, Dr George O'Brien Davenport (affectionately known as "GOD"), was himself a living embodiment of his belief that a boy's education should comprise a wholesome balance of both the intellectual and the physical. Consequently, Wednesday afternoons at Netherbridge were dedicated to sport, and every Saturday morning throughout the winter months saw as many as five rugby teams, five football teams and three cross-country teams turning out in the distinctive red and green livery. Cricket, tennis and athletics were similarly represented during the Summer Term, and even the 'walking wounded' were expected to help with equipment, refreshments or simply cheering the teams on.

It was Dr Davenport's proud boast that the School "ran itself". But this illusion of 'autopilot' was largely due to the quiet efficiency and dedication of his secretary, the elegant and self-effacing Miss Martha Wolf, who as the sole female on the premises, also acted variously as mother, sister, aunt, nurse and confidante to the boys, and occasionally to the masters too!

During his time at the helm, from 1936 to 1966, the School acquired an enviable academic reputation, with some half-dozen or more gaining open scholarships to Oxford or Cambridge every year, many of whom being products of Dr Davenport's beloved Scholarship mathematics class. So great was the demand to get into Netherbridge that entrance tests were held during the first week of the Easter holidays, with some 200 aspiring ten- and eleven-year-olds competing for the 90 first-year places available for the following September. One waggish Old Netherbridgeian claimed that it was harder getting into Netherbridge now than into Oxbridge. And, of course, getting in was no guarantee of remaining there, for as Dr Davenport always maintained, the School was as ready to welcome worthy late-developers as it was to bid farewell to those who (heaven forbid!) had patently failed to fulfil their promise.

In the only HMI inspection of his reign, in October 1964, the School was taken to task, much to his amusement, for its "over-stringent selection procedures" and "the unrealistic demands made upon its pupils"; but during the ensuing weeks his amusement changed, first to derision, then cynicism, and finally indignation, which emotion was given full vent in his address at the annual

Prize-giving Night held the following February as usual at the Netherbridge Town Hall. With characteristic vigour and plain speaking, he not only demolished the HMI Report's main tenets, but left a capacity audience in no doubt as to how he saw the future of the School. The address, so unlike the usual catalogue of compliments, was given front-page coverage in the *Netherbridge Chronicle,* and the concluding remarks quoted verbatim:

In my travels about the country, I cannot help but notice the insidious and relentless spread of egalitarianism in our schools and universities, a phenomenon often masquerading under that fashionable mantra, 'equality of opportunity'. Politicians seem to talk of little else these days but replacing our fusty, antiquated grammar schools with resplendent, modern *high* schools, which, in the words of our dear Prime Minister, 'will deliver a grammar school education to every child'. There are also plans afoot to create myriad new universities to accommodate the hordes of bright young things produced by these brave new institutions.

Moreover, the daily press is replete with the war cries of those who would denounce such subjects as Latin and Greek as atavistic and irrelevant in a twentieth century Britain. I am convinced that such assertions, far from serving the best interests of Britain, or indeed our young people, are motivated largely by what Francis Bacon called, 'that vilest and most depraved of emotions' – envy.

Finally, ladies and gentlemen, apropos Her Majesty's Inspectors' Report, let me leave you with this one thought. Contrary to what certain people may propose, as long as I am the Headmaster, there will never be room for mediocrity at Netherbridge. Our boys, many of whom, like me, come from solid working class stock, are hand-picked, as are the masters. Each deserves the other. Thanks to the unfailing support of their families, and an education at Netherbridge Grammar School, (whose quatercentenary, incidentally, we shall be celebrating in a few weeks' time) a great many of them will make their mark in one of the learned professions, or as captains of industry, or in some other worthy enterprise. This school is about educating the next generation of thinkers and leaders - or it is nothing.

Heaven knows, today we need leaders who can think as never before.

But even as he sat down to a rapturous applause, far from being beguiled by his own eloquence, and certainly not one to indulge in triumphalism, he already felt the heavy, cold hand of fate resting on his shoulder. Leaning towards his loyal and ever-present assistant, he asked anxiously, "Was that all right, Martha, or did I over-egg the pudding?"

To which she replied mischievously, "I would say the pudding was delectable, Dr Davenport!"

Although this brought a brief smile to his face, sadly, it needed more than Martha's reassuring words and smile to quell the nagging doubts and endless self-questioning that tormented him at that moment. Was the content of his speech too academic, or too political? Had he spoken for too long? And might it not have been said more directly, more personally, and therefore more effectively? Was the language too emotional? He knew that he had always been inclined, despite his mathematical training, to be as anxious about the sound of his words and phrases as their meaning! But more fundamentally, and more seriously, had he perhaps grown out of touch with the real world? He had always tried to keep abreast of the latest developments in the worlds of industry and commerce, as well as in his own field, education, but was there now something of the King Canute about his whole stance? Maybe many of the assumptions he had made throughout his career were at last *passé* and irrelevant. Indeed, was the very concept of "the grammar school" outmoded in this rapidly changing post-war world, and was "comprehensivisation" *the idea* whose time had come?

Surely, people like Wilson and Crosland weren't fools: they were intelligent and well-educated men, and so on and so forth.

Although he himself still believed passionately in the ideas and sentiments he had just expounded, he was also all too painfully aware of the overwhelming political and social pressures militating against them. Only a month earlier, on the 21st January 1965, to be precise, the Government had declared its objective to reorganise Butler's tripartite state education system "along comprehensive lines", and the newly appointed Secretary of State for Education, Anthony Crosland, had adopted this transformation as his personal crusade. In his wife's biography of him (1982), he is quoted as saying, "If it's the last thing I do, I'm going to destroy every f------ grammar school in England; and Wales; and Northern Ireland." And all this despite having himself benefited from a highly selective kind of education at the prestigious Highgate School in leafy North London, which, albeit since 1871 a fee-paying school rivalling Eton, Harrow and Winchester, was originally founded on the same lines, and coincidentally in the same year (1565) as Netherbridge Grammar School, and rejoicing in the august name of The Free Grammar School of Highgate!

Be that as it may, in July 1965 (indeed, the very month when NGS was celebrating its quatercentenary) the Department of Education and Science published its *Circular 10/65*, which 'requested' all local education authorities "to draw up and submit plans for reorganising all their secondary schools on comprehensive lines". Some half dozen models were laid out in the document, and each authority would have to determine which model best suited its own particular circumstances.

Although there was no specific reference to 'direct grant' grammar schools, Dr Davenport anticipated that it was only a matter of time before centrally funded schools like NGS would be required to choose between becoming a comprehensive school under local authority control or independent and funded almost entirely by endowments and fees. Accordingly, together with a handful of loyal parents and Governors, he immediately set about fighting to procure independent status for NGS by trying to persuade Old Netherbridgians, local businesses and parents to lend their support as was being done at neighbouring Manchester Grammar School by his friend, Peter Mason, the High Master, and also at Oldham Hulme Grammar School.

However, owing to the ground swell of public opinion, especially among middle-class parents whose sons had failed to gain a place at NGS, and perhaps more significantly the socio-economic profile of the Netherbridge catchment area, all their efforts came to nothing. After much consultation and debate (some of it very acrimonious), the Governors eventually succumbed to the local authority's arguments and lavish promises of resources, including a substantial building programme.

ONE WOULD have thought that someone as prodigiously gifted as George Davenport would have brimmed over with self-confidence and *joie-de-vivre*, but in fact one could hardly have met a more self-critical and insecure human being, who throughout his life had sought the reassurance of friends and colleagues.

From his very earliest schooldays in Altrincham,

Cheshire, this only child of a railway carpenter and a district midwife had astounded his hapless teachers with his needle-sharp intelligence and astonishing all-round abilities. It was as if Mother Nature had squandered her whole treasury of talents on one unassuming *wunderkind*.

Young George excelled at everything, effortlessly and unpretentiously. Having perfect pitch, he sang like a lark, and from a very young age played the piano well enough to accompany the hymns at morning assemblies. His stories and poems, even when composed as class exercises, were invariably entertaining and beautifully written, while his drawings and paintings were so extraordinarily accomplished as to belie his years. But perhaps most astonishing of all was his ability to perform complex arithmetical calculations in his head. Furthermore, and infuriatingly for his contemporaries, his supremacy was not confined to the schoolroom: his natural athleticism enabled him to run faster and jump higher and farther than many who were a head taller than he; and of course, any ball-game came to him as naturally as leaves to a tree.

Yet, curiously, he never seemed to take much delight in any of these accomplishments, being always more preoccupied with the peccadilloes that might rob him of perfection. Whilst his teachers could only marvel at this phenomenon in their midst, predicting in their mundane way, "one day George Davenport will be a millionaire", the boy himself wore his cornucopia of attributes but lightly, often finding the universal praise cloyingly embarrassing, and harbouring secret longings to be 'normal' like everyone else. Indeed, his headmaster once remarked that such a rare combination of excellence and humility seemed to ascribe to his sobriquet something more than a fortuitous set of initials.

In 1913, at the tender age of ten and a half, and to the relief of his beleaguered teachers, the young prodigy moved to the recently founded County High School for Boys nearby, where his reputation had preceded him. Fortunately for him, the Governors had secured the services of a young Oxford mathematician as their first headmaster, who was to make such a deep impression on him, both as a teacher and a person, that in later life he unwittingly adopted him as a professional role-model. As soon as this headmaster recognised the awesome talent that had newly joined their ranks, he took him under his wing, along with two other exceptional scholars, providing all three whenever possible with the appropriate extra tuition and assignments necessary to fulfil their potential. All three relished this intense academic milieu, and for the first time in his young life George was able to enjoy a true comradeship of minds seasoned with a generous measure of healthy rivalry. His hunger for learning seemed insatiable, and unencumbered by such modern contrivances as radio and television, his main source of entertainment (and enlightenment) was books. He read avidly and widely, availing himself of the well-stocked libraries both at the school and in the town, while instinctively observing Bacon's precepts in *Of Studies*: "Some books are to be tasted, others to be swallowed, and some few to be chewed and digested". Thus, even by his mid-teens, he had no need of the "much cunning to seem to know what he doth not", because reading "histories (had made him) wise; poetry, witty; mathematics, subtle; natural philosophy, deep; moral, grave; and logic and rhetoric, able to contend". In short, reading had already made him a "full man"!

Needless to say, his academic progress was meteoric, not only in mathematics, in which, thanks to his enthusiastic tutor, he had mastered much of the Cambridge Mathematical Tripos course long before he went up to Christ's College in 1920, but also in as broad a range of subjects as the newly established school could provide.

But was it Thomas Carlyle who defined genius as "the infinite capacity for taking pains"? It was certainly so with George Davenport, whose constant striving after perfection knew no bounds, nor unfortunately the depth of his despondency when outcomes fell short of his own impossibly high standards. His attention to detail bordered on the obsessive, for to him nothing was good if it could be better. Unsurprisingly, therefore, his written assignments were also calligraphic masterpieces, and if a single errant stroke of the pen were ever to blight perfection, a whole page would have to be rewritten. Likewise, a small scuff-mark on a polished toe-cap, or being delayed for an appointment, or even the fear of missing a train distressed him greatly, and his tortured soul agonized long and inconsolably over his own or someone else's unwittingly hurtful, remark or gesture. Once in his second year at the school he wept bitterly after gaining only 95% in an end-of-term Latin exam, and during his final year before going up to Cambridge, he once sat up all night rewriting an essay on Hamlet's madness, after coming across a copy of Prof. AC Bradley's newly published lectures, *Shakespearean Tragedy*, wherein Hamlet's prevarication and disgust with life is attributed to what is now called "bipolar disorder", symptoms of which he also recognised in himself.

Even in the gymnasium or on the games field, where his prowess was no less spectacular than in the classroom, his quest for flawlessness dogged him continually. In his final year at the School, he was invited to captain a representative Cheshire Schools Football XI against a professionally coached Manchester Youth team, and despite having almost single-handedly saved his side from a humiliating defeat, his immediate reaction after the game was to thank each of his fellow-players and then ask the Master-in- charge if *his* performance had been "all right".

UP TO THE TIME of the Great War, all the masters at NGS had been, almost *ipso facto,* 'Oxbridge' men, embracing broadly the same values and prejudices. But with the cream of a generation lost in that war, and the ever-increasing demand for school places, the Governors had had to recruit from farther afield, first from Durham and then, *faute de mieux*, from the new, 'redbrick' universities of the industrial Midlands and the North.

The 'Old Brigade', that is, those appointed before the turn of the century, had shaken their heads in disbelief at the changes undermining the very fabric of their little world. These entrenched academics, often unmarried and living in lodgings, had always regarded the Masters' Room as their very own cloistered domain, a kind of private gentlemen's club where they convened daily with their briars and pouches of St Bruno to tackle *The Times* crossword, play bridge, and deplore the plethora of newfangled ideas threatening western civilisation, until importunately summoned by bells to lead their young charges into "the realms of gold".

As the School expanded during the 1920s, it also became more competitive and less complacent. The new breed of master was more business-like, ambitious, and eager to improve his standard of living. He also saw the School less as a vehicle for propagating his own academic enthusiasms than as a means for intelligent and highly motivated boys from a less privileged background to fulfil their potential and make their way in the world. But by the time of Mr Whitworth's retirement in 1936, when most of the 'Old Brigade' had long departed, these one-time trench-hardened iconoclasts had themselves now become the 'elder statesmen', with their own *weltanschauung*. They worked hard and played hard, and expected everyone else to do likewise. It was as if the harrowing experiences of the War had invested them with a potent authority to demand the best of their pupils, as they did of themselves, and many came to regard this period as NGS's "golden era".

The School's burgeoning reputation spread throughout the North West bringing with it yet more demand for places. Extra classrooms had to be built and extra staff appointed. In one of the many tributes to Mr Whitworth at his farewell dinner, William Ravenscroft, the then President of the Old Boys' Association, and a fairly recent addition to the Governing Body, remarked on how the School had changed during Mr Whitworth's reign, and how the role of Headmaster had also changed. "When he first arrived at the outbreak of the War," he recalled, "I was in my final year, and he and my father were co-managing directors of the Ravenscroft Mill. And yet he still managed to find time to run the School. Of course, there were only two hundred boys then, and a dozen or so masters. But how times have changed! I'll give you one little example. At that time the masters were paid in cash on the last Thursday of the month, and I remember my father saying that if a young master for whatever reason found himself short of funds before the due date, he would go to Mr Whitworth for a "sub" to tide him over; and provided he put a convincing case and did not make a habit of it, Mr Whitworth would hand him a pound or two from his wallet and make a note in a little pocket book.

"But when my father died, Mr Whitworth had to relinquish his interest in the mill to concentrate solely on the School, and as is patently obvious today, the mill's loss was the School's gain. Under his leadership, the range of subjects has almost doubled, and the demand for places has grown apace. Currently, we have three hundred boys, taught by twenty masters of the highest calibre, and the facilities, especially the two new science laboratories and the gymnasium, are second to none. The new Headmaster will have a hard act to follow, but, thanks largely to Mr Whitworth's foresight and leadership, he will also have a firm foundation on which to build."

AFTER TEN gratifying years teaching Mathematics at Manchester Grammar School during the Douglas Gordon Miller era, Mr Whitworth's successor, George O'Brien Davenport, arrived, unheralded and unassuming, but possessing impeccable credentials, and soon proving more than equal to the "hard act".

For all his self-doubt and anxieties, he had gained a Double First in 1923, before going on to work on the electron theory under Ebenezer Cunningham, receiving his PhD in 1926. This was in the same year as his enigmatic contemporary, Paul Dirac, one of the greatest mathematical thinkers of all time, as reflected by his incomparable *curriculum vitae*: FRS, (1927, aged 25); the fifteenth Lucasian Professor of Mathematics (1931); and the Nobel Prize for Physics (1933) for his masterpiece, *The Principles of Quantum Mechanics*.

Dr Davenport, too, had once contemplated a career in *academia,* but despite all the plaudits and commendations, he doubted if he was temperamentally, or even intellectually, equal to the demands of the ivory tower. Besides, Cambridge in the 1920s, he felt, was awash with brilliant young theoretical physicists, such as Shrödinger, Oppenheimer, Kapitza, Heisenberg, Max Born, Charles Darwin (the grandson of the great biologist) and of course Paul Dirac himself; and as much as he had relished being part of that pioneering research into the nature of matter, he never felt he truly belonged to that elite group of young men who were destined to change the nature of science for ever. Accordingly, being ever grateful for the opportunities bestowed on *him* as a young boy, he eventually convinced himself that perhaps, after all, he would be more usefully employed in discovering and nurturing the next generation of thinkers.

As many an Old Netherbridgian fondly recalled, "GOD" truly had an aura of the divine about him at that first school assembly in April 1936. Addressing his young audience in quiet, almost apologetic tones, he exuded natural and effortless authority. It was the first of countless riveting assembly talks, each with a cogent, simple 'message', elegantly encapsulated in a memorable anecdote.

During the next decade under his enlightened tutelage, and despite the seismic hiatus of the Second World War, when many of the young masters were called up into the Armed Forces, their posts temporarily filled by nuns from a neighbouring Convent School, a retired naval officer and a clergyman, the School flourished as much as ever. In 1946, Dr Davenport successfully applied for membership of the Headmasters' Conference, and the following year, mainly owing to the widespread renown of his Mathematics Scholarship class and the after-school Radio Engineering Club, he was approached by a group of enthusiastic parents to see if some of their more able daughters currently attending the Netherbridge Grammar School for Girls could transfer. Despite much resistance from the older masters and, interestingly, some parents, the idea was eventually tried and proved so successful that Dr Davenport considered extending it to other Sixth Form Science classes; but, unfortunately, for practical reasons, this was doomed to remain a dream.

AFTER THE Second World War, the Masters' Room at NGS lost almost all of its former character, becoming increasingly heterogeneous and congested. Some of the younger masters wore sports jackets and addressed each other by their first names, and some preferred to remain in their classrooms during morning breaks, or indulge in some "vulgar sporting activity", such as 5-aside football or weight-training in the gymnasium, and on account of the thick tobacco fug, only visited the Staff Room (as it was now sometimes referred to) for official Staff meetings. The one prominent exception, of course, was the new Senior Crafts Master, who made it his business to be seen there as often as he possibly could.

Every morning, he would arrive at the School earlier than most, hoping to catch the Headmaster's eye, but also to ensure a parking space for his much admired 1938 SS100 Jaguar underneath the covered walkway between the main building and the refectory, and right next to Dr Davenport's 1927 Hercules Roadster bicycle! Having flung his leather flying-jacket onto the hook behind the Woodwork room door, he would then make his way to the Masters' Room (as *he* always called it), a copy of *The Times* tucked visibly under his arm, and making sure to sit or stand next to someone of acknowledged status like the Senior Modern Languages Master, or at least someone whose star he deemed to be in the ascendant. Likewise, during the lunch-hour he would foist his less than welcome presence on the bridge table, or perhaps interrupt an erudite conversation in the Classics corner with a jarringly inappropriate quip.

Eventually, in order to alleviate the problem of congestion, and possibly to restore something of the old sense of unity among the masters, Dr Davenport suggested that morning coffee be served in the Refectory, but unfortunately with little effect. The inexorable fact was that times were changing and people had to change with them. As usual, Dr Davenport was among the first to recognize this, maybe secretly welcoming it, for, despite his qualms about Nobbs, he could see the benefit of engaging staff from a more varied background, and accordingly, made a few unexpected appointments of his own, including of course Frank Fairclough.

One of the most controversial of these was a young Welshman called Philip Evans, an energetic and intense individual who delighted in ruffling received opinion with provocative assertions like, "The world would be a far better place if everyone were shot at sixty". He arrived at the School like a whirlwind in September 1958, after National Service with *The Welch Regiment* in Cyprus, and often proclaimed thereafter his good fortune in having experienced, albeit briefly, the "last oozings" of NGS, if not of Netherbridge itself as a working cotton and coal-mining town.

Newly married, he and his wife, Shirley, a library assistant at Stockport Public Library, whom he had met at the Freshers' Ball at UCW Aberystwyth, had managed between them to scrape together the prohibitive £180 deposit for one of "Seymour's Starter Semis" on the western fringes of the town, with mostly coal-miners and cotton-mill workers as neighbours. Answering a call of nature in the small hours on their first night in their new home, he happened to look out across the 'Moss' towards the cotton mills lit up like cathedrals along the Netherbridge branch of the Bridgewater Canal. He was smitten like Wordsworth on Westminster bridge: not only were these gigantic edifices the mainspring of the town's economy, where many of his pupils' mothers worked, they were themselves objects of breath-taking splendour. This strange landscape, overshadowed by majestic chimney stacks and green domes, and so different from Cyprus or his native Cardiganshire, captured his imagination, and over the next twenty years he developed a lasting affection for its intimidating beauty. It was his daily indulgence to walk to school along the canal past these structures, never ceasing to marvel at their scale and symmetry, and reflect on how over a century ago each one of those red Accrington bricks had been exquisitely tapped into place by some unsung master craftsman, who also had a very good head for heights.

Less imposing, but no less entrancing for Philip, were the long narrow streets of red brick cottages running at right angles to the canal, with their tiny cake shops, fish and chip bars and two-roomed public houses, which were little more than converted cottages, albeit emblazoned with august names like *Crystal Palace*, *The Royal Sovereign* and *The Golden Fleece*.

But it was the three mighty mills – *Belmont*, *Ellesmere* and *Ravenscroft* – that fascinated him the most, especially the way they dominated the town, both the place and the people. From time immemorial, the last week of June and the first in July had been designated "Netherbridge Wakes Weeks". Originally a religious festival, this annual event took place when the mills closed for the workers' annual holiday and the machines were overhauled and cleaned. But in fact, tradition decreed that almost everything else in the town closed down too because the bulk of the population, even those not connected with the mills, joined the mass migration, mainly by train, to a specified seaside destination like Rhyl, Blackpool or Whitby, leaving only skeleton services for the few left behind. One or two shops opened briefly mornings and evenings for essentials such as milk and bread, and news-vendors operated from hand carts at strategic street-corners in the town.

This time-honoured tradition had such a marked effect on attendance at NGS that the time-table of lessons was suspended during this period. The masters usually spent the mornings marking examination papers, completing end-of-year reports, while the few remaining boys got on with their private reading. The afternoons were devoted to keenly contested masters-versus-boys cricket, tennis and chess tournaments. In short, it was a most agreeable time of the year at the Grammar School, with public examinations over for another year and the long summer vacation barely two weeks away; and no one enjoyed it more than the new young English master from Wales.

Having graduated in English from the University College of Wales, Aberystwyth in the mid-1950s, Philip had first thought of becoming a journalist, perhaps starting as a junior reporter on the *Cambrian News*, and eventually moving on to a more prestigious daily. But inveigled by the starting salary of school mastering, the long holidays, a five-day week, the job security and a handsome pension, he finally succumbed, like so many before him and since, "stumbling upon the profession rather than choosing it", as he once put it.

But for all that, he made quite a good fist of it, having also fortunately stumbled upon an institution with whose traditions and ethos he felt completely at ease, and where energetic and resourceful individuals were given their head. Although lacking the intellectual credentials of some of his colleagues, he was academically inclined, deriving deep satisfaction from researching texts thoroughly before introducing them to his pupils. But perhaps his greatest assets were his energy and his enthusiasm, both for his subject and for extending education beyond the classroom.

Though no great sportsman himself, he soon adopted the Davenportian philosophy of *mens sana in corpora sano*, and most lunch-breaks could be found in the gymnasium together with a dozen or so colleagues, all exorcising personal frustrations with the world (and each other) by engaging in something purporting to be 5-aside football but containing more than a hint of Cumberland all-in wrestling! Always an avid student of human nature, Philip observed at first-hand how quickly intelligent and cultured grown-ups could transmute into mindless thugs in the name of so-called sporting supremacy. Furthermore, some took delight in inflicting actual bodily harm on their physically inferior colleagues, while others saw fit to settle old scores with well-directed assaults on the more vulnerable parts of the anatomy. This unbecoming spectacle continued for some half-hour daily until interrupted by the registration warning bell, when an ungainly mass of bloodied and sweaty bodies dispersed and charged towards the cold shower cubicles, to cool the elevated temperatures and tempers before resuming academic dress and a suitably sober mien.

More purposefully, Philip also became a devotee of Frank Fairclough's Weight-training Club, and helped out with the junior gymnastics and athletics teams. He officiated at Dr Davenport's annual Inter-house Boxing Tournament, and whilst no great swimmer himself, 'inherited' from an elderly though disingenuous medievalist the organising of the Inter-house Swimming Gala, held during the penultimate week of the Michaelmas Term at the Netherbridge Public Baths.

In addition to these commitments, during his second

year at the School he was also asked by the Senior English master to take over *The Netherbridgian*, the School's magazine, which reputedly had run continuously in some form or other since its inception to celebrate Queen Victoria's Golden Jubilee in 1887. Of course, Philip saw this as an ideal opportunity to indulge his journalistic instincts; and for good measure, he himself started a hugely popular monthly magazine of Sixth form creative writing and cartoons, entitled *Shoots*, typed up by the boys themselves and duplicated on Martha's Gestetner.

When Jim Allen, one of the housemasters, left NGS to become the headmaster of an independent school in the Somerset in the summer of 1960, Philip thought it would be a nice gesture to arrange a surprise buffet evening in his honour at the *Boar's Head*. The following Friday he suggested to Jack Higginbottom, the landlord, who warmed to it at once, "That's a gradely idea, Philip lad, the missus could do you a reet good supper for two bob a head."

And so, during the following week Philip went round all the masters in turn explaining his plan and where possible collecting their florins. He was pleasantly surprised: most thought it a splendid idea, though one or two had other commitments that evening or had genuine excuses, like transport difficulties. One or two others had been wary at first, but changed their mind when they learnt that the Headmaster would be present. But a hard core of some half-dozen were resolutely against the idea because it had never been deemed necessary before. In the event, this inaugural get-together proved an enormous success, and thereafter became a regular end-of term feature on the Staff calendar, along with the Annual

Boxing Tournament, the Prize-giving Evening and the Old Boys' Association Dinner.

But perhaps Philip's most ambitious and successful extra-curricular venture was his Theatre Club, which began tentatively when he invited some half-dozen Sixth-formers to accompany him to see a production of Chekhov's *The Seagull* at the Library Theatre in Manchester. Without any prompting from Philip, requests soon followed for further theatre visits, and, with Dr Davenport's wholehearted support, he decided to form what became known as the Senior Theatre Club, whereby he would reserve tickets and arrange transport for the first Wednesday of every month to attend a play at one of the many professional, and amateur, theatres in the North West. Live theatre proved such an exciting novelty that he extended the Club to include fifth and then fourth form boys, and demand always outstripped supply. At one point Frank Fairclough complained that he was losing his weight-trainers because they preferred "to go and see some poncey actors wearing make-up and tights." In the end he was obliged to change the Weight-training Club evening, and ironically started accompanying Philip on the Theatre trips!

Again, making the most of his journalistic instincts, Philip began designing and posting notices around the school to publicise each "Play of the Month", and such was the response that he soon had to book a 54-seater coach, then two, and finally two double-decker buses. The final reward for those who had attended the requisite number of monthly theatre visits was a trip to the Royal Shakespeare Theatre in Stratford upon Avon at the end of the Summer Term.

BUT PHILIP'S youthful energy and enthusiasm did not always meet with his colleagues' approval. Dyed-in-the wool academics looked askance at such "capers", denouncing this new preoccupation with "extra-curricular activities" as time-wasting distractions.

One lunch-break when Philip had taken two 'O'-level English Literature classes to see a production of *Julius Caesar* at the Liverpool Everyman, feelings ran high in the Masters' Room. "No wonder standards are falling," pontificated one of the bridge-players, who had lost a free period that morning covering one of Philip's classes, "we always managed without this sort of nonsense before."

"Enough time for the theatre and such like when they've got their qualifications and are settled in jobs!" echoed his friend.

"What next?" said a third, "Ski trips to Switzerland... or field-trips to Amsterdam, eh?"

"Of course, we know what's really behind all this, don't we?" chimed in a fourth, lending a sharper edge to the sarcasm. "Feathering his own nest, that's what, embellishing his brag-sheet for his next job. The sad fact is, there's no call for good, old-fashioned schoolmastering any more – nor for fellows who really know their subject and how to put it across. Oh, no, you've got to be a bit of an *impresario* now – that is, if you want to get on. Showmanship...that's the name of the game, I'm afraid. All I can say is, it's all a bit late for me, and I'm glad I've only got two years to go. I'll soon be marking off the days on my locker!"

"By the way, what's this latest idea the old man's got about a... Parent Teacher Association?" exclaimed another. I think the less we see of these parents, the better.

Give some of them an inch, and they'll be taking over our jobs. It all started when those bossy women talked him into letting their so-called "clever daughters" join the Science Sixth. That's when the rot started."

Such barbs did not emanate exclusively from the "old contemptibles". Equally acerbic gibes came from the golfing set, the bridge table, and especially from a peculiar 'in-group', dubbed by Dan Carrington, the Music Master, as the "Banger-Forty Club", presumably on account of its members' age and obsession with old motor-cars. Unsurprisingly, Nobbs was one of its founding members and staunchest adherents.

DIAMETRICALLY opposed to the "Bangers", was the less intrusive, but no less dynamic, "Gang of Four". This was a bunch of incorrigible young cynics comprising: Dan Carrington, the said Music Master, a portly and good-natured Liverpudlian; Peter Halliwell, a gangly and somewhat youthful-looking French Master with a passion for Traditional Jazz and motor-cycles; Charlie Aldridge, a Physics Master with a first from Dr Davenport's *alma mater*, Christ's College, Cambridge; and finally, Philip Evans. With his gentle and forbearing disposition, Charlie Aldridge seemed something of a misfit in the group, but he loved an intellectual argument on any subject and was a past master at drawing fine distinctions or exposing logical fallacies. These four had arrived at the School on the same day in September 1958, and being young and new to the profession, had sought comfort in each other's company. With the passing weeks and terms, their friendship grew, forming strong bonds, which were visibly resented by many of the other masters. Apart from

Philip, they were unmarried and living in apartments or lodgings within walking distance or a bus-ride from the School.

When not on duty, they usually took lunch at a small table in the far corner of the Refectory, and after school met for a pot of tea and a toasted tea-cake at Tiplady's, a splendid, old-fashioned dining establishment in the centre of the town, built in the same neo-Gothic style and from the same York stone as the Town Hall opposite. On most Friday nights they could also be seen putting the world to rights at the *Boar's Head*; but whatever the venue, the discourse was always vigorous and the topics wide-ranging and unpredictable. When no matter of great import occupied their thoughts, they often aired grievances about the ways of the world, and occasionally their little world at NGS, where wayward pupils or unhelpful colleagues frequently tested their patience.

ON THE FRIDAY before the Lent half-term of 1963, with the whole country in the grip of the severest winter of the twentieth century, Dr Davenport decided to close the school early. This often happened during the winter months to afford the buses extra daylight to negotiate their routes home through the dreaded sulphurous smog, a phenomenon that plagued Netherbridge like all other industrial towns before the Clean Air Act came into effect. But now the drivers had the further hazard of treacherous ice to contend with.

Few objected to that particular early closure: young married masters hurried back early to their families and firesides, while small boys bicycled or skated home, less hurriedly, along the rock-solid Bridgewater Canal. In the

Masters' Room, the chess and bridge contingents reassembled at their respective tables, while others relaxed with a pipe and the Staffroom copies of *The Times* or *New Statesman*, or even took the opportunity to catch up with some marking or other routine task. Accordingly, despite the encircling gloom and the god-awful weather forecasts, in general, all seemed well with their world.

Ice, fog or even hell-fire notwithstanding, the "Gang" had arranged to meet as usual at Tiplady's, though Dan Carrington would be late, because of a meeting with the peripatetic woodwind teacher. When he eventually arrived, breathless and not a little discomfited, he recounted how, on returning to the Masters' Room, he had found Dr Kendricks, the distinguished Senior Classics Master, frantically searching for a mislaid set of Sixth form reports, and had stayed behind to help him look for them. When they were eventually found – in his briefcase – Dan distinctly overheard Tony Titchener, the Senior R.I. and occasional English Master, saying to Nobbs and his cronies, "Silly ol' bugger! About time old farts like him were put out to grass!"

"Quite!" agreed Nobbs *sote voce*, "... should never have been in this job in the first place... and why does Fatso have to be so bloody nice to everybody? He gets on my f------ wick."

This incident crystallized in Dan's mind the vague sense of irritation he had felt all along about Nobbs's entourage; and after recounting it to the other three over a pot of tea, he privately vowed to seek revenge somehow for the unwarranted affront to both Dr Kendricks and himself. Over the weekend, various ideas occurred to him, including a satirical ballad, which he could sing at the end of term function at the *Boar's Head*, but in the end he settled on a spoof 'proclamation', couched in the inflated jargon well-beloved of petty bureaucrats. A copy could be posted on one of the school notice-boards, or possibly included in Philip's *Shoots*.

And so, on the Sunday evening, still smarting from the insult, a glass of whisky and an enormous coal fire as his sole companions, he set about this most agreeable of tasks with the zest of an inspired author. By midnight he had completed quite an acceptable draft, which Philip later kindly agreed to edit and type up on his newly acquired portable *Imperial*, and making two carbon copies for good measure. In the first instance, it was decided to pin one copy of the final draft on the Masters' Room notice-board, which Nobbs would be sure to see, because he always checked the notices daily – a habit ingrained in him during his orderly clerk days at Donnington.

THE BANGER-FORTY CLUB

Inaugural Report (February, 1963)

This is a well-established, though badly-publicised, association which evolved for the express purpose of affording opportunities for mutual admiration between certain individuals, who, for obvious reasons, must remain anonymous.

Ironically, what began by accident has since been so carefully nurtured that it could now be described as an inviolable unit with powers of endurance defying the most advanced psychological or sociological explanation. Even more phenomenally, its members are probably unaware of its existence; and membership is so exclusive, so jealously guarded, that none, except the most perceptive of observers, would detect any vestige of activity - if, indeed, that is a suitable term to use. But although the proceedings of this occult and highly esoteric organization takes place, in the main, at the sub-conscious level, the astute student of middle-age may, with patience and application, obtain occasional glimpses of fleeting yet unmistakable manifestations, subtle and cryptic though they be.

For the benefit of non- and aspiring-members of this unique coterie, a word of advice might not be inopportune at this juncture: as a result of painstaking research, a certain scholar was able to glean some information from the Club's unwritten rule-book. Again, for obvious reasons, the reader is warned that owing to the extremely confidential

nature of this information, he is to treat it
honourably, and wear it as near to his heart,
as if he were - vain ambition - an actual
member of this respected and 'respectable'
clique.

RULES OF ENTRY AND MEMBERSHIP

1.   It has been laid down from time
immemorial (or at least from about 1950) that
any member who omits on any occasion to
acknowledge, honour and respond to a
plaisanterie, however pedestrian, or more
commonly, platitudinous, perpetrated by a
fellow-member shall be deemed unworthy of the
Club.

2.   Members must assume the dire
responsibility at all times of furthering the
public esteem, and uphold the reputation,
however tenuous, of fellow-members; not
necessarily by crude and palpable means such
as public eulogy, but preferably by such
negative, yet highly effective, techniques as
failing to acknowledge the efforts,
achievements or remarks, however witty or
meaningful, of non-members.

3. Members must, as far as their consciences
will allow, endeavour to praise and uphold
the values, conditions and standards of
yesteryear, both directly, and by
vociferously deprecating current values,
standards and conditions. All changes – post
about 1950 – are detrimental; any innovation
must be regarded with grave suspicion,
particularly if the innovator appears to lack
the proper respect due, if not by divine
right, certainly by age and experience, to
the Club's members, and instinctively felt
by aspiring non-members who act unconsciously
as a kind of shield and defence-mechanism for
the chosen few.

4. Members must never allow themselves to
forget that this Club is only as big as the
sum of its members, and no member is as big
as the Club. Accordingly, it is each
member's responsibility, each according to
his means, to promote the well-being of the
Club; chiefly by setting impossibly high
standards of entry; indeed, the whole concept
of territorial expansion is not only vulgar
but contravenes the purpose for which the
Club was established. Therefore, membership
shall at no time exceed five in number; and

women, of course, by definition are
ineligible.

NOTE

(a) This Report was compiled some four years
ago; but owing to the atavistic and
anachronistic attitudes and 'policies' of
this Club, nothing of note has occurred,
predictably of course, to alter any detail.
(b) The point made in (a) is only incorrect
insofar as one interesting 'development'.
Though Rule 4 remains intact, it has been
observed that a system of peripheral admiring
non-members have been tolerated of late. Many
of these sycophantic parasites are often the
most unlikely candidates, incompatible by
attitude, creed, educational beliefs, or
aspiration, but somehow have been blinded,
moth-like, by the resplendence and charisma
of this esteemed group.

Readers will be kept thoroughly informed with
triennial reports.

 The document remained posted on the Masters' Room
notice-board for several days, arousing little overt
interest, until at last, Brian Blackwell, the Junior
Chemistry Master, a proud owner of a 1936 MG TA

Midget, and one of Nobbs's closest allies, asked Philip casually if he knew anything about the "Report". Was it official, or was someone "taking the piss"? At first Philip prevaricated, but then acknowledged that he too had seen it. "In fact, I found it quite informative..." adding with a knowing wink at a disinterested bystander, "that is, if you want to learn about social interaction within a closed, all-male community." The following day, however, it suddenly disappeared, and Dan Carrington felt totally vindicated.

NO ONE, except possibly Dr Davenport, could have imagined the changes that would befall NGS before the next triennial "Report" was due, but curiously certain things remained immutable: the Gang of Four's afternoon teas at Tiplady's, and the smug, self-serving demeanour of "The Banger-Forty Club", to name but two.

One Friday evening at the Boar's Head and three years to the week after the publication of the "Inaugural Report", Charlie Aldridge asked Dan if he had forgotten about the promised second report. Much to his surprise, Dan assured him that everything was under control, and that he intended to present the copy to his editor the following Monday morning.

BANGER-FORTY CLUB

Triennial Report (February, 1966)

At a recent secret meeting of the above Club

a motion was tabled as a minor concession to accuracy that it be re-named the "Banger-Fifty Club". Needless to say, the motion was defeated on two counts:

That it implied change, thereby contravening Rule 3 (See Inaugural Report, 1963.)

That it did little to further the public esteem of the Club - another breach of the Code (Rule 2).

At the same meeting, held in the collective imagination of the five members, it was unanimously acclaimed that the Club continues to thrive. An impartial observer could not but agree.

While the Club remains apparently immune to all the vicissitudes of twentieth century living, individual members have followed dissimilar paths according to how they viewed the world and interpreted the Code. A brief résumé must suffice.

Disillusioned by events, one sought his destiny in foreign parts, where his wonderfully inflated ego might be more spaciously accommodated. Another, more subtle, saw fit to engineer a sinuous though profitable path at home, miraculously promulgating two opposing philosophies simultaneously. In a similar vein, a third - perhaps the wiliest of all - earnestly embraces as many orthodoxies as there are hands to applaud him; while yet a fourth, politically less deft and embittered by a tardy realisation that honesty is not the best policy, nurses a cancerous dejection. The Club, alas, which once served him well, could offer but flimsy protection against the philistine cannonades exploding about his ears, and less still against the satanic engines and machinations which threaten the very foundations of his beliefs. Alas, belatedly, the chickens of the 'sabre-tooth curriculum' have indeed come home to roost. The last member of the 'old contemptible' quintet stands alone, doggedly glum, yet curiously affable and remarkably unaware of his unique role in the greater drama.

The last three years have witnessed wave upon wave of would-be 'counter-coteries' rearing their truculent heads as they seem to challenge the Club's supreme authority. Some of these may rightly be disregarded on grounds of intellectual arrogance, blatant dishonesty or in some cases sheer incompetence. A timely word of advice was issued to all such upstarts: 'If you must board a bandwagon, first make sure it is heading in the right direction, and secondly, don' t fall off the bloody thing' .

In Note (b) of the first report (1963) readers will recall a brief but significant allusion to a novel phenomenon in the life of the Club: the appearance of a clutch of self-appointed novitiates who deluded themselves into believing that devout and constant admiration of the glorious five must eventually lead (vain ambition!) to true membership. Alas, despite faithful and long adulation they must instead remain eternally ostracized, because the Club' s chief function of intramural, self-perpetuating and mutual congratulation by definition precludes all forms of annexation. Consequently, the said posse of toadies, having grown sullen and bewildered by their idols' wanton indifference, have been seen to cast a lascivious eye at other, more accessible and proselytizing factions.

All in all, therefore, the Club (albeit slightly diminished in number) seems to have little to fear, and can look forward to another five years' consolidation. Members may find themselves at times wooing the giddy mode of the hour and variously seeking personal advancement with discrete opportunist overtures, but when the common enemy glowers, whatever innovatory badge he may wear, and threatens the corporate well-being of the Club, they shall not forget where their prime duty lies.

Readers will be kept thoroughly informed with the next triennial report in 1969.

Philip had another reason for not spending too much time on Dan's "Report". Unbeknown to the other members of the "Gang", he had recently embarked on a literary effort of his own. Inspired by Dan's foray into the realm of satire, he had pondered long on how he might trump his friend's tour de force.

During his second year at Aberystwyth, he had briefly shared a room with a History research student from London with the then improbable name of Peredur ap Iorwerth. His father was a minister at one of the large Welsh Presbyterian churches in north London, and from all accounts a formidable preacher in the grand, though by now outmoded, incantatory style. Both Peredur and his sister had been raised entirely through the medium of Welsh and imbued with a love of all things Welsh, especially Welsh literature. Often before "lights out", he would read aloud or recite pieces of Welsh poetry, mainly for pleasure, but also to demonstrate to Philip the Welsh language's unrivalled capacity for poetic expression. His favourite form was the *englyn*, whose succinctness and intricate alliterative and rhyme patterns, he insisted, surpassed any poetic form in the English language, including Shakespearean blank verse. One of his very favourites was by the early twentieth century eccentric, Dewi Emrys, called *Y Gorwel*, (The Horizon):

> *Wele rith fel ymyl rhod – o'n cwmpas,*
> *Campwaith dewin hynod;*
> *Hen linell bell nad yw'n bod,*
> *Hen derfyn nad yw'n darfod.*

Understandably, Philip was more than a little in awe of Peredur, not only his academic credentials and metropolitan upbringing, but more particularly his impeccable pronunciation of both the English and Welsh languages – a rare accomplishment this, because the mother-tongue usually casts a shadow over any other. Nevertheless, Philip countered with a spirited defence of his adopted language, and demonstrated the flexibility and splendour of the "iambic pentameter" by quoting the whole of (the blind) John Milton's sonnet, "Methought I saw my late espoused Saint", his eyes moistening with the final poignant line, "I wak'd, she fled, and day brought back my night."

"Now, there's a sonnet for you," exclaimed Philip triumphantly.

"Yes, but *we've* got some wonderful Welsh sonnets, too, like R. Williams Parry's *Y Llwynog* (The Fox)!"

"Well, I'll have to take your word for that... but what about the "heroic couplet" then? Surely this is one of the finest poetic forms in any language... it wasn't called "heroic" for nothing."

Some fifteen years later, while preparing Pope's *The Dunciad* for his 'A' level English class, Philip recalled fondly those stimulating, late-night disputes with the urbane Londoner, albeit squirming now at his own painfully naive and inadequate defence of the "heroic couplet". But it was while re-reading some of Pope's incisive portrayals in *The Dunciad* that he hit upon the ideal vehicle for giving vent to his feelings not only about the 'Banger-Forty' bunch, but other colleagues as well.

Accordingly, he settled on a mock-heroic poem in the vein of Pope's *Dunciad*, and with a format akin to that of Chaucer's *Prologue to the Canterbury Tales*. Adopting a mediaeval scenario, he imagined himself as a wandering minstrel who happens upon a northern royal court ruled by a kindly, wise but not altogether happy King George. The baronial hall where the knights reside would stand for the Masters' Room at NGS, and the knights themselves, the masters. He was satisfied that this setting would provide ample scope for both satirical and laudatory observations, and the framework unlimited flexibility.

(The poem was too long to be included in its entirety, but the following fragment should give a flavour of Philip's droll sense of humour.)

A CELT AT THE COURT OF KING GEORGE

Preface

This poem is a fiction, but should any of the
characters resemble any real-life personalities so as
to cause offence, the author reserves the right to
congratulate himself, for in part that was his express
intention. At the same time, he wishes to exonerate
himself from all responsibility, and thereby declare
recriminatory immunity on the strength of having
performed a service beneficial to the individual, and
the community at large.

   Since art is a selective process, the gallery of
portraits is perforce incomplete. The author has
attempted no more than could be achieved within the
bounds of time, interest and purpose. Some characters
were felt to be so 'stock' as not to merit a
mention, while others, alas, were ignominiously
dismissed in a line or obscure couplet. If anyone
feels slighted by dint of omission, let him consider
himself fortunate, for since our profession seems
prodigally indiscriminate in its rewards, he saw it
fit to sprinkle his compliments scantily on the
deserving few. Finally, let the 'victims' not wince
too much or too long, for the present writer was more
exercised by felicity of expression than with venting
his spleen.

Prologue

Four summers past I left my native Borth
To spread my rustic wings, and travelled north,

And scarce but two days' march from Offa's Dyke
I soon discovered what the north was like.

I came upon a court renowned for miles
Whose inmates greeted me with nods and smiles:
  'Nowhere in all the land,' they said, you'll see
A court so full of grace and amity.'
The King – a "parfait gentil" king withal –
Welcomed me warmly to his noble hall.
Beside him stood his second-in-command,
Who drawled 'Oh yes', and made to shake my hand,
When like a badger to his sett withdrew
To check his old stock and release the new.
(How fallen are the mighty, blunt their blades,
When viceroys gladly ply such menial trades!)

Thus, friend, if love and pity have you none,
  'Twere best this court, like pestilence, you shun;
But if your mind is sound, and nerves are strong,
I'll show you where our modern peers belong.

The Portraits

First meet Lord Pallisan, (God comfort him),
Bulbous of belly but too lean of limb,
Who gained at Bolton Tech his HND,
And mourns each day that he has no degree.

But lo, who next in smugness sits serene
Mocking with comely words and jibes unseen,
Assumes omniscience, perorates and sneers,
And cannot see why we have doubts and fears?
What boots two lovely eyes and chubby cheek,
When round the nether regions vestments reek?

And yet, he generates such high esteem:
Both lord and knight alike him worthy deem.
Nightly he prays as down he lies to rest
What type of central heating suits him best.
This is a knight with no distinctive mark -
Prize product of the English public park.

Towards him leans all clad in seagull grey
Thrice-blessèd darling of the month of May:
Three knights, it seems, congested in one lump,
Few knights in court are blessed with such a rump;
A mountainous paunch, a prairie for an arse,
No woman bore this knight - he came to pass.
Yet, let not flesh conceal the fire and fight
That stirs his spirit and directs his bite.
From Skelmersdale each day he hails with speed;
The Devil take the stirrup - God the steed!

But now with boredom let your eyes alight
To scrutinise a 'constipated' knight,
Yearly he doffs the pedagogic gown,
Incites his greenhorn yeomen to lampoon
The clichés they will peddle all too soon.
A glutton for print, he reads all that is writ,
Sad chance he's not rewarded with more wit.

Thus, let us pass and briefly scan the room
For freaks that Nature nurtured in her womb.
First mark a weather-gnome in charcoal grey
Who keeps the minutes for the PTA;
And round Sir Ron, the alchemist-in-chief
Whose frequent litanies show great belief;
Much greater piety indeed than he
Who's paid to inculcate divinity.

I speak, of course, of him whose stunted frame
Was hammered out to play some 'vulgar game'.
Tiptoe all day he struts about the hall,
And prays in vain that God will make him tall.
First, muscles flex while chairs are borne aloft,
For fear a fool should think that he is 'soft';
Meanwhile he bides the bell with likely tales
Of Jonah's strange experiences in whales,
Or makes the welkin ring with solemn strains
As saintly heroes bear their Christian pains;
But worse, with poignant irony recites
How Madeline performed her nuptial rites,
If Keats but knew, he'd hire old Hildebrand,
(Dwarf against dwarf) to crush this charlatan.
As well for Caliban to speak blank verse,
Or Goneril the agèd Lear to nurse:
Such complexes this vicious midget twist
That noble rank no longer spurns the fist.
O, for an oracle to tell me why
The King picks infidels to teach RI!

Now meet a different knight who needs no trace
Of outward pomp to justify his place.
Without a boast, without a herald's gong,
This learned thane enriched the noble throng.
Slow to opine, reluctant to pronounce,
But in defence of right, not slow to pounce.
Those hackneyed knights his gothic robes mistake
For senile decadence and wits opaque.
One can but wonder at the Royal ruth
And wisdom that embraced this man of truth.

As terms glide by like palfreys at the fair,
Duke after duke resigns, and moves elsewhere;

85

Some seeking headships, some a graded post,
And others sinecures on the coast.
Replacements come like rabbits from a hat;
More lords rush in to grab the dangling sprat,
Full of ideals and "visual aids" untold,
Such as yon Teuton with the teeth of gold.

Now, patient friend, forget such mundane things,
And come away with me on fancy's wings,
Where you will find two noble paragons
Whom Mother Wit may proudly call her sons.
The first, a tall and comely youth behold,
Whose one regret in life is growing old,
Though youth has cost him many a stinging sneer
And frequent sharp rebuffs from duke and peer.
Slow to dispute, unwilling to offend,
This gentle thane appreciates a friend,
But lacks a tolerance of tedious souls
Who do not share his whims, or see his goals.
But age may yet instruct his fiery breast
The wisdom to accept an alien guest.

His partnered princeling had a wistful mien,
Who, when at court, preferred to toil unseen:
And finally, when bored with boors, took wing,
Winning the palm to serve another king.
Now he is gone, let me at least record
His gentle scabbard housed a valiant sword...

Few can be judged by what is manifest,
And simpletons alone omit to test
What lurks insidiously beneath the flood;
But, honest friend, for all his noble blood,
To damn this knight on sight is not unkind,

For infant looks denote an infant's mind.
In Wales we have an ancient tale,
Depicting in a mad Atlantic gale,
A brace of handsome ravens gliding home
To nest high up above the seething foam;
And as they reach that dreadful, dizzy height,
The mother says, "Behold, my child is white!"
Remorseless Fate denied the noble dame
Who whelped this knave the love to do the same.

Rarely does Fate inflict a triple wrong,
But cast your eye again among this throng,
And see three sterile souls with good degrees –
And ask, 'Did He who made the Lamb make these?'

PHILIP'S *magnum opus* had taken him the best part of six months to complete, and throughout that time he had managed to keep it to himself until it was ready for publication.

His wife had berated him many a time for wasting his time and energies on such a pointless and puerile exercise.

"What good will it do you – or anybody else, for that matter? It certainly won't further your career. And, by the way, have you thought about the libel implications? You should be applying your talents to earning some extra cash. Remember that article you wrote for the *Cambrian News* about our cycling holiday in France... and the editor kept asking you for more? Or what about something for the *Manchester Evening News* about... oh, I don't know... modern youth, perhaps, or anything fashionable? Or what about a book of short stories about Army life? You're always going on about that when we have people in. And what about that novel you were always going to write? You could set in a grammar school... plenty of possibilities there!"

Shirley was probably right, he thought: he *should* be putting what little talent he had to better use. But for now, no other reward, financial or otherwise, could provide the thrill and satisfaction he had derived from his "pointless and puerile exercise", *A Celt at the Court of King George*.

Chapter Four

Morning assemblies at Netherbridge Grammar School were unpretentious affairs – a hymn, a Bible reading and a prayer, followed by a short address. And yet, these gatherings often had a longer-lasting impact on the boys than many of the actual lessons because they set the tone for the day, and reinforced the "grammar school virtues" of working hard, playing hard, and putting duty and self-sacrifice before instant-gratification.

Tuesday, 19th April 1966 was the first day of the summer term, and apart from the general excitement of a new term, nothing seemed unusual about that morning's Assembly, but for many of those present it was to prove extraordinary.

At five to nine prompt, the boys, supervised by the prefects and form masters, file in quietly into the historic assembly hall redolent of freshly-waxed furniture and tradition. On the platform, on either side of a massive oak lectern (a gift from Mr Whitworth's late widow, and exquisitely constructed and carved by Taff Jenkins) sit the Senior Master, Mr Joseph Riley, and the Head Boy, Neil Pemberton, who has just won an open scholarship to read Modern History at Magdalene College, Oxford.

The hall clock strikes nine, and Dr Davenport, immaculate as always in a black suit and gown, but this morning curiously without his customary red carnation, enters stage left and walks to the lectern, whereupon all conversation ceases and everyone stands. "Good morning, everyone," enunciates the great man, and the whole school responds as one with dignity and reverence. In an effortless, self-effacing way, he exudes a potent, charismatic presence, which once experienced leaves an indelible impression. Even physically he is impressive: a smidgen over six feet tall, with the lithe musculature of an Olympic athlete, and, as Frank Fairclough once remarked, still looking capable of going ten rounds with Rubin 'Hurricane' Carter!

The Senior Master announces the hymn like a vicar: *Blest are the Pure in Heart*, and a promising young pianist from the first year strikes up the first few bars of *Franconia* on the magnificent Broadwood grand, before the whole school bursts into lusty song. At the end, everyone sits for the Head Boy's reading from St Matthew's Sermon on the Mount:

Blessed are the poor in spirit: for theirs is the kingdom of heaven... Blessed are they that mourn: for they shall be comforted... Blessed are the meek: for they shall inherit the earth, etc...

Followed by the prayer:

Almighty God, give us grace to be gentle and forgiving in our dealings with one another. Endow us with humility that we may each esteem the other better than himself; for the sake of Jesus Christ our Lord. Amen.

And so, at last, the moment everyone has been waiting for arrives. Dr Davenport discards the lectern and steps forward to the front of the stage to be more at one with his audience. As usual, he carries no papers, preferring to speak from the heart, his style more conversational than declamatory – a chat rather than an oration.

"Thirty years ago, almost to the day," he begins, "I stood on this platform for the very first time, and, as you can imagine, like most beginners I felt more than a little anxious. I also happened to be following in the footsteps of that great headmaster, Mr Henry Whitworth, who had worked so hard over many years in a quiet and unassuming way to make this school one of the leading academies in the North of England. And thinking about Mr Whitworth's self-effacing manner reminded me of a most edifying encounter I experienced a little over a year ago.

"An old college friend had telephoned me that he had two complimentary tickets for the premier of the ballet, Romeo and Juliet at the Royal Opera House, Covent Garden on February 9th. He stressed that the choreography was by the outstanding Kenneth Macmillan, and that it would be a wonderful chance to see the then rising star, Rudolf Nureyev, in partnership with the legendary Margot Fonteyn. As it happened, I had several other engagements that week, but this seemed too good an opportunity to miss, especially as Fonteyn was appearing for the opening night only. So, I rearranged things, and on the 6th caught an afternoon train to from Manchester to Euston, where my friend was duly waiting for me. We took a taxi directly to the theatre, and arrived with only minutes to spare.

"The performance turned out to be spell-binding, and by way of acknowledgement the packed audience gave a forty-five minutes' standing ovation during forty-three curtain-calls – something, I feel sure, that will be talked about in ballet circles for years to come.

"Now, this friend happens to have close links with the Royal Ballet, and after the performance, to my great surprise, we were invited back stage to meet the great lady herself and show our appreciation in person. I fully expected to see a prima donna luxuriating in all the adulation, snowed under with flowers and countless telegrams from well-wishers. Dame Margot's dressing room certainly was festooned with the many bouquets she had just received on stage, but curiously she herself was not among them, nor was she busy opening telegrams. Indeed, she was not in her dressing room at all, but, curiously, in the practice room next door rehearsing with her dance coach an intricate sequence of steps from one of the scenes she had just performed to such overwhelming approbation."

At this point he pauses, but even the softest whisper or cough dares not sully the riveting silence. He stares into the middle-distance momentarily as if considering matters beyond the here and now, and then re-addresses his spell-bound audience.

"Coincidentally, but very appropriately as it happens," he continues, "the theme of this morning's reading and prayer was humility, and an important aspect of humility, I believe, is to be mindful of one's shortcomings, and to be always striving to remedy them. That must be especially difficult when the whole world is singing your praises.

"We all know that each one of you in this hall this morning possesses real potential to achieve great things in life – that is why you attend this school. Some of you will go on to gain national and possibly international recognition, emulating many of those who passed through these doors before you. One or two of you, maybe, will be rewarded, like Dame Margot, with the CBE, or a knighthood, or possibly a Nobel Prize. Who knows? But whatever the future holds for you, let me finish with the same piece of advice that Margot Fonteyn herself once gave to a group of promising ballet students: 'Take your work seriously – but never yourself'".

Then something strange and unprecedented happens: an Upper Sixth boy at the back of the hall stands up without warning and starts clapping spontaneously. Then, two or three of his friends do likewise, and then the Head Boy also stands up and vigorously joins in the applause. Suddenly the whole school rises to its feet and erupts into frenzied applause. Embarrassed by such fulsome acclaim, Dr Davenport stands there visibly ill at ease, and raises a self-conscious hand to quell what he regards as an unwarranted tribute, but to no avail. He tries again, but again to no avail, and when the third attempt fails, this supreme embodiment of both achievement and humility bows politely, turns, and slowly leaves the very platform he has graced ever since anyone can remember. As he disappears into the wings, the applause continues for a while before reluctantly abating. At last, the Senior Master gives the signal for the dismissal, and the hall begins to empty quietly and solemnly.

Presently, a palpable gloom seems to descend on the whole school, with even the masters making their way in silence to their respective bases, as if to say anything at all would constitute a profanity.

"Well, f--- me!" chortles Nobbs to a fellow Forty-Banger, as they swagger back to the Masters' Room, "Fancy 'God' entering Fonteyn's inner chamber! I always thought he were a dark 'un!"

VERY SOON after Dr Davenport had entered his study, an all-pervading gloom engulfed him too, and he began to sob loudly and inconsolably. Martha had heard him coming in, and had been looking forward to their usual cup of tea and chat about the work schedule for the day, but even she was taken aback at this sudden reversal of mood. Had anything happened during Assembly to upset him? He had been in such high-spirits immediately before, even repeating that old joke about the farmer, the prize sow and the wheel-barrow, which seemed to improve with every telling.

But she left him alone for a while, having learned from experience how best to deal with his unpredictable, and of late more frequent, 'turns', as he called them. After a few minutes, she ventured to knock gently on the adjoining door. At first, all she could hear were pitiful sniffs and groans, and then eventually an apologetic and self-conscious "Come in, Martha."

"Are you ready for your cup of tea, Dr Davenport?" she asked with as much normality in her voice as she could muster.

"Yes, that would be very nice, Martha, thank you." But as soon as she closed the door softly behind her, she heard another heart-rending sob.

These dreadful, black bouts usually struck without much warning, and often at the most inconvenient times. Once, while delivering the keynote speech to an educational conference in Exeter, he had broken down just as he was warming to his theme.

Usually, the attacks were triggered by some trivial detail, often connected with his father, who had died tragically, aged 63, a few days before his son was due to start at the County School. Being well into his middle years, he had never expected to find a wife, let alone have a child of his own, but he did acquire a wife, and moreover a young and beautiful one, who duly presented him with a marvellously gifted and sweet-natured son. He adored them both and they him, and yet he always wondered why the Good Lord had seen fit to bless him, George Davenport, an ordinary working man, so prodigiously and so undeservedly. One would have thought that someone so blessed as he would have had little to feel dejected about, but the truth was that the father was prey to the same mental and emotional aberrations as the son was doomed to endure.

Mrs Davenport had always taken every care to shield her boy from the worst episodes of his father's infirmity, and especially the electric shock treatment he had undergone at Winwick Mental Hospital a few months before he died, telling the lad that he was working away on a new railway bridge at Netherbridge. Likewise, for several years she had successfully concealed the truth about his death: he had not in fact been killed accidentally by a runaway coal wagon. It was something she said unwittingly many years later that had aroused young George's suspicions. He had never quite understood the awkward silences nor been entirely convinced by the facile explanations. This highly intelligent and inquisitive teenager desperately needed to know when, where and how this tragedy had taken place, and whose fault it was.

"It was no one's fault, George dear," implored his mother, "just a terrible accident. The ambulance took him to the hospital, but it was too late; the injury to his head was too severe. The doctors said they had tried their best, but in the end, they could do nothing for him."

Despite his mother's impassioned plea, young George was never fully persuaded, and had had to make do with her account until he was in his final year at school. It was at about that time that he himself began to develop morbid thoughts and feelings of worthlessness, which in turn rekindled his curiosity about the circumstances of his father's death. The nagging doubts that had always dogged his young life intensified, until one day his mother let slip with, "I hope you're not getting like your father."

He brooded all night long on that remark, and the following morning vowed to find out the truth. At first, he had no idea how to go about this, but the ever-helpful lady at the Town Library, suggested that he looked up the obituary and inquest reports in past copies of The Altrincham Guardian, which were stored in one of the back rooms of the Library. He knew exactly the date of the accident, and after some patient rummaging eventually managed to home in on the relevant issue of the newspaper and the inquest report. Although he had long suspected that something untoward had surrounded his father's death, he was shocked to have his suspicions confirmed so suddenly and categorically in print:

Recording a verdict of suicide, the presiding officer, Dr L.P. Clarkson, said,

"Mr George Davenport, a railway employee of Navigation Road, Altrincham, had killed himself while the balance of his mind was disturbed. I am satisfied that this was a deliberate attempt by Mr Davenport to kill himself."

The report then went on to give an account of the manner of death:

"The sole witness, Mr David Bowden, a signalman at Netherbridge Railway Station, confirmed that at approximately 7 am on Tuesday, 6th September, 1913, he noticed from his signal-box what he believed to be a trespasser meddling with the brake mechanism of one of the empty 20 ton Hopper coal wagons, which had been shunted onto the slightly inclined siding about 200 yards away from his box. He rushed out to investigate, and as he got nearer to the scene, he recognised the trespasser as Mr George Davenport, a carpenter in the Bridges Department.

"At this point, the witness was visibly distressed and asked for a glass of water, whereupon the presiding officer ruled that the inquest be adjourned for ten minutes so that the witness could collect his thoughts.

"On continuing his evidence, the witness testified that Mr Davenport had partially released the brake on the wagon, enabling it to move slowly down the slope. Ignoring Mr Bowden's attempts to attract his attention, he then ran ahead of the wagon and knelt down at the track side with his neck on the rail. Being still some 30 yards away, Mr Bowden could do nothing but watch in horror as the wagon rolled forward and the front wheel virtually severing Mr Davenport's head. According to the witness, by the time he reached the scene Mr Davenport was clearly beyond medical assistance, and his main concern was to make the wagon safe for fear it ran down and obstructed the main line. Accordingly, he hurried to reapply the brakes properly, and then covered Mr Davenport's upper body with his jacket. He then ran back to the booking office. and asked the booking clerk to cycle to the police station to report the incident to the duty officer.

"P.C. Saunders, the duty constable on that fateful morning, then read out his report of the incident, specifying how he and Mr Bowden had carried the mutilated body on the station stretcher and locked it in the Porter's Room, until a doctor arrived to certify the fatality.

"HERE YOU ARE, Dr Davenport, this will make you feel better," said Martha, as she re-entered the study breezily. She placed a tray down on the desk, and poured two cups of tea before settling into her usual chair opposite him.

"I made these scones early this morning... especially for the first day of term... I know they're your favourites."

He cut a sad figure sitting there, red-eyed, hunched and disconsolate, with his magnificent head buried in those huge, powerful hands, more like a miner's than an academic's.

"It's hopeless, Martha, I can't go on... I'm not worthy... you should be sitting here, and I pouring your tea. You see to everything... you practically run the place... sometimes when I'm travelling to London, I feel it would be better if I never returned... and how wonderful it would be to fall between the..."

"Now, Dr Davenport, you mustn't..." began Martha, but he cut across her and continued his monologue.

"The mind is a very funny thing, Martha... I can feel it all welling up inside me now... I'm so sorry, Martha, I shouldn't be putting you through all this... perhaps you had better leave me for a while." And with that he broke into another pitiful sob.

Martha said nothing, but instinctively reached across and took his hand, stroking it gently. They sat there for a few moments, avoiding each other's gaze, and then she got up and tactfully left the room, leaving this magnificent wreck of a man in lonely despair. On the way out she quietly recalled snatches from Ophelia's lament for her demented Hamlet, a part she had once played at school: "O! What a noble mind was here o'erthrown... /Now see that noble and most sovereign reason, /Like sweet bells jangled, out of tune and harsh..."

AFTER HER husband's death, Anna Maria Davenport had coped with the shock and grief by immersing herself in her work. She was still young and attractive woman with much of her life left over to live and a burgeoning genius of a son to support and cherish. She decided to remain at their terraced house in Navigation Road because of its proximity to the railway station and also because it retained so many happy memories for them both. The two accepted their fate stoically, often comforting each other by reliving the good times all three had had together, especially the annual rail trips the length and breadth of the land, from Ilfracombe to Inverness, Durham to Dunstable, or wherever the wanderlust took them, courtesy of George Davenport's annual rail 'passes'. Not unexpectedly, George Junior had acquired a detailed knowledge of all the regional railway networks and time-tables, and from a very early age had harboured an ambition to drive an express train from Manchester to Edinburgh.

He had loved the Scottish trips best of all, especially the ones on the little West Highland railways to Kyle of Lochalsh or Mallaig, but held especially fond memories of their last visit to Aunt Sarah, his father's widowed sister, in Fraserburgh during that gloriously hot August of 1913, barely a month before the blackest day of his life. When alone, he often recalled in detail what they had done each day. On the first Sunday, young George, aged ten, had won instant celebrity at the open-air Fraserburgh Swimming Gala by winning the Boys'under-15 race across the harbour.

He had handed the little silver cup to his mother for safe-keeping and for many years it had enjoyed a prime position between the two pot dogs on the mantel-piece in their neat, comfortable parlour. But, against his father's wishes, he had insisted on holding on to the shiny new half-crown piece – until disaster struck. On their way back to Aunt Sarah's, and momentarily distracted by two seagulls squabbling over a piece of fish, young George made his first intimate acquaintance with a cast iron lamp post. Stunned and disorientated by the sudden jolt, he lost his grip on the coin, which he then saw rolling tantalizingly towards a drain grid before vanishing into the murky depths.

George Senior was not pleased, and had it not been for his wife's calming presence, might well have exacted summary justice. However, unbeknown to them, a local lad two or three years older than George, and neatly rigged out in his Sunday best, had also witnessed the little drama. With quiet confidence he took off his jacket, and lifted the heavy iron grid. He then rolled up his right sleeve, reached down into the drain, and felt all round until he had found the errant coin. This he then dried on a clean handkerchief before handing it back to its rightful owner. He then re-buttoned his sleeve, put on his jacket and quietly melted into the afternoon crowd. Young George could not thank him enough, and throughout his life never forgot that little unremembered act of kindness.

It was also on that holiday that he had first seen the inside of a lighthouse – the Kinnaird Head in Fraserburgh. Aunt Sarah attended the same kirk as the keeper, who had agreed to show them round. Unfortunately, the youngster's persistent questioning stretched the poor man's patience (and intellect) to breaking point, eventually prompting an admonitory warning from George senior!

He had always held especially fond memories of

getting up at dawn to see the herring-boats returning to harbour with their night's catch. The gulls' frenetic squawking and the bitter-sweet odour of fresh fish engulfing the town were still vivid in his memory, as were their own fishing expeditions to catch mackerel, or more usually rock-salmon, with a simple hook and line and bits of fresh mackerel for bait bought at the harbour front tackle store. The best spot, he remembered, was off the reefs beneath McChonokies fish-factory, whose effluent attracted enormous specimens from all corners of the North Sea. With hardly any effort or skill they seemed to leap on to the hook barely before it had landed in the water, and most were thrown back. Equally memorable but how different were those cold, damp Saturday afternoons sitting with his father beside the Canal in Altringham, catching nothing but his father's zeal and infinite patience.

"I THINK I'll have that cup of tea now, Martha, and those cakes certainly do smell good," said Dr Davenport, desperately trying to brighten up, if only for Martha's sake; though in reality tea and cakes were the last thing on his mind.

"I'll make a fresh pot," said Martha, and quickly retreated to the makeshift kitchenette at the back of her office.

Over the years, the great man had experimented with various strategies for combating the disease, one of the most effective being intense physical exertion. This was largely why he had kept up the daily training schedule throughout his life, including an early morning run on Netherbridge Moss, the intense skipping and heavy bag routines, and finally the mandatory cold bath. No wonder his aspiring young pugilists at the school were in awe of him whenever he turned up for their twice-weekly practice sessions. (It was he, of course, who had founded the renowned NGS Boxing Club and the annual Inter-house Tournament, and for that reason it was very close to his heart.)

But a more readily accessible and most helpful ploy he had accidentally discovered was to simulate normality by telling jokes, of which he had a seemingly inexhaustible supply, ones suitable for any occasion or company. Of course, he had always taken particular delight in making Martha laugh with his double-entendres or risqué anecdotes, many recalled from his Cambridge days or more recent ones heard at the Netherbridge Cricket Club and on his many travels. But she knew when the humour was natural and when contrived.

"Goodness! That was quick, Martha! You know, as I've often said, you would have made someone... indeed still might... what am I saying?"

She knew very well what he was saying, and blushing slightly arranged the blue willow-patterned tea things on his desk a second time. He watched her every move, admiring her delicate features in profile, her full bosom and the fecund veins in her long slim arms and capable hands – so very like his mother's, he thought. Then his eye alighted briefly on the specific details in the willow pattern on his plate: the three little fishermen on the bridge reminded him of a joke Tom Molesworth had told at the Old Boys' Dinner in March.

"Did I ever tell you the one about the three sisters, Martha?"

"No, I don't think you did, Dr Davenport," she replied, wondering what was coming next, but relieved that he was beginning to sound a little more like his normal self.

"Well, anyway, they were called Sally, Kathy and Fanny, and all three were slim and strikingly beautiful. But unfortunately, their beauty was somewhat compromised by disproportionately large feet. Sally wore size eleven shoes, Kathy, size twelve, and poor Fanny, size fourteen.

"One Saturday evening, Sally and Kathy went out as a foursome with two boys from the neighbouring street, and half-way through the evening one of the boys, no doubt emboldened by drink, suddenly exclaimed, 'How come you two have such big feet?'

"Whereupon Sally replied, 'If you think we've got big feet, you should see our Fanny's!' "

Just as Martha was recovering from choking on her buttered scone, there was a gentle knock on the door.

"Importunity knocks, Martha! Come in."

The door opened slightly, which Martha took as a cue to withdraw tactfully.

"Ah, come in, Joe. I was about to come and see you. Martha has made some delicious scones especially for the first day of term. Would you care to join us?"

"Oh yes, that would be lovely... thanks very much."

At this point Martha returned with an extra cup and asked if they would like a fresh pot of tea.

"No, really, this is still quite hot, thank you, Martha," said Dr Davenport, "I must say these scones really are delightful. Have another one, Joe."

"I shouldn't, really... Dr Kinloch says I should cut down on cakes and puddings... But go on, then... I'm sure one more won't kill me!"

After a brief and slightly awkward pause, he went on, "I had a phone call from our Ian last night... wishes to be remembered to you, as always... was very pleased with himself because at last he's made it to Senior Research Officer... Going down to the Royal Marsden proved a very good move for him in the end. But unfortunately, his good news was marred somewhat... I could tell he was upset about something. At last, he told me... his favourite research monkey had developed an untreatable abscess, and he'd had to euthanize him. Apparently, every morning, old Percy would offer him his left arm through the bars of the cage to receive his daily experimental injection, and immediately afterwards reach for the banana with his right! Well, yesterday, poor thing, he presented his left arm as usual, but unbeknown to him, of course, there was to be no banana... I don't know about you, George, but that brought a tear to my eye. Perhaps I'm getting soft in my old age!"

After another anxious pause, he continued, "Oh yes, I'd nearly forgotten... what I really came to see you about was that strange business at this morning's assembly. I thought it was quite extraordinary...to coin a phrase, 'a spontaneous overflow of powerful feelings'. In my whole time schoolmastering I've never known anything quite like that."

After a slight pause, Dr Davenport felt obliged to say something, "Yes, it took me by surprise too, and I wasn't sure how to deal with it. I was very touched, of course, but also a little embarrassed, and wondering what exactly had triggered the whole thing?"

"Your guess is as good as mine, George, but whatever

the cause, the boys' and the Staff's universal respect and affection for you was unmistakable. Oh yes... not that it was ever in any doubt, of course!"

"Oh, it was probably just the reference to my first assembly sparking off an emotional reaction, that's all. We sometimes forget how impressionable young lads of this age can be; and they're always encouraged nowadays to express their feelings openly, which in our day of course was frowned upon."

"O yes, things were very different in 1936, George. That sort of thing was just not done then. Still, I suppose we've got to accept change in our line of business... I'm told it's called progress... and it's no use fighting it! It's all part of the grand new order of things, driven largely, I suspect, by this wretched 'pop' culture, which, like everything else cheap and nasty, originates in America. But what really gets to me is the perversion of our language... I cannot abide some of these new slang words I keep hearing around the school, like, 'bread', meaning money, and 'cool' or... or 'groovy' as terms of approval. And then you've got 'hang out', and 'dude', not to mention 'hippie', 'teenager' and 'rock and roll'... there's no end to it, somehow. It's an epidemic infecting our language. And I don't know where this drug business will end up either. I do hope we never have that problem at NGS. I hear they've already got it at the Secondary Modern across the road. I often reflect that those blasted Yanks stationed here during the war have a lot to answer for!"

"Don't let it get to you, Joe. Remember, our boys still do the old school proud; they work hard, play hard, and if they do kick over the traces a little more than we did at the weekend, well, I'm sure come Monday they're back at their studies duly refreshed. Remember, we've had more Oxbridge acceptances this year than at any time I can remember. Furthermore, the first XV ended the season unbeaten; and this year's First Cricket XI also looks pretty promising, especially now that the Rylance twins are back fighting fit after that meningitis scare. If the current bunch were called up to serve their country like the class of '39, I bet they'd give just as good an account of themselves. And by the way, Joe, talking about pop music I have a feeling that 'rock and roll' is pronounced as one word! Incidentally, although I wouldn't claim to be an expert, I'm amazed how this Liverpool band, The Beatles, keep coming up with so many highly original and memorable tunes. They've also developed a very distinctive sound, which I believe will stand the test of time. And on that one I think I'm in good company: both Martha and Charles Groves of the Liverpool Phil happen to agree with me!"

"You mean the... Fab Four... oh yes, they may very well have something, though I don't think they're in the same league as Irving Berlin and Cole Porter... or Gershwin. And they're certainly not more popular than Jesus just yet, as one of them claimed recently! But they are clever with those guitars, and their harmonies are certainly easy on the ear – not like that raucous lot from down south... Rolling Stones, I think they call themselves. With a name like that I doubt if they'll last beyond Christmas! By the way, I only recently discovered that 'Beatles' is spelt with an 'a'. Something to do with 'beat music', I believe, and the 'beat generation', another American abomination. Young Stanton from my Lower

Sixth class tried to explain it to me the other day, referring me to an article in the November 1952 edition of The New York Times Magazine... I ask you!"

"Well, all I can say is, Joe, I hope Mr Stanton sets you a stiff test on it, and asks for a resumé with a fully referenced critique! Talking of the different generations reminded me of something I heard in last year's HMC Conference. (By the way, Joe, it mightn't be a bad idea if you went in my place next year. I think you'd enjoy it). Anyway, one of the guest speakers was a young man from Virginia who gave a thought-provoking lecture on the post-war generation gap. I won't bore you with the details, but he began with an amusing little story. An old man, he said, was sitting on a park bench enjoying the afternoon sun, when a young fellow (probably one of your 'teenagers', Joe!) came along on his roller skates and sat down beside him to adjust one of the skates. He had an elaborate bouffant hairstyle arranged in red, yellow and green sections. Taken aback, the old man stared hard at him, and when the young fellow looked up, he said, 'What's the matter, old-timer, never done anything wild in your life?' After some thought the old man replied, 'Got drunk once... and had sex with a parrot... and I was wondering... if you could be my son!'"

Martha's full-throated chortle from her office was even louder than Joe Riley's.

"Well, Joe, time's running on, and I'm afraid I'll have to leave the ship in your capable hands again today. If you need me, which I very much doubt, Martha can ring me at home. There are a couple of things I've got to attend to in the next couple of days, and I'll get more peace and quiet there."

He thanked Martha for the cakes, and wished them both au revoir. Then after exchanging his black gown for the black gabardine coat hanging behind the door, he briskly stepped out into the long, dark corridor.

"He's in a jolly mood today, isn't he?" said Joe. Martha said nothing.

Then after a slight pause he added, "Is there anything special you need me for this morning, Martha? If not, I'll get back to my stock-take. Oh, by the way, when you have a moment, could you please remind some of the usual culprits about their requisition forms? I don't want to be last minute with all that again this year."

"Yes, certainly, Mr Riley, I'll see to it this afternoon."

"Thank you... that would be a great help".

An uneasy silence hung over the office after the two men had left, and Martha immersed herself in routine matters. She cleared and washed the tea things, and then tidied up Dr Davenport's desk. Unusually, he had left his Conway Stewart fountain pen behind – a gift, he once told her, from his mother on his tenth birthday, ready for "going up to the County School". She put it away carefully in the top right-hand drawer of his desk, where he kept one or two other personal treasures, including a pencil sketch of his father fishing in the Canal at Timperley, signed and dated Sat. 16/9/1911, when he would have been eight and a half years old. There was also a small silver-framed photograph of his mother, aged twenty-six, standing on the steps of the Halfpenny Bridge in Dublin; and his father's horn-handled pocket-knife, with "Joseph Rodgers, Sheffield" and the Maltese cross trademark emblazoned on the blade.

Though partly relieved that he had managed to haul

himself out of the trough of despair, Martha was still upset at having seen him, again, so utterly distraught; she knew that the jocularity was a mere cover, and done largely for her benefit.

She glanced at the wall-clock and realised gratefully that soon it would be morning break when the corridors and play areas would once again come alive with a distracting bustle.

As Dr Davenport made his way along the long, main corridor, he was obliged to pass Nobbs's 'Graphic Design Workshop'. Outside the door stood a very small first-form boy standing bolt upright and with his face against the wall. When he saw the Headmaster approaching his eyes filled with tears.

"Forgive me, young man," said Dr Davenport gently, "but you're Magraw, aren't you? And the latest, I hope, in a fine line of scrum-halves!"

"Yes, sir," sniffed the boy, with as much dignity as he could muster.

"And why are you standing in the corridor?"

"Mr Nobbs, sir... he said my pencil was too short, sir, and had the wrong lead as well... it should be 3H, and mine was HB, sir. I did try to explain, sir, but he smashed it on the workbench with a mallet, and told me to go and stand outside the door until the end of the lesson, sir... and..."

Leaning down and putting a protective arm round the boy's shoulder, Dr Davenport said conspiratorially, "I'm sorry to hear that, Magraw. I remember something similar happening to me when I was your age. I'd left my fountain pen at home, something I never did normally, but our Scripture master, who was very strict about such matters, would not listen to excuses. Instead, he bent me over a chair there and then and gave me 'six of the best', as he called them, with a horsewhip he kept under his desk to teach bad boys like me a lesson! His name was Mr Savage, a very apt name, we all thought!"

By now the boy's tears had given way to a broad smile.

"I tell you what," added Dr Davenport, reaching into his jacket pocket "Why don't you take my pencil? I won't need it again today. That should be long enough. I don't think it's a 3H, but it's got a good sharp point on it. Let's see what Mr Nobbs has to say, shall we?"

And with his arm still cradling the boy's shoulders, he knocked gently on the Woodwork room door, and opened it tentatively to reveal the latter-day Savage enthroned behind a larger version of the pupils' workbenches, and the guilty mallet still ready to hand. All the boys, of course, stood up when they realised they had a visitor, especially this visitor, as did Nobbs himself, reluctantly.

"Sorry to disturb your lesson, Mr Nobbs," tendered the great man, choosing his words carefully, "but we managed to find another pencil for young Magraw here. I think he has learnt his lesson, and, with your permission, would now like to re-join the class."

Nobbs, of course, had no choice but to accede, notwithstanding the vengeful resentment seething inside him.

As he was already in the room, Dr Davenport took the opportunity to take a look at the wall displays and talking to some of the pupils, and as he worked his way towards the front he could hear Nobbs making a great show of explaining to "young Magraw" in the most ingratiating tones the task which had been set while he was standing in the corridor.

"The Woodwork room looks very neat and tidy, Mr Nobbs"

"Well, thank you for that, Dr Davenport. Let us say, it's an improvement on what it used to be. I like to lead by example. Ordnung ist das halbe Leben and all that!"

Dr Davenport said nothing, but turned to the class and bid everyone good day, before leaving the room, closing the door gently behind him. After waiting a moment or two, he continued on his way down the corridor to collect his bicycle from its usual place next to Nobbs's Jaguar and Frank Fairclough's Vincent.

His usual route home was along the canal towpath as far as Northcott Lock, and then up a short, steep path to join the busy main Manchester Road, but today he felt an urge to make a short detour past the railway station, pausing briefly on the bridge on which his father was once said to have worked. Many a time as a boy, and also during the past thirty years, he had stood on that bridge, relishing the thrill of heavy trains from Manchester or Liverpool thundering underneath and momentarily shrouding his world in a heady mix of steam and smoke. And in between trains his gaze would wander across to the signal box and the shunting yards beyond to watch a brace of tank engines intent on their hectic little manoeuvres. But today he had to be content with a smug little diesel unit, dead on time, snaking prosaically over the points, full of busy, faceless people all going somewhere, but oblivious to the weed-strewn sidings mourning their glorious past.

Chapter Five

When Dr Davenport was appointed Headmaster of Netherbridge Grammar School, tradition dictated that he live within two miles of the School. After much searching and self-searching, he was eventually persuaded to take out a mortgage on *Elsinore*, No 7 Lancaster Avenue, a handsome three-storey Edwardian property on the southerly edge of the town, and brought his mother, then aged sixty and newly retired, to live there with him.

Compared to their house in Altrincham, this was a veritable mansion, with seven bedrooms, three bathrooms and a spacious cellar. Guests would be greeted in the magnificent entrance hall, their eye drawn ever skywards by the winding staircase towards the multi-coloured glazed roof.

On the eastern side there was a separate coach-house, where the previous owner had kept a brace of Bentleys; and on the western side a multi-tiered, hexagonal tower, culminating in an all-round observation chamber, gave the building a castellar aura.

Clearly, no expense had been spared in making the house the envy of the neighbourhood. The internal fittings and decor were of the finest quality, though perhaps a little lavish for the Davenports, and the extensive grounds had been landscaped in the manner of the day with manicured sunken gardens arranged in geometric patterns, a large fish pond with water-lilies, several neo-classical statues, and a rich variety of shrubs and trees, including a gigantic magnolia which when in flower enshrouded the entire front of the house in an ethereal haze. To the rear of the property a large conservatory had been added, in which Mrs Davenport took a special interest. In sum, *Elsinore* was indeed, as Jack Higginbottom of The Boar's Head once declared, "a gradely house, George – a proper headmaster's house".

But George Davenport himself was far less sure of his choice, often lying awake at night wondering if he had decided wisely. Would looking after it be too much for his mother? He would certainly have to engage a gardener and possibly a cleaner, though he could not see his mother's readily agreeing to that. And really there were far too many rooms for just two people. But, then, they didn't all have to be used. There was also the cost of heating and maintaining such a large building, and he wondered if they could advertise for a lodger or two; or possibly a 'live-in' factotum? But more than anything at first, he felt embarrassed about the resplendent life-style such a residence implied.

His mother harboured no such anxieties, and was altogether more sanguine about their new life in the grand house. She relished the open spaces both inside and out, having spent most of her life in cramped surroundings. "Oh, George," she said after the first week, "I feel I belong here already. I know I'm going to be happy here, and so will you, once you've got used to it. It's a shame your Da isn't here to share it with us. He would have loved this garden and the coach-house. It's as if it had been waiting for us all these years. I can't believe how lucky we are, and I want to grow old here!" And with that she did a little Irish jig around an antique sundial that overlooked the fish-pond.

As long as his mother was happy, George felt he could muddle through somehow despite his doubts and self-questioning, and after a while he became so engrossed in his work at the School and its related commitments that, by default, he delegated the management of *Elsinore* entirely to his mother, who being an excellent cook, housekeeper and a natural organiser, relished her new vocation.

It is remarkable how quickly living creatures adapt to altered circumstances, and so it was with both George and his mother. Presently, the perceived embarrassment of space metamorphosed into a solution looking for fresh problems. By the end of their first year there, the pantry, the larder, the scullery, the kitchen, the laundry room, and the breakfast room had been remodelled into one large working kitchen area – or the 'engine-room', as Mrs Davenport called it.

In a similar vein, George had converted the parlour and the adjoining store-room into a library and study, largely to accommodate his huge collection of books; and to this end he had commissioned Taff Jenkins to cover three of its four walls with solid oak shelving. A Kranich and Bach parlour grand piano on one side of the fireplace and a late Victorian writing desk (both gifts from the widow of a colleague at Manchester Grammar School) on the other, complemented the shelving admirably. Finally, the addition of a reconditioned Chesterfield three-piece suite created a restful environment for study, leisure, or business, and George came to spend much of his spare time there.

He also set up his personal observatory in the tower, and after a long train journey, or a demanding day at school, he could often be found there peering through his six-inch Broadhurst Clarkson celestial telescope, which the Manchester Grammar School Old Boys Association had bought him when he left, in recognition of the time and energy he had invested in the School's Astronomical Society.

And then, of course, there was the coach-house, which George, as the 'man of the house', had commandeered from the outset. Besides, his mother would have had no use for such a barn of a place clearly in need of some new, manly purpose. But from its polished parquet floor to its colossal oak beams, it still seemed to mourn the departure of the majestic Bentleys, and yearn for worthier tenants than George's work-a-day bicycle and his physical fitness paraphernalia. The over-sized beams were specially designed to support a block and tackle set, which the previous owner had used to lift the massive twelve-cylinder engine blocks when they needed repairs. Since George could find no obvious use for this finely-crafted piece of machinery, he adapted it as an item of weight-training equipment; and on the other beam he hung the heavy punch-bag on which he worked every morning after his training run.

But over the years, and especially after the onset of his mother's dementia and eventual death on Christmas Day, 1957, the old coach-house had become something more than a gymnasium for him: more akin to a private purgatory to which he felt drawn daily before breakfast, or whenever he felt the need to pulverize Cerberus's three heads of remorse, futility and despair.

THE REMAINDER of that first day of the Summer term played out without incident: Martha opened and filed Dr Davenport's mail, made a few phone-calls, and typed some letters and references; Joe Riley almost completed his annual stock-take; Form Two Alpha made their first acquaintance with the ablative absolute; and Phil Evans checked that everything was in order for his trip to Stratford-on-Avon on Wednesday the 27th to see Peter Hall's production of Hamlet.

Wednesday also proved equally calm and uneventful – that is, until lunchtime. Taff Jenkins had always spent his lunch-breaks in the Boiler Room playing pontoon and three-card brag with the Caretaker and the Groundsman, but when the new Technology Block opened in April 1957, he had preferred to stay put in his modern and splendidly equipped workshop. He was particularly enamoured of the wood-turning lathes, and most days after consuming his 'snap' and a monstrous mug of tea, he could be found ankle-deep in shavings experimenting with different shapes and grain patterns, usually with very pleasing results. Not unexpectedly, these lunchtime sessions attracted a coterie of devotees, some wishing to try their hand at this novel art form, others simply to watch the maestro performing minor miracles with Burma teak.

From time to time, Nobbs, largely to assert his petty authority as the 'Senior Crafts Master', would grace Taff's workshop with his besuited presence, and on occasions, much to Taff's annoyance, even intervene in the activities.

On this particular Wednesday, Phil Evans was on yard duty, and as was his wont, stopped by to see Taff, who happened to be engrossed in showing a second-former the correct method of mounting a facing-plate on the lathe. At that moment Taff was called away to the telephone, and Nobbs, who had been hovering nearby took over. But in his eagerness to demonstrate that he too knew something about wood-turning, he failed to check that the boy's turning block had been mounted securely. When Taff returned, his mind still preoccupied with the good news he had just received about his pension, he assumed that Nobbs had carried out all the correct safety checks, and let the boy proceed – with disastrous results. At the first bite of the chisel the wood block flew off its mountings, striking Taff directly in the face with such force as to demolish the greater part of his nose.

Phil immediately rushed to the telephone and asked Martha to call an ambulance. Nobbs ordered everyone out of the workshop, while Phil fetched a towel and bandages from the First Aid cabinet. When he returned and saw the blood and the extent of the damage, he felt physically sick, while Taff sat in a chair, numb with shock and fear at the sight of so much of his own blood.

Very soon the ambulance arrived and Taff was rushed

off to Netherbridge Infirmary. Meanwhile, Nobbs had set about entering a report of "this unfortunate incident" in the School Accident book, ensuring to couch the account in such detailed, yet ambiguous, terms as to exonerate himself of all responsibility for "the regrettable outcomes", adding that "lessons would have to be learned so that this kind of thing would never happen again."

After phoning for the ambulance and informing Joe Riley, Martha tried to telephone Dr Davenport, but there was no reply. Where could he be? He did say that he would be at the School by lunchtime, unless, of course, he was actually on his way.

Her next thought was to contact Jack Higginbottom (now the Chairman of the Governors). Jack of course was horrified, and wondered if there had been something wrong with the machine, because Taff was always so safety-conscious, especially when children were involved. And could Martha please check the insurance policies? He added that he would try and call round later if he had time, and would be sure to visit him that evening whether he was still in hospital or at home. And had Martha informed his wife? And no, he hadn't seen Dr Davenport since Sunday lunchtime when he called in for his pint on the way home after putting fresh flowers on his mother's grave. After things had quietened down at the pub he would try and get hold of him, and get back to her.

WHEN DR DAVENPORT arrived home on the Tuesday morning, he wheeled his bicycle down the drive as usual, past the magnolia tree and entered the coach-house through the side door. He then parked the bicycle carefully in its customary place beneath the railway clock he had recently bought at auction when a nearby station had fallen victim to Dr Beeching's 'axe'. Then standing back to admire the old bike in the bright mid-morning sunlight he noticed with dismay that the lens of his front dynamo lamp had developed a crack and could not fathom how or when it could have happened. But he was sure he had a spare lens in one of the drawers, and he would replace it that afternoon.

After closing the coach-house door carefully, he went into the house, picking up some letters from the vestibule floor on the way. One was an electricity bill from NORWEB; the second, a Thomas Cook holiday brochure; the third, an invitation from the Old Boys' Association to attend their Annual Dinner Dance on Friday, 15th July. That was the last day of term, he recalled, and also the night of the Brazil v Hungary game at Goodison Park. Lastly, there was an interesting looking personal letter with a Dorset postmark addressed simply to G.O.D, *Elsinore*, Netherbridge, Lancashire, and written in a beautiful and instantly recognisable italic script. But the sender's juvenile use of the acronym still rankled.

He put the letters down on the breakfast counter while he made himself a mug of coffee, and switched the oven on ready to heat up what was left of Monday's shepherd's pie. After two or three sips he sat down at the kitchen table and opened the personal letter. He was surprised and delighted to hear from Dick Spence again, a colleague and a close friend in the Mathematics department at Manchester Grammar School, who had left the teaching profession in his mid-forties to retrain as an Anglican priest. After several years as a curate, and later a vicar, in a remote corner of Worcestershire, he had eventually been rewarded with the lucrative parish of Grafton-on-Sea, a retirement resort on the south coast with a preponderance of elderly folk and frequent funerals. But whenever anyone lamented the passing of yet another well-loved and faithful parishioner, Dick's stock reply was, "Yes, it is sad, but don't forget, madam, it's also my bread and butter!"

Dr Davenport took another sip of his coffee and began reading:

My dear George,

I trust this missive finds you in the pink, and looking forward to your imminent and well-deserved retirement. With the cataclysmic changes planned by Messrs Wilson, Crosland et al, I suspect it cannot happen too soon for you.

I have been meaning to write to you for some time, but you know how it is, so much to do and not enough hours in the day – especially now with one or other of the grandchildren coming to stay almost every weekend. By the way, the powers-that-be have finally seen the light and made me a canon! Better late than never, what!

Mary and I have been thinking, it would be nice if you came down here for a few days during your summer vac. We have plenty of room, and it really is a lovely spot, with the sea front, country walks and (most important) a choice of three excellent pubs within walking distance of the rectory. "Devoutly to be wished", you might say! It's *five years now since we had a good powwow, setting the world to rights, and all that. I do miss those fantastic discussions we used to have about whatever took our fancy, and often late into the night. And no matter how late, or how many bottles of ale we'd consumed, <u>you</u> were always up at first light in your tracksuit and plimsolls pounding the pavements like a maniac. I never discovered your secret!*

Mary often said that I should do the same, if only to keep my ever-expanding waistline at bay. But in my view that kind of thing is best left to the young, and besides, if the good Lord had intended me to have a sylph-like figure, he would <u>not</u> have blessed me with such a healthy appetite – and a good-cooking wife!

Be that as it may, like you I'm sure, I'm looking forward to the World Cup in July. Bill, our eldest, has tried to get some tickets, but without much luck, so far. Still, it's not the end of the world, and in many ways you can see the action better on TV these days, albeit in black and white – roll on colour TV next year! After performing wonders at Ipswich, I think Ramsey was the right man for the England job, and I have a hunch he may well surprise us all, and more especially those b----- continentals. Let's hope so, anyway.

Looking forward to hearing from you, and I do hope you'll be able to visit us this summer.

Ever yours,

Dick.

Dr Davenport read the letter twice, pondering a little on

Dick's use of the phrase, "devoutly to be wished". But hearing from Dick again, so unexpectedly and after such a long time, was a joy. Dick had always had that effect on him. And he was so glad that his bizarre change of career had worked out well for him. At least, he sounded happy enough, but then Dick always was an incorrigible optimist. They had started at MGS on the same day in 1926, and had struck up an early, albeit unlikely, friendship. Though both gifted mathematicians with many shared interests, temperamentally they were complete opposites – Dick, the genial prankster and George, a cerebral introvert. And yet, George had been Dick's obvious choice of best man when he married Mary, and godfather for their first-born, but he had politely declined the latter because, as an agnostic, he had felt unqualified, and in any case, quite inadequate for the role. Some of George's happiest times had been the long weekends he had spent with them in their cold, ramshackle parsonage in Worcestershire, and even better when they had visited him at *Elsinore* while his mother was still alive. Yes, those certainly were happy times.

Despite the buoyant tone of Dick's letter, it had deepened George's despondency, and all of a sudden he had little appetite for the lunch he had been looking forward to. Instead, he went upstairs, changed into his training kit, returned to the coach-house and put himself through a gruelling forty minutes of punishing strength-building exercises, followed by ten minutes on the heavy bag, seeking with each blow to destroy his malevolent doppelgänger.

After executing this masochistic ritual to the point of exhaustion, he slumped down, breathless and sweat-soaked, on a tiny boxing-ring stool with his head between his knees, and sobbed, once even calling out for his mother. His cries were sufficiently loud and persistent to draw the attention of Mrs McAllister, a kindly old lady from No 5, who had been a very good friend of Mrs Davenport.

"Is everything all right, George?"

"Yes, everything's fine, Mrs McAllister, thank you," he replied, half hiding his face in a large towel. "I've probably been overworking of late, and overdoing my exercises. I must try and be more sensible with everything," he added with a forced smile. "Thank you for asking, but really, I'll be all right once I've had a bath and changed. By the way, do you need anything from the town this afternoon? I'll be going in later to post some letters. Give me a shout if you think of anything."

After she had gone, he got up and went back into the house, pausing for a moment by the front door to savour the cool, damp scent of spring, and a brief burst of the noonday sun on his bare shoulders. He then took the usual cold bath, and though feeling temporarily cleansed, the 'thing' was never far away, lurking in the wings, as it were, eager to usurp the throne of his "sovereign reason".

His expiatory ablutions completed, he raced up the magnificent oak staircase, three steps at a time, to his bedroom, and got dressed in his old green corduroy trousers and one of the three red and green roll-neck jumpers his mother had knitted for him during the harsh winter of 1946-47 – and in NGS colours too, as she always used to say! He glanced at himself briefly in the mirror as he left the bedroom – in fact only very briefly, because he always felt appalled at the briefest glimpse of that wrinkly travesty of his former self staring back at him reproachfully, as if to say, "you disgusting charlatan, you imposter! Admit it, George, the School needs a young man at the helm now, someone more in tune with the times, more capable of steering a steady course through these stormy waters. Remember Yeats: 'An aged man is but a paltry thing/ A tattered coat upon a stick...'"

The sudden burst of activity had strengthened his resolve to get on with things – and reawakened his appetite for the remains of the shepherd's pie! And so, like a skittish toddler free from its mother's restraining hand, he straddled the banister and slid down all the way into the hall, finishing the descent with an elegant dismount. He then returned to the kitchen, switched the oven on again, and sat down to re-read Dick's letter.

He found the word 'retirement' in Dick's first paragraph curiously comforting, the very sound and rhythm of it as well as its meaning – a kind of return to the womb. And the word called to mind a host of associated comforting words some of which seemed especially apposite at that moment: 'release', 'repose', 'freedom', 'acquittal', 'deliverance', 'discharge', 'relief', 'exoneration,' 'forgiveness'... Retirement too now sounded like something devoutly to be wished. Hitherto, he had always dismissed hanging up one's gloves as something old men did... the ultimate capitulation... in the ring it is for someone else to throw the towel in on your behalf. But Dick had made it sound desirable, especially now that the 'comprehensive' war was as good as lost.

He was woken from this brief reverie by the timing buzzer on the electric oven, and as he carried the pie from the fridge a preposterously puerile play on words brought a bashful smile to his face, "The pie's the thing/ In which to catch the conscience of the king".

There were other letters he had planned to write that afternoon but a reply to Dick's had inadvertently jumped the queue. And so, after several false starts, he eventually settled on the following:

Dear Dick,

It was a delight hearing from you again, especially after such a long silence, for which I hold myself equally culpable.

Regrettably, I have not felt very much "in the pink" of late with one thing and another, and as you rightly imply there is much to be said for retirement, and in my case it might be better to bow out sooner than bow to the inevitable later.

Not unexpectedly, my representations regarding the imminent changes have fallen on deaf ears, and, apart from a loyal few, the Governors and the leading lights on the PTA have been won over by the silver-tongued rhetoric and fulsome promises from our political masters.

However, I am very pleased that your masters have "seen the light", and more generally, that your bold decision to change careers in mid-stream has worked out well for you. Clearly, you were wise to ignore my ardent protestations! Alas, I too must now consider my future. I have the obvious escape route, of course, but what then? NGS has been my life and I can envisage no other.

126

At this point Dr Davenport took a break: he needed the toilet and he had not eaten anything, apart from Martha's scones, since seven o'clock that morning, and the humble pie did smell good. He also felt emotionally drained by the restraint he had had to exercise while writing the first paragraphs of the letter, and the hard bit was still to come, though he had a good idea how he wanted to say it. While he was eating, he heard William Hardcastle announce on The World at One that the trial of the Moors Murderers, Ian Brady and Myra Hindley, had begun that morning at Chester Crown Court. Their alleged crimes had sickened Netherbridge and indeed the whole nation for months, and now the whole nation was baying for its pound of flesh. Furthermore, to add to the gloom the weather forecast for the next few days promised an unseasonably cold spell with heavy showers in the northwest. Thinking about those children's gruesome deaths quelled any appetite for a dessert, and instead he made do with a very strong cup of black coffee, before resuming the concluding paragraphs of the letter:

I am very grateful to you and Mary for your kind invitation. It would have been most enjoyable and an ideal opportunity to catch up with events and so forth, but regrettably it won't be possible.

Yes, I agree, Ramsey <u>was</u> a very good appointment. Furthermore, he has an excellent pool of players to choose from, and given the host nation's 'home advantage', I am optimistic of a resounding victory at Wembley on July 30th.

But, sadly, Dick, I shall not be joining in the celebrations, for it is with a leaden heart and with great difficulty I have to tell you that this is the very last communication you will receive from me, for by this time tomorrow I will have made my quietus, sailed to Byzantium... choose your own euphemism.

My very best wishes as always to you both and to your expanding family,

George.

Curiously, searching for the right words to express his resolve to end it all had temporarily lifted the gloom. He had few qualms about the act itself, as he did not share Hamlet's fears of what dreams the "sleep of death" might bring: they could be no worse than the nightmares he endured throughout most of his waking hours. His sole concern was the impact it would have on those whom he held most dearly, two of whom he would spend the afternoon composing even more difficult letters, beginning with Taff Jenkins:

Dear Taff,

You know already how much I have valued your friendship and your down-to-earth common sense over the years.

Furthermore, I want to thank you for all your hard work and for allowing so many organisations and individuals in Netherbridge and beyond to benefit from those wonderful skills of yours, the parish church, the YMCA, our School, to name but a few, and of course me personally.

I am so glad the investment in our new workshops have proved so worthwhile, and more particularly that you and your enthusiastic band of 'apprentices' derive so much pleasure and satisfaction from the modern lathes.

I also want to thank you for all you did in the "Save Our Grammar School" campaign. If only there had been more like you, and fewer fifth-columnists, we might have won through. But, alas, it was not to be, and no one, I know, was more disappointed than your good self.

However, a small chink of light "amid the all-encircling gloom": I understand you will shortly be hearing some good news regarding your pension. You have waited patiently for long enough, and in the end the Governors in their wisdom have made a sensible and much deserved concession.

My love to Elizabeth, and I wish you both a long and happy retirement. Unfortunately, this is something I cannot contemplate for myself, at least not in that sense.

You see, Taff, by this time tomorrow I shall have "gone west", (as you might have put it).

Sincerely yours,

George.

The afternoon sun had now moved round to the rear of the house, leaving the kitchen in relative gloom. He heard the old wall clock in the study strike three and decided to move there and refresh himself with a second cup of strong coffee. He was surprised to discover how under the circumstances he was able to muster enough sang-froid to put pen to paper at all, let alone so lucidly: it was as if some external force were guiding his hand and the right words appearing on the page of their own accord without any need for revision.

He stood up and went to the window and looked out on the neat lawns, the blaze of daffodils and the shimmering pond. His eye fell finally on the sundial around which his mother had danced a jig all those years ago. But none of it gave him any solace now; merely reminded him of the third letter that now had to be written. He sat down with his coffee in his favourite leather chair and set about completing his afternoon's work:

Dear Martha,

Writing this letter is one of the hardest things I have ever had to do, and to be sure the result will be but a poor reflection of my feelings and thoughts at this moment.

No one knows better than you that I have not always been the most congenial of colleagues, but, my dear Martha, with your tact, forbearance and intelligence, you have always managed to make amends for my shortcomings, and for that I am deeply grateful.

I still remember vividly your interview for the post in 1946, and the favourable impression you made on everyone present. You were still awaiting official confirmation of your release from the Services, and, if I may say so, you looked very fetching in your WRNS uniform!

I also remember your first day at the Grammar School, and feeling anxious on your behalf, as the only female on the premises! But my disquiet was, of course, utterly unfounded, for within a very short space of time people were wondering how on earth we had managed before; and, ever since, you have made the role your very own and become all but indispensable

But as you know too well "the old order (certainly) changeth", and you will need to call on all your talents, including your tact, your forbearance and your fine intelligence to handle the formidable slings and arrows that lie ahead. Beware, in particular, of certain self-seeking, treacherous iconoclasts in your midst, and their lackeys, an equally dangerous bunch of time-serving boot-lickers. I predict that Harold Wilson's political slogan of a "grammar school education for all" will turn out to be just that, a political slogan.

As you have probably sensed already, this letter is a valediction: not just to our dear old School and all it stands for, and all the good people it has been my privilege to know and work with over the years, especially you, Martha, my... non plus ultra. *But it is also my personal valediction to the heartache and the thousand natural shocks that flesh is heir to.*

I wish it could have been different. But my dearest Martha, by the time you read this letter I will have shuffled off this mortal coil.

Ever yours,

George Davenport.

P.S. You will find a copy of my "last will and testament" in the top drawer of the writing desk in the study, together with some suggestions for the funeral arrangements.

It was now approaching half past four, and doleful clouds began to glower over *Elsinore*. He had taken the first important steps, and felt exhausted, though curiously relieved. He had already planned to miss the five o'clock collection from outside the main post-office, so that the letters would not arrive until Thursday morning. In the meantime, he had one or two little things to do, such as repairing the lens on his bicycle lamp, and calling on Mrs McAllister to see if she needed anything from the town.

But first, it was time to feed the fish and replenish the bird tables and then perhaps take a final reflective stroll around his large and beautiful garden. He wanted especially to visit the secluded retreat where he used to sit with his mother and watch the sun go down on warm summer evenings. He rarely went there now, because the feeling of loss was too painful.

He had envisaged – and in his mind acted out – these final hours many times, but now that it was for real, he had a strange awareness that events were developing their own logic and momentum. He found the inevitability of it all simultaneously daunting and comforting, almost as if he were a spectator at his own execution.

The gathering clouds confirmed the weatherman's prediction, and the evening chill made him glad of his mother's woollen jumper. There was also another reminder of happier times he needed to visit – the rowan tree which his mother had planted in the autumn of 1936 in loving memory of George Davenport Senior. She had chosen a rowan, she said, because in Irish folklore it protects against misfortune and evil spirits; but its appeal to George was more aesthetic: its mathematical 'rightness', its pentagram leaf shape, and its luscious berries – and all in NGS colours, of course! But for all that, he had always referred to it as "the magic tree", and it was now just coming into bud after another long winter.

By the time he got back into the house it was past five o'clock, and he remembered about the broken lens. He went straight into the coach-house to see to it, and after fitting the replacement, stood back to admire his old friend, a true marriage of form and function, or, as Jack Higgingbottom once put it, "like its owner, solid and dependable – not like these modern lightweights".

After checking that both the front and rear lights were working, he wheeled it carefully out of the coach-house and leant it against the trunk of the magnolia tree while he went inside to change into something more respectable. Then with the three letters safe in his pocket, he set off towards the town, but turned back after a few yards to see if Mrs McAllister wanted anything from the town. He rang her bell three times, but there being no reply, he presumed she was in the summer house at the far end of the garden relaxing as was her wont, with a pre-prandial sherry and the Manchester Evening News for company.

It usually took him between six and eight minutes from his house to the town centre, depending on the strength and direction of the wind, but this evening, despite the indifferent weather, he felt in no hurry, relishing every tarmacked inch of the road, and even dismounting once or twice to chat to friends and acquaintances.

His first stop was Fred's (or to give the shop its full alliterative title, Fred Challinor's Fish and Chips.) He and Fred had much in common: born in the same month of the same year, they both hailed from Timperley and had been close friends at their primary school. Furthermore, they had rekindled their friendship in 1936, the year that Fred had started his fish and chip business in Netherbridge and George was appointed Headmaster of the Grammar School. Indeed, more than once during the 1950s, he had approached Fred about joining the Board of Governors of the Grammar School, but Fred had always declined because of his presumed lack of education and social standing in the town.

George had always found the piquant aroma emanating from Fred's most alluring, but the self-denying ordinance of his eating and training regimes had invariably intervened. However, his fraught afternoon's work and now the cold evening air had weakened his defences, and he took advantage of being the first and only customer in the shop. Besides, he had another reason for calling on Fred: he wanted to congratulate him and Betty on their elder son's Scholarship to read Physics at Keble College, Oxford. He knew how proud they were of his scholastic achievements, and he assured them that this latest was nothing less than what he deserved.

Without a trace of false modesty, Fred replied, "George, I'm telling you, without that Grammar School, our Stephen would have ended up in a bank, or the Town Hall, or who knows... even frying chips! You've all been

134

absolutely brilliant, especially you, George. As you know, after a shaky start he's come on in leaps and bounds, and we can't thank you enough, can we, Pat?

"And now... those buggers up in Preston want a slice of it... want to make it "comprehensive", whatever that means. If something is working well, don't meddle with it... that's what I always say. We're just hoping it won't happen until our Peter's gone through. I don't know... these politicians... they need bloody shooting. Pardon my French, George, but that's how I feel. And after all you've done for that place... you must be devastated. I suppose you'll retire now, though, won't you? Or have you got some other plans?"

While Fred was ranting, George was quietly demolishing his shilling bag of chips, but had no stomach for Fred's chip-shop polemic. He had already fought his corner, in town halls, committee rooms, bars, or wherever he was called to do so – and all to no avail. Accordingly, he merely said, "Fred, these are the best chips in the North West... now, don't you go changing the recipe!"

As he was leaving the shop, he was hailed from across the road by two of his promising fourth-form pugilists. (This kind of thing had become a growing phenomenon of late: he could rarely appear in public without being button-holed by someone simply wanting to say hello, shake his hand, discuss the weather, or simply share his personal space for a moment or two. In some ways, he missed the 'distant' mystique he used to enjoy in the early years, but the age of deference was fast disappearing, and of course in general he celebrated that fact more than anyone.)

"So, this is your elixir vitae, sir!" teased the smaller of

the two.

"Oh, I don't know about that, Higson! But anyway, good luck to you both on Saturday. Unfortunately, I can't be there myself; but you'll be in good hands with Mr Travis."

"Thanks, sir. It's a shame you won't be there, though, but we'll give it our best shot... for you, sir."

He did not bother mounting the bike again, preferring to push it along the pavement over the canal bridge, and stopping on the crest to watch a coal barge chugging underneath towards Salford. He waved and smiled at the well-wrapped bargee, who waved and smiled back, and George envied him his apparent contentedness and job-satisfaction.

As he continued along the main street, past the Coliseum cinema, the Baptist chapel and the Midland Bank, the last few yards seemed never-ending. At last he could see the letter-box looming menacingly ahead.

He leant the bike carefully against the nearest tree, and a young girl scurried past him dragged along by a powerful Alsatian dog. He then reached into his jacket pocket for the letters, and checked the addresses and the stamps one last time. He then inserted them, one by one, into the box's gaping maw, first Dick's, then Taff's, and finally, after planting a lingering kiss on her name – Martha's.

Then, without any further delay, he switched the dynamo lights to 'On', remounted the bike and set off homeward, pedalling furiously against a brisk easterly breeze, his heavy heart strangely lighter for having completed this irrevocable step.

On arriving home, he wheeled the old Hercules to its

usual place in the coach-house, and patted it gently by way of a life-time's 'thank you, old friend, and a good night'. (When he bought it new in 1927 from John Howes and Sons of Cambridge for the considerable sum of £5: 18: 6, it had been guaranteed by the manufacturer at the Britannia Works in Birmingham for 50 years. With ten years still to run, clearly, this had been no idle boast!) On the way out he glanced up briefly at the gleaming block-and-tackle gear suspended from the beam, then switched off the light, and locked the side door as he left.

He then went into the kitchen and made himself another cup of coffee. While waiting for the kettle to boil, he made two phone-calls, one to thank the Vicar for his help and support in securing Taff Jenkins's pension enhancement; and one to Martha checking that nothing untoward had occurred during the day, not that anything ever did, but he liked to be reassured, and it was an excuse to hear her voice! He said that he still had one or two things to attend to, but he hoped to be back in school before lunchtime the following day; and if there were any change he would let her know.

He then took his mug of coffee into the study, and played the second movement of Beethoven Seventh Symphony on the radio-gramophone he had built for himself in the mid-1950s. Quite recently, he had treated himself to a modern Bang and Olufsen 'hi-fi' system, but he rarely used it because, he said, his old equipment produced a warmer, more authentic sound.

All in all, then, Dr Davenport's first day of term had gone reasonably well, albeit a little tiring. However, in order to calm his still over-active brain he reached down a well-thumbed copy of Tennyson's Poetical Works and read some of his favourite cantos from In Memoriam. He then went up into his 'observatory' to take a final peek at the clear night sky, the magnificence of which never ceased to astound him. Then, within minutes of setting the alarm clock for the usual 5 am reveille, he drifted off to sleep, with little care for the morrow.

Chapter Six

Evening visiting at Netherbridge Infirmary was from seven until eight, and at one minute past seven Phil Evans was shown into the Men's Ward by a young nurse. He found Taff sitting up in a bed next to the French windows, decked out in regulation NHS pyjamas. He was watching a flock of starlings squabbling over some kitchen waste the cook had just put out on the patio.

"How's tricks then, Taff?" inquired Phil, in as nonchalant a tone as he could muster.

"Could murder a pint," grumbled Taff, without turning his head, "but I'm not allowed a drop of anything until the M.O.'s been. And worse still, they've confiscated my smokes."

At last, he turned to face Phil, who could barely hide his revulsion at the open gash where the bridge of his nose used to be and the smile twisted by the facial swelling into a grotesque gurn.

"Hey, what's up, Phil? You've gone a funny colour! Bloody 'ell, it's only a bit of a scratch... nothing to get peaky about. I've had worse in the boxing booths down in Tredegar. I'm a quick healer, you know. You watch, I'll be as right as rain in a day or two. You should have seen some of those poor buggers out in France. My butty on the Vickers got half his bloody face blown off."

"No, it's just me, Taff. The smell of antiseptics always gets me this way," he lied tactfully, "though I was a bit concerned about that 'Ivor Novello' profile of yours... you know, with the end of year photos coming up, and all that!"

"Cheeky bugger! You're no bloody oil painting yourself!"

At this point Jack Higginbottom and Joe Riley walked in, they too barely able to hide their dismay.

"What happened then, Taff?" inquired Jack, matter-of-factly.

"Oh, the bloody chuck plate flew off, didn't it... and caught me right on the snozzle. Should have checked, I know, but there you are, these things happen. At least the lad wasn't hurt, that's the main thing. Thinking about it, I suppose I was so chuffed about the pension... and now you're here, Jack, I must thank you for everything you did... I know you and the gaffer pulled out all the stops. It'll make a big difference to me and Liz. I'll buy you both a pint when I get out of here, right? And you too, Phil, if you behave yourself, though I think it was your turn to buy me one when you left suddenly last Friday."

"Oh, never mind that now," replied Jack. "It was nothing, the least we could do after all you've done for the School."

140

It was now approaching half past seven and the swing doors opened again, this time by Taff's wife, Liz, followed by Martha. Liz rushed forward to hug her husband, and although quite used to seeing horrific injuries, struggled to conceal a slight wince. Martha held back to allow them their private moment before coming forward herself and kissing Taff on the mouth.

"Bloody hell, Martha, what have I done to deserve that? Don't tell the gaffer, whatever you do, or he'll start... By the way, where was he today? I haven't seen him since yesterday morning. Anyway, if you see him before me, tell him how grateful I am about the pension."

After exchanging knowing glances with Jack, Martha managed to say, "He said he was going to work from home for a couple of days, but I haven't spoken to him since yesterday evening."

This awkward situation was rescued by the unmistakable roar of Frank Fairclough's Black Shadow entering the car park, followed soon afterwards by his syncopated footfall in the corridor.

The swing doors opened to their full extent to accommodate his broad shoulders. "I'm sorry I'm late, Taff," he said, as he put his helmet down on the bed, and handed him a conciliatory bunch of grapes. "I didn't hear about it until I got home. So I got you these on the way here just now."

"Oh, thanks, boyo, I was just telling this lot how I could kill for some nice juicy grapes! Hey, folks, it'll be chucking out time in five minutes, but if you like, I can whisper something in the Sister's ear."

Martha saw her chance to make a quick exit. She had so much to think about and some phone calls to make.

"Would you like me to drop you off, Elizabeth? Or would you like to stay a little longer? I'll call on you again tomorrow, Mr Jenkins. But perhaps the Doctor will have discharged you by then."

BY THE TIME Phil had arrived back at school after escorting Taff to the Infirmary, his first period of the afternoon (which Joe Riley had covered) was all but over. So he made straight for Martha's office only to be told by the Caretaker that she had just left the building in some hurry.

The fact that Jack Higginbottom had no idea either of Dr Davenport's whereabouts had made Martha very uneasy. Had the dreaded moment arrived? Surely not, there had to be some explanation. But she was determined to find out one way or another, and without a moment's delay.

As she sped along Manchester Road, a jumble of horrific scenarios flooded her brain, and at one point she even surprised herself by saying a little prayer out loud that what she feared was simply her mind playing tricks on her.

Curiously, Jack Higginbottom had had the same premonition, and had driven off from *The Boar's Head* with little concern for speed limits. The two arrived almost together, and without anything being said, knew instinctively the nature of their mission. Could he be saved, or were they too late?

Martha had always had a full set of keys to *Elsinore* and volunteered to look inside the house, while Jack went to check the (unlocked) coach-house. As he entered, he could see Dr Davenport in his tracksuit seemingly standing with his back to him underneath the block and tackle mechanism, his head and shoulders leaning forward as if he were looking for something on the floor.

"Oh, there you are, George, you weren't answering your phone," said Jack with huge relief; and when Martha heard him she convinced herself that she could hear two men talking, and rushed into the coach-house to join them. But her joy was cruelly short-lived when she saw Jack standing next to his old friend and shaking his head sadly in her direction.

Martha rushed towards him and uttered the most heart-rending shriek Jack had ever heard, and perhaps for the very first time she gave vent to her true feelings. She sobbed uncontrollably, and then the two hugged each other tightly, seeking some kind of reassurance that the whole world had not gone mad.

It would appear Dr Davenport had been dead for several hours, and presumably by his own hand, unless of course there had been some freakish accident during his exercise routine. They decided not to touch the body and leave everything to the doctor and the police, both of whom arrived very soon after Martha's emergency phone-call. When the police had completed their routine questioning and investigations, they arranged for the body to be taken to the chapel of rest at Blackstone and Snead, Funeral Directors.

As soon as they had gone, Jack and Martha went round every room in the house to check that all the windows and doors were securely locked. They then sat in silence in Martha's Mini for several minutes in a deep state of shock. Both had suspected for a long time that this kind of thing was a real possibility, but both had also hoped to be spared its grim reality. After a while even the silence became unbearable, and Jack said simply, "What a man! What a waste!"

Martha felt too numb to say anything.

Then he continued tentatively, "Perhaps you could let Joe know as soon as you can, Martha, because as from now, of course, he will be the acting Headmaster?"

Martha nodded.

"And *I'll* try and let all the Governors know this afternoon. And perhaps everyone at the School can be told formally in tomorrow morning's Assembly?" Then after a short pause he added, "I wonder how Taff's getting on? I must pop over and see him this evening. Would you like me to pick Liz up, Martha? It's not far out of my way."

"No, it'll be all right, thanks. I've already arranged to call for her soon after seven."

WHEN MARTHA got back to the School it was nearly four o'clock, and a good many of the masters had already left. She still felt numb, but needed to catch Joe before he left too. Fortunately, his little black Ford Popular was still in the car park. She first tried the Stock Room, then the Masters' Room, but with no success. Eventually, she found him in the Boiler Room, still discussing Taff's accident.

"Oh, there you are, Mr Riley, I'm glad I caught you. You couldn't spare me a couple of minutes in private, please, before you go?"

"Certainly, how can I help? Taff's no worse, is he?"

"No, not as far as I know. No, this is something completely different."

As they walked together back to her office, Martha was steeling herself for the task of imparting the dreadful news, while Joe's mind was still preoccupied with how Taff's absence would affect the substitute rota. Would they have to appoint a temporary replacement or could they juggle things around a bit, since it was after all the summer term, with three weeks of public examinations followed straight after by the Wakes fortnight? But, of course, he would have to discuss it all with George before making any decisions.

"Do sit down, please, Mr Riley. I'm going to make a pot of tea. I'm feeling quite parched after the afternoon I've had."

"Yes, I can well believe it. I've not had a moment myself."

"You'll have one too, won't you? I'm afraid I've only got chocolate digestives today."

What a difference a day makes, she thought, as she brought the same willow-patterned pots out again, while desperately stifling a sob.

"Help yourself to milk and sugar. I'll go and get the biscuits."

"Oh, yes, nasty business, this accident. He could well be off for the rest of the term. It's never just the physical injury; it's the shock to the system that does the damage, especially for someone his age. Mind you, if anyone can bounce back from a thing like that, Taff will."

"Yes, let's hope so, anyway. I phoned Elizabeth as soon as the ambulance left, and said I'd take her to see him this evening. She left me a message in the office when I was out; apparently he was due to see the ENT consultant later this afternoon, but he's got to come all the way from Liverpool.

"Anyway, I'll join you at the Infirmary this evening, Martha. Between seven and eight, isn't it? Would you like me to bring Liz? I'll be going right past their flat, and it's a little bit out of your way."

"No, I'll be fine, thanks, Mr Riley, and anyway it'll help me take my mind off things... which brings me... to what I've got to tell you. Let me pour you another cup, and do have another biscuit."

"Two cups, Martha, this sounds serious!"

"Martha took a good half-minute to gather her thoughts.

"Yes, I'm afraid it is, Mr Riley, I'm the bearer of even worse news. Something else horrible has happened today."

She paused again to stifle yet another sob.

"After the ambulance took Mr Jenkins to the Infirmary, I tried to phone Dr Davenport to let him know, but there was no reply. I then phoned Mr Higginbottom to inform him, and to see if he had seen or heard anything of Dr Davenport, as he wasn't answering his phone. Well, I just had this uneasy feeling that he might have fallen or something, and couldn't get to the phone. Anyway, I hope you don't mind, but I asked the Caretaker to mind the Office while I drove over to Dr Davenport's place. As I was approaching the entrance to his drive, I saw Mr Higginbottom's red Cortina coming from the opposite direction and turning in just in front of me. Apparently, he'd also had the same weird feeling after I'd phoned him. Anyway, I went straight into the house and Mr Higginbottom tried the coach-house."

At this point she stopped, swallowed hard and

breaking into a sob wailed, "And Mr Riley, there he was. It seems he'd taken his own life with that blooming pulley thing."

Joe Riley was speechless, and took another biscuit from the packet.

"When do you think it actually happened then?" asked Joe, feeling obliged to say something, anything, the enormity and the practical consequences of the tragedy not yet having sunk in.

"Of course, they won't know anything for certain until they've done a post mortem, but Dr Winstanley, who was called to the scene, guessed probably early this morning. Dr Davenport did phone me last night to check everything was all right at school, and he seemed all right then. But of course, you can never tell with him. I don't know if he ever told you, but he suffered dreadfully from sudden mood-swings. In fact, he had a bad attack straight after Assembly yesterday morning, just before you came into his study."

"Oh, yes, come to think of it, he did mention something to me a couple of years ago, but at the time I thought nothing of it. I remember telling him that I feel low sometimes too when things aren't going too well, as most people do from time to time. I remember telling him that I'd felt very down after Mrs Riley passed away. But then I've always believed that time is a wonderful healer, and that helped me get over it."

Martha said nothing because clearly Joe had no conception of what she was talking about, nor of the living hell poor Dr Davenport had had to endure.

"I suppose I shall have to make an announcement in tomorrow's Assembly. But, of course, I shan't mention the... suicide."

"Good heavens, no!" interrupted Martha. "There'll have to be an inquest first, and we'll have to wait for the coroner's report. And anyway, if they can't determine absolutely the cause and circumstances of death, they usually return an "open verdict". Of course, it is feasible that he had an accident with that contraption, because he did use it regularly for his exercises... and he was dressed in his tracksuit. He might have slipped or something," she added unconvincingly, "and before he could do anything he might have lost consciousness. We didn't find any suicide notes near the body or in the house. Of course, by now the police may know more than we do. Dr Winstanley was pretty sure it was suicide, but, as I say, coroners still tend to avoid that verdict unless there is indisputable evidence. I suppose there's still a stigma attached to it even though it's no longer a crime, as such."

"Oh, yes, I agree," said Joe. "But there has always been a tendency towards that, even before the 1961 Act, often because of insurance payouts and what have you. I remember reading many years ago about a young woman's body found on the beach in Morecambe, and in fact she had even posted suicide notes to several of her friends and relatives, but the coroner still returned an "open verdict" because he couldn't know for certain how the body came to be on the beach. Anyway, there's no point in speculating at this stage; we'll just have to wait and see what transpires? So, for tomorrow morning then, I'll keep it simple and stick to the facts as we know them. All they need to know is that our Headmaster passed away suddenly at home on Wednesday morning, and further details will be given when all the facts are known. But of course, in all this I mustn't forget to say something about Taff Jenkins's accident, and how we're all wishing him a speedy return to rude health... and so on. But at least, I can be a little bit less circumspect about that."

All of a sudden, Martha felt very sorry for him, this little old man being thrust willy-nilly into the hot seat at such a difficult time. She feared for him personally, and for the School under his command. But she simply said, "Oh, Mr Riley, just for you to know, Mr Higginbottom and I will inform the Governors about Dr Davenport."

"Oh, that's excellent! My goodness, look at the time! And Martha, thank you for everything. I don't know how I would cope without you. But haven't I heard that said before! But for now, I'll love and leave you. We've both got a lot to think about. It's been a horrible day, no two ways about it. But together, Martha, we'll win through. Anyway, see you shortly at the Infirmary."

AFTER DRIVING Elizabeth Jenkins back to her flat, Martha stayed to keep her company for a little longer than she had intended. But in reality, she was in no hurry to return home in her present state of mind and was glad to have someone as sympathetic and reassuring as Elizabeth to share the day's hurt. All too often, when she called on her, Taff dominated the conversation, but this evening the two women were able to talk freely and relax in each other's company with a pot of tea and some of Liz's cakes.

Throughout her stay Martha wondered at what point she should raise the matter of Dr Davenport's death. Clearly, events were beginning to tell on poor Elizabeth, not only her husband's injury, but also his imminent retirement, with the inevitable formalities, the tiresome dinners, the dressing up, the presentations, and all those long-winded speeches. It was not her style at all – nor really his either. If only they could leap-frog the next three months, go for that long-promised holiday in Porthcawl, and then settle into the serene and leisurely life that they had always talked about. And with this latest news about the enhanced pension, perhaps they could even consider farther afield, say, Pembrokeshire – she had always wanted to see Pembrokeshire again.

The evening had gone so well, and so quickly, that Martha was reluctant to leave, and even more averse to spoiling it by disclosing her dreadful secret. Could it wait till tomorrow? Or should she get the wretched thing over with tonight. It was bound to upset Elizabeth, especially in her present nervous state, but better for her to hear it from herself that from some gossip-monger at the bus stop. And anyway, tomorrow morning would be too hectic at school for her to be making phone-calls, and this kind of news was better imparted face-to-face.

Accordingly, when there was a slight hiatus in their animated chatter, Martha ventured gingerly, "Elizabeth, I know today has been a dreadful day for you... for us all... but I'm afraid... what I'm going to tell you now will only add to your distress. You see, something else horrible happened today, and it's fallen on me to have to tell you about it. It's about Dr Davenport."

She paused for a moment to find the right words, and being so mentally exhausted she wished that she had waited until the morning. But she sensed right away that Liz knew what she was about to say. Eventually, she heard her own, almost disembodied, voice enunciating the hackneyed phrases "Elizabeth, there's no easy way to say this, but... I'm afraid Dr Davenport has... left us."

"Oh, Martha!" she replied, and rushed forward to hug her friend and gently patted her on the back. And then, as if trying to make things easier for Martha, added, "Was it... was it what we always thought?

"Yes," sobbed Martha, and then once again gave full rein to her emotions. "You see, I tried to phone him... to tell him about Mr Jenkins's accident... but there was no answer. So I rang Mr Higginbottom before driving over to his house. Mr Higginbottom must have thought the same, because he had driven there as well, and we both arrived more or less together, and found him... in the coach-house."

"God, I don't know what to say, Martha. What a shock for you. How the poor man must have suffered... for him to do that. It's hard to imagine the state of mind he was in. But then we had been half expecting it for a long time. Actually, I thought he might have done it when his mother died, because they were so close, but in a strange sort of way he seemed to get over that quite quickly."

"Well, he'll be at peace now," replied Martha simply.

"How on earth I'm going to tell Taff, I don't know," said Liz. I'll have to get across there in the morning or something, before he hears it from someone else. Perhaps I'd better have a word with the Sister before I go to bed."

"Would you like me to go and tell him, Elizabeth?"

"No, I think it would be better coming from me. But thanks all the same. God, he idolised the "Gaffer", and this will be like a 'double whammy' for him, and won't help his recovery one bit."

"Would you like me to come with you, then?"

suggested Martha.

"No, I'll be all right, really. And anyway, you'll have plenty on your plate tomorrow at the School. He'll be very upset, I know. He thought so much of him. But then didn't we all?"

"We certainly did that," sighed Martha, getting up to go, and added deep in her heart, especially me.

"Would you like a nightcap before you go, Martha?

"No, thanks, I'd better go now. It's getting late, and I've got to ring Mr Higginbottom as soon as I get in. Anyway, thank you for your company this evening, Elizabeth."

"Well, thank *you*, Martha, please call any time. I've always got a fresh supply of Welsh cakes on the go, they're his favourites. Good night."

"Good night. And give him my love when you see him in the morning."

AS SOON AS Martha had left the flat, Liz went out and phoned the Infirmary from the telephone box across the road to inquire after Taff, and was relieved to hear that he was now "sleeping like a baby". The ENT specialist had eventually arrived, and apart from a slight heartbeat irregularity, he had given Mr Jenkins an encouraging report. Apart from a slight irregularity of the heart, he had a robust constitution, and barring any set-backs would be able to go home in a few days. He would be seeing him again in about a week and decide then whether reconstructive surgery would be necessary or indeed advisable.

Cheered by such a promising outlook, Liz asked if it was possible to come and see him first thing in the morning. As a retired nurse, she realised that this was irregular, but there was something very important she needed to tell her husband before he heard it from anyone else. Given that they were abnormally quiet, she felt sure Mrs Jenkins would be able see her husband for a few minutes, say, about eight o'clock the following morning.

All in all, despite the trauma and the heartache, she felt her day had concluded on a slightly more positive note than she had feared, and after a large cup of cocoa laced with a tablespoonful of whisky she retired in as tranquil a state of mind as could be expected, and was soon sound asleep.

The following morning, she arose early to prepare herself for the ordeal. Even as she bathed, she rehearsed aloud how she would break the ghastly news to him, but the task did not get easier with practice. Shortly after seven o'clock, she went out to the kiosk again to ring Martha and tell her the good news about Taff, and how they were letting her see him that morning.

"Look, I'll call for you and drop you off on the way to school, if you like; it's not much out of my way. It'll save you waiting for a bus, and they're so busy at this time of day."

"Oh, thank you, Martha, provided it's not too much trouble. That would be a great help."

And so, at eight o'clock precisely Liz found herself entering the massive oak portals of Netherbridge Infirmary, looking forward to seeing her husband again, but not to what she had to say to him. As she entered his ward, she could see him sitting peacefully in an armchair next to the partly open French windows, basking in the early morning sunshine that promised another warm day.

"Bloody hell, Liz, how did you get here so early?"

"Oh, Martha gave me a lift."

"God, she's a good girl, that one; can't do enough for people. It's a shame she never married; would have made a wonderful wife, and mother too."

"You keep saying that, Taff; but perhaps she never wanted to get married. Anyway, I've brought you your shaving kit and a tin of your favourites."

"Oh, smashing!"

"I hear the specialist was pleased with you."

"Well, yes, he gave me, you know, the once over, and said all my important bits were working O.K. But you'll be pleased to hear, I've got to cut down on the fags. Anyway, I've been thinking, I can go one better than that; I'm going to give them up altogether, especially now we'll be living on a pension."

"Ho, ho! How many times have I heard that?

"No, Liz, I really mean it this time."

"Well, yes, it would be fantastic, if you could. You'd certainly feel a lot healthier, and the flat would smell nicer. *And*, think about it, all that spare dosh you'd have... to spend on me!"

"Anyway, how did you wangle your way past the guard room at this time of day?"

"Oh, I might have whispered in the Sister's ear, or something!"

"At this point the Day Sister, who had just started her shift, came into the ward and remarked how much better Mr Jenkins looked. The swelling had gone down quite a bit already, and the wound had formed a good strong scab. "He'll soon be up and about, Mrs Jenkins. The plan is for him to go home tomorrow or Saturday, that is if you feel up to it, of course, Mr Jenkins. Mr Charlton wants to see you again next Wednesday. And then we'll take it from there."

"So it looks like you're going to be round my feet sooner than I expected," said Liz, giving him a tight hug.

"Ooh, it's nice to know you're wanted, isn't it, Sister?" retorted Taff.

"Now listen, Taff, joking apart, I've come here early this morning for a reason. I've got something very important to tell you."

"Oh! You're not thinking of running away with the milkman, or anything, are you?"

At this point the Sister felt her presence was becoming an encumbrance, and withdrew quietly.

Poor Liz was finding it hard enough to break the news to him without his irrepressible flippancy. So, she thought she might as well come straight to the point. "O, shut up with your nonsense, and be serious for a moment. Taff, I'm afraid something far worse than your accident happened yesterday... George Davenport died. And it looks like... well, you know."

Taff said nothing for a full half minute.

He turned his face slowly towards hers, his eyes full of tears. "I knew it... I bloody knew it... I guessed something was up last night when I saw Jack and Martha looking funny at each other. Oh, bloody hell... Poor bugger... How? I mean, how did it happen?"

"Jack and Martha found him... in the coach-house... hanging from that pulley contraption."

"It was always on the cards, I know, but it's still one hell of a shock. I remember him telling me once that he had tried it before with pills, more than once in fact, but had chickened out at the last minute." And after a long pause, he added, "I always thought he was sort of too good for this world somehow. God, he was like a brother to me." And with that he broke down and hid his face in Liz's bosom.

"Everything all right, Mrs Jenkins?" inquired the Sister, who re-entered just as the distant half-hour chimes of St Mary's clock wafted in through the French windows.

"No, it's not *all right*," snapped Taff through his tears, "not bloody all right at all."

"Shush," said Liz apologetically, "a very good friend of ours has passed away suddenly." Then quietly to Taff, "Perhaps I should have waited till you got home, but I didn't want you to hear from someone else."

"Liz, no, you did right. I needed to know as much as anyone, perhaps more so. I'll be all right in a minute. You go now. See you again at seven, yes? Oh, and you couldn't bring that big crossword book with you? It gets a bit boring in here with no one to talk to."

"Will do," she replied soothingly, and as she hugged him again she could feel the tremors of the sobs shaking his whole frame. The "little bit of a scratch" on his nose had now become just that, and very much yesterday's story already.

As she was leaving the infirmary gates, the Number 12 bus was just arriving, and she was back in the flat shortly after nine, by which time the postman had been. All the letters were addressed to Taff: a brown one from the Ministry of Pensions and National Insurance; three "Get Well" cards which had been pushed through the letter box; and a white one hauntingly addressed to "Mr

156

Dafydd Jenkins" in a distinctive copperplate script. She decided to open the Pensions one straightaway in case it needed a prompt response, but the others she would take along to the Infirmary that evening.

Meanwhile, Martha's morning at school was proving just as hectic as she had expected. She, of course, had left the house before the post had arrived, and thus was dumbfounded to receive a trunk call from Dorset just as Assembly was about to start. It was from the Revd Richard Spence, inquiring about a most distressing letter he had just received from his old friend, George Davenport, post-marked, 18th April, and whether the appalling prediction contained in the letter had in fact come about. Martha gave him a brief résumé of events, adding that the School was in utter shock. She also promised to contact him again when the cause of death and so on had been ascertained, though from what she had seen and heard, it looked as if Dr Davenport's prediction was indeed authentic.

JOE RILEY'S first Assembly as Acting Headmaster of Netherbridge Grammar School was one of the briefest in living memory. Not being a gifted public speaker, he had decided to keep things, as he said, simple. Indeed, this morning he dispensed with both the opening hymn and the reading. The poor fellow had been up most of the night rehearsing his little speech and by nine o'clock he knew it by heart.

Firstly, he felt sure that most of them had already heard about Mr Jenkins's accident. But he was glad to report that when he went to see him at the Infirmary he seemed in very good spirits and waiting to see a specialist. But his return to School was not envisaged for a while, and alternative arrangements would have to be made for his classes.

Then, taking a deep breath, he braced himself for the second announcement, that it was his painful duty to inform the School that Dr Davenport had passed away suddenly at home. Its unexpectedness, he continued, meant that there would have to be a post mortem and an inquest, and when all the facts were known there would be a further announcement.

He then asked the whole School to stand for a minute's silence, and then join him in saying the Lord's Prayer and the Grace.

Finally, he trusted that the events of the past two days would not prey on people's minds or impinge unduly on their studies. The best balm in such circumstances was to continue working and playing hard, and as far as possible carry on as normal, which, of course, is what Dr Davenport himself would have wanted. Then, after bidding everyone "Good Morning", he left the platform and walked briskly back to his office, leaving the Head Prefect to direct the dismissal.

JOE'S 'office' comprised one end of a long, narrow storeroom attached to the rear of the gymnasium. This was his private fiefdom to which only a select few were allowed access. His 'desk' consisted of a piece of surplus laboratory benching lying across a matching pair of Army-surplus filing cabinets. The only sources of natural light were a small skylight directly above his armchair and a small hatch, through which he issued items of stationery to the boys. It was in this room that he also checked and stamped new books and pieces of equipment as they arrived from the educational suppliers, and rumour had it that it had not been cleaned during his twenty-six years' tenure because he would never entrust anyone else with the keys.

As soon as the bell rang for morning- or lunch-break, nervous supplicants were obliged to form an orderly queue outside his hatch, hoping, often against all odds, to persuade Joe that this or that exercise book was indeed full, and needed replacing, only to be rebuffed with "Call that full, boy? You could get the 119th Psalm in there... and the Sermon on the Mount to boot, if you used smaller handwriting." New boys soon learned to accept the old fellow's quaintly uncompromising manner because, well, Joe was Joe, and he was unlikely to change during their time at the School.

And so, after delivering his first oration as Acting Headmaster (he even found the title overpowering) it was to this inglorious and dusty grotto that he gravitated, and not to the "Headmaster's Study", as most in his position would have done. He felt unworthy of sitting in that hallowed chair, despite his Double First from Durham and a starred M.A. from King's College, London.

About a week later, Jack Higginbottom called at the School to discuss a letter he, as Chairman of the governors, had received from County Hall. He first knocked on the Headmaster's study door, but on receiving no response, then tried Martha's door and fortunately found her in, busy filing documents.

"Hello again, Martha, how are things with you by now? I've come to see Joe Riley, actually, about this letter. Is he about, or is he teaching?"

Martha cast her eye over the master timetable on the wall above her desk and replied wryly, "No, Mr Higginbottom, Mr Riley's not teaching", and then added with a smile, "I expect he'll be in his counting house counting out his pencils!"

Appreciating the irony, Jack replied, "Well then, Martha, I wonder if you would kindly persuade him to stop counting for a moment and honour me with his presence in the Headmaster's study – where he now belongs."

As she had intimated, she found Joe literally counting coloured pencils into sets of thirty, and not a little discomfited by Jack's ill-timed summons.

"I wonder what letter that would be?" inquired Joe, as they walked back to her office.

"Oh, it came yesterday, Mr Riley. There's a copy in your in-tray."

"O, hello, Joe. How are you today? Sorry to trouble you at such short notice, but I thought we'd better have a chat about this letter."

"To be honest, Jack, I haven't had a chance to look at it yet."

"It's from Preston... we're invited to a 'working lunch at County Hall to have pre-preliminary discussions' about this comprehensive thing. Apparently, they want to start the ball rolling as soon as possible. More haste, less speed, I say. And God, if only for the sake of decency, you'd have thought they'd have waited until after the funeral. But there you re, that's a sign of things to come, I expect."

"Oh yes, Jack, we'll have to get used to a very different regime in due course, I'm afraid."

"Anyway, give it some thought, Joe, and let me know when you've got something definite in mind. There's no rush."

"Oh yes, but let's get all the exams over with first, shall we? Then we'll have more time to... chew the fat with the great and the good."

At this point, Martha brought in the customary tea and biscuits.

"Oh thanks, Martha," said Jack, "that's lovely. By the way, Joe, don't get me wrong, but I really think you should move out of that store room pronto. George is not coming back, and *you're* now in the driving seat. And to be honest with you, it would be a lot easier for everyone if you relocated. Everything would be at hand here – including Martha!"

"I have given it some thought, Jack, and you're probably right. But I'd rather wait until after the funeral, if you don't mind. I'd feel less presumptuous then. But more importantly, we'll need to get together to sort out Taff's temporary replacement, and perhaps also find someone to look after the stock until the various positions are decided."

"Have you anybody in mind in the short term?"

"Well, there are one or two, but it is important to get the right person."

"Well, I'm off... it's nearly opening time. Thanks, Martha, for the tea, and keep me informed about any developments."

"I must be off too, Martha. Thanks for the cuppa. I'll take the mail with me, and then we can deal with it together after lunch. Is that all right?"

"Yes, that'll be fine, Mr Riley. Things should be a little

quieter by this afternoon, anyway."

No sooner than Joe had sat down to go through the day's correspondence, there was a knock on his door. Assuming it was someone impatient for some foolscap file-paper or a new rough-book, he called out, "Look, I'm very busy at the moment, and unless it's absolutely essential, come back at half past twelve."

However, Joe's visitor was not a pupil at all, but someone with a most unlikely offer of help. If it had been Phil, or Frank, or Len Travis, say, he could well have understood, but...

"I know you're very busy, Mr Riley, but you couldn't kindly spare me a moment or two?"

"Yes, of course, Mr Nobbs, come in," replied Joe, with as much composure as he could muster.

Closing the door behind him, and sitting down (uninvited) on a stool next to Joe, Nobbs smiled warmly inwardly and bethought himself of Brutus, "There is a tide in the affairs of men. Which, taken at the flood, leads on to fortune..."

"Please don't take this the wrong way," Nobbs began, "but it's obvious you've got a hell of a lot on your plate at the moment, with being Acting Headmaster as well as doing your old job. And I was thinking last night, since I've got some spare time, now the exams have started, I could give you a hand with something... anything, if that's all right with you."

"Well, yes," said Joe, baffled by this sudden outburst of altruism, "that's very kind of you. Yes, as a matter of fact I am a bit pushed, and a little help would not go amiss."

Pressing home his advantage, Nobbs then continued,

"Well, then, what if I helped out with something here, to start with. You could then concentrate on running the School."

"Yes, that would be very helpful. Being here every break and lunchtime is a bit of a tie, I must admit."

"Right, I'll make a start this lunch-time, then, if that's okay with you? Oh, by the way, what's the latest on Taff Jenkins?"

"Well, I called on him last night after school. He's home now, of course, and he's due to see the specialist again later this week. He's coming along, slowly, but I doubt he'll be back this term. So we may have to think about a stand-in. Have you got anyone in mind that might fit the bill *pro tem*?"

"Yes, as a matter of fact I have, but really I can manage on my own for a while yet. And we don't want to be spending money unnecessarily, do we? Anyway, I'll see you here at about 12.30, then, okay?"

"Yes, thank you, Mr Nobbs, that'll be fine."

As he got up to go, he added as an afterthought, "By the way, I liked your Assembly... very succinct, and to the point, if I may say so."

"Oh, thanks. It wasn't easy, I must admit, and I thought the less said the better, in the circumstances."

"Keep up the good work, Joe. I can call you Joe, can't I? Whatever anybody else thinks or says, you've always got *my* support. If I can help in any way, all you've got to do is ask."

"Thank you," replied Joe, "I'll bear it in mind,"

"Well, as my dear old father used to say, 'Do the thing that's nearest, my boy, though it's dull at whiles, helping when you meet them, lame dogs over stiles.'"

Chapter Seven

As soon as Joe Riley's first assembly had finished, and the classes had dispersed for the first period of the morning, Martha wandered over to the Stock room, where she found Joe already ensconced in his armchair, surrounded by piles of file-boxes and ledgers.

She knocked gently as she entered, and said, "I've just had a telephone call from Dr Davenport's old friend, Mr Spence."

"Oh yes, Dick Spence! Good sort, Dick. Maybe a little too fond of the bottle, but there you go, it takes all sorts. Anyway, what did he want?"

"Apparently, he'd received a letter from... Dr Davenport this morning saying that... by the time it had arrived, Dr Davenport would have... would no longer be with us. He put it less delicately than that. And he wanted to know if it had actually happened, or not. It occurred to me that maybe Dr Davenport had sent this kind of letter to other people... to you for instance, or Mr Higginbottom... or possibly me?"

"The post hadn't come when I left. Of course, there might well be one."

"Well, would it be all right if I popped home later to check *my* mail? I wouldn't be more than twenty minutes."

"Yes, of course, Martha. You might as well go right away, before the phone starts ringing again, and you could put that little 'Back Shortly' notice in your window. Or, I'll tell you what, I'll bring some of these papers over to your office. I can work on them there just as easily. Then you wouldn't have to rush. Yes, you go now, Martha."

And so, for the second time in less than twenty-four hours Martha found herself speeding along Manchester Road, her heart pounding audibly, and her mind barely aware of the other traffic scurrying to and fro.

She almost burst the latch of her front door in her eagerness to get into the porch, and there, on the floor among some dull-looking business letters lay a long, white envelope with her name and address elegantly written in that impeccable handwriting.

As she reached down to pick it up, she convulsed with another sob, and she was torn between opening the letter there and then and waiting until she got back to school where she could read and re-read it at leisure. In the event, she put it in her handbag and returned post-haste to relieve Joe of his office-minding duty.

AS APRIL gave way to May, and May to June, Taff Jenkins continued to make a steady recovery. The consultant was very pleased with him, but had advised against reconstructive surgery on account of his age and the slight heart problem. And so, by 20th June, his sixty-sixth birthday, for which Phil had arranged a surprise "chicken in a basket" supper at the *Boar's Head*, the wound had healed as much as it ever would. Although the damage to his nose-bridge hampered his breathing, especially at night, he held this as a minor inconvenience compared with the ordeal of the self-imposed smoking ban, and a battle he might well have lost only for Liz's uncompromising stand.

He had also tried to convince himself and everyone else within ear-shot that he would be returning to school before the end of term, even though both Jack Higginbottom and Dr Winstanley had advised against it; and, of course, in some ways he agreed with them. Ending his professional life on the same day as "the Gaffer" had a certain neatness about it; and, anyway, he knew that things changed for ever on that fateful Wednesday. Old Joe was a capable boatswain, but what the School needed was a proper skipper. Taff also knew that there would be very little he could do at that time of year that a "stand-in" could not do as easily, and, of course, there would be no financial gain in it for him. He was also quietly gratified to hear one evening at the *Boar's Head* that the Governors, with Joe Riley's blessing, had decided that his workshop should remain closed until they had appointed someone else with the necessary skills and experience to operate the machines safely. Thus, the urge to return, he concluded, was mainly emotional: for the past forty-five years NGS had been his reason for getting out of bed in the morning: it had provided fulfilling employment with a good livelihood, a superb bunch of friends, and not least, a legitimate escape from Liz's manic cleaning and polishing. He had often wondered in recent years if there was life after NGS, and whether there would be enough to do when the initial euphoria of retirement had faded; and now he was about to find out, and much sooner than he had expected.

"IS EVERYTHING all right, Mr Riley?"

"Yes, it's been very quiet, actually. There was just the one phone-call, from Elizabeth Jenkins, asking for you. She said she'd ring again later. Anyway, did you find what you were looking for?"

"Yes, I'm afraid I did, but I haven't opened it yet".

"Anyway, I'll leave the shop in your capable hands now, Martha. If you need me, you know where I am."

As soon as he had gone, Martha went through to Dr Davenport's office in order to read the letter in peace. She took out his old pocket-knife from the desk drawer, and carefully slit the envelope open. She could hear the pounding of her heart as she pulled out the immaculately folded, crisp sheet of white note-paper, her quick eyes scanning the beautiful black handwriting to elicit its main message.

At least now we know, she thought, and besides, Dr Davenport was far too cautious to have died accidentally.

The bell for morning break sounded, heralding the usual flurry of queries about bus passes, dinner money, items of lost property, and masters wanting to use the duplicating machine or the telephone, but as soon as it was over, Martha for the first time that day was able to sit down with a cup of strong tea and one of her home-made flapjacks, Dr Davenport's favourite. She took the letter out of her handbag again and read it slowly two or three times, savouring every turn of phrase, and every punctuation mark, and especially each time he had written "Martha". Her eyes filled with tears at "*non plus ultra*", and by the time she had reached the closing, she had run the whole gamut of emotions from pride, gratitude, admiration, love, grief, misery, and finally anger that God in his infinite wisdom had seen fit to mould this paragon of humanity in the first place, and then after submitting him to a lifetime of torture, destroyed him with seemingly wanton delight. Yes, in her book, this God of love, and compassion, and forgiveness had a lot of explaining to do.

While she was thus reflecting on this latest manifestation of the Almighty's mysterious ways, the telephone rang. It was Liz Jenkins.

"Oh, Martha... won't keep you... I know you're busy. Just to let you know how I got on this morning. He took it quite well, really, considering. He was obviously very upset, but, as he said, it was always on the cards.

"Sorry I missed you, Liz, but I'd popped home to check my mail."

"Did you get a letter too?"

"Yes, I'm afraid I did, and it was just as we thought."

"Well, by the time I got home after seeing Taff, about nine o'clock, the postman had been, and there among some brown envelopes was this white one addressed to Taff in that lovely handwriting. Of course I haven't opened it. I shall take it along with me tonight during visiting. Do you know if there were any more?"

"Yes, his friend from Dorset, Mr Spence, rang the School this morning inquiring about a strange letter he'd

168

received from Dr Davenport. So, that makes three that we know of. There could be more."

"To think that he could sit down and write such letters in the state of mind he must have been in. It's unbelievable."

"Yes, it is. Anyway, would you like me to call for you at about seven again this evening?

"Oh, yes, please, Martha, that would be lovely, thanks very much. Bye."

"Bye."

The letter was still in her hand, and she read it quickly once more before there were any more interruptions. Then her eye fell on the postscript:

You shall find a copy of my "last will and testament" in the top drawer of the writing desk in the study, together with some suggestions for my funeral arrangements.

Typical, she thought, nothing left to chance, and amidst all the turmoil, his last thoughts were to make things easier for me. God, I'm going to miss him.

THE OFFICE clock had barely moved since she last looked: it was still not twenty-four hours since Mr Higginbottom and she had made their grim discovery, and less than forty-eight since Dr Davenport had bid them "*Au revoir*".

Through her window she could see the long line of daffodils dancing in the breeze – *his* daffodils. She gaz'd and gaz'd, but today her heart could not join in their dance.

With another glance at the stubborn clock, she began

busying herself almost automatically with routine matters until lunchtime, and, apart from a brief consultation with Joe Riley, spent the afternoon likewise, typing up requisition forms and (poignantly) the very last of Dr Davenport's business letters.

Although the school day ended officially at 4.15, Martha rarely left the premises before five o'clock, but today she left promptly at 4.30 and drove straight to *Elsinore*. After parking her car beneath the towering magnolia, she hurried towards the front door and the sanctuary of the entrance hall, consciously averting her eyes as she walked past the dreaded coach house. Once inside, she fondly half-expected him to leap out of a cupboard wearing a silly hat, but of course his practical jokes and that sonorous sound of his voice would have to be consigned to her treasury of memories now.

She went round every room checking for signs of a break-in, as Mr Higginbottom had advised, and once she was satisfied that all was well, she finally plucked up courage to enter his study. The magnificent writing-desk was secured with a simple but very effective locking device that he himself had designed with a numerical code incorporating his and his mother's year of birth. At first she blundered with one incorrect digit, but at the second attempt the top drawer unlocked with an efficient clunk, revealing a large brown envelope addressed to "Miss Martha Wolf". As she lifted the envelope out of the desk, she was amused to notice that his ornate "M" in "Miss" could easily have been mistaken for a "K"!

It was a good half-minute before she could bring herself to slit the envelope open, wherein she found two further envelopes, one marked "Will" and the second curiously, "If you will". She opened the envelope marked "Will" first, and began to read:

WILL

OF

GEORGE O'BRIEN DAVENPORT

OF

7 LANCASTER AVENUE NETHERBRIDGE

IN THE COUNTY OF LANCASHIRE

DATED *13th November 1965*

THIS IS THE LAST WILL AND TESTAMENT OF ME

GEORGE O'BRIEN DAVENPORT of "*Elsinore*" 7 Lancaster Avenue Netherbridge in the County of Lancashire

1. I REVOKE all prior wills and Testamentary Dispositions made by me

2. I APPOINT my friend MARTHA WOLF as my sole Executrix

3. IF she is unable or unwilling to act or if she dies before proving my Will I appoint the REVEREND CANON HERBERT RAMSBOTTOM as my Executor and

Trustee

4. I GIVE the sum of £5000 to the DEPARTMENT OF NEUROSCIENCE AND PSYCHIATRY at ADDENBROOKE'S HOSPITAL CAMBRIDGE

5. I GIVE to ST MARY'S CHURCH NETHERBRIDGE the sum of £1000

6. I GIVE the sum of £1000 to THE ROYAL SOCIETY FOR THE PREVENTION OF CRUELTY TO ANIMALS of Wilberforce Way Southwater Horsham Sussex (registered charity number 219099) for its general purposes

7. I GIVE the sum of £500 to my friend REV CANON RICHARD SPENCE

8. I GIVE the sum of £500 to my friend MR DAFYDD JENKINS

9. I GIVE the sum of £500 to my friend MR JOHN HIGGINBOTTOM

10. I GIVE the sum of £500 to my friend REVEREND CANON HERBERT RAMSBOTTOM

11. IF MARTHA WOLF survives me for thirty days I give the whole of the remainder of my estate to her including the property known as "*Elsinore*" 7 Lancaster Avenue Netherbridge and the contents thereof.

12. IF this gift fails the following provision shall apply:

13. I GIVE the whole of the remainder of my estate in equal shares to ST MARY'S CHURCH NETHERBRIDGE and the DEPARTMENT OF NEUROSCIENCE AND

PSYCHIATRY at ADDENBROOKE'S HOSPITAL
CAMBRIDGE

IN WITNESS whereof I have hereto set my hand to this my Will

this *13ᵗʰ* day of *November* 1965

SIGNED by the Testator

George O. Davenport

The said GEORGE O'BRIEN DAVENPORT

as and for his Last Will and Testament in our joint presence and by
us both in his presence:

Daniel Newsome   56 Hand Lane
Netherbridge

Anne Monks   115 Ashley Drive
Netherbridge

Newsome and Co

Solicitors

17-19 Podmore Street

Netherbridge

Lancs

Dr Davenport had drawn up his first will soon after his mother died, and had asked Martha to act as his executor, "should something happen to me", as he put it. And now, it suddenly dawned on her that that "something" had actually happened, and that she would have to prove as good as her word. She noticed under Item 3 that she could still abnegate the responsibility, if she so wished, whereupon it would then fall on Canon Ramsbottom, but for all her emotional turmoil and confusion, Martha was absolutely clear about one thing, that she could never let her great friend and mentor down.

She had always imagined benefiting in some small way from the will: a few books or records perhaps, or even an item of furniture she had always admired, though her own little house was already over-furnished. She also knew that substantial legacies were designated for his cherished charities, especially the RSPCA and Addenbrooke's Hospital, but the unsparing generosity shown towards her personally took her by surprise.

While still in a state of euphoric bewilderment, she ventured to open the second envelope, marked, "If you will". Inside, she found a note, dated 13th November 1965, the same as that of the will.

Apropos my funeral arrangements.

I entrust you, Martha, with all decisions regarding my funeral arrangements. However, should you find yourself wondering what the old rascal would really have wanted, I offer the following suggestions:

- *A basic committal service with <u>a minimum of fuss</u> at Altrincham Crematorium, taken by Canon Ramsbottom, if available. A short reading and a prayer, followed by an uplifting piece of music would be ample. <u>No</u> eulogies.*
- *Likewise, things to be kept low-key at the School.*
- *£100 to be deposited behind the bar at the Boar's Head, and Jack to arrange a "gradely bite" after the service.*
- *The ashes to be scattered on my mother's grave in St*

Mary's churchyard. We left a space on her tombstone for the added inscription: "Also her loving son, George O'Brien Davenport (1903 -)".

- In the middle drawer of the desk you will find up-to-date details of all my financial affairs, arranged in alphabetical order.

- Furthermore, I have listed the names, addresses and telephone numbers of all the agencies you will need to notify.

- Perhaps you should contact Dan Newsome as soon as possible and be guided by him regarding probate etc.

I am truly sorry to burden you with all this drudgery, Martha; and I am eternally grateful to you.

The funeral service was held at Altrincham Crematorium on Saturday morning, 23rd April. Martha had arranged it for the previous day, but Canon Ramsbottom had forgotten that he had an extraordinary diocesan meeting on the Friday, and Martha had insisted on his services.

In his introductory remarks Canon Ramsbottom

observed wryly that there might have been an element of divine intervention in the change of date, the Saturday being St George's Day. Thereafter, he followed Martha's instructions to the letter, bringing the private and understated service to a close with Holst's *Jupiter* played on the crematorium's barely acceptable music system.

However, the proceedings were not to everyone's taste, Jack Higginbottom especially. He felt that his old friend deserved something more worthy, and during the lunch afterwards at the *Boar's Head* he prevailed on Martha to arrange another service later in the summer, to celebrate his remarkable life and achievements, especially while at Netherbridge. Martha protested that she had mixed feelings about the idea, because it contravened Dr Davenport's last wishes, but over the next few days she persuaded herself that perhaps it did not constitute a betrayal so much as meeting a deep and commonly felt need. Accordingly, after a short ceremony for scattering the ashes the following Friday, again performed exactly as Dr Davenport had requested, she arranged with Canon Ramsbottom to hold the kind of service at the Parish Church that Jack Higginbottom had suggested.

This service eventually took place at two o'clock on Friday, 3rd June, a glorious summer's day, and was given front page coverage in the *Netherbridge Chronicle*:

Memorial Service
Dr George Davenport
Head Master
Netherbridge Grammar School
1936-1966

"On the Friday of Whitsun week, several generations of pupils, masters, parents, and friends of Netherbridge Grammar School packed into the St Mary's Parish Church to celebrate the life of the town's most distinguished adopted son. An equally large gathering listened to the service on the public address system outside the church.

The Vicar, Canon Herbert Ramsbottom, extended a warm welcome to the largest congregation he had ever seen at the church, adding that it was a clear indication of the great esteem in which this remarkable man was held. He added that whilst it was generally known how George Davenport had always loathed his "silly nick-name", as he called it, it was also generally agreed that if any human being deserved this sobriquet it was he.

Canon Ramsbottom felt blessed to have known Dr Davenport for well-nigh 30 years, and during that time, like countless others, had benefited immeasurably from his wisdom, loyal friendship, and lively sense of humour.

Further tributes followed from the current head prefect, Neil Pemberton, and several distinguished alumni. Each in turn regaled an appreciative audience with fond memories and amusing anecdotes, illustrating the great man's many qualities: his superb intellect; his quiet authority; his moral rectitude; his sense of duty; his capacity to inspire; his sense of fair play; his compassion; and his utter selflessness.

After one or two pertinent readings and prayers, the service concluded with a hearty rendering of *Guide me O Thou great Redeemer*, followed by some closing remarks and the blessing by Dr Davenport's former colleague and friend, the Rev Richard Spence."

"Well done, Martha," said Jack Higginbottom, as they walked back together to the car park, "that was more like it... a proper Headmaster's funeral... a gradely send-off for the "Gaffer". Now, aren't you glad you listened to your Uncle Jack?"

"Well, yes, it *was* a nice service, if a funeral can ever be called that. And you were right... the cremation service was a little cold... but then that was what he'd asked for."

"Anyway, we got the best of both worlds in the end, and this afternoon will stay in people's minds for a very long time. By the way, I was very impressed with young Pemberton. He's going places, that lad."

And with that they both went their separate ways, he back to the *Boar's Head*, while Martha, quietly pleased with the way things had gone, drove back, more slowly this time, to her own little house to ponder what the future held for her. It was too early even to imagine what life might be like as the lady of *Elsinore*, or whether it might be more prudent to sell it off and stay put in her own house. There were so many factors to consider, but more immediately, as the will's executor, there was still much letter-writing and telephoning to do, and so many people to consult.

Martha had noticed with some satisfaction that nearly all the masters had made the effort to attend the service, and that most had been in no hurry to leave. Many had enjoyed meeting old colleagues and past pupils, several even repairing afterwards to various hostelries in the town to continue their reminiscing. However, there were one or two interesting absences; namely, Mr Tony Titchener, the diminutive R.I. master, who claimed he had a long-standing golfing commitment in Wales, and Mr Nobbs, who apparently had taken his wife to Scarborough as a surprise birthday treat in his new Mark X Jaguar.

After a substantial evening meal, Martha dozed off in front of the television. She had had a tense and emotionally draining day. She awoke with a start to find it was eight o'clock, time to carry out her nightly checks at *Elsinore*. After a cloudless day, the sun was setting gloriously over the Cheshire plain, and as she drove the short distance from her house to Lancaster Avenue, more slowly than usual because of the low trajectory of the sun, it dawned on her that putting Dr Davenport's house on the market, let alone exchanging it for money, was tantamount to prostitution. This was not just a beautiful house in an exquisite setting: it was the former home of a beautiful and exquisite human being, whose praises had been sung so volubly that very afternoon,

No, she made up her mind in that instant to live in it herself, painful though it would be, and to sell, or possibly rent, her own house. Perhaps Taff and Liz would be interested? She would charge them a very reasonable rent. Liz would have plenty to occupy her with a much larger garden to tend, and Taff could make the garage into his own private retreat where he could carve and turn wood to his heart's content, safe from Liz's chiding. Martha had a lively imagination and saw possibilities where others threw up their hands in despair, and during those brief ten minutes an irrevocable decision seemed to have implanted itself in her head.

After parking her mini in its usual place underneath the magnolia tree, she walked down the drive towards the front door. As she was about to insert the latch key, she heard a woman's voice calling from the boundary hedge. It was Mrs McAllister.

"Hello, Martha, I'm so glad I caught you... a young gentleman called this morning... an agent or something, from Manchester... he wanted to know if *Elsinore* would be up for sale soon. He said he knew the former owner had recently passed away, and he was looking around on behalf of a customer... Oh, I did enjoy the service this afternoon, and so well attended. I couldn't believe it when

I saw all those people arriving... a good job I went when I did, otherwise I would never have got a seat. George *would* have been proud of you, Martha."

"I don't know about that, Mrs McAllister, but we did our best, and it seemed to go down quite well," replied Martha, eager to escape her clutches, but at the same time curious about the mysterious estate agent. How would an agent from Manchester know about *Elsinore* so soon? This had to be more local than Manchester, she reckoned.

"What did this gentleman say exactly, Mrs McAllister?"

"Not very much really, beyond what I've told you, but he did leave this card, in case you wanted to get in touch with him. I told him that a young lady was looking after the house until it was sold, and I would give her the card."

"Oh, thank you, Mrs McAllister. If I get time, I might phone him over the weekend, although I've quite enough on my plate at the moment without any extra pressure."

As Martha worked her way methodically through the rooms, checking every door and window, she grew more and more irritated by this mysterious speculator. Besides, she had now decided to move into *Elsinore* herself, and this latest development only hardened her resolve. As far as she was concerned, it was still Dr Davenport's home, and this unsolicited inquiry was premature and impertinent. Furthermore, she felt distinctly unnerved by it, and in order to deter any other intruder or busy-body, in future she would leave the curtains drawn in one or two bedrooms and the lights on in certain areas of the house. On the way home, she also made up her mind to see to Dr Davenport's will sooner rather than later, and accordingly made an appointment with the solicitor the following morning to inform him of her decision not to sell *Elsinore*.

WHEN THE SCHOOL reopened after the Whitsun break, Joe Riley moved across to Dr Davenport's old study. Now that the funeral ceremonies were all completed, he felt a little more comfortable about the idea.

Nobbs had been exerting subtle and sycophantic pressure on him for several weeks, simply so that he could inherit his desirable little hideaway; and almost before actually gaining possession, he had begun the task of converting it into a modern office, using self-assembly kitchen cabinets, shelving, and worktops. Thus, poor Joe's makeshift 'desk', along with all his other archaic accoutrements, were unceremoniously consigned to history via the Netherbridge Municipal Dump, and replaced with an up-to-the-minute work-station, befitting an ambitious and controlling stock-controller. Joe's *modus operandi*, devised in a bygone age, may have stood the test of time, and served the School well enough in the past, but it belonged to that abominable *status quo* that Nobbs abhorred, and had to go. If dissenting voices were raised in the Master's Room, they would be silenced with well-rehearsed quotations by the likes of Churchill ("progress is impossible without change"), Shaw ("to improve is to change; to be perfect is to change often"), or even the current Prime Minister, Harold Wilson ("the only human institution which rejects progress is the cemetery").

ON ASSUMING the headship of Netherbridge Grammar

School, Joe Riley's most pressing task was to produce a time-table of lessons for the following school year. In most schools a new time-table had to be written annually, and towards the end of June the headmaster would withdraw from the real world into his study, protected by a prominent sign on the door, "DO NOT DISTURB, UNLESS ABSOLUTELY NECESSARY"; and woe betide the miscreant who took liberties with the words, "absolutely necessary". Thus, safely cocooned in a mystical world of grids and symbols, and sustained with a generous supply of a favourite condiment and beverage, he would often remain incommunicado for days on end, juggling different combinations of rooms, periods, classes and masters, until a workable arrangement eventually emerged.

Constructing the school time-table had been one of Dr Davenport's annual delights, not least because it often lent a little spice to what could sometimes be a vapid tail-end to the school year. Curiously, he had learned the basic principles as a third former in Altrincham County School, when the (overworked) headmaster had invited him and a fellow pupil to try their hand. Together, the two boys managed to develop a simple but ingenious template, which had served him well throughout all his time at Netherbridge.

But for Joe Riley, albeit quite familiar with interpreting a time-table, say, for the purpose of the daily substitution rota, the mere thought of constructing a new one from scratch filled him with consternation, and he had always dreaded the day when he might have to practise the black arts himself. Indeed, Dr Davenport's robust constitution had teased him into believing that this eventuality was highly improbable, and little did he think on that first morning after the Easter break, when the two had spent their last half-hour together in that very room, sharing jokes and putting the world to rights, that the cup would be passing so soon into his inadequate hands. Admittedly, he had often of late helped Dr Davenport with the rudimentary mechanics of the task, but the more creative aspects, such as making the most of one's resources, distributing lessons so as to maximise their learning potential, allowing for any specific demands or requirements and so forth, were uncharted waters.

Accordingly, to give himself ample time in this novel and unwelcome situation, he decided to make an early start, first, by raiding his old store for a good supply of HB pencils, rubber erasers, and sheets of graph paper. Unfortunately for him, Dr Davenport had left no written record of how he had approached the task, mainly because he used to work a great deal of it out in his head while on his cycle journeys to and from School!

After several false starts and fruitless attempts, he concluded that perhaps time-tabling might never be his *metier*; and maybe he should break with tradition and delegate the task to a younger and aspiring underling. He could advertise on the Masters' Room notice-board or approach likely candidates individually. Of course, he realised that in some respects this would offer hostages to fortune, but as far as he was concerned, the suddenness of the circumstances and his own lack of appropriate skills justified that sacrifice. He even considered creating a new post, something on the lines of, "with special responsibility for the time-table and the substitution rota", but of course this would have required the Governors' approval, and besides, the "sub-rota" had always been the responsibility of the Senior Master (as the time-table had been the Headmaster's).

Poor Joe was in a quandary, and in desperation he took a brand new HB pencil from the box and started jotting down some possible names on a blank sheet of graph-paper. The first two or three sprang to mind readily: people like Frank Fairclough and Phil Evans were always volunteering to do things, and would probably fit the bill admirably now, but it would be good if he could persuade someone new, someone fresh, who also had an aptitude for organization. While he was thus engrossed in considering his options, there was a gentle knock on his door.

"Come in," he barked with an unconvincing note of authority.

"Mr Riley," began Nobbs, "I hope I'm not cutting across anything, but I hear on the bush radio that you could do with some help with next year's time-table.

(Now, how the devil did he know that? thought Joe, he must have been eavesdropping or has spies on the premises.)

I don't want to sound pushy or anything," continued Nobbs, "but I thought perhaps *I* could give you a hand... I did a week's course on time-tabling at York University a couple of years back, and I wouldn't mind putting that knowledge into practice... And on a practical level, I've got all those facilities in my workshop to draw up some blanks on large sheets of drawing paper... they'd be much easier to use than those tiny sheets of graph paper. Of course, if you wanted to be really professional, you could send away for a time-tabling system, with a custom-built wall-board and coloured pegs to represent all your variables... you know, the classes, rooms and what have you. They demonstrated one in York, and I've often seen them advertised in one of the publishers' catalogues. They're a bit expensive, but I'm told they are very good. But, what the hell, I could save you all that expense... I could knock something similar up from a sheet of peg-board, and then we could buy coloured pegs from Stanhope's on Chester Street... Anyway, I happened to be passing, and for what it's worth, I thought I'd offer my services. Of course, you may have other plans, but, remember, the offer's always there, if I can be of any help... tell you what, why don't you come up to our place this evening? We could discuss it further over a bite to eat. I managed to get hold of some nice quails on Saturday, and I think Mandy's braising them with wild mushrooms for supper. Perhaps we could have a good chat about things then."

"Well, thank you, Mr Nobbs, that's very kind of you. I'm taken aback, really. Yes, I have heard about these special boards, but for this first effort I thought perhaps it would be best if we stuck to the 'pencil and rubber' way that Dr Davenport used. Indeed, I would also prefer if we kept as close as possible to this year's model, with no changes except where absolutely necessary.

"Well, yes, of course, if that is what you want... there's a lot to be said for the tried and tested... but, anyway, don't forget, if I can be of any assistance, you know where I am."

"Oh yes, thank you very much... and thank you also for the very kind invitation to supper... it's very much appreciated. But I'm a bit tied up most evenings at the moment... when things quieten down a bit, I would like that very much... I don't think I've had the pleasure of meeting your good lady."

"That's all right... I quite understand... but don't go kicking it into the long grass now... you see, I've been here knocking on twenty years now, and I really should be getting to know more of my colleagues... and, naturally, I thought I'd start at the top, Joe, if I can call you that!" Then after a slight pause he added, "You know, I feel about this time-tabling business like a monk feels about sex... although I've never done it, I think I might be quite good at it!"

Joe smiled politely at this old chestnut, while Martha, busy in the adjoining office, pretended she had not heard.

After Nobbs had left, Joe asked Martha what she made of his offer. To which she replied, "Don't let me put you off, Mr Riley, but I should be wary of Greeks bearing gifts, especially that one. He's wily, and Dr Davenport always kept him at arm's length."

"Yes, I agree with that, Martha, but, you see, I could use all the help I can get at the moment, and a lot of what he said did make sense. And it would save having to formalise matters. No, give the devil his due, or possibly, enough rope... Oh, God... sorry, Martha, that wasn't in very good taste. But in fairness, he has made a first-class job in the Stockroom and all in double-quick time; who knows, he could be equally good on the time-table. Mind you, I'm glad I refused his invitation to supper; that, I believe, *would* have been a step too far... although, you know, it would have been interesting to get another perspective on things! Anyway, we shall see. Oh, I nearly forgot, now we know Taff's definitely retiring, we'll have to get an advert in for his replacement. I suppose I'd better consult our Mr Nobbs on that one... we'll sort out the wording, and then I'll get back to you as soon as I can, Martha."

ALTHOUGH NOT usually one to look a gift-horse in the mouth, Joe spent the remainder of the day and much of the following night weighing up Nobbs's offer. He appreciated Martha's unambiguous note of caution, and in all honesty he himself had never quite understood the fellow. One thing that puzzled him was why someone with such easy charm and bonhomie had so few friends in the Masters' Room. Presumably, George, and now Martha, had solid grounds for their suspicions: perhaps they knew something that he didn't. To be fair, Nobbs had always been respectful towards him, and as far as he knew towards his other colleagues. He wondered if it might be the same kind of ingrained prejudice that existed in the Masters' Room when he was first appointed. But for goodness' sake, this was the 1960s, not the 1930s. And, besides, most of the 'old brigade' with their built-in academic snobbery had long departed. He remembered well their reaction when he first arrived in 1930, simply because he was not "Oxbridge", and had an, albeit modified, Geordie accent. But neither George nor Martha could ever be accused of such snobbery, so could there be something else? Of course, there might also be an element of jealousy in some quarters. People did wonder where on earth he got his money from. No one could sustain such an affluent life-style on a schoolmaster's salary: those suits were not from British Home Stores, and the new Jaguar, how much did that cost? And someone said his house was enormous, with all the latest gadgets and expensive Swedish furniture. Certainly, no Cyril Lord carpets for our Mr Nobbs, thank you very much, only the premier grade Wilton or Axminster. And apparently his wife didn't work either... most mysterious. Rumour had it that he had won a tidy sum on the pools, or that his father had died and left him a fortune.

But prejudice and jealousy were not part of Joe's nature. As a no-nonsense northerner, unless he had good reason to think otherwise, he took people as he found them. Nobbs evidently did have more money than the average schoolmaster, enjoyed the good things in life, and for good measure, had a very attractive wife, twenty years his junior! But that did not make him a villain. Good luck to him! And if he was prepared to go the extra mile and get Joe out of that hole, well, who was he to say him nay? Obviously, he was a capable organizer and had the confidence and hopefully the know-how to sort out this time-table business. No, Joe's mind was made up. He would accept his offer of help with good grace.

After school assembly the following morning, Joe called Nobbs into his study to inform him of his decision. And one never knows, enthused Joe, but he (Nobbs) might also benefit from the experience... it was always useful to have such things on one's *curriculum vitae*. Furthermore, having mulled it over and slept on it, he was persuaded to go down the 'do-it-yourself' route with the wall-board and the coloured pegs from Stanhope's. And if Mr Nobbs would kindly obtain the necessary materials, perhaps they could make a start together during the Wakes weeks... Oh, and could he be sure to get all the receipts and pass them on to Miss Wolf?

Accordingly, during the last week of June and the first in July, two of the most unlikely work-mates, the tall and well-groomed wheeler-dealer from Oldham and the bald, diminutive academic from Durham – Dick and Joe – put their heads together inside the newly reorganised Stockroom to make a time-table for the 1966-67 year. It took a little over a week to complete, and Joe was thrilled with the end-product, especially after being flattered into believing that it was *he* who had made all the important decisions and resolved all the dilemmas and clashes. Thereafter, some half dozen boys the second year technical drawing class were volunteered to transcribe the details from the wall-board onto a large, prepared sheet; and by the time normal school resumed on July 11th, all the individual time-tables had been extrapolated and distributed, but most important of all, Joe Riley was able to sleep soundly in his bed again – but not for very long.

On Tuesday, July 12th Joe received a letter from Martin Shaw, his dentist, and now President of the Netherbridge Rotary Club, inviting him to become a member. This was now another problem Joe could have done without, and he wrestled with it for the best part of a week before penning his reply:

Dear Martin,

First of all, may I thank you from the bottom of my heart for your kind invitation for me to join the Netherbridge Rotary Club.

I have always acknowledged the mutual benefits of maintaining close links between 'town and gown', and, as you know, no one did this better than our dear late friend and colleague, George Davenport. As one of the Club's founders and one of its central pillars, he himself sometimes used these links in practical ways. Indeed, I often heard him say how useful he found the little blue book of members' addresses and telephone numbers when the School needed access to specialist equipment or skills.

However, as for myself, after much thought and self-questioning, and with much regret, I feel obliged to decline, on account of age, my new responsibilities and heavy work load.

(Indeed, there may have been some truth in all this, but the real reason for his refusal was his aversion to the whole business of 'socialising', or indeed any kind of enforced fellowship and jollity. At heart, he had always been a private person, preferring to spend his leisure hours pursuing his own interests, or with his family.)

I must stress that I regard the Rotary movement very highly indeed: its motto, Service before Self, happens to be very much in tune with the ethos of our School. I also know many of the Netherbridge Club's members, some of whom are old Netherbridgians, and as individuals I have always found them to be friendly and honourable. But joining their ranks was not something I had ever aspired to!

(Joe felt fleetingly tempted to cite Groucho Marx's famous quip when placed in a similar situation: "I don't care to belong to any club that would accept people like me as a member"; but lest he be taken for a frightful curmudgeon, he desisted, and instead concluded on a constructive note.)

Accordingly, Martin, might I make a suggestion, that the Club break with tradition and accept another, younger and indeed more suitable member of our staff as the School's representative. If this be acceptable in principle, I should gladly recommend a suitable candidate.

Thank you again,

And with my very best wishes,

Joe Riley

During morning break the following Friday Joe invited Nobbs into his office. "Do come in, Richard, I won't keep you... I know you're busy. Look, I'll come straight to the point... I'm in a bit of a quandary... and I was hoping that you might be able to do us both a favour. How do you fancy becoming a Rotarian... representing the School at the Netherbridge Club?"

Nobbs was nonplussed by this unexpected proposition. Like Joe, he had always regarded himself more as an individual than a "clubby type", even as a young boy in Oldham. It might have been the "Jewish thing", but whatever the reason, he had always felt an outsider, even though he was never short of company.

"Well, this is a bit sudden, Joe, I must say, but do you know what, for *you* I'm prepared to give it my best shot."

"Look, Richard, you don't have to decide right now.

Sleep on it... talk it over with your good lady... but you'd be doing me a big favour."

Nobbs had often hankered after some such accolade. Membership of Rotary might be the very thing to bring him and Mandy a modicum of social respectability: for some reason, despite the lavish dinner-parties they had given, he had never felt "accepted" by the "people who mattered" in Leigh. And for some reason, an offer such as this had never been forthcoming.

"I think you'd enjoy it, Richard," continued Joe, "When Dr Davenport was away, I occasionally took his place at lunch-time meetings, which, of course, I gladly did. Sometimes the talks were very interesting, but being a proper member, well, I'm probably too old to start that sort of thing now anyway. But you, Richard, you'd be ideal, and I'm sure you'd find it very fulfilling – Dr Davenport certainly did – and I'm sure the contacts you'd make would be very useful. Anyway, you'd be doing me and the School a big favour. The School definitely benefits from the links, and so does the club. It's not really *my* cup of tea, and besides, I can't really afford the time... but I thought it would be right up *your* street... you know, dressing up, dining out, having a few drinks at the bar and all that... anyway, you have a think about it, and perhaps we'll discuss it again in a few days... and if you're still keen, I'll put your name forward."

"Well, thank you, Joe... for thinking of me, that is... I'm sure there were plenty of others you could have asked. But as I've said before, if I can ever be of assistance, all you've got to do is to ask. As Charles Dickens put it, 'No one is useless in this world, who lightens the burden of another.'"

As soon as Nobbs left the office, Joe shuffled across to Martha who had overheard most of the conversation. She was standing by the window watching a pair of collared doves feeding near the flower beds that Dr Davenport used to admire at this time of year.

"Well, Martha," said Joe a little triumphantly, "I think we may have done our friend a grave injustice. This last fortnight he has been a revelation to me, which suggests perhaps we should never pre-judge people. He's worked like the proverbial... we were here some nights until nine and ten o'clock. And the thing is, he's so handy with all that drawing equipment. It's half the battle getting the blank tables and charts drawn up before you start. And what I like about him, he's always so positive, so supportive... he brings me solutions, instead of problems. I know he can be a little... you know... over the top at times... but none of us is perfect."

"No," agreed Martha wearily, as she gazed out at the towering Ravenscroft Mill, its red bricks aglow in the mid-morning sun. Yes, the looms were alive again after the Wakes, but for how much longer? But more to the point, what fate awaited her dear old Grammar School? Had she not just glimpsed the "rough beast, its hour come at last", beating a monstrous path towards Netherbridge?

Chapter Eight

School re-opened for the Michaelmas Term on Tuesday, September 6th. It had been an indifferent summer, apart from the last week of August, when the garden thermometer at *Elsinore* had reached 85°F on five successive days.

Joe Riley had spent the first three weeks of the vacation down in Torquay at his sister's, following England's progress in the World Cup on her new 21 inch Murphy. His morale, already high after the surprisingly agreeable end to the Summer term, was further boosted on the 30th July by the gratifying defeat of the Germans by Ramsey's band of immortals, especially those two fellow Geordies, the Charltons.

And then the euphoria of July was enhanced on August 6th by the Governors' letter confirming his position as Headmaster. Whilst only a formality, it brought him great joy: if only Janet had been there to share it with him. But, at least, Ian would be very proud of his father.

However, two hurdles still remained, either of which could wreck his *annus mirabilis*: the 'A' level results on the 11th and the 'O' levels on the 18th. In fairness, that year's Upper Sixth (which included such luminaries as Fred Challinor's son, Stephen, and the outstanding Head Prefect, Neil Pemberton) had always invited comparison with the *Inexsuperabiles* of 1957, whose record of 14 Oxbridge entrants still stood. As it turned out, Joe's insomnia proved unwarranted, for the Class of '66 did not disappoint. All 73 candidates secured the required grades for their respective universities, with six heading for Cambridge and five for Oxford. Furthermore, Joe was overjoyed that the three who had chosen to read his subject, Classics, at his *alma mater*, St John's, Durham, had also been successful.

And so, it all now hung on the 18th. Surely, Fortune would not desert him so near the winning post. But the night before Wednesday, the 17th yet again proved how the stress of examinations never diminishes with the years, and he whiled away the small hours emulating the young Harold Macmillan lying wounded in a trench on the Somme in 1916 by reading Aeschylus' *Prometheus Unbound* in the original Greek!

George Davenport had often warned against getting carried away with the glamour of 'A' levels; the 'O' level results with their wider range of subjects and candidates, he maintained, gave a truer snapshot of a school's academic fitness. Whilst acknowledging George's point, Joe had become increasingly irritated by the recent craze of 'O' levels being amassed like Scout badges: "As many as fifteen in some cases!" he grumbled. "It's quite

196

unnecessary... and the cost of it. In my experience, eight is ample, providing they include the matriculating subject requirements. But Dr Davenport had taken a more lenient view, arguing that the trend generated harmless competition, and, more importantly, broadened pupils' perspectives before embarking on their specialist Sixth form subjects. Indeed, in an ideal world he would have liked a broader curriculum in the Sixth form too, recalling how reading English literature and history up to university entrance level at Altrincham County School had complemented his mathematics and physics wonderfully.

JOE RILEY unlocked his office door at seven o'clock prompt, and had boiled the kettle and made the tea by the time Martha appeared at 7.30. He had always done this on results day because he enjoyed the rituals of receiving the packages from the postman and opening each one himself so that he could familiarise himself with the details and work out some averages and percentages before Dr Davenport and the madding crowds of anxious parents and pupils came knocking on the door.

Sadly, of course, George would not be here today to share the excitement, (or question his arithmetical endeavours), but Fortuna (or Tyche, as Joe preferred to call her) had not forsaken him. She smiled on him as she had done on Alf at Wembley, so that her modest little favourite would not wilt beneath his inordinate yoke.

In the event, judging by the Davenport yardstick, NGS's levels of fitness had never rated more highly than in 1966 when the 93 Fifth formers harvested a grand total of 987 passes, most of which were at grades one and two.

Interestingly, Joe was decidedly coy when Peter Halliwell, the young Physics master, pointed out that 36 of the grade ones had been obtained by three boys alone!

THE MOOD IN the Masters' Room on the first day of term was also buoyant, if not self-congratulatory. Some had feared, wrongly, that the tragic events of mid-April would have impacted harshly on the examination results. But they had reckoned without the resilience of youth, and its acceptance of death as a fact of life that brings with it change and exciting new possibilities. Besides, the pupils' tragic loss was not germane to the immediate business of growing up and their aspirations in the adult world. And, of course, this was exactly how the great man would have wanted it.

However, beneath the general bonhomie, certain mutterings were heard regarding Joe Riley's first time-table, if indeed it was Joe's. Many resented Nobbs's involvement at all, except that perhaps without him it might not have been ready on time. His 'bloodless coup' of the Stockroom was tolerated good-humouredly as a long overdue updating of a fairly low-status part of the institution, but the time-table, that was a different matter altogether. This had always been the Headmaster's territory: 'God's ordinance', as it were, handed down from on high on the first day of a school year, for lesser folk to accept and marvel at, but never to meddle in.

Even the diminutive Dr Morrison, the easy-going Senior Mathematics Master (train-buff and Secretary of the PTA) dismissed the overall schema as having as much to do with education as a railway timetable.

In the same vein, Fred Fielding, a Junior German Master,

198

(Phil Evans's "yon Teuton with the teeth of gold") thought it "mechanistic": "Dr Davenport always made sure that modern language periods were distributed evenly in singles throughout the week, and not bunched together in doubles and triples, as we have here. It's an absolute mess!"

Even Jim Nuttall, the elderly and long-suffering Biology Master, complained that many of the decisions were arbitrary, if not downright inconsiderate: "You need double periods for practicals... surely Joe must know that."

"What have *I* done to upset Joe?" lamented Ian Moore, the Senior Games Master, "he's only gone and put all my free periods on a Monday! I'm bound to be clobbered for the sub-rota every week. And anyway, I'll lose most of them to half-terms and bank holidays. Thanks a bunch, Joe, you're a treasure! You wait until the next cross-country races; I'll put you right out on the Caldwell tip!"

When some of these negative observations filtered back to Joe, he took them as a slight on his general suitability for the role of Headmaster, thereby tarnishing his hitherto glorious summer and promising start to a new term. He agonized for days over how he might make amends, until Nobbs told him not to be silly. "You always get one or two awkward sods," he exclaimed, "and after all, this was your first one... and it works... that's the main thing. Perhaps next year you can put in a few bells and whistles just to silence the 'moaning minnies', but for now, tell 'em to lump it. Bloody Hell! I don't know how some of this lot would have coped in the Burmese jungle!"

"Well, as someone who was spared such horrors by

my indifferent eyesight, I'm not really qualified to give an opinion on that," replied Joe, little knowing the true impact of his remark.

"Anyway, don't you let their whining get to you, Joe... remember, you're not as young as you used to be... and we don't want another... do we?

Whilst acknowledging Nobbs's (somewhat crass) attempt to allay his anxiety, Joe felt distinctly uneasy in his presence. What the devil did he mean by "we don't want another..."? In June, when he was clutching at straws, he had somehow managed to brush such feelings aside, but now he was beginning to wish that he had heeded Martha's advice. And he resented all the 'Joe this' and 'Joe that' business, and being patronised as a pathetic old man floundering in a morass of ineptitude. It seemed that familiarity had indeed bred contempt, and he would now find it hard to disentangle himself from this self-appointed counsellor's grappling hooks.

Meanwhile, oblivious to the disgruntlement simmering in the Masters' Room, the playground resounded, as always at the start of a new term, with excited voices, and especially this time with talk of the World Cup, and how the gods had favoured the English brave on that glorious Saturday in July. Knowledgeable opinions were exchanged on this player and that: Hurst's opportunistic hat trick; Banks's acrobatics in goal; the majestic Bobby Moore; not to mention their indefatigable local favourite, Nobby Stiles.

Others enthused, perhaps less effusively, about England's cricketing exploits that summer: there was no shame in losing 3-1 to a West Indies side containing Hall, Griffith, Gibbs and Gary Sobers; and winning the last

Test at the Oval so convincingly vindicated the wholesale changes, especially their new captain, Brian Close.

But over and above this frenetic chatter was everyone's perception of a sudden rise in seniority. Hitherto, the lower sixth, their rich haul of 'O' levels the previous summer notwithstanding, had had to defer to their seniors in the upper sixth for nine long months, but today *they* were the new aristocracy, catapulted into the School's academic and social stratosphere, from which vantage point they would be expected to lead by example. From among their ranks all the School's officers would be appointed, the Head Prefect and his Deputy, the Captains of each sport, and the Presidents of each society. But more importantly, every individual would have to develop his talents to the full and help maintain the general standard of academic attainment, sporting prowess, and gentlemanly conduct for which the School was rightly famed. Furthermore, as future leaders, they would need to put duty before self-gratification, and immerse themselves in their chosen disciplines as ends in themselves, as much as gateways to careers.

Of course, similar adjustments, albeit less dramatic, were made by all year-groups as they matured and edged up through the forms, but nowhere were these felt more acutely than by first-formers. These poor wretches, newly bereft of *elite* status at their former institutions, once again had to endure the indignities of benighted neophytes, at the mercy of their elders' teasing and posturing. It was ever thus, no doubt, even for the School's legendary cartoonist, William Postlethwaite, *circa* 1674, and, who knows, possibly for the fledgling William Shakespeare at Stratford Grammar School, some hundred years before that.

It was certainly the case at NGS in 1966, when an over-bearing second-former, called Simon Tranter, was seen to take great delight in intimidating a clutch of credulous eleven-year olds about the horrors awaiting them: the incomprehensibility of Greek grammar; the inedibility of school dinners; the cruelty of the cross-country run; the inhumanity of prefects; and worst of all, the sadistic propensities of certain masters, especially 'Nobb'ead' and 'Titch'. Indeed, by Christmas they'd be wishing they'd failed their entrance exams.

"And I'll tell you something else, my friends," he declaimed to his already demoralised audience, "it will be much worse for you, because GOD isn't around any more to keep an eye out for you. *You've* missed out big time... because last year *we* used to see GOD every day."

After a slight rhetorical pause, during which his captive audience looked more bewildered than ever, the incipient demagogue continued in quasi- religious tones, "He was brilliant, was our GOD... what he didn't know wasn't worth knowing... omniscient, if you like... but he wasn't a big'ead or anything... no... just an ordinary bloke like my dad supporting Everton on a Saturday afternoon, or going to the boxing at Belle Vue with his mate, Mr Jenkins. And there's another great bloke who's no longer with us. Nobody messed about in his class, I can tell you... I don't know why... he was never nasty or anything... we just... sort of... respected him. *He*'s still alive, mind, but he had to retire this summer after an accident over there in the Technology Block. My mate saw it happen... a piece of wood flew off a lathe and hit him in the face... he said there was blood everywhere. My dad said there should have been an inquiry, but everything was hushed up, for some reason.

"But GOD left for another reason... he went and topped himself last Easter. Why he had to do a thing like that, God knows... but then they do say gods move in mysterious ways! Of course, GOD wasn't his real name, you know... his real name was Dr Davenport, Dr George O'Brien Davenport, G...O...D... geddit? Our late Headmaster... And now we've got... huh... 'Old Mother Riley'."

Mercifully, the bell spared the perplexed gathering any further torment, but they had much to ponder over as they trooped back to their respective classrooms.

MARTHA SPENT much of her spare time during June and July attending to Dr Davenport's will, and as soon as probate was granted, she contacted all the beneficiaries to impart the good news. They were all nonplussed by their sudden stroke of good luck, especially Taff, who had visions of a life-time's trip to Madison Square Garden, to see the Joe Frazier-Oscar Bonavena fight in September. But Liz had other ideas. In the first instance, she would take him along to Graysons, the Gentlemen's Outfitters on Podmore Street, to have him measured for a new suit, and some fashionable casual wear ready for their proposed holiday to Pembrokeshire in September. He had not worn his 'best suit' for several years, because, thanks to the ravages of Liz's cooking and his loyal attendance at "Jack's", as he called *The Boar's Head*, his once inverted triangular torso had acquired a distinctly ovoid configuration.

Friday, July 15th was Taff's 66th birthday, and Martha

invited them both over for supper to celebrate the occasion, but she also had a hidden agenda. They arrived promptly at 7 o'clock with the usual bottle of Blue Nun and an enormous bouquet of tiger lilies.

"Oh, you shouldn't have... they're absolutely gorgeous... anyway, happy birthday, Mr Jenkins," said Martha, before hugging them both firmly and kissing them on the lips. "Welcome to my little retreat!"

When Taff had recovered his breath and composure, he declared, "Look, Martha, it's about time we stopped this "Mr Jenkins" nonsense. From now on I'm "Taff", all right?

"Well... yes... if that's what you want... old habits die hard though... but I'll try to remember!

While Martha went out to look for a receptacle for the lilies, Taff rummaged in his mackintosh pocket for a carefully wrapped little parcel. Liz had known for some time that something was afoot but had thought it best not to inquire.

"And this is a little something extra for you," said Taff to a bemused Martha, when she returned with the lilies, now neatly arranged in a large earthenware urn.

"What is it? I hope you haven't gone to a lot of expense."

"No," said Taff, "it didn't cost anything... it's just something I made."

She then proceeded to open the parcel, or at least tried to do so.

"You've packed it very well, Mr... erm... Taff."
When he saw her struggling with the sticky tape, he lent her his pocket-knife, which was large enough not to look out of place in an abattoir. Beneath the outer packaging

there was another protective layer of ribbed cardboard which she removed carefully to reveal a most exquisitely carved jewel casket in Burma teak – what else?

"Oh, it's absolutely beautiful... I don't know what to say..."

"You don't need to say nothing, love, the look on your face says it all. Besides, it's me that should be thanking you. It's just a little 'thank you' from me and Liz for all you've done for us, especially at the time of the accident. And making it helped to take my mind of things when I was feeling fed up. As it happened, I had a nice little piece left after a job I did at the Baptist chapel, and I kept it in case it came in handy for something."

While he was talking, Martha's eyes were irresistibly drawn to her surprise present: its elegant curves and smooth edges; the symmetry of its floral images; the precision of its tiny dovetail joints; its tiny brass hinges and clasp, with all the screw-heads pointing the same way. How very Mr Jenkins, she thought.

"Open the lid," urged Taff.

She gave a little squeal of delight to find that the inside surfaces were all lined with purple velvet padding. She caressed the casket gently on her cheek, relishing its silky smoothness and the wholesome aroma of French polish.

"Oh, and have a look underneath," said Taff, adding almost apologetically, "I checked with Joe about the Roman numerals!"

She turned it upside down, and read the inscription out loud,

MARTHA
MCMLXVI
TJ

"Oh, that's lovely... thank you, thank you... there really was no need, you know... it's gorgeous, and I shall treasure it forever. As a matter of fact, I haven't got much jewellery as such, but what bits I've got, mainly after Mum and Aunt Hilda, couldn't have a more beautiful home...", whereupon emotion got the better of her.

"Yes, Brenda did love her jewellery, didn't she?" said Liz. And it's funny, you're quite the opposite."

"Martha's lovely enough as she is," rejoined Taff.

"Look, I must get you a drink," said Martha at last, "I'm sure Liz will have her usual dry sherry, and I've got some bottles of Bass in for you, Taff... unless of course you'd like to join us in a sherry!"

"No, the Bass will do me fine, Martha fach, thank you."

"I tell you what," said Martha," let's go outside, shall we, and enjoy the last of the sun? It's a shame to be indoors on such a beautiful evening."

She had been busy all week planning this little get-together, and the garden looked at its best, the borders neat and a mass of colour, and the lawn freshly cut: indeed it was a perfect setting for what she had in mind. And the birds joined in the celebration.

"You've got this place looking really nice, Martha, and it's so quiet here... apart from those sparrows in that hawthorn bush, of course!" enthused Taff. "You know, anybody would think we were right out in the country. And the garden's so neat and tidy. Do you do it all yourself?"

"Well, I try to keep on top of things, though I wouldn't call myself a gardener. I got a man in last year to lay this patio and enlarge the rockery..., so everything's a lot easier to manage now. Anyway, have a wander round while I go and get the eats. There's a tremendous crop of Victoria plums this year, and the gooseberries and black currants seem to be doing well too. So there'll be some nice tarts to look forward to soon. Anyway, have a look round."

"Wasn't it good of her to invite us round like this on your birthday?" said Liz. "You kept pretty quiet about that box. *I* could do with something like that to keep all my necklaces and bangles together. Anyway, it was a very nice gesture, Taff, and I could see she really appreciated it."

"Well, I wanted to show her how *we* appreciated all that running around she did. I couldn't think what to get her at first, and then all of a sudden one morning while I was shaving it came to me."

Their musings at the bottom of the garden were brought to a sudden halt when Martha, with the authority of a seasoned bugler, put her right fist to her mouth and gave a creditable rendition of the mess-call.

She had laid out a sumptuous buffet on the patio table, and the three tucked in with gusto.

"Now, this is what Jack would call a 'gradely bite'", said Taff. "You've been very busy, Martha."

"You certainly have, that," said Liz, "I really don't know how you find the time. And this is more than a bite... it's a banquet."

"Oh, I don't know about that. Help yourself to another

beer from the fridge, Taff, while Liz and I clear the things away. I'll wash them up later. Ooh, I don't know about you, but I'm feeling a bit chilly, now the sun's gone down. Let's go inside, shall we?"

When they were settled comfortably in the living room, momentarily mulling over the recent past and their hopes for the immediate future, Martha decided to the broach the subject of her hidden agenda.

"Look, I've been thinking...I've got a proposition to make to you, and I'd like you at least to consider it, even if in the end you decide against it."

Both Taff and Liz looked at each other, wondering what "proposition" she might have in mind.

After a slight pause she continued, "I haven't told anyone else yet, and I would appreciate it if you also kept it to yourselves for the time being. When Dr Davenport died, everyone assumed that his house would be sold. After all, it's a family house, really. Of course, it suited him all right, because with all his interests he was able to make use of all the rooms and facilities; and besides, he could afford the expense of its upkeep.

"But between you and me, I don't think he wanted it to be sold, because why else would he leave it... to *me*, Martha Wolf, spinster of this parish?"

"Lady of the manor, more like!" exclaimed Taff, "and in more senses than one! Good on you, girl! You bloody well deserve it, an' all."

"And so say all of us," echoed Liz.

"At first, I did think selling was the sensible option, and perhaps reinvesting the proceeds in something less grand, or possibly in something completely different. But anyway, on the evening after the Memorial Service, when

I was on my way to do the usual security checks, I suddenly had this feeling that selling it was wrong, immoral almost. It felt like selling the family silver, or selling this beautiful jewel casket. And another thing... just as I was about to go in, the old lady from next door... you know... Mrs McAllister... called out to say that a man had called earlier wanting to know if it was for sale. Well, that really put the *kibosh* on things. The idea of some stranger lording it in Dr Davenport's old home, I ask you. But wait, it gets more interesting... and *you'll* like this, Taff. You know me, I'm like a Jack Russell with a rat when it comes to delving into mysteries... and in less than 48 hours I'd discovered the identity of our would-be buyer. Well, it turned out that the caller was acting on behalf of someone else, someone, Mr Jenkins, you might know better than any of us... but not necessarily admire ..."

"Oh, no, don't tell me it's. !" exclaimed Taff.

"Yes, I'm afraid so, the very same... yours truly... Mr Richard Nobbs."

"Bloody hell, I've heard it all now," exclaimed Taff. There's no end to that bugger's cheek! The nerve of it! He's not fit to share a planet with the 'Gaffer', let alone live in his house."

"Now, calm down, love. I'm sure Martha is quite capable of sorting out our mutual friend."

"Well, actually, our mutual friend did me a massive favour. If I had any lingering doubts about *Elsinore*, he managed to sweep them all away. And so, there it is, my friends... decision made... I shall live in it myself, and if necessary, sell this little house. I know it sounds daft, and I realise that it will be ridiculously big for my needs; but then, Mrs McAllister's is about the same size, and she seems to manage all right. Besides, I don't have to use it all. A good half of it could be blocked off, or even rented out. And think of that garden and all the parties I'll be able to throw! There are minuses, I know, but think of the pluses, the main one for me being that I'll be keeping Dr Davenport's memory alive."

"Well, this *is* a surprise," said Liz, you seem to have made your mind up very quickly. I know it's none of our business, but shouldn't you wait a little before doing anything rash?"

"Well, actually, Liz, I'd like to *make* it partly your business," replied Martha. "The bigger question for me is what I should do with this house when I move. I hate the idea of selling it, because of all the wonderful memories this holds for me as well, and I've spent quite a bit of late on improvements, and they tell me you don't get all your money back when you sell. Anyway, selling it is out of the question, so the only alternative is to rent it out... which brings me back to my proposition. Look, I'll come straight to the point... what I would really like is for you two to come and live here. It would be ideal for you. I know you're happy in your flat, and you've got it exactly as you want it, but you've often told me, Liz, that you'd like somewhere with a proper garden... and a garage or shed for Taff to do his woodwork... instead of the spare bedroom. Well, you'd have both here. What do you think, Taff? You're very quiet."

"I *thought* our little Martha was up to something! Well, I don't know what to think, really. It sounds almost too good to be true... I don't think Liz would take much persuading... and if she's happy, well it's okay with me.

God! So much has happened these last three months, bad and good, but everything's turning out great at the moment... and, do you know what... I can't help thinking the Gaffer's still looking after me, even from up there."

"There's just one thing, though," said Liz, "Have you thought how much rent you'd want? Perhaps we wouldn't be able to afford it, on our pensions!"

"I haven't actually, but there's no need to worry about that... I certainly wouldn't want any more than you're paying at the moment. I tell you what, you sleep on it, and if you still think it's a good idea tomorrow, then we can get down to the nitty-gritty. But please don't think I'm pushing you... you can take as long as you like. As far as I'm concerned, I shall be moving into *Elsinore* as soon as I can, and then I can empty my stuff out of here pretty quickly. I would dearly love you to take it, but only if you're happy with the idea."

"Goodness, look at the time," said Liz, "It's past Taff's bed-time!   But I don't think I'll be able to *sleep* on it tonight!"

"Why don't you come round for coffee tomorrow morning, and have a proper look around?" said Martha.

"Well, thank you so much for the lovely evening, Martha, and yes, tomorrow at about 11 o'clock would suit us fine... you haven't got anything on tomorrow, have you, Taff?"

"No, nothing that can't wait," replied Taff, as he turned towards the front door, which very soon, he thought, would be their very own.

"I'll get your coats, and then I'll run you home. You could be waiting ages for a bus at this time of night."

Chapter Nine

Martha Wolf was born in Shrewsbury on November 18th 1920. Her father, Charlie, had worked on the railway since leaving school at 14, first as a porter, and later as a signalman-porter at Dorrington station on the Shrewsbury-Hereford line. When military conscription was introduced in 1916, he enlisted, aged 23, in the KSLI, and served with the Second Battalion, fighting the Bulgarians in Macedonia.

On his return home in March 1919, his euphoria was scotched by the news that his younger brother had died a week earlier from the so-called Spanish flu, a month short of his 20th birthday. He had been wounded while serving with the KSLI's First Battalion during the German Spring Offensive of March 1918, and being severely debilitated, had succumbed to the virus while receiving treatment in a field hospital. Charlie himself had emerged from the War unscathed physically, but had never come to terms with the mental wounds, especially that last one, and very rarely talked about them.

However, albeit haunted by what he always referred to as "that bloody, stupid war", he resolved to restore order and purpose to his life, and very soon became re-acquainted with a fine looking Shropshire lass, called Brenda Marsh, from nearby Bayston Hill, with whom he had stepped out briefly before his call-up. Evidently, the still glowing embers of their relationship soon rekindled, and an intense courtship followed, resulting in a pregnancy and a shot-gun wedding in the summer of 1920.

After demobilization, Charlie had felt no great urge to return to his old job, even if there had been a vacancy: surely, he thought, he was capable of something better. Consequently, he spent the first eighteen months "clearing his head and earning his crust" doing various things such as window-cleaning and helping out during busy times on local farms. Like many ex-servicemen, he had grown disillusioned because the England he had fought for was not in reality the "country fit for heroes" promised by Lloyd George. He felt especially betrayed that those who, for whatever reason, had avoided serving in the war had in the meantime leapfrogged their enlisted colleagues and secured most of the desirable jobs. Indeed, when things seemed at their bleakest for him, he did consider emigrating to New Zealand or South America in search of better opportunities.

However, much to his surprise, shortly after he had got married, he received a letter from his old employers, inviting him to meet them at Shrewsbury station. They were keen for him to continue working for them, assuring him that his "knowledge of the railway, together with his commendable war record" would stand him in good stead, and offered him the position of relief signalman based at Shrewsbury. With three mouths now to feed, he welcomed this opportunity, and often worked extra shifts on Saturdays and Sundays. His enthusiasm and reliability did not go unnoticed, and in September 1924 he was called for interview again, and offered a clerical position in the main office at Shrewsbury station. Here again he showed so much energy and flair that the Station master recommended him for further training to prepare him for promotion, which eventually transpired in April 1926, only days before the General Strike, when he was made a relief station master for the stations west of Shrewsbury as far as Moat Lane Junction.

Meanwhile, he had settled with his little family, "the Wolves", in a ground floor flat on Underdale Road in Shrewsbury, overlooking the River Severn. Having no siblings, little Martha found a surrogate brother in Tom Bradfield, a boy of similar age from Ashley Street around the corner, and from early childhood the two were inseparable. However, following the eleven-plus examinations, Martha won a place at the Girls' Priory Grammar School, where she shone from the outset both academically and in sport, whilst Tom had to make do with the nearby Monkmoor Senior School. Nevertheless, this enforced separation in no way affected their friendship, and indeed, as they matured, they became more than friends – much more.

Inspired by the sea-faring tales of W. H. Kingston and Captain Marryat, Tom became enamoured of a naval career, and as soon as he was old enough, joined the Royal Navy training ship, *Indefatigable*, moored at Rock

Ferry on the river Mersey. Meanwhile, Martha continued to flourish at the Priory, and after a creditable set of School Certificate results, embarked on her Higher School Certificate studies with a view to reading modern languages at Liverpool – until, that is, two days after her eighteenth birthday, when suddenly one morning her father collapsed and died of an aortic aneurism, aged 45.

Martha, of course, was inconsolable, and with Tom away at sea, she lost all interest in higher education. She continued, somewhat half-heartedly, with her Sixth form courses, still managing to gain reasonable grades in all three subjects, but she was adamant that there would be no university. Instead, ignoring her mother's and her teachers' pleas, she enrolled on a two-year Secretarial course at the town's old Technical College and Art School near the English bridge, a short walk from her home.

As expected, she shone there too, and qualified with high levels of proficiency in all the business and administrative skills in June 1940. She was 'head-hunted' almost immediately as a private secretary to the senior partner of an old established Law firm in the town, and started work on the 1st July. She did think briefly of applying for university again, to read Law, but it was 1940, with Britain embroiled in a full-scale war. Furthermore, rumours were rife that conscription for women was imminent, and indeed when the second National Service Act was passed in December 1941, "unmarried women and childless widows aged between 20 and 30" did become eligible for call-up.

With Tom on anti-submarine patrols in the English Channel and the North Sea, she spent much of her time at work worrying about his whereabouts and the dangers he had to confront. In a way, the office tasks served as a distraction; but even though she had always feared the worst, little did she imagine what ghastly news awaited her on Monday evening, the 29th July.

She was making her usual way home shortly after 5.30 pm, down the Wyle Cop, over the English bridge, past the Abbey Church, and then along Holywell Street and finally Underdale Road, looking forward to her tea, followed by an evening curled up with Jean Paul-Sartre's much acclaimed first novel, *La Nausée*, when she was met at the front door by her distraught mother. Tom's father had called earlier with the dreaded telegram: *HMS Wren* had been sunk by German air-fire on Saturday evening, 27th July. Some survivors had been picked up by mine-sweepers, but, sadly, Tom was not among them, and together with 36 of his ship-mates, he was "missing, believed drowned".

Although utterly numbed and heartbroken by these blunt facts, Martha put up a stoical front at first, as she tried to persuade herself that perhaps the telegram was premature, and that he might have been picked up by a foreign ship, or even taken prisoner. But all too soon, the bleak reality of the news began to close in on her, and the prospect of an empty life without him stretching out into rheumy old age threw her into a fit of deep despondency. The two men who mattered in her life had been snatched from her. If there *is* a God up there, she mused, I hope He knows what He's doing.

Nevertheless, she managed somehow to report for work the following morning, albeit in no state to concentrate on the detailed assignments awaiting her.

After a vacuous half-hour watering the office plants and rearranging items on her desk, she finally ventured to knock on her boss's door to tell him about Tom. As it happened, he had just heard the dreadful news from another source. It helped that he himself had also served on a Royal Navy destroyer during the Dardanelles Campaign of 1915, and could relate genuinely to Martha's distress. In the event, he decided, despite the firm's heavy commitments, that she should take a week's leave with immediate effect, and dismissed her voluble protests about letting the side down, and that carrying on would be the best palliative. He would have none of it.

That afternoon, her mother wrote to her sister, Hilda, who kept a guest-house in Aberdyfi, asking if she and Martha could go to stay there that week instead of the last week in August as planned. The reply came back by return saying that all the rooms were booked, but provided they didn't mind "roughing it" in the chalet at the back, they were very welcome.

The war was now intensifying by the day, and after the fall of France, ordinary people, even in sleepy Salopia, feared that a German invasion was possible, if not probable. The Dunkirk evacuation of May-June had been a further reminder of Britain's vulnerability, and the continuing bombardment of shipping in the English Channel and the North Sea suggested that Hitler meant business. Good job Churchill was now Prime Minister; *he* would stand up to him, if anybody would. News bulletins advised holiday-makers to keep away from eastern and southern coastal resorts, which resulted in an unprecedented influx to Scotland, the Lakes, and West Wales. Thus, on Wednesday, 31st July, when Martha and her mother boarded the 8.57 'down' train at Shrewsbury, seating was at a premium, and they were obliged to squat on their suitcases in the corridor until a couple of kindly airmen, about Tom's age, offered them their seats.

Martha had made this journey countless times, but the ever-changing landscape never failed to enthral her. She cherished it all the more because of her father's connections with it, and the stories he used to tell her about the 'characters' and the 'happenings' at the various stations, including, of course, the appalling collision of two Cambrian Railways trains outside Abermule station in January 1921 killing 17 people and injuring 17 more. She had always felt a deep sympathy for the implicated staff on the day of the tragedy, especially the relief stationmaster, Frank Lewis. Her father had always maintained that, despite his gross negligence in not checking the train tablet himself, he had also been the victim of a complex set of coincidences.

Their train swept ever westward, stopping at Welshpool, Abermule, and Newtown, and then rising gently along the Severn valley to Moat Lane and Caersws. Here the flat flood plains gave way to bosky hillocks with their urgent little streams, where peasant farmers eked out a living on thistle-strewn sheep-walks, seemingly heedless of the death and devastation being meted out from the skies above the fertile fields of Kent and Sussex. The train stopped dutifully at every little station, each with its uniformed signalman and stationmaster, neat little flower beds, and imposing polysyllabic name-plate, which Martha always endeavoured to enunciate as authentically as her Shropshire burr would allow... Pont-dol-goch... Carno... Tal-erdd-ig... Llan-bryn-mair...

Commins Coch... Mach-yn-lleth. She wished *she* could speak the lingo properly, like some of her friends in Aberdyfi.

The rhythmic de-de-de-dum of the wheels induced a soothing drowsiness, and despite her distraught state of mind, she managed to exchange a contented smile with her mother as they approached Dovey Junction, where they would have to heave themselves out of their comfortable seats and change trains for the last, but the prettiest stage of the journey.

At last, they alighted at Aberdyfi station, and as soon as Martha caught that first whiff of salt and seaweed, she felt at peace in her own little heaven; indeed, as they walked with their suitcases along the sea front, past Bodfor Terrace and Glandovey Terrace towards Aunt Hilda's, the place had never looked more welcoming. It was barely conceivable that a mere two hundred miles away a deadly last-ditch defence of the realm was being fought. Could the Dyfi's tranquil waters be part of the cruel sea that had taken her Tom from her? No gun-boats here, and no mines; no torpedoes and no *Schnellbombers*; only seagulls gliding over chimney pots, and a lonely dinghy returning with its catch on the midday tide.

AUNT HILDA was Martha's mother's younger sister, who had also married a railway man, a loco fireman based at the depot in Machynlleth. His name was Harry Sutcliffe, and unlike his brother-in-law, who went to work in a smart tailored uniform, he brought home a set of heavily soiled overalls every week for his mother to scrub. The family had moved to Aberdyfi from Coventry when Harry was twelve, with a view to setting up a guest-house business and hoping that the sea air would improve his father's failing health. However, whilst the business flourished, Harry's father's condition deteriorated, and all too soon T.B. had claimed yet another victim.

Harry's mother soldiered on for three more years until she found the washing, the ironing, the cooking and the cleaning too much even for her, and suddenly, one morning he found her lying inert and barely conscious on the bedroom floor, having suffered a major stroke in the night. She survived in an insentient state for nearly a week, before finally fading away peacefully.

Harry was twenty-three, and utterly lost without his mother, but somehow, he had to grow up very quickly, doing his own housekeeping and getting to work on time. Being an only child, he inherited the guest house, where he lived alone for some time until he met an attractive young woman by the name of Hilda Marsh, who served in the Refreshment Rooms at Shrewsbury railway station. After a brief courtship, they got married at Bayston Hill Parish Church on Saturday, 27th March, 1926, with her sister, Brenda, as matron-of-honour, and Jack Pugh, one of Harry's fellow firemen at Machynlleth, as the best man. Charlie organized the whole event with military precision, hindered and abetted by six-year old Martha, who nevertheless performed her duties on the day as a bridesmaid with charm and aplomb.

Perhaps 1926 was not the most auspicious year to re-launch a guest-house business, but Hilda proved to be a shrewd businesswoman, and by dint of hard work and unstinting support from her husband, she soon built up a loyal clientele of factory-workers and their families from the Midlands. Depending on his shifts and the weather,

Harry sometimes found it more convenient to lodge overnight in Machynlleth, but when he was at home he usually spent his leisure hours helping Hilda with the washing up, shopping, and any heavy chores.

Both having come from small families, they longed for children of their own, but sadly this was never to be, and Martha inevitably became a most treasured surrogate daughter for them. Throughout the late 1920s and 1930s, she would spend weeks at a time, sometimes on her own, during school holidays at Aunt Hilda's, helping around the house and running errands, and she became so attached to the village, its people and, of course, the estuary, that she often wished her parents would also move to live there, away from "boring old Shropsbury", as she used to call it. The only drawback with that dream, of course, was Tom. If only he could come as well… (Indeed, unbeknown to Martha at the time, her fantasy very nearly materialized, because shortly before her father's untimely death, he had been offered a post of permanent Station master at Tywyn,)

THE FOLLOWING morning, Martha was woken early by seagulls feeding their chicks on Aunt Hilda's roof. Indeed, despite being physically and emotionally drained, she had been kept awake much of the night by her mother's incessant snoring. By six o'clock she could bear it no longer, and quietly slid out of the bed, and padded across the yard and into the kitchen to make the first cup of tea of the day.

As everyone else in the house seemed fast asleep, she filled the kettle very carefully, and was sure not to replace the whistle. She then lit the gas stove, and returned to the chalet to look for something suitable to wear. Eventually she plumped for a pale-blue blouse and the Marlene Dietrich-style navy slacks her father had bought her on her seventeenth birthday.

Ironically, now that she was up and about, the snoring had ceased, and the culprit blissfully unaware of the annoyance she had caused. Martha had often wondered how on earth her mother could sleep through such a loud and cacophonous racket, whilst she herself was obliged to repress a cough or remain frozen in an uncomfortable position lest she be rebuked with, "For goodness sake, girl, stop fidgeting and go to sleep!" And, furthermore, why was it that Aunt Hilda never snored at all?

Duly replenished by the tea and one of Aunt Hilda's rock cakes, she closed the door gently behind her and set off down towards the sea-front, relishing every sight, sound and scent on the way. If only Tom were there too. She sobbed quietly to herself as she recalled the last time she had walked along that pavement, and he alongside her holding her hand. But that was then, and all she could do now was cherish the memory.

She turned right into the main street and made her way towards the slipway, nodding and smiling at several familiar early morning faces, some more familiar than others, but the joy of yesteryear could never be recaptured. And then, all of a sudden, her mood changed.

At the bottom end of the slipway, she could see a very familiar figure already at work: Ellis Williams, the ferryman, preparing *Sea Spray* for yet another busy day on the river. He had his back to her, and was engrossed in topping up the boat's fuel tank, while she approached noiselessly along the sand. She crept up behind him and

222

with her usual mischievous humour clapped her hands over his eyes, saying, "Boo! Guess who?" followed by an irrepressible and unmistakable chortle.

"Duw! Martha!" exclaimed Ellis, before even turning round. "You didn't half give me a fright. *You're* up early."

"Oh, I couldn't sleep, so I thought I'd have a little walk before breakfast."

"Best time of the day," said Ellis, and after a slight pause, added, "I was *so* sorry to hear about Tom... *'rhen Dom druan*... I don't know... this damn war...it's an awful business... and I'm afraid it'll get worse before it gets better."

Martha knew that Ellis spoke from experience because he had served as a gunner on a mine-sweeper off the Shetland Isles during WW1.

"News travels fast," said Martha.

"Yes, Martha *fach*, especially bad news. Harry told me last night, and he also said you and your Mam were coming over for a few days. When do you have to go back by?"

"My boss said to take a week off, so Mum arranged with Aunt Hilda to stay until after the Bank Holiday. So, *dyma fi!*"

Seeing Ellis standing there in his white naval cap and with the early sun catching his bronzed, handsome face, proved to be a life-defining moment for Martha. He had always been the kindly uncle-figure for her, and her greatest joy as a little girl during her holidays in Aberdyfi had been helping him on the ferry-boat. Eventually, she became sufficiently skilled that he would let her pilot the boat on routine crossings to Ynyslas, while he chatted to the passengers as he collected the fares.

However, the trips were rarely mere crossings. They usually included an additional "pleasure" dimension, involving a triangular course that varied with the tides, the weather, and sometimes the passengers' wishes, A popular version was to go down-river beyond the bar buoy and into the open sea almost to Borth, before returning to Aberdyfi via Ynyslas; or conversely, up-river as far as Trefri and then downstream home, again calling at Ynyslas, if there were passengers waiting to cross to Aberdyfi. At high tide, the boat could reach up the Leri as far as the little wharf next to the Ynyslas road bridge, but at low tide, passengers had to disembark on the sand bank near the Refuge platform where the river Leri passes between Craig y Penrhyn and Traeth Maelgwyn. Passengers, some of whom had bicycles, would then have to trudge across half a mile of soft sand to reach the main road. The original (wooden) Refuge had been built to mark the ferry's landing point at low tide, but with the arrival of the railways in the 1860s and the expansion of the ferry services, it was replaced by a more elaborate structure, which could also serve as an actual place of refuge for waiting passengers from the treacherously fast-moving tides. In 1934, this structure, too, was replaced by another (iron) Refuge, which was used by holiday-makers at Borth and Ynyslas as a superb and safe viewing point, or for hailing the ferry from Aberdyfi!

Martha loved the Dyfi when she was unruly and skittish, with *Sea Spray* pitching and rolling like a bucket; but the high-spot of her summer was the moonlit trip on a high tide upstream as far as Glandyfi Castle, although she would miss it this time because the full moon was not until the 18th. This expedition, of course, required Ellis's detailed knowledge of the river's quirks, especially its sandbanks, and specific navigational skills learnt from his father, such as lining up the tip of the mast with this particular chimney or that oak tree on a hillside opposite.

"Well," said Martha, after a moment's reflection, "I must get back, or else they'll be wondering where I've got to… although Mum will probably have a good idea! So long, then… I'll try to come down again this evening."

"*Cymer ofal, Cariad*," replied Ellis, "and give my love to Brenda."

"I will."

This chance meeting with Ellis had lifted Martha's spirit. He always had that effect on her. When she was tearful as a little girl, usually after a stiff telling off from her mother, she would wander off to Ellis for a word of comfort. His friendly voice and rock-like presence reassured her that her little world was not about to collapse. But she had never needed his comforting words as much as now.

By the time she got back to Copper Hill Street, her mind was made up: the best way to deal with Tom's loss was to do something for her country. She felt sure that he would have approved, and volunteering for the newly-reformed WRNS would also be a way of remaining close to him in spirit, and continuing his good work. Even the word, "Wren" helped in that respect. Her first-hand knowledge and love of boats would surely help her to get in, even though her experience was limited to the Dyfi estuary. Yes, as soon she got back to Shrewsbury, she would make inquiries – whatever her mother said.

As she walked up Copper Hill, she could hear the

clock on St Peter's Church striking seven, and the air was thick with the aroma of fried bacon. By the time she reached the house, it was abustle with guests, some queuing for the bathroom, others making their way to the dining room. Her mother was also up and dressed, giving her sister a much-needed helping hand.

"Hey, where did *you* get to, madam? I didn't hear you get up."

"Well, I tried not to wake you, Mum, but I couldn't sleep, so I took a walk down to the front. And guess who I saw?

"Not *Ellis*."

"Yes… and he sends his love."

"That's very nice of him. Did you tell him about Tom?"

"He already knew. Uncle Harry had told him last night."

Martha helped herself to a plateful of eggs, bacon and mushrooms from the range, and sat down at the kitchen table. She ate in silence, while her mother scurried back and forth with the guests' breakfasts. Then the next time she returned to the kitchen, Martha thought she would test the water.

"Listen, Mum… sit down a minute… I've got something to tell you.

Brenda was relieved that her daughter seemed more like her normal self, and sat down.

"Promise you won't be cross!"

"Oh dear, what have you been up to *now*?"

"I've not been *up* to anything. But I've been thinking…"

"Oh, yes?"

"Well, you do know, don't you, that after next March, all single women between eighteen and thirty have to register for war work?

"Yes, I did read about that somewhere."

"Anyway, while I was down by the slipway talking to Ellis just now, it suddenly came to me… if I signed up now, instead of waiting until March, I'd stand a better chance of getting to do something I really liked. And anyway, I can't see myself settling back in that office job… not the way I feel now, anyway. It just wouldn't feel right."

"What! Surely, you wouldn't let Mr Tisdale down, just like that. You've only been there five minutes… and you know he speaks very highly of you. And look how good he's been, giving you the time off now."

"Oh, Mum! I know all that. He's an excellent boss. But that's not the *point*, is it?" Everything's changed since last Saturday."

"Well, yes, of course, love… but… please don't do anything rash. You're not in a fit state to make important decisions just now. Maybe when we get back home next week, you'll feel different. You're just like your father… with him everything had to be done by yesterday. His favourite saying was 'Procrastination is the thief of time'. And *he* enlisted before he had to an' all, just because "all the lads" were doing it… I don't know. But I do know one thing… he wouldn't have wanted *you* to do the same… I'm certain of that. Look, Martha, I know these last two years have been horrible for you… and for me, too, remember. But at least we've got each other. And now we've lost Tom, we'll need each other more than ever… But, Heaven forbid, if I lost you too, I couldn't bear that…

227

I just couldn't… so please, please don't… I beg you…"

Martha's eyes filled with tears. She had never known her mother being so openly emotional. She got up from the table and hugged her tightly, and said, "Mum… it's all right… I promise you… I won't… I won't court disaster. I'll wait my turn… like a good girl! It will come round soon enough, anyway, and maybe by then we'll have a better idea of how things are shaping up. It was just that… you know, how I've always loved coming here since when I was little, and helping Ellis with the ferry and things… and it was a brilliant idea of yours bringing me here now… it was just what I needed… and I'm very grateful. But when I saw him in his white cap by the slipway this morning, it felt like someone up there was trying to tell me something… and all of a sudden, I thought since I *have* to serve my country with this war effort, what better way than in the 'Wrens'?"

"Well, you know best, love, but all I say is, don't rush into it."

And then after a slight pause she looked at Martha and said, "By the way, I didn't snore last night, did I?"

"No, of course not, Mum… just the odd snort, that's all!"

As soon as breakfast was done and all the guests had dispersed, the two of them spent most of the morning, as usual, helping Hilda with the clearing and cleaning, and then after a light lunch they took themselves off on their favourite walk, up the steep incline to Penybryn. They sat in silence for a good few minutes near the shelter relishing the breathtaking panorama, from Penhelig and Trefri to their left, across the, now, sandy estuary towards Cors Fochno and the blue foothills of Plynlimon, and to their right, out towards the Aberdyfi bar and Cardigan Bay. Martha shed more than one discreet tear as she recalled the last time, almost a year ago, she and Tom had sat at that spot, and he had looked into her eyes and for the first time uttered those three magical words, "I *love* you.", and then kissed her passionately. In her mind's eye, she indulged herself by recalling every detail of that precious afternoon; how he, ever the gentleman, had lent her his jacket against the chill sea breeze; and how on the path down through chest-high bracken, she had made him walk in front of her for fear of being bitten by an adder or some other deadly creature lurking in the undergrowth! Oh, how she missed him…

After a while, she said, "Mum, do you really believe there's a heaven?"

"Well, yes, I think so… well, I hope so, anyway… and one day we'll all be together again, like one happy family. What made you think of that, all of a sudden?"

"Oh, nothing… only, if there *is*… Oh, look… there's *Sea Spray* coming round Penhelig Point. And Ellis is having a good day by the looks of it… I suppose everybody's taking advantage of these last few days before… Let's wave and see if he spots us!"

But they were too far away, even for his keen eyesight.

Martha suggested they made their way home via the hillside path she had taken with Tom, with her leading the way until they reached the stretch of chest-high bracken, where she managed to step aside adroitly so that her mother found herself at the front ready to ward off snakes or other beasties lurking in the undergrowth! Then they followed the narrow path down until it joined the main road near the railway bridge, and were back in good time to help Hilda prepare for the guests' evening meal.

ON THE TUESDAY after the Bank Holiday, Martha and her mother returned to Shrewsbury on the early morning train after a busy but uplifting week by the seaside. They also felt pleased to have been of some help to Hilda on one of the busiest weekends of her year.

However, Martha's relatively good cheer was short-lived because of what was waiting for her on the mat in the porch. Among sundry letters and packages, there was also an ominous-looking one from H.M Admiralty. She handed all the mail to her mother, and disappeared to her bedroom.

When she eventually emerged, her mother had opened and read all the mail except for the official letter, which she handed to her. "I think you should read it first, love… the Bradfields must have gone out and they've very thoughtfully put it through our letter-box in case we got back before them. I expect it'll be one of those official sympathy letters they always send… I remember the one they sent about little Johnnie in 1919… your Gran kept it behind the pot dog on the mantel-piece for years… I don't know what happened to it when she died."

Martha took the letter carefully out of its envelope, sat down in her father's old leather armchair, and read it two or three times through, striving to elicit any significant sub-text from the bureaucratic jargon:

Dear Mrs Bradfield,

    By now you will have received the sad news

of your son's death. I am writing to assure you of my deep sympathy with you in your sorrow. I am very grieved about him. He was a highly rated member of the ship's team of artificers, and was in every way a most excellent man in my company.

On the 27 July, HMS Wren, in which your son served, was providing anti-aircraft protection for minesweeping operations off Aldeburgh, Suffolk. She came under heavy and sustained dive bombing attacks by 15 Junkers Ju 87 aircraft and was damaged by several near misses which holed her below the waterline. Collapsed bulkheads caused heavy flooding which led her to sink quickly, killing 37 of her crew.

You will in due course receive his pay due to him, and any remaining personal effects.

I firmly believe he suffered very little at all.

It may be some time before you will receive his unpaid pay &c. as these things can take a long time to clear up.

Assuring you again of my very sincere sympathy,

I am yours very truly

(Signed)　S. T. R.　Westerdale

"It doesn't say much more than we knew already," remarked Martha matter-of-factly, as she handed the letter back to her mother. "But there again, when they've got 37 of these to write, I wouldn't expect much more than the bare facts."

THE FOLLOWING day Martha returned to her office job at Tisdale and Coop, but with little enthusiasm: if only she could have stayed on in Aberdyfi to help Aunt Hilda. But the tourist season was drawing to a close, and Aberdyfi would soon be losing its summer vibrancy and preparing for hibernation. On the other hand, with the war effort things might be different this year. Indeed, Uncle Harry had heard that the area was to be used for Commando training, and that the War Office had contacted Ellis regarding a contract ferrying equipment and personnel for rocket testing and anti-aircraft training at Ynyslas. Now that *would* be interesting… better than being cooped up in an office!

Mr. Tisdale welcomed her back like a long-lost daughter, and hoped that the short break had helped in some small way. He also reassured her that if she needed more time off, all she had to do was ask. Privately, Martha was sorely tempted, but of course she knew that under the circumstances that was out of the question, as her in-tray was already full. Accordingly, she resolved to knuckle down to whatever dull, repetitive tasks that landed on her desk.

Mr. Tisdale made sure that she had little time to brood, for although the work was not intellectually demanding, the high volume often meant having to stay behind after hours to "clear her desk". After a while, her mother started complaining, "You might as well take your bed there." To which Martha's retorted, "Perhaps I *am* taking after Dad: you know, not putting off till tomorrow what I can do today!"

September and October came and went, and still no German invasion, but the newspapers were full of the Luftwaffe's massive bombing raids on London and other cities, purportedly to demoralize the workforce and the civilian population before an invasion. However, the RAF, buoyed by their recent success in the Battle of Britain, was retaliating with equally devastating raids on German ports and cities.

Mercifully, Shrewsbury escaped the "Blitzkrieg" altogether, and apart from the inconveniences of blackouts and rationing, life trundled on much as it had always done. Martha was as good as her word, remaining with Tisdale and Coop until March 1st 1941, when she proudly volunteered for the 'Wrens', and much to her delight on June 2nd a letter arrived from the Director of the WRNS with instructions to report to the Naval Base at Plymouth on Tuesday, July 1st. So, this was it then, at long last – life on the ocean wave, just as Tom had experienced – and Mr. Tisdale – and Ellis too.

After a long and exciting rail journey across the heart of England, she found herself walking, somewhat nervously, along Platform One towards the Exit at Plymouth North Road Station, with her gas mask over her left shoulder and all her other worldly possessions neatly packed in the new, navy-blue valise her mother had bought for her at the Della Porta store the previous Saturday. The train was met by a Royal Navy troop truck, driven by a fully-fledged and uniformed Wren, who drove an envious Martha and three other girls to the training base on Seymour Road with perhaps a little more *panache* than Martha would have wished!

The following morning, she underwent a thorough medical examination, followed by an in-depth interview with a "very posh sounding" WRNS officer, who finally asked if she would be willing to train for a special job, about which she could not give her any information at the moment, because the work was "highly classified". Assuming that it would somehow involve boats or small ships, and intrigued by such open-ended prospects, Martha readily agreed, but was warned that her acceptance would in any case depend on how she performed during her initial two weeks' basic training, after which she could be rejected as unsuitable, or she could leave of her own accord.

Given her good academic and sporting credentials, Martha could never have countenanced either option, and the first week passed quite agreeably, with physical training, route marches, drills, marching, and naval procedures, including how to salute correctly. In-between, there were also lectures on naval organization and history, and on the crucial role played by the WRNS during the Great War, but more particularly how much more was expected of the service now, with the future of the British Empire in jeopardy.

The second week, however, proved more dispiriting than edifying. Up at five every morning, all the recruits were required to undergo two hours of chores before breakfast under the menacing supervision of a humourless Petty Officer 'Wren': scrubbing insanitary latrines "until they gleamed", scraping grimy floorboards with their own eating knives and then re-polishing them until they also "gleamed", and indeed any other dirty jobs their uncompromising mentor could find or devise.

Towards the end of the second week, Martha was called in to see the "posh" lady again, to be informed that she had "passed her probation period satisfactorily". On hearing this news, Martha was thrilled, and fully expected to be assigned to a specific boat crew, possibly in Plymouth itself, and perhaps finally discover the nature of this exciting, top-secret venture, for which apparently she had proved herself to be "suitably qualified". Instead, she was instructed to pack her bag, and collect a single train warrant from Plymouth to Bletchley in Buckinghamshire.

"Bletchley?" exclaimed Martha, "but that's inland!"

"Bletchley," repeated the posh lady laconically.

The following morning, Martha found herself being steam-hauled across the heart of England a second time in a month. She was met at Bletchley station by an impossibly tall young police officer, who whisked her away in a police van the short distance to a beautiful, but heavily guarded, country mansion. There she met several other equally mystified young 'Wrens', each desperate to discover what they had let themselves in for.

After being issued with security passes, which they were to guard with their lives, they were taken into a low building adjacent to the mansion, where a severe-looking 'Wren' officer welcomed them to Bletchley in fairly unwelcoming tones. She proceeded to explain at length without giving very much away that they had all been carefully screened and selected to undertake very important work connected with the war effort. She also warned them that this work would entail long and unsocial hours, would be mentally taxing, and at times quite boring. Nevertheless, if the Nazis were to be defeated, it was essential that they all undertook their respective tasks enthusiastically and painstakingly.

The 'Wren' officer then stressed that perhaps the most trying aspect of the work was the high level of confidentiality demanded from each one of them. To that end, they would be required to sign the Official Secrets Act. Thereafter, on no account was anyone to divulge anything at all about their work or environment to anyone, not even amongst each other outside their own specific building. Indeed, the punishment for breaching this fundamental regulation was imprisonment. If anyone should ask them what they were doing, they were to say that they were War Office filing clerks, or training to be war correspondents. Likewise, the content of all letters home would have to be of a very general nature, revealing nothing that could directly or indirectly damage the Allied Forces' war effort, or help the enemy. They, more than anyone, were always to be mindful of the slogan, "Careless Talk Kills" and be on permanent guard against the "enemy within".

Some of them, she said, looking specifically at Martha, or so she thought, having enlisted in the 'Wrens', would be disappointed not to be serving in the Navy as such, but she reassured them that what they were about to undertake was absolutely crucial to the war effort, and that they had been hand-picked for the job.

After the lecture, the girls were escorted in batches of two or three into a small room to sign the Official Secrets

Act document, which made them feel very special if a little bemused and subdued. As soon as this formality had been completed, they were transported in troop lorries some ten miles farther out into the country to another country mansion, called Woburn Abbey, where they would be billeted throughout their time at Bletchley.

The following morning, after an early breakfast they were brought back again to Bletchley Park in troop trucks, and then allocated to their specific work stations in the wooden huts situated in the grounds. Clearly, these had been built in a hurry and were not exactly luxuriously appointed, and the heat from the machines made life in uniform a little less than glamorous.

Martha, herself, was assigned to Hut 4 where the German messages were translated and meticulously typed up before being passed on to the tele-printer operators. She enjoyed the camaraderie, and especially working alongside brilliant young Oxbridge linguists; she was also well attuned to the uncompromising discipline that pervaded the entire establishment, but throughout her time at Bletchley she never became acclimatized, psychologically or physically, to the eight-hour shift system, especially the dreaded midnight till 8 am shift, with breakfast at 11.30pm, lunch at 4 am, and supper at 8 am. Furthermore, like many of the other girls, she did find much of the work tedious and mind-numbing, especially with the six-day week regime and only one week off four times a year.

From time to time, some important visitors would call, largely, they presumed, for morale-boosting purposes. Perhaps the most memorable of these occurred in September 1941, not long after Martha's arrival, when

Prime Minister Churchill, himself, came to pay his respects and encourage his "geese (to continue laying) their golden eggs".

One of their more frequent visitors was a tall, handsome man in his late thirties with a slight northern accent. *His* visits were certainly morale-boosting, and the female hearts in Hut 4 went all aflutter as he meandered among their work stations. He called several times during Martha's first few weeks at Bletchley, and subsequently during school holidays and half terms. He clearly knew Messrs Turing and Alexander well, and focused mainly on the deciphering work in Hut 8. Nevertheless, since Huts 8 and 4 were closely linked, the latter never felt snubbed. Martha felt sure that he paid her particular attention, but so did her rivals, Susan and Mary and Kath on the adjacent desks! He was always meticulously turned out in a black suit with a red carnation in the lapel, a fact which induced much stifled giggling amongst the less inhibited. But to Martha he was someone she began dreaming about when the days were at their dreariest.

Ever since she was a little girl, Martha had always loved letter-writing: first, aged 5, from her one-armed doll, Margaret-Jane, to her beau, Mr Teddy; then to her parents downstairs when she was ill in bed with measles; to Aunt Hilda, after a fortnight in Aberdyfi; to her father, when he was working away; and to Tom, of course, wherever he was.

Throughout her late teens she had also enjoyed corresponding regularly with two pen pals, a Helène, in Rennes, and a Renate, in Bremen. She had been given these contacts by her languages mistress in the fourth form at the Priory, and had corresponded with them both, usually at great length from 1935 until the outbreak of the War, they in English, and she in French and German respectively. Naturally, therefore, she found it frustrating not being allowed to regale her mother likewise with detailed accounts of her life in the 'Wrens', and instead having to engage in so much chicanery and tell so many white lies. It offended her sense of openness, and honesty. But in times of war needs must, she supposed, and like everyone else, even the boy soldier sweating and bleeding at the battle front who lied through his teeth that he was "in the pink" and everything was "hunky-dory" so as to give his distraught mother a faint hope of his safe return, she too succumbed to the great collusion, producing endless bland weekly missives such as this first one:

Dear Mum,

This is just to let you know that I am keeping well, but missing you very much.

You'll be glad to hear that I passed my basic training satisfactorily, and was selected for special duties elsewhere.

We landed at our new posting last week, and so far I am enjoying the work, doing something useful at last to help win this war.

I'm sorry I cannot give you any details, as we are not allowed to discuss anything to do with work, not even with our families.

They work us very hard, but we are well looked after, and are comfortably billeted.

I have made two good friends already, Susan and Mary, both Londoners, so I come in for a bit of ribbing about my accent! But as you know, I can give as good as I get! But they're a good sort really, and we have a lot of fun together. When we are off duty, we sometimes go for walks in the nearby woods or go to the local picture house if there is a good film on. But the highlight of our week, if we are free, is the Saturday night hop, where we girls are always very much in demand!

Keep your chin up, and I hope to see you before Christmas. We haven't been given any dates yet.

Please give my love to Tom's parents.
From your loving daughter,
Martha   xx

Chapter Ten

Joe Riley's reign as headmaster was not the fiasco that many had feared. Obviously, he lacked his predecessor's powers of leadership, and had few ideas beyond perpetuating the *status quo*, but with Jack Higginbottom's encouragement and Martha's constant support, he managed to survive the early slings and arrows with fortitude and *sangfroid*.

The School's academic and sporting successes continued as before, with 1970, especially, comparing well with some of the vintage Davenport years. The cynics maintained that this was entirely due to historical momentum, and when the finely honed fly-wheel finally came to rest, the Riley reign would be seen for what it was, purely titular.

Among his chief weaknesses was his fear of being unpopular, despite knowing full well that trying to please everyone usually meant pleasing no one, as Nobbs, of course, delighted in reminding him.

"Look Joe, the trouble with you is you're too bloody soft... I'd make the buggers sweat a bit, if I were you... there's only so many hours in a day... I don't like to see you rushing about like a blue-arsed fly just because some pillock wants his payslip checking. Bloody hell, you'd never see Davenport doing that... he always left that sort of thing to you... or Martha."

"Oh yes, I know," replied Joe, "but, in any case, I would never dream of comparing myself with George."

"Yes, but what I mean is... and I hope I'm not talking out of turn here... let's be honest, Joe, Whittaker *could* get off his fat arse a bit more... after all, he *is* your number two... isn't he?"

"Yes," replied Joe, meekly, "and you may have a point... perhaps I *should* delegate more."

"Well, if I've told you once, I've told you a hundred times... when you're really pushed, all you have to do is ask *me*."

"Yes, Richard, I know, thank you... I'll bear it in mind," replied Joe noncommittally.

Ever since the time-table business, Joe could never make his mind up about Nobbs. To most of the masters he was just an over-bearing and boorish anti-intellectual whom they loathed. Perhaps one or two of the younger ones tolerated him, with caution – even the "forty-bangers" could no longer be sure of his goodwill – but, strangely, Joe found his mercurial blend of charm and menace captivating. And yet, whilst envying his many attributes, especially his *chutzpah*, he could never bring himself to trust him, and had never yet accepted an invitation to supper at the big house.

Like many others, Joe was also intrigued by the

fellow's extraordinary affluence, and often wondered how he had come by it. When he first joined the School after the War, with the country bankrupt and ration-books taking precedence over cheque-books, young masters typically lived in lodgings or rented a room on a convenient bus route for the School. Few could raise the deposit for a mortgage or even a down payment for a bed or a cooker. Indeed, for many, the very word *mortgage* still held negative connotations, akin to "buying on tick" or "the never-never". "Getting on the property ladder" was decades away from becoming a national obsession. A young master on the threshold of life and a career needed to be free to follow his proclivities, not trammelled by the cares of "bricks and mortar". Moreover, two years were generally considered long enough to stay in one's first post – long enough to learn the trade, but, with luck, not long enough for one's frailties to be rumbled – and certainly not long enough to take out a mortgage.

But, of course, Richard Nobbs was not a typical young master. By inclination and example, he had acquired a taste for gracious living from early childhood in a grand, detached house in the Coppice area of Oldham, with a Daimler in the drive, a bank of mechanical bells in the basement, and a maid at the ready to dance to their every jingle. The only child of Oleg and Veronika Dunobsky (hard-working refugees from the post-WW1 Russian pogroms), he had never wanted for anything, and for good measure he had also assimilated some sound northern maxims, such as, "brass is king" and "do owt for nowt, except for thissen".

His unremarkable achievements at Oldham Hulme

Grammar School had less to do with academic ability than with his devotion to turning a shilling into three without breaking sweat, a knack he mastered while still in short trousers. Dismissed by the School's 'old brigade' as a "bloody fool", or no more charitably by the younger masters as an "obnoxious cocky dick", he himself concurred with his Headmaster, that his talents would be more profitably deployed elsewhere. Accordingly, one fine morning he was called into the big man's study to be given some kindly, but unequivocal, advice about his future career.

"Look here, Nobbs, let's not beat about the bush, shall we? I'm afraid it's decision time. I know your parents have always seen you as an architect or a lawyer, or something... but, let's be honest, Nobbs, can you honestly see that happening? I've just been reading some of the comments on your last report... not exactly inspiring, are they? So, let's cut to the chase. What do you say to a traineeship with an insurance company, or a bank? Your father tells me you're good with money... well, I happen to know the manager of the Midland Bank through Rotary, and I could put in a word."

AFTER A DISMAL performance in his School Certificate examinations in 1938, which he had taken purely to please his mother, Nobbs bade farewell to education, as he thought, for ever, and decided to live at home for a while to reflect on his options, helping out when required in his father's thriving fruit and vegetables business.

In 1940, when the spectre of military service threatened, his parents persuaded him to join the Oldham

Borough Police Force as a cadet, believing that that might qualify him for exemption. Being tall and of an upright bearing, he certainly looked the part on point duty opposite the newly rebuilt Gaumont Cinema on Saturday evenings; but, alas, he liked the police discipline even less than that of the Combined Cadet Force at school! However, he persevered with it in the knowledge that should he be called up, 'retainer' payments would be payable throughout his period of war service. In the event, his mother saved all these weekly payments for him in a high-interest saver account at the Oldham branch of the Midland Bank, so that on demobilisation he would have a "tidy sum to put down on a house".

On the day Nobbs was appointed to the staff of Netherbridge Grammar School, his father gave him a further £200 in cash towards his first home. In reality, he now had enough to buy outright a modest three-bedroom town house in the centre of Netherbridge. But Nobbs Junior, with his canny eye for a business opportunity, had other plans, and took out a mortgage on two large semi-detached houses near the railway station, with a view to living in one and letting the other out unfurnished. This proved a most astute decision, for thanks to the post-war marriage and baby booms, there was no shortage of good tenants, and the rental income more than covered the mortgage repayments on both properties. Furthermore, having no other financial or personal commitments, he was able to keep his outgoings to a minimum, and furnish his home piecemeal with valuable antiques, usually bought at bargain prices in auctions or from second-hand warehouses.

The exceptionally favourable post-war interest rates

enabled him to expand his property portfolio rapidly, using rental income to service the mortgages, and by his 29th birthday in 1951 he already owned five properties, three in Netherbridge and two retail premises near Mumps Bridge in Oldham – all tenanted. However, despite his burgeoning wealth, he remained in his first house for several years, partly because of its proximity to the shops, and the *Duke of Edinburgh*, where he dined most evenings, but mainly to dispel the tax inspectors' suspicions. To this end, very few people had ever stepped over his front doorstep, and those who had were astonished by the contrast between the house's modest exterior and its interior opulence.

Despite his early aspirations, Nobbs had long concluded that the promotional prospects of an "emergency trained" Crafts master at a highly academic grammar school were, to say the least, slender, and consequently he decided to concentrate on his lucrative extramural interest, thereby also vindicating his old headmaster's blunt but prescient counsel. Indeed, it was largely as a waggish compliment to his old mentor that he named his rental company *Shaw Enterprises*.

The country's improving economy during the 1950s and the continuing low cost of borrowing benefited northern towns like Netherbridge substantially, with several small factories and businesses springing up, which in turn created a steady stream of factory workers and young professionals seeking temporary accommodation until they could afford homes of their own. Whilst not quite as unprincipled as his notorious contemporary, Peter Rachman, Nobbs shared much of his ruthlessness as a landlord, and especially his *penchant* for exacting exorbitant rents. His default response to requests for repairs or extra time to find rent money was, "Certainly not... I'm not a charity, you know". Consequently, by 1960 his income from rents was making his monthly cheque at the Grammar School seem like a pittance barely worth collecting, and, unbeknown to anyone, he was on the verge of resigning his post, when his life took a sudden turn.

DESPITE Nobbs's blanket reticence about his financial affairs, he rarely missed an opportunity to hold forth on his amatory encounters. But sadly, now fast approaching his fortieth year, he was beginning to sound more like a wistful monk than the Casanova he saw gazing back at him every morning from his bathroom mirror. Indeed, few actually believed his extravagant tales, but after three or four pints at the *Duke* on a Saturday night some of his more impressionable hangers-on found his telling of them hugely entertaining.

For instance, was the one-night stand during the School's First XV's Easter tour of the Midlands in 1954 fact or fantasy? According to Nobbs, the hotelier's beautiful young wife had seduced him while her husband was away on a skiing holiday. She had taken a shine to him when the party had first checked in, and during dinner had pressed a note into his hand with the tantalising message, *1 am Yours* – which he took to mean either "I am yours", or perhaps more realistically, "1 o'clock in your (room)".

Anyhow, according to Nobbs, on the stroke of one, the diaphanous seductress slinked into his bedroom and beckoned him to follow her into her own marital bed, where intense activity ensued throughout the small hours until the pair, still inextricably entwined, collapsed into a deep and refreshing slumber.

However, as dawn was breaking, they were awakened by loud voices, and more particularly that of the lady's husband, at the front door, directly beneath their bedroom window. Needless to say, our hapless Lothario was obliged to beat an undignified retreat, leaving his poor paramour to simulate sweet innocence and delight at her husband's unexpected return.

All would have been well except that in the heat of the moment, our hero left his watch on the lady's bedside table. Half-way through breakfast, *mine host* entered the dining room to greet his guests, and to express his sincere hope that they had all rested well. Then, almost as an afterthought, he added that an expensive Rolex watch had been found, and if anyone present had mislaid it, it could be collected from him personally at the reception desk!

BUT THERE was nothing fanciful about Nobbs's chance meeting with one particular young lady during the day after St Valentine's Day, 1960. Nobbs had driven to the neighbouring town of Leigh quite early that day to enquire about a disused warehouse on Twist Lane with a view to converting it into flats. While he was ensconced in an armchair waiting to be served at the Bradford Building Society office on Bradshawgate, perusing leaflets about this and other properties, another customer was at the counter having a heated conversation with an elderly sales adviser. She too was enquiring about a property, one of the small semi-detached bungalows being built on a new estate off the St Helens Road, a stone's throw from Pennington Park.

All of a sudden, Nobbs lost all interest in his warehouse conversion, his eyes now feasting on architecture of a different order. Being fair-skinned, he had always envied those with a dark, 'Mediterranean' complexion that never turned a fiery pink in the sun. And who would have expected such a splendid example in murky old Leigh in February? Behold, thought Nobbs, a true marriage of form and function: *Shall I compare thee to my Mark Nine Jag*, he began promisingly, *Thou art more lovely...* before reverting to the standard clichés of car-marketing: *thy full-sculpted headlamps, well-turned rear, firm chassis, and soft, voluptuous curves...*

Then, as if sensing peering eyes, the divine form pirouetted in mid-sentence, catching poor Nobbs *in flagrante* as it were; and as their eyes met fleetingly, he lowered his with feigned insouciance and renewed interest in his leaflets. But during that millisecond he knew that some magical spark had been struck.

She was having a difficult, and all too public, altercation about her mortgage application. What was her annual income? How old was she? What was her job? Did she have the deposit? Who was her guarantor?

"Look, I don't believe I'm hearing this... anybody would think it was 1860, not 1960. I'm over twenty-one; I've just got myself a good, secure job; yes, I've even got the deposit, and my monthly income is more than three times the repayments... Why do I need a guarantor?

"Yes, yes, yes, Miss Green, I quite understand your frustration... but, I'm afraid, rules is rules."

"*Are*," corrected the feisty Miss Green, "rules *are* rules,"

"Yes, well... all the same, as things stand, you are unmarried... and an unmarried woman needs a *guarantor*. Let's face it, anything can happen... you could lose your job or, forgive me, but you could ... erm...have a baby. These things do happen, you know, even to the best of us. What happens then, eh? Who would make the payments then? And in any case even if you *were* married, and let's say, for the sake of argument, you earned more than your husband, which, of course, *can* happen in this day and age, our calculations would still be based on your husband's earnings. It may sound odd to you, Miss Green, but that's how things work, I'm afraid, even in 1960."

"Well, sir, for your information, I have no immediate plans to get married, and I certainly have no intention of having babies... well, not for a long time yet, anyway... and as a newly-appointed primary school teacher in Leigh with a £450 deposit saved up, I believe I'm a good bet for a £1500 mortgage! The trouble with you Bradford Permanent lot, your brains seem *permanently* locked as well – in the Bradford of the Victorian age, when "little wifey" did what her lord and master told her. Well, I'll tell you one thing for nothing, *I've* no intention of *ever* being a mere adjunct to any lord and master. And again, just for your information, *I* was quite happy to rent a property, until my father called it "dead money going straight into the pockets of some grasping landlord". He told me to get a mortgage in my own right, and failing that, he would act as my guarantor."

"Well, that's all right, then. Why didn't you say so in the first place? Now, if you could ask Sophie here to arrange an appointment for you and your father to come along and fill in the forms, then we should have everything sorted in no time at all?

"Thank you, kind sir," she replied icily, "and if there wasn't another person in the room, I might be inclined to say something more in keeping with my feelings. Anyway, I won't waste any more of your precious time. I must catch the 11 o'clock train for Manchester."

"Look," interrupted Nobbs, rather awkwardly, having overheard most of the young lady's tirade, *I've* got to go into Manchester later. I could give you a lift, if you want. My car's just round the corner, and it would save you a lot of hanging about at the station. The name's Nobbs, Richard Nobbs."

"Well, thank you, Mr Nobbs," said the doughty young lady, as she shook the tall stranger's outstretched hand, "Amanda Green... pleased to meet you."

"Tell you what," said Nobbs, reaching up to his full height, "it's blooming cold out there... let me buy you a coffee or something to warm us up, and then I'll run you to Manchester. How does that grab you?"

"Well, that would be lovely, if it's not too much trouble."

"My pleasure," replied Nobbs.

As he escorted her along Bradshawgate towards the nearest cafe, Nobbs was unusually quiet, for fear of saying something that might ruin the moment.

"Do you *live* in Manchester?" he ventured, after a while, deeming that a safe opening gambit.

"No, Chester, actually," she replied, "but I need to do some shopping in Manchester... there's more choice there, and there are always plenty of trains back to Chester."

The coffee took a little longer to arrive than expected,

and the conversation grew stilted, with long awkward pauses. For once, poor Nobbs's ready tongue had forsaken him.

"What do *you* do for a living?" she asked, at last.

"You won't believe this," he replied, "but I'm in the same line of business as your good self."

"What do you mean, b*usiness*?"

"Well, for my sins, *I'm* also in the teaching profession... at Netherbridge Grammar School... have been for far too long... since I was demobbed in '47, to be precise."

"That's not all that long."

"Well, it seems long enough to me. Besides, I've been thinking that maybe it's not my true *métier*. At first, I was prepared to try anything, well, anything at all that didn't involve snakes, and bullets... and mosquitoes. Then I remembered some of those old fellows back in my old school... they didn't have such a bad time of it... not many snakes or bullets there!"

"What do you mean, 'snakes and bullets'?"

"Oh, nothing... I just did my bit, that's all, like everyone else... you know, Slim's "Forgotten Army"...Burma? Anyway, never mind all that, the fact is, I thought I'd give schoolmastering a go, but after a while I found it too..."

Nobbs was spell-bound by this goddess sitting opposite him, as were several others in the cafe, apparently. For once in his life words kept failing him. There was something other-worldly about her face, as if Mother Nature had had her *eureka* moment, finally sculpting perfection after a million years of experimenting. And yet, despite her glossy brunette tresses... her mesmerising hazel eyes... her perfectly symmetrical teeth, and flawless complexion, her manner was utterly unaffected.

"Too... what?" said Amanda.

"Well... when I... when I left school," he continued, having almost forgotten what he was about to say, "I joined the Oldham Police Force... to make a career of it... not a bad number, really, all things considered... and you retire on a good pension after 30 years... still young enough to start another career. But then the War came... my call-up papers arrived... and that was that. Could have gone back to it afterwards, I suppose... and my army training and commission would have done me no harm... but, you know how it is, after five years leading patrols through hot, steamy jungles, who'd want to patrol the back streets of Oldham during that harsh winter of '47? Anyway, that's enough about me... what about you?"

Amanda barely heard the question, for she was so beguiled by the voice and the ice-blue eyes piercing her very soul, she simply sat there speechless for several seconds like a little girl too shy to ask James Stewart for his autograph.

"Me?" she said at last, "Oh, god, don't ask! Nothing very exciting there, I'm afraid. I've done nothing... yet! I was a prefect in my last year at the Queen's, Chester, if that means anything... then two years at Chester Training College, where I rose to the dizzy heights of vice-captain of the first hockey team. How dull is that! But hopefully, from now on things should get a bit more interesting... though, I was beginning to wonder at the Estate Agent's. Ooh! I could've throttled the old booby."

"Yes, so I noticed! I was just about getting ready to

defend the poor chap!"

"Are *you* looking for a house in Leigh, as well?"

"No, not a house, exactly... How can I say? Although school- mastering is my *official* occupation, I have been thinking of packing it in of late, and concentrating on my business."

"That sounds interesting."

"Oh, it's nothing much, but it helps pay the bills... well, it pays better than schoolmastering anyway."

"And?"

"Do you know what, I can't believe this! I've only known you ten minutes, and here I am, about to tell you something I've never told anyone else in my life. Do you always have this effect on people?!"

"Only on some!" she replied, with a disarming smile.

"Well, it started off as a side-line, but over the years it's developed into something bigger than I imagined."

"So, are you going to tell me?"

"Your father wouldn't approve!"

"Oh dear, that sounds dodgy. You don't have to tell me, you know... unless you really want to!"

"No... it's perfectly legit."

"So, you can tell me, then."

"Well, let's put it this way, if your father hadn't given you such good advice, you might well have been doing business with me, or someone like me."

"Ah! You mean renting? I get it... you're one of these 'grasping landlords'!" she teased.

"Well, not grasping."

At last the coffee arrived, just as Nobbs was beginning to regret revealing so much so soon to a complete stranger. It wasn't his style. But he had never met anyone quite like this before. Not only was she eye-wateringly beautiful, but her tireless vivacity reminded him of all the happy days of his life rolled into one. And, thanks to the little Latin he still remembered from his Hulme days, he thought what an apt name – *Amanda* – 'she who should to be loved'!"

"So, if you're not buying a house, what is it then, a cotton mill?"

"Hey, that's not a bad guess. An old warehouse, actually... to convert into flats. That's the future, I'm told, multi-occupancy. That's where the money is."

"But won't that mean a big expense for you?"
My god, she's even taking an interest in my financial affairs now, he thought.

"Yes, that's true, but, if I get a good deal, and manage to get, say, five units out of it, or even six at a push, I'd soon make it back."

"Oh, it's all beyond me, I'm afraid, but I must say it sounds quite interesting... like playing Monopoly, with real money!"

"Well, it keeps me out of mischief. Perhaps *you'd* like to try your hand at it one day?"

Nobbs pulled back the sleeve of his bespoke tweed jacket to reveal his gold Rolex. "Hey, it's nearly 12 o'clock. Shall we make a move, Amanda?"

"Most people call me Mandy."

"Well, Mandy it is, then... and I'm Rich."
As they made their way towards the door, he was conscious of a bank of eyes trained on them. They certainly made a striking couple, and he had even left a small tip.

As soon as they reached the door, he helped her with

her coat.

"Oh, thanks," she said, "you're right, it has gone colder."

"Never mind, we haven't got far to walk."

As soon as they turned into Vernon Street, one car stood out regally among all the other workaday delivery vans, rusty Morris Minors and Fords – a pristine white limousine.

"Don't tell me... it's the big, white one, isn't it?"
He nodded, complacently.

"God, it looks like a wedding car!" she said excitedly.

"You might be on to something there!" he teased.
He opened the front passenger door for her, and as she lowered herself elegantly onto the luxurious burgundy leather seat, he could not help staring at her muscular, brown thighs disappearing above the hem of her miniskirt, but he quickly averted his eyes when she looked up.

"This *is* a beautiful car, Richard. I've never been in a Jaguar before, and these seats... it's like sitting in your own front room! You must be very proud of it," she said.

"Well, what's good enough for Stirling Moss is good enough for yours truly! I've always had Jags, but I must say this Mark Nine is as good as it gets."

When she was safely inside, he crossed over to the driver's side, and after closing the heavy door with an efficient clunk, made himself comfortable behind the huge steering wheel. He then made great play of checking the gauges and adjusting switches like an airline pilot, before finally starting the motor and blipping the throttle gently to demonstrate its obedient response. When he deemed everything to be in perfect order, he began the

256

intricate manoeuvres of easing the Jaguar out of its tight parking space, before pulling away silently along the narrow side-street. Meanwhile, Amanda, a privileged witness to all these rituals, was entranced by the brave new world of polished walnut and leather, wherein the insistent ticking of a tiny inset clock was the only audible sound above the docile whirr of the powerful 3.8 litre engine. The silence was uncanny: this car did not strive and grunt like her father's Morris Eight, but conveyed its passengers effortlessly with a smug purr, its huge wheels and springs cushioning them from any bumps and shocks along the way.

Soon, they were floating elegantly over Butts Bridge and picking up speed along Warrington Road towards the Greyhound and the 'East Lancs' road, where our would-be Stirling Moss gave the 'big cat' free rein. She noticed the speedometer edging towards seventy... then eighty... and finally ninety.

"You all right?" asked Nobbs at last, "you're very quiet... not too fast for you?"

"No, I'm fine, thanks." Then after a pause, she added, "Only, I was just thinking... two hours ago, I didn't even know you existed... and here I am now hurtling along the East-Lancs with you at ninety miles an hour! How weird is that... I don't know what my Dad would say!"

"Never take lifts from strange men in Jaguars, I expect!"

"Very probably... but seriously, I hardly know you, do I? Nor you me... and already I'm putting my life in your hands."

Nobbs reduced his speed to a pedestrian forty-five, while he thought of an appropriate answer.

"Mandy, you're absolutely right, of course... you don't know me, and I don't know you... But then, it depends what you mean by "knowing". Some say it takes a lifetime to get to know someone properly... but back in that estate agent's this morning, I knew instantly that standing in front of me was the most beautiful woman I'd ever set eyes on, and also one with the most delightful personality."

"Flattery will get you everywhere, Mr Nobbs!" she replied, waving a finger in mock admonition, "Damn! I've forgotten what I was going to say now... but it doesn't really matter."

"Perhaps it'll come to you another time? Where exactly would you like me to put you down? Will here do, near St Peter's Square?

"Yes, this is fine. And thank you again so much for the lift... and the coffee."

"My pleasure... oh, by the way, I'm coming up to Leigh again on Friday... what about another coffee, same place, same time?"

She replied with an understated smile, and a charming little wave.

"Friday, eleven o'clock it is, then!" said Nobbs, triumphantly.

After watching the white limousine glide away and merge with the city traffic, she stood on the pavement for a good half-minute, a bundle of confused thoughts and emotions. Shoes were no longer at the forefront of her mind, but she needed to buy two new pairs for work, regardless.

That night at home in Chester, she was uncharacteristically quiet.

"Everything all right, dear?" asked her mother, "How did you get on with your mortgage?"

"Oh, don't ask. I gave the manager a piece of my mind... Dad's got to be a guarantor... otherwise there's no deal."

"Never mind, dear, I'm sure he'll sort everything out."

"But I didn't want him to sort everything out."

"Yes, I know... it must be very annoying for you. Things were very different in my day." Then, after a slight pause, she added, "There's something else, isn't there?"

"Why do you say that?"

"I can always tell when something's bothering you... you're just like your father."

"Well, if you must know, I've had a weird sort of day. While I was in the Estate Agent's office, this man offered me a lift to Manchester."

"What sort of man?"

"Ooh, where do I start? Tall... good-looking... well-off... smartly-dressed...

"Yes, I get the picture, but what was he really like?

"He seemed a very nice person, Mother... good conversationalist... nicely mannered... well brought-up... house-trained... what else would you like to know?"

"Sounds a bit too good to be true, if you ask me... how old was he?"

"Well, older than me, obviously."

"Well, yes, but how much older?

"Mu'um, you're impossible... *I* don't know... I never asked him. Did you ask Dad that on your first date? He was in the War, though... so he's a *good* bit older... but does that matter?

"About forty, would you say?"

"Has to be, I suppose... but he didn't look it.

"Anyway, I hope you didn't accept the lift?"

"Oh, Mum... yes, I did, as a matter of fact... and guess what... it was this beautiful, white Jaguar!"

"I hope he didn't drive too fast."

"Yes, he did drive fast, but you could tell he was a very good driver, and, if you must know, slowed down when I asked him too."

"Well, as long as you didn't come to any harm..."

"He wants to see me again on Friday."

"What! And you agreed? Tell me, what does this... man... do for a living?"

"He's a school master... at Netherbridge Grammar School.

"Oh... that sounds better. What's his name, or didn't you ask him that either."

"Richard... Richard Nobbs..."

Amanda said nothing about the rental business, and decided to have an early night to avoid further interrogation.

"Well, I'm off... good night. Tell Dad I was very tired, and I'll explain about the mortgage in the morning."

"Okay, love, good night and God bless."

THE FRIDAY tryst was duly kept, and yet another one the following Friday. Indeed, the Bradshawgate coffee-shop became the glamorous couple's regular meeting-place, a convenient and neutral venue free from gossiping tongues. By the fifth meeting, Amanda was persuaded that her white knight in the shining Jaguar had honourable intentions, and was now ready for some objective scrutiny from her mother and widowed Aunt Polly. In the event, barring Aunt Polly's caveat, "when you're his age, Mandy, he'll be drawing his pension", "the lad" did pass muster with these most demanding of arbiters. Meanwhile, her father, who kept his opinion on the matter to himself, had now signed the mortgage guarantor forms so that his daughter could move into her new bungalow well before taking up her teaching post after the Easter break.

The couple's courtship was brief and intense, concluding ironically with a low-key wedding at Chester Register Office on Nobbs's birthday, Saturday, 25th March 1961, and a simple reception at a rural hostelry near Delamere Forest. The only witnesses, apart from Amanda's parents, were Amanda's long-term school friend, Denise Sheldon, and Nobbs's best man, Martin Shaw.

In his short, but well-rehearsed, speech, Nobbs apologised wholeheartedly for his parents' absence. Despite all his best efforts, he had failed to persuade them to attend. In fairness, he elaborated, neither of them had been in good health lately, and travelling any distance beyond the weekly trip to the shops was proving increasingly difficult.

But in truth, the *problem* lay with Nobbs, not his parents, and the picture he had painted was a total fabrication. Despite all the smoke and damp of winters in Oldham, both his parents enjoyed robust good health. Indeed, Mr Nobbs, a tall, athletic-looking man with a magnificent head of white curly hair and beard, could often be seen during the summer months taking his good lady on day trips to Southport in their pale-blue Daimler Conquest Convertible.

But Nobbs had always felt uncomfortable that his parents were 'different' – that they were immigrants, had a "weird" accent, and wore "old-fashioned" clothes – and their presence at his wedding would have been acutely embarrassing for him. Accordingly, he had decided that it would be better for everyone if they were not told about the ceremony at all. Naturally, Amanda had been disappointed not to meet them, but he did promise to take her as soon as the weather improved.

In the days before it became almost *de rigueur* to honeymoon in the Caribbean or on some remote Greek island, Nobbs treated his beautiful young bride to a chilly but exhilarating ten days of touring Devon and Cornwall in the "wedding car", staying a night or two here and a night there in small hotels just as the spirit moved them. Nobbs had kept the event secret from everyone in the School, with Martha alone suspecting that something more than a change of scenery lay behind his sudden change of address and the preponderance of carefully wrapped parcels and bouquets of flowers filling the back seat of his car.

Clearly, the happy couple's living arrangements needed careful consideration, with Nobbs insisting that remaining in Netherbridge would be far too public, and in any case, impracticable for Amanda. From all the options available, they eventually decided to buy a large, red-brick block of a house on the St Helens Road in Leigh, opposite Pennington Park. It was far more spacious than they needed, and certainly more than Amanda had been used to, but the rooms were light and welcoming, and the gardens interesting, if a little overgrown. Furthermore, it was only a short bus-ride from her school.

Nobbs brought most of the antique furniture from his home in Netherbridge, but gave Amanda free rein with new purchases, which resulted in a quirky mixture of the old and the new: Louis Seize and Regency rubbing shoulders with G-plan and Parker Knoll, and an exquisite Turkish rug complementing a fitted maroon Wilton in the living room.

Amanda's own little bungalow, a quarter of a mile away, was now, of course, redundant; but in keeping with Nobbs's golden rule of never selling a property unless the proceeds could be invested more profitably, it became subsumed into the *Shaw Enterprises* portfolio, but with Amanda retaining its sole management rights. Her first tenants were two young mistresses at the Girls' Grammar School, who wanted time to find a suitable house to buy together in the area, and she was surprised by how much she enjoyed the whole business of being a landlord.

Despite their age difference, their relationship flourished. They had eyes only for each other, and were rarely seen apart. He never ceased to wonder at his good fortune in 'landing such an exquisite catch', and never missed an opportunity to show her off in public, whether escorting her in Pennington Park on a warm summer's evening to see Joey, the grey African parrot, or ostentatiously holding the Jaguar's passenger door for her while she eased her mini-skirted legs demurely in or out of the passenger seat. She too delighted in his attentiveness, and of course relished her dramatically enhanced standard of living. Indeed, even her mother eventually put aside any lingering doubts, and accepted an invitation for her and Mr Green to stay for a few days during the summer holidays of 1961 at "Chez Nobbs", as

Amanda teasingly dubbed it.

Our hostess had prepared a splendid roast beef and Yorkshire pudding for her parents' first evening at the "big house". The men shared a flagon of Robinsons *Old Tom*, and the ladies a bottle of *Mateus Rosé*. After the meal, Nobbs took Amanda's mother out to the garden "to show her to his roses", as he gallantly put it, but more pertinently to exhibit his newly-acquired enthusiasm for matters horticultural.

"Yes, Richard, lovely, everything looks fine and dandy," she exclaimed, as she politely examined the tomatoes and the cucumbers. "But... I hope... you're not going to keep us waiting too long for our first grandchild?"

"Oh!" said Nobbs, utterly thrown by such an unexpected, and no doubt wine-driven, inquiry, "Um... we... that is... Mandy and I haven't actually got round to discussing that yet. It *is* early days."

"Discuss? No need to discuss it... just get on with it... and the sooner the better, I say. None of us are getting any younger, and the best time to have a child is when it happens, and the sooner the better! I don't agree with all this family planning nonsense. Leave it to Nature, I say."

"Yes... well... you may be right, Mrs Green," replied Nobbs diplomatically, "No doubt it *will* happen... in its own good time. But to be honest, I don't think Mandy feels quite ready yet, with just having started her new job. And anyway, we want a bit of time to enjoy each other first... and freedom to see the world... before complicating things."

"Well, don't leave it too late, that's all I'm saying. Of course, in our day things were different. I always thought

264

the whole point of getting married was to have children. I would have loved another brother or a little sister for Mandy, but unfortunately it wasn't to be. I suppose me and Ted were a bit late getting married... and then we lost Keith ... our first... a lovely little boy... dark, just like Mandy he was... cot death... broke my heart... but thankfully Amanda came along quite quickly, but then there were complications... and after that, sadly, we couldn't have any more. That's why I always tell young couples to get on with it!"

"Well, the one you did have was pretty special, Mrs Green, and I'll always be grateful to you and Mr Green for that. She's got her mother's good looks and her father's intelligence."

"Well, thank you, kind sir! A good job it wasn't the other way round, though, isn't it?"

At this point Amanda appeared, having finished the clearing up. "What are you two nattering about out here?"

"Oh, I was just admiring Richard's gardening skills... quite the Percy Thrower, isn't he?"

"Steady on, Mum... or he'll start believing you. Anyway, it's gone quite chilly now. Let's go inside and join Dad... I've just lit the gas fire."

Chapter Eleven

Reorganising secondary education on comprehensive lines had always been dismissed by die-hard NGS parents as some sort of madcap experiment dreamt up by "a bunch of champagne socialists from down south". Surely, no right-thinking person would condone the destruction of such a famous beacon of excellence as *their* school, not even those parents whose boys had been denied entrance – or would they? Clearly, these clever politicians had no idea how ordinary folk cherished "a grammar school education", if only as a means of escape from the back-breaking toil of the pit and the mill. Besides, why should Latin and Greek be the sole preserve of the rich?

The masters, on the other hand, had consoled themselves that the process would take years to accomplish, by which time many of them would have retired, or be too old to care; and a few fondly believed that a change of Government would secure an eleventh hour reprieve.

But when the Government did change in June 1970, hopes of such a reversal of fortunes were short-lived, for despite having a carpenter's son as Prime Minister, and a grocer's daughter as the Secretary of State for Education and Science, and both prime products of the grammar school system, it soon became clear that the political momentum of comprehensiveness was now unstoppable. As Dr Davenport had rightly concluded, it seemed very much "an idea whose time had come".

By Easter 1971, there was talk of little else in the Masters' Room, everyone with his own perspective and weighing up his options for when the inevitable did happen. In fairness, Joe Riley had kept his staff well abreast of developments throughout, especially the various "models" being considered in high places. "There'll be winners and losers," he kept proclaiming, safe in the knowledge that he himself would have completed his "two-score years" long before "C-day".

Even Jack Higginbottom, a comprehensive denier *ad ultimum*, eventually had to accept the inevitable, likening it to the Black Death infesting their little town, or a grotesque juggernaut trundling down the M6, destroying centuries of glorious tradition in its path. It was just too distressing to think about. In fact, Jack was convinced that their masters-to-be had a special agenda for NGS: to gain maximum revenge for decades of ruthless selection by that fascist autocrat, George Davenport. "I don't like their attitude one little bit," said Jack, "I think the buggers want to make an example of us, and claim us as a gradely scalp for Percy Lord's trophy cabinet."

MEANWHILE, something less political was exercising Joe Riley's patience – the plethora of correspondence arriving daily from both Central Government and County Hall. He had never enjoyed dealing with officialdom, any more than Dr Davenport had, but now that the hyenas were closing in on the spoil, he felt obliged at least to become acquainted with their language and ways. Oh, how he missed old George now!

"Jargon-ridden balderdash!" he declared one morning, as he flung yet another circular from Preston into his overflowing pending tray. "No wonder this country's in a mess. By the way, Martha, what *is* the correct noun from *comprehensive*? *Comprehension* sounds a bit archaic to me... in this context at least. Mightn't *comprehensiveness* be more precise? Or *comprehensivity*? And have you noticed all these American terms creeping in... *educator*... *pastoral care... guidance... pedagogy... students*?" He spat each one out with as much venom as his soft north-eastern vowels would allow.

"And I ask you, what's a blooming *school counsellor* when he's at home? What's wrong with the Queen's English, Martha?

As usual, Martha maintained diplomatic neutrality during Joe's struggles with "officialese", although a discerning eye might have noticed an ironic smile playing around her mouth.

But more irritating for Joe than even the correspondence were the so-called *visitations* from the "Forward Planning Group". These comprised carloads of young men from County Hall in fashionable suits drawing up in the school yard with the express purpose of "forward planning" and reassuring the benighted Staff of

NGS about the wonderful world of comprehensive education. "Very forward," declared Joe, "but not very reassuring."

Then one day, as if he had nothing more pressing to see to, an invitation arrived, the first of many, to attend "a consultative meeting at County Hall, and to bring along one or two of his senior management team in order to facilitate in the cascade process of dissemination". Joe's reaction, of course, was predictable, but even Martha was surprised by its violence. Poor Joe, like his faithful old Ford, had never ventured onto the 'East-Lancs', let alone the M6; and, of course, Jack had better things to do than "waste a day chewing the fat with that toffee-nosed lot up in Preston." Accordingly, when Nobbs offered to chauffeur the party there and back in his new Jaguar XJ, Joe could not believe his good fortune: yet again the white knight had come to his rescue.

During the 1971-72 school year, Joe's very last at the School, these trips to Preston became a regular feature in his diary; and, contrary to expectations, he thoroughly enjoyed them. As Dr Davenport's Number Two, he had felt always obliged to be "available at the school", and had found it difficult to change his ways when he became Headmaster. But now, with retirement beckoning, he had decided to listen to his son's advice and delegate some aspects of the work to younger colleagues, many of whom had surprised him with their willingness to "go the extra mile to help old Joe".

In the event, he thoroughly enjoyed the novelty of high-speed motorway travel, sitting back in the front passenger seat of the luxurious limousine, watching the Lancashire plain go speeding by; and the *smorgasbord* lunches at the County Hall were a definite improvement on the workaday fare served up in the NGS refectory by Mrs Musgrave and her doughty bunch of dinner-ladies. But he was less enthusiastic about the actual business of the meetings, leaving much of the detail to Martin Shaw, now the Deputy Chairman of the Governors, and Jim Whittaker, the Senior Master.

The Jaguar attracted much attention in the County Hall car park, up-staging the Victors and the Cortinas, just as the "chauffeur" up-staged his passengers. When the motley quartet arrived the first time, the honey-tongued Education Officer responsible for the Netherbridge area took the tall and distinguished gentleman in the smart suit for the Headmaster, instead of his elderly and diminutive companion in the over-worn sports jacket and crumpled grey flannels.

"No, indeed," declared Nobbs, eager to laugh off such a preposterous assumption, "I'm just the driver, your humble servant, Richard Nobbs. May I introduce you to my boss, and very good friend, Mr Riley... the Headmaster... and Mr Whittaker, the Senior Master, and this is Mr Martin Shaw, the Deputy Chairman of the Governors."

"Well, very pleased to meet you all, gentlemen," said the Officer, nodding at each one as they were introduced. My name's Whittingham, Tony Whittingham, and I've been given the special honour of looking after you today, and hopefully for some time to come. Anyway, first things first, I'm sure you could all do with a cup of coffee after wrestling with the horrendous morning traffic on the M6."

"Oh, Mr Nobbs is an excellent driver," interjected Joe,

"we spent most of the journey in the outside lane, sailing past everything in sight! That's why we're here so early. Oh, and you couldn't make mine a tea, please, Mr Whittingham? I find coffee repeats on me... there's always one awkward one, isn't there? Ha! ha!"

ON THEIR first wedding anniversary, Nobbs treated his lovely young wife to a marathon drive across Europe to Montreux, where they stayed in a stylish hotel overlooking Lake Geneva. Amanda had never been abroad before, and like most first-time visitors was almost as impressed with the sheer cleanliness of the bathrooms as with the grandeur of the scenery. After the tiring journey, they spent much of the week lazing by the lake or on it in *bateaux pédalos*,

Despite the joyous occasion and idyllic setting, Nobbs seemed uncharacteristically quiet, pondering whether to resign his post at the Grammar School at the end of the year in order to concentrate on his property empire. Amanda had never approved of this plan, and on the eve of their return journey, while they were out on the terrace enjoying a quiet drink before dinner she broached the subject again, this time from an unexpected angle.

"Rich," she said sweetly, "I've been thinking..."

"Oh, yes... and I can guess what about."

"Can you just listen for a moment, please? Now if you give up your job at the School, you'll be throwing away a golden opportunity."

"What... of becoming a miserable old fart like Taff Jenkins?"

"Hear me out. Forget about the damn woodwork... obviously, there's no future for you in that. What you need is a complete change of career... *within* the profession."

"What do you mean... re-train... for Maths or Physics... or Classics? God, no dice there, Mand! I'd be up against a whole brigade of Oxford brain-boxes."

"No, Rich! Not Maths... not Physics... not Classics... nor any damn subject, for that matter... you must think outside these little boxes. Think the big picture... think... *management*... that's your thing, Rich... *man-management*. I'm sure Dr Davenport didn't get to be Head master just by being good at Maths. No, he's the full package... can't you see? The height... the looks... the voice... oh my god, that voice... the intelligence... the charm... the confidence... the bearing... you name it... he's got the lot. And do you know what, Mr Man of Property... so have *you*!"

"God, that's some speech, Mand... you really mean it, don't you? As you know only too well, nothing would please me more than fulfilling your dream... but unfortunately you're forgetting one little problem... before they even consider those other qualities you mention, you need some qualifications. Let me give you an example... let's suppose Davenport got run over by a bus tomorrow. Do you know what would happen? That doddery old fool, Riley, would step right into his shoes.... that's what. Why? Well, he's got the effing bits of paper that open doors for you in the Grammar School, that's why."

"Yes, okay, okay... point taken... but... there *is* another option,"

"O, yes, and what's that, then?"

"Well... getting out of the grammar school altogether,

272

that's what. Look, only about twenty-five per cent of kids go to a grammar school anyway... what about the other seventy-five? Don't they need educating too?

After a slight pause, Nobbs stood up and said "Bloody hell, Mand, why didn't *I* think of that? Yes, you're damn right... and there must be three 'sec mods' for every grammar school, which means three times as many chains of command... you know what... you're a little genius, you are... and wasted in that school!"

"But, you are right about one thing, though," said Amanda, "First, you'll have to get some qualifications... not the posh, academic sort you're on about... no, the ordinary ones, with lots of letters in them! I've seen some American degrees and diplomas advertised in the Sunday papers... anything would do to start with... most people can't tell the difference, anyway, and wouldn't bother asking. And let's face it, what actual use is a degree in Maths or Greek for running a secondary modern school... or any school, for that matter. So, perhaps while you're at it, you might as well get a qualification that might be of some use in the job... like, you could enrol on a diploma course in *business,* or *management* at somewhere like Manchester Poly... and in three or four years' time, bingo!... you might have your own school, and I'd be Mrs Headmaster! How do you fancy that, eh? You know what they say, 'cometh the hour, cometh the man'...well, in my book, Mr Nobbs, the hour is nigh... and you are the *man*... trust me. We make a good team, you and I... in more senses than one! And from now on you listen to your little Mandy, right?"

"Oh, come here, gorgeous!"

"Not here, Rich... not now... people are watching!"

Nobbs was speechless, but a smile had replaced the pensive frown, as he looked out across the lake dreaming of running a school and a business from the headmaster's office like a latter-day Harry Whitworth. Now, that *would* be something, he thought.

After the waiter had been to clear their glasses, Nobbs said, "You may not believe this, Mand, but, during these last few months I've been doing a lot of weighing things up... and one thing has become pretty obvious to me... making money for its own sake is pointless in the end. Okay, at first, it does get you nice things, like a decent house, a good car and holidays abroad... but one thing it can't do... it can't buy you things like... respect... and status. Being a master at the Grammar School does give you a bit of that, I suppose... until they find out you're only an effing Woodwork master! That's where the 'big cat' comes in handy! You know... I've never forgotten what Jack Higginbottom said at my interview way back in 1947... he asked me how would I go about *earning* the respect of "our gradely Netherbridge lads", as he called them. Now, looking back, that was quite some question... I can't remember what I said exactly, but I remember I had to put my thinking cap on pretty sharpish to think of an answer! Yes, Mand, *respect*, that's what *we* could do with.... and *status*... and, thanks to you, I think we'll get them."

As soon as they arrived back in Leigh, Nobbs could think of nothing except those elusive "bits of paper". If only he had listened to his dear old Dad, and taken his schoolwork more seriously... even a decent "matric" would have done him no harm now. But, on the plus side, he was still only forty, and thanks to his clever and adorable wife, wonderful new prospects had suddenly opened up.

Accordingly, the draft resignation letter was consigned to the flames, and promptly replaced by a frantic search for suitable courses – correspondence, evening, weekend, residential – anything related to managing a secondary school, and preferably ones leading to a grand sounding qualification. And Mandy was right... many of the parents would be more impressed with the number of letters than with what they stood for.

All of a sudden, collaborating with his wife on this ambitious project had injected new vigour into Nobbs's waning career. Even *he* had eventually accepted that an elite institution like NGS was not really for the likes of him, who could only ever be spear-carriers on such an exalted stage.

The following afternoon Amanda visited the town library to look up suitable courses in the various college brochures and magazines, and made a list of several they might consider. When she arrived home, Nobbs was in the garage simonizing his Jaguar. "Look, Rich," she said excitedly, "I think I've found the very thing for you...what about the Royal Society of Arts? It says here for a small registration fee and an annual subscription, you can get F.R.S.A. after your name. That would be a start, wouldn't it? And then there's always the old Royal Geographical Society. Wow! I can see it now... *Mr Richard C. Nobbs, F.R.S.A., F.R.G.S., Headmaster*, on your office door. Not bad, eh? And 'Mr' sounds classier than 'Dr'... like with surgeons... once they get their F.R.C.S., they call themselves plain 'Mr' again. Anyway, take a look yourself, while I get the meal on..."

"What are we having?"

"Oh, I fancy some shepherd's pie...what do you think?

"Yes, that would be fine, love... a nice change after all the marinated mushrooms and coq au vin last week!

With the dinner menu settled, Amanda disappeared into the house, leaving Nobbs to his polishing, and (she hoped) dreaming of the glorious future she was mapping out for him. He continued burnishing the paintwork obsessively, periodically standing back to admire how the deep lustre set off the limousine's long alluring lines. He also admired his own reflection in the paintwork, turning his head this way and that, better to appreciate his classical profile, perfect teeth, and glossy, blond mane... like a Greek god's, he thought, adding under his breath, "Eat your f------ heart out, Davenport, you wrinkly b------!"

All the talk about qualifications reminded him of the time when Joe Riley shocked the Masters' Room by calling the Oxford M.A. a "Mickey Mouse degree". According to Joe, all you had to do for that was to keep your name on the register for so many terms after graduating... no research... no exam, or anything. So, thought Nobbs, why should *he* bother with membership fees, and the rest of it, when this sort of jiggery-pokery went on in high places? Come to think of it, why couldn't he make up his own f------ letters? M.A. (Master Artificer), MM (Mandy's Man), TD (Top Driver)... or he could even use I.A.M. (Institute of Advanced Motorists)... the possibilities were endless... and chances were nobody would ever query them! He further concluded that titles and handles were a "load of bullsh-t" anyway... what really mattered was, could you do the job... So... *he* wasn't going to lose sleep over qualifications. He wouldn't even consider the bogus degree market, because the way he saw it, a D.I.Y. fake was no less a fake than a real fake... a fake was a f------ fake, whichever way you looked at it. Q.E.D! Okay, maybe he'd do this R.S.A. thing just to please Mandy... but, one thing was for sure, whatever happened... one day he'd show those university b------s who was f------- boss.

"It's ready, darling!" intoned Amanda seductively over the inter-com, "Come and get it while it's hot."

THROUGHOUT that rock-hard winter of 1963, when the Beatles were only warbling their way round the cotton towns of Lancashire, the normally gregarious Nobbs was leading a far less flamboyant social life: Amanda had enrolled him on a night school course in *Business Studies* at Wigan Technical College. Indeed, he even missed the Beatles' much heralded "gig" at the Leigh Casino Ballroom on February 25th, though from all accounts that had been no great loss, thanks to the frenzied screeching of a claque of hyperventilating schoolgirls.

Furthermore, weeks of ice and fog had made driving conditions so treacherous that the 'Mark Nine' had had to remain in its garage alongside the old 'S.S.' from mid-January until early March, while poor Nobbs threw himself at the mercy of Leigh Corporation Transport. This often meant walking the last smoggy mile home to Pennington late at night, with eyes and nostrils encircled with soot, after the driver had announced unequivocally somewhere near the Miners' Welfare Institute, "I'm not going no further tonight... can't see 'tlamposts!"

Being naturally averse to "book-learning", Nobbs

found the seminars and the role-play much more to his taste, and being older and more confident than the other students, he could not resist foisting his overbearing personality and opinions on the proceedings, whatever the subject might be. After a while, this generated considerable resentment and not a little muted sniggering behind his back; but no one, not even the lecturer, had the confidence to disillusion him.

He also took delight in flirting with two teenage girls on the course, informing them in stage whispers that he had done quite well in property... and now wanted to give something back to society... and as his next project was planning to buy a disused mill or warehouse and setting up his own school... and having had his own education interrupted by the war, he now needed to bring himself up to speed with the management and business side of things... although, of course, in due course he would be advertising for full-time staff... a bursar... and (adding with a wink) some young female office staff.

Much to Amanda's surprise, he had also taken to dipping into her old teacher-training textbooks and manuals, "just to familiarise myself with the jargon, like", he explained coyly. If truth be told, ever since his grand epiphany in Montreux, he had become a monomaniac bore, rarely missing an opportunity to steer the conversation towards the 1944 Education Act and the iniquities of the 11-plus.

Not unexpectedly, he was equally dismissive of formal examinations: "All they do, Mandy, is flatter a select few into thinking they're more intelligent than the rest of us... and they're not. I'll tell you one thing for nothing... because I've seen it at first hand... a man with an Oxford degree can strut and swagger as much as he likes, but, as someone once said unless 'he write a better book, or preach a better sermon, or make a better mousetrap than his neighbour, the world will (not) make a beaten path to his door', or again, as it says in the Good Book, 'he is become a sounding brass or tinkling cymbal'. At the end of the day, as Einstein himself said, 'education is what remains after one has forgotten what one has learned in school'... and not how many exams you've passed."

Even Amanda was beginning to tire of his rants, and once or twice had to warn him that people were staring and shaking their heads. "Let the buggers shake whatever part of their anatomy they like, Mand, it's about time someone told it like it is. God, effing grammar schools have been around since the Middle Ages... they were probably all right in their day, teaching Latin and Greek grammar to priests and lawyers. But, whether you like it or not, times have changed... and you can't stop progress... It's like with cars... things are improving all the time... and schools, like everything else, have got to move with the times!"

"Yes, yes, I know, love... and please don't get me wrong... I really *am* glad you didn't hand in your notice... but, don't go over the top with the politics of it all, that's all I'm saying... leave all that to the politicians... it'll make you ill... you just concentrate on getting your promotion. Your turn will come, you mark my words... but first, you've got to get those bits of paper... then, bingo!"

But Amanda's emollient words had little effect on her husband's fervour: if anything, his harangues grew noisier and more confrontational with the passing months. He behaved like a man possessed, totally convinced of his own rightness and impervious to the most blatant rebuff or gibe. Armed with his evangelical zeal and a "little learning", and energised by the perceived hurt of his own educational failures, he led a one-man crusade against the accepted educational order. "Stands to reason," he shouted at the world in general, "grading kids of eleven into 'eggheads' and 'blockheads' for life is just plain bloody stupid. And you don't need a degree from Oxford to tell you that."

Clearly, this line of argument found few adherents at NGS. If there was one principle that kept even the most liberal within the pale, it was the principle of *selection by ability*; this was sacrosanct and immutable.

"I don't think I'd have the patience to teach nincompoops, Carrington," declared Phil Evans's "constipated knight", shaking his few remaining locks in horror at the thought.

"Nor I!" concurred Long John, his bridge partner, "What the devil's got into the fellow? Should keep his nose out of things that don't concern him... you never hear Taff Jenkins talk this kind of tripe."

"Quite agree!" exclaimed the 'prize product of the English public park'. "I think the Old Man should have a quiet word with him, don't you?"

"Huh! I shouldn't hold your breath," grumped 'round Sir Ron'.

"If you ask me, he's an all-round bad egg," declared Phil's "thrice-blessèd darling of the month of May", "never liked the fellow... and now, with all this subversive talk... it's bad for staff morale, if nothing else."

"And he's infecting some of the boys with his left-wing nonsense as well, I shouldn't wonder," concurred

"John the Maps".

Indeed, even some of Nobbs's "Banger" chums were beginning to look askance at his endless tirades. Some had even taken to leaving the Masters' Room, when they heard him vociferating outside the door; and if he button-holed some hapless soul in the refectory, the flimsiest excuse was invoked to effect a speedy escape.

NEVERTHELESS, for all the opposition Nobbs encountered within the School, with the passing months, his 'anarchic' views grew more in tune with the nation's mood, and when the Labour Party took office in 1964, determined to fulfil their manifesto promise of eliminating selection at eleven years, Nobbs felt fully vindicated. Although it was a vision the Conservatives had also toyed with, albeit half-heartedly, ever since their landslide election victory under Macmillan in 1959, it had taken a Labour Prime Minister, a northerner and an ex-grammar schoolboy to boot, to bring it to fruition.

Some Labour-controlled authorities in the industrial north, like Lancashire and Liverpool, made an early start with submitting plans for "going comprehensive". Others were less enthusiastic, but when Labour won a bigger majority in the 1966 election, everyone assumed that the process would be expedited through compulsion. In fact, it took another four years to draft a bill, and when Labour lost in 1970, the bill was lost too.

Interestingly, thanks largely to Dr Davenport's natural compassion for the 'underdog', and his innate sense of fair play, NGS had long enjoyed good relations with its neighbouring schools, especially the "Secondary Modern" across the road. Privately, as both Martha and

Joe Riley later testified, he too had never felt entirely comfortable with rigid selection at eleven – the arbitrariness of the age and the unreliability of the measuring instruments – but far worse, and far too often, the finality of the verdicts. Despite every effort on his part, the harsh dilemma always remained: reconciling the late transfers *into* the Grammar School with the necessary but traumatic *exits*. Once after a particularly difficult day reviewing borderline cases, he said with a deep sigh, "Gray was right, Martha, 'Full many a flower is born to bloom unseen/ And waste its sweetness on the desert air'; even one is one too many."

Chapter Twelve

Whenever Joe Riley retired in the summer of 1971, Nobbs arranged a party for him at "the grand house". As expected, he went to considerable trouble and expense, including erecting a marquee on the back lawn, and engaging Taylors, the renowned local caterers, to lay on "a banquet fit for royalty", as Joe graciously described it.

The guest-list made interesting reading, as did the list of those who declined, some less apologetically than others. Joe himself would have preferred a cup of tea and a bun in the School refectory, with some amusing anecdotes about "the good old days". Moreover, having always made great play of never succumbing to Nobbs's style of persuasion, he had found this unavoidable acceptance doubly irksome.

But, for all his shortcomings, Joe was not a boor. Besides, he felt Nobbs had been a loyal and supportive colleague for some years, and the least he could do now was accept his kind gesture in the spirit it was surely intended. Furthermore, breaching his self-denying ordinance this once might help shed light on this most intriguing of characters.

Much the same could be said of Martha, except that she had felt no moral obligation to accept. Indeed, her immediate reaction on receiving the invitation was to invent a 'prior engagement', but after some consideration, she changed her mind. Despite all the animosity she had felt towards Nobbs since their first encounter in 1947, and more recently, his underhand attempt to wrest *Elsinore* from under her nose when she was at her most vulnerable, she could not actually bring herself to refuse, partly for Joe's sake, and partly because to her it would have been a gratuitous insult. Besides, if she were really honest, she had always found Nobbs's supreme self-confidence and dominant personality strangely fascinating.

And so, like Joe, she too had an ulterior motive. Ever since her Bletchley days, distinguishing *what seems* from *what is* had always been something of a preoccupation for her, and indeed one that had often stood her in good stead in her subsequent career. Who *was* this intriguing character with whom she had shared the same place of work for a quarter of a century, but who was just as much a stranger to her now as he was when he first arrived? She had never met anyone who could charm and offend in equal measures, sometimes simultaneously. And again why should anyone as privileged and as well-endowed as he harbour so much resentment against the world? And why should a supposedly intelligent man of mature years behave like a back-street bully? By nature or design – or possibly both – here indeed was a bundle of contradictions – and perhaps observing him on his own territory might help unravel some of the threads.

Then there was the question of the "dark lady". From all accounts, she was so breathtakingly beautiful and accomplished that all the princes and moguls of the western world might have come knocking on her door. Moreover, despite holding strong opinions and expressing them forcibly when required, she had opted for an inconspicuous life of domesticity, honouring and obeying her lord and master, even to the point of giving up a promising career before it had really begun. Those who had met her also spoke of her delightfully lively and outgoing personality, but as far as Martha knew, she had never accompanied her husband to any school function. Was that her choice? Here was another bundle of contradictions.

After deciding not to continue as a school governor after Joe's retirement, Jack Higginbottom too felt obliged to attend. He had heard flattering reports about the "hospitality at the Nobbery", and was particularly interested in what Taylors could bring to the feast. He brought Phil and Shirley along with him in his car, so that they could have a noggin of something exotic from the grand cellar, though he knew Phil would have preferred a game of darts and a quiet pint with Taff Jenkins in the *Boar's Head*. Not unexpectedly, Taff himself had found "better things to do", such as attending to his vegetable patch, or working on one of his superb teak squirrels or owls ready for the Summer Fair at St Mary's, and had asked Liz to send their joint apologies. Besides, she and Taff were already planning a surprise retirement "knees-up" for both Joe and Jack at their cottage in late

September.

The hundred and five hand-written invitations Amanda had sent out had produced 69 acceptances, which Nobbs counted as "a result", even though he knew that acceptances were often as disingenuous as the invitations themselves, and that for many, celebrating Joe's retirement would *not* have been the chief criterion.

Amazingly, Frank Fairclough had agreed to "show his face". Like everyone else, he had heard much about these "grand hob-nobbings" on St Helens Road, and thought he might as well "have a dekko" while he had the chance. As it happened, he had an 'away' match at the Boothstown Bowling Club that Saturday, but he could call in on the way home after visiting his mother on Holden Road.

The acknowledged "academics" on the staff had declined almost *en bloc*, some having genuine excuses, like caravanning in France, or walking in Scotland. But most, like Dr Kendricks (who had never forgotten Nobbs's caustic jibe on that cold afternoon in February, '63), "would rather be run over by a bus than fraternise with that impudent oaf". In much the same vein, Dan Carrington, the Senior Music master, "suddenly remembered" that he had to give an organ recital at the Orrell Parish Church that Saturday; whilst his friend, Peter Halliwell, had to go to Didsbury to look at a second-hand Norton Commando he had seen advertised in the *Manchester Evening News*.

But their two friends, Charlie Aldridge and Ken Travis, were not quite as dismissive, and devoted a pot of tea and two toasted tea-cakes at Tiplady's to the matter, eventually agreeing on an uneasy compromise of "putting in a brief appearance out of respect for Joe, and perhaps having one drink, but certainly nothing to eat".

Needless to say, the "Forty-Bangers" were present and correct to a man, despite the recent cooling off in their adulation of their leader. Each had been allocated a specific role, such as welcoming guests as they arrived; supervising the parking in the drive; manning the drinks bar, the ultimate responsibility for which had been entrusted to the "little R.I. man", Titchener; helping with a safe and orderly exit into the busy St Helens Road at the end; and finally wishing everyone a safe journey home.

Among the 69 guests, there were many who had wrestled with their consciences over their R.S.V.Ps, but had ultimately succumbed to Nobbs's potent cocktail of allure and menace. Furthermore, many feared that, with his network of connections in high places and his educational views, he might well "feature (possibly prominently) in any future developments", and nothing would be lost by displaying some semblance of loyalty.

For others, "nosh at the Nobbses" was a regular, though not necessarily welcome, event, and they would be familiar with the customs and practices of the great house, including their host's propensity for humiliating guests with jokes at their expense, and (ostensibly good-natured) bullying. But, like all bullies, he himself could not brook being the butt of any joke, however harmless.

It was rumoured that most of these regulars were attracted more by Amanda's couture than by her cuisine; and as there would be no call on her culinary talents on this occasion, she could concentrate on "making an impression", as Nobbs put it, especially on people who mattered, for to him this was no ordinary jamboree.

Among the VIPs were the Rev Canon Ramsbottom

287

and his good lady, Josephine. As soon as they arrived, Nobbs leapt across the room to greet them, making a great show of escorting them to a pair of black leather "G Plan" reclining swivel chairs incongruously placed between a Louis XVI escritoire and a William and Mary long-case clock by *Thos. Wheeler of London*,

"There you go, Vicar," declared Nobbs, "a pair of Mandy's specials for you...and according to the manufacturers, the *world's most comfortable chairs...* reserved tonight for my two very special guests."

"Well, thank you, Mr Nobbs, you're most kind," replied the reverend colossus, as he steadied himself nervously before lowering his Brobdingnagian bulk onto the risibly inadequate contraption.

When he had attained a modicum of equilibrium, Nobbs urged him to sample "the full Gomme experience", helping him to raise one leg and then the other onto the accompanying footrest until he lay almost supine as if awaiting the dentist's attentions. Naturally, this droll spectacle triggered much hilarity among the assembled gathering, including Josephine, who by now had herself assumed a similar position of recumbence in the matching chair alongside her husband's.

"Ee, by *Gomme*!" exclaimed the clergyman good-naturedly, gasping for air with the effort, "we're like a pair of effigies on a tomb, Jo. Yes, Mr Nobbs... an extraordinary example... of modern design... and maybe indeed... '*the* world's... most comfortable chair,' but we old Ramsbottoms... well... let us say our bottoms are more accustomed... to the solid old chesterfields at the Vicarage.

Nobbs allocated a good ten minutes to the

Ramsbottoms, inquiring variously after the organ fund; Taff Jenkins's latest *chef-d'oeuvre*; the "holy dusters" (who made sure everything was sparkling and ship-shape for Sunday); and indeed, all the lovely folk of St Mary's. "Not many black sheep in this good shepherd's flock, eh, Josie? I *can* call you Josie, can't I? We *did* miss St Mary's when we moved up here... we really did, but... that's how it is."

(The Vicar cast a knowing look at his wife, as if to say, "I did warn you, dear!")

"But rest assured, if we ever move back to Netherbridge, we'd be like the *lost* sheep, safely back in your fold before you could say Judas Iscariot. I don't know about the rejoicing in Heaven though, but you know what I mean. By the way, Vicar, how are *your* numbers holding up at the minute? I know the C of E's going through a dodgy patch... trouble is it's the young folk... they don't want to know about the Sabbath... or God, for that matter... Black Sabbath and *Sympathy for the Devil* is more to their taste... and the only hymns they hear now are *Abide with Me* at Cup Finals, and *Guide Me O Thou Great Jehovah* at funerals... I've often thought the School could do a bit more an' all... you know, a proper religious input from a proper priest... because these lads don't get much of it at home, do they? And as I was saying to Mand only the other day, perhaps we could all make a bit more effort of a Sunday... otherwise it'll become like any other day, and that would be a great pity. It's the same here in Pennington... dwindling congregations... very depressing for the clergy, I'm sure. Anyway, on that depressing thought let me get you a drink. Don't get up... I'll get someone to come across to you right away... and *I'd* better start spreading myself about as well... see you anon."

"Gosh," whispered Josephine, "doesn't he go on?"

"Yes, he does rather," said the Vicar with a chuckle, "but he *means* well."

Josephine kept her counsel.

As Nobbs 'worked the room', he spotted Martha sitting alone on a window-seat, people-watching from a good vantage point.

"Hell-oo, Martha," he said ingratiatingly, kissing her on both cheeks, "*soo* glad you could come, especially with your Aunt, and all that. But you could have brought her along, you know... or is she... struggling? A fall like that can knock the stuffing out of you when you're getting on... look, your glass needs topping up."

(How the devil did *he* know about Auntie Hilda's fall, or even that she was staying with her at *Elsinore*?)

"Thank you, Mr Nobbs, but no, really," replied Martha, "I must go easy... you don't want to get me breathalysed on the way home, do you? And may I also thank you... and of course Mrs Nobbs... for the invitation... it's very kind of you both to arrange this get-together... you've gone to a lot of trouble."

"No trouble at all, Martha... besides we couldn't let such an occasion pass without doing *something*... and anyway, we love entertaining. And I must say we're very touched by the wonderful response... I'll miss old Joe when he's gone... as, I'm sure, we all will... they broke the mould when they made the likes of him. Yes, it'll be a sad day when the 'old brigade' have all gone."

Martha repressed a sob by changing the subject. "You've got a beautiful home here, Mr Nobbs... you must be very proud of it."

"Well, it was the best available at the time, Martha. Mandy's put a lot of time and effort into the decor and the furnishings, so it's beginning to take shape now. But *you've* got a lovely house too, especially that fabulous garden. That's what *I'd* really like, a house something like this, but with about an acre of land attached, where you could have some water features and things. One day, maybe, when my ship comes in, eh!"

"*Elsinore* is rather big just for one person," replied Martha, "but I manage, with a little help from one or two very good friends... and it holds very special memories for me."

"Yes, I'm sure," replied Nobbs, nodding piously. "Oh, I don't believe you've met my wife, have you? Let me see if there's any sign of her. She's about somewhere... I think she must be in the tent... keeping an eye on developments, I expect... not much gets past her! Oh, and speak of the devil... Mand, over here... I want you to meet..."

All heads turned as the lady of the house walked graciously across the room, dressed in an arresting, gold-coloured mini-dress and very high stiletto heels.

"Something in the way she moves," crooned Titchmarsh pretentiously, as his eyes gazed lasciviously at the enchanting creature passing before him. Then a muted wolf-whistle from the bar area was heard above the hub-hub. Clearly, Nobbs was not amused, and showed his disapproval by scowling menacingly in the direction of its source. But after a brief awkward hiatus, he continued nonchalantly, "Everything okay, Mand?"

"Yes, I think so... they said about another ten minutes."

"That's good. Now, I'd like you to meet someone very special... may I introduce you to my special colleague and friend ... the one and only... Miss Martha Wolf."

"Oh, please," sighed Martha, *sotto voce.*

"Pleased to meet you, Miss Wolf," said Amanda, with a warm, sympathetic smile, "I'm so glad you were able to come.

"Well, it's lovely meeting you too, Mrs Nobbs," replied Martha, reaching to shake her hand, "I've heard so much about you."

"Nothing too terrible, I hope."

"Oh, very much the opposite," said Martha.

"Well, *that's* a relief. But I wouldn't believe everything *he* tells you. And, *please* call me Mandy."

The two women continued chatting naturally long after Nobbs had moved on. Martha found her refreshingly forthright, and with her dark, intelligent eyes, and delightful chuckle, she reminded her a little of Mrs Davenport. Indeed, here was someone Martha would very much like to know better.

Meanwhile, Nobbs had joined two ill-assorted individuals engrossed in some matter of great importance – Jim Whittaker, the Senior History Master and now the interim headmaster-designate, and Nobbs's new pal from Preston, Tony Whittingham.

"We've got a good man here, Tone," interrupted Nobbs, slapping Jim a little too heartily on the back, "Been round the block a few times, has Jim... a very safe pair of hands, I would say... and do you know what, a nice bloke to boot."

Jim Whittaker managed to smile politely at Nobbs's fulsome compliments, whilst "Tone" himself seemed a little more circumspect. "Well, we'll certainly need an experienced hand at the helm in these uncharted waters. But, as you know, Jim, you won't be alone on the bridge... you can always count on me, as your pilot, so to speak, to help weather the storm... and Richard here will always be on hand to help you navigate a steady course... as he did, I believe, when Mr Riley first took command of the ship."

"Well," said Nobbs, "I've said it before, and I'll say it again, 'No one is useless in this world who lightens the burdens of others'."

THE BEATLES' *Abbey Road* album had been playing softly on the sound system throughout the afternoon, and as the last strains of *All you need is love...love is all you need* faded for the fourth or fifth time, a treacly voice came over the Tannoy – it was Ken Aspinall, one of Nobbs's fellow classic cars enthusiasts, and 'Lord Pallisan' in Phil Evans's poem, who was acting as some kind of master of ceremonies for the event.

"Ladies and gentlemen," he drawled. "if I could have your attention for a few moments, please.... before we move across to the marquee, our kind host, Richard, would like to say a few words. Rich?"

"Oh, thanks, Ken. Good evening, one and all... yes... just before we eat, I'd just like to say thank you to each and every one of you for joining Mandy and I on this important occasion."

During the polite applause, Nobbs waved to Joe Riley to come forward to the microphone, and much to the latter's discomfiture, he lent over him and put his arm round his shoulder, as if reassuring a first-former not to worry, because everything was going to be all right.

"As I was saying to someone earlier," he continued, "they broke the mould when they made Joe. We can call you Joe now, can't we?

Joe nodded obligingly, even though proper modes of address were the least of his concerns at that moment.

"But, really, friends, it doesn't matter what we call this gentleman, because to us he always was, and always will be, the same, reliable, good old Joe... no airs and graces, always even-tempered... and, sadly, we shall never see his like again. I shall miss you, fella... as will we all.

(As Nobbs looked across the room to see how his 'speech' was being received, he noticed Phil whispering something in Jack's ear, and Phil also noticed that he had been caught in the act.)

"Now a little bird tells me," he continued, with his arm still disconcertingly around Joe's shoulder, "you're going to be spending some of your time in retirement writing a book... a memoir, I believe, of your time at the School... I know you'll have plenty of marvellous stories to tell, Joe, and I for one will be at the front of the queue to buy a signed copy when it is launched... who knows, I might even get a mention in it myself!"

Joe smiled politely again, and one or two of Nobbs's cronies tittered dutifully. That jest was also the pre-arranged sign for someone to hand him two neatly wrapped parcels and a homemade jumbo-sized retirement card, on which everyone who worked at the school, even the cleaners and the refectory staff, had kindly signed, and written some personal comment.

"And now, ladies and gentlemen, for the exciting bit... Joe, on behalf of us all and in acknowledgement of all you've done over the years, I'd like you to accept these small tokens of our appreciation. We all know you don't reckon much on trinkets and baubles... so we decided to get you some useful and practical things instead. In this red parcel...wait for it... we've got one half-dozen Staedtler HB pencils with built-in rubbers; one Boston Champion pencil-sharpener; and one half-dozen reams of broad-lined foolscap file-paper... also an expanding file to keep everything together. And then in the green parcel... well... Mandy thought it would be a good idea, Joe, if you had a typewriter for when you're ready to type it all up. So we got you the very latest Imperial portable."

Poor Joe had been dreading this moment for weeks, and had spent some time composing and then memorising a brief but elegant farewell speech. But Nobbs's "theatricals" had utterly thrown him. He was so daunted by the ambience, and Nobbs's controlling manner, that when he tried to adapt his speech to express his gratitude, his emotions defeated him. All he could manage at first was a perfunctory "Thank you, everyone... and thank *you*, Richard... and of course thank you, Amanda... for arranging this wonderful evening... It is much more than I ever expected. I don't know what else to say, really, except also to thank everyone for coming, and for these much-appreciated gifts... not only will they be useful, but they'll be a constant reminder of all the good people I've been fortunate enough to have worked with at NGS over the years."

Then, recalling a snatch of his prepared speech, he added, "As we are all very much aware, big changes are afoot in education, and it's only right that men of my generation move aside to make room for those more in tune with these changes. We are living through very volatile times, and no one can truly predict the outcomes. But as I've said many times, there will be winners and losers, and I should like to wish each one of you the very best in your future careers."

He had wished to say a little more, but a sudden burst of applause led by Nobbs persuaded him that perhaps there was no call to continue. He therefore gladly handed the microphone over to the waiting 'Lord Pallisan', who clearly seemed far more at ease with the "infernal gadget".

"It's obvious," gurgled the good 'Lord', with a cheesy grin, "that they all love you, Joe, and on behalf of us all again, may *I* too wish you a long and happy retirement... you thoroughly deserve it...also my own special thank you for everything you've done over the years... no two ways about it, Joe, you're going to be missed... a lot."

At this juncture, a very much relieved Joe Riley felt free to make his way back to his seat next to Martha, who duly complimented him on his "nice little speech", while 'Pallisan' concluded this formal phase of the ceremony. "And now, ladies and gentlemen, I am reliably informed that the food is ready... and you, I'm sure, are ready for the food. So, if you would, please, be up-standing while Canon Ramsbottom says grace, then we can make our way into the marquee, where, I assure you, a feast awaits you. Thank you very much."

TAYLORS HAD indeed prepared a feast – for all the senses. As instructed by Nobbs, they had "pulled out all the stops", with many of the dishes so exotic that only the one or two *bon vivants* amongst the guests could recognise them. Moreover, everything inside the octagonal tent had been arranged with almost geometrical precision, ready for the photographer from the *Journal*.

When the first guests entered the marquee, there were audible gasps of wonderment at the centre-piece – an enormous pyramid of mouth-watering savouries gracing the central table. Nobbs had positioned himself strategically next to this, ostensibly to help 'serve the troops', but in reality, to avail the 'tea and bun' brigade of his superior gastronomic erudition. On the opposite side stood Amanda, herself a feast of elegance and exquisite beauty, kept the queue moving with charm and effortless efficiency, whereas her husband impeded the flow with detailed explanations about the piquancy of this particular comestible or the source and unique attributes of the other.

When it was Phil Evans's turn to choose from the plethora of delights, seeing Nobbs standing beside this culinary showpiece, impeccably accoutred and coiffured, reminded him of another self-publicist, Ramesses II, and Shelley's cruelly ironic caption: *My name is Ozymandias, King of Kings;/Look on my works, ye Mighty, and despair!*

"Right, Phil!" interrupted the latter-day Ozymandias, "*you've* been to France plenty, haven't you? Let's see if you can name this little beauty."

As it happened, Phil knew his Roquefort from his Bleu d'Auverne, and his Camembert from his Brie de Meaux, but on no account was he prepared to take part in Nobbs's petty mind-games.

"Oh... I don't know," he said at last.

"Go on, have a guess," persisted Nobbs.

"Looks like Dairy Lea to me," said Phil with a serious

face, "or it could be Philadelphia... they're very similar!"

"*Very* funny, Mr Evans... *very* funny," replied Nobbs... and then, after a slight pause, added, "F------- 'hell, Phil, have you noticed? If your hair line recedes any more, it'll end up as your arse line!"

"*Not* very funny, Mr Nobbs," countered Phil. "My hairline is as Nature intended... which is more than can be said of your waistline."

NOTWITHSTANDING any implicit or explicit criticism of Nobbs's 'do', by the end of the evening even the most cynical had to concede that all in all it had been an outstanding success. "Fair play," they said, "the fellow's made an effort... you've got to hand it to him... okay, he's obviously got the facilities and the means to lay on this sort of thing... but there's not many would have gone to this trouble for a bloke he'll hardly ever see again." Almost everyone made a point of thanking him, or Amanda, personally, with even Jack showing his appreciation of the "right gradely grub", wondering only if the baps had been "Taylors' own, or bought in"!

When Martha realised how late it was, she, too, joined the grateful throng. "I've *really* enjoyed myself, Mr Nobbs... it's been *very* interesting, and the food... well... that was top drawer." She was tempted to add, "You must come to me next," but quickly thought better of it. Amanda for morning coffee would be lovely... but Mr Nobbs? No, that would be a step too far... for now, at any rate.

As Martha turned to go, she overheard Nobbs asking his wife, "I wonder what happened to Fairclough... you know... the ageing biker with the gammy leg?"

"Mr Fairclough *certainly* said he was coming," replied Amanda, "maybe he got delayed, or something... but why do you have to be so unpleasant about people?"

At that moment, almost on cue, the Vincent's thunderous grunt was heard entering the Nobbses' drive. In fact, Frank *had* been delayed for a considerable time by a nasty accident near the Greyhound hotel on the East Lancashire road. At first, he had thought of giving the party a miss, and telephoning to apologise, but in the end, he decided to get it over and done with that night, and it was a good thing that he did.

Martha suddenly noticed that Joe had been gone some twenty minutes after telling her that he needed to "go and see a man about a dog". She was about to go looking for him when Frank appeared in the hallway apparently in no mood for niceties.

With all the cars blocking the drive, he had left his bike near the main gate, and as he was making his way towards the front door, he had heard strange noises coming from behind a large laurel bush. On further investigation, he found Joe Riley on all fours retching and heaving and seemingly very much the worse for drink. Now, Frank knew that Joe was not given to excessive imbibing, even when it was free. A gill of ale perhaps to be sociable, or a glass of sherry at a wedding usually sufficed. Frank deduced (correctly as it happened) that someone (and two or three names sprang to mind) had decided it would be "a good laugh to get J. R. plastered".

After turning his patient round into a sitting position, and ensuring he was in no imminent danger of missing out on his pension, Jack put his motor-cycling jacket round Joe's shoulders, and told him not to move until he came back. He then hobbled as quickly as he could through the great portals and into the entrance hall, where he saw Martha still inquiring about Joe's whereabouts.

"You'll find Mr Riley, Martha, slightly the worse for wear, sitting behind a bush near the main gate," said Frank with the faintest of smiles, "I'll be with you as soon as I can."

Then apart from one or two cursory nods, he ignored the assembled company and made straight for the bar area where Titchmarsh and his crony, Blackwell, the knight, according to Phil, with "two lovely eyes and chubby-cheek" were still supposedly minding the shop.

"Right, you two!" said Frank, as if addressing a pair of obstreperous third-formers, "you come with me... now!"

When Frank spoke in that special tone of his, no one dared say him nay. The two straightened up as well as their befuddled condition allowed them, and followed him out like a pair of guilty apple-scrumpers caught red-handed by the village constable.

"Well? said Frank, as soon as they were outside in the cool evening air, "did you, or did you not?"

"Did what?" bleated Titchmarsh.

"Do I have to spell it out? Did you, or did you not, spike Joe's drink? Come on... I haven't got all night."
Titchmarsh glanced up at his accomplice, and after a short pause whimpered, "Look... we just wanted Joe to have a good time... right... that's all... didn't mean any harm, like... wanted him to loosen up a bit, like everyone else... he's all right, in't he?

"Well, no, not exactly... in my book, spewing your guts up is not *all right*, especially when you're sixty-five years of age," replied Frank.

With Martha's help, Joe had managed to get to his feet, but was incapable of doing much else.

"Everything's going round and round," he groaned in a pronounced north-eastern accent, "must have eaten something, like... that foreign scran... too rich... O lordie, I'm ganna hoy up again. *Non solum mala*, Martha."

The 'foreign' contents of Joe's innards manifested themselves in their multi-coloured splendour on Nobbs's manicured lawn.

"Better out than in!" said Frank half humorously, "and how about you two... why don't you make yourselves useful instead of standing there... and give Mr Riley a lift up to the house... I'll go on ahead and explain to the hosts."

As he approached the house, Frank could hear Nobbs's saccharine tones in the hall 'good night-ing and god bless-ing' his departing guests, while outside on the drive, he saw a stylishly dressed young woman (whom he assumed to be Mrs Nobbs) bidding Martin and Wendy Shaw 'goodnight and a safe journey home'.

"I'm sorry I'm late, Mrs Nobbs," he said, "I presume you are Mrs Nobbs... my name's Fairclough... and it seems I missed a great party... a bad accident on the East Lancs, at least two fatalities, and we had wait for ages for the ambulances and the police to arrive."

"Oh, I *am* sorry, Mr Fairclough, how awful for you... no need for you to apologise... these things happen... the important thing is that *you're* all right... And yes, for my sins, I *am* Mrs Nobbs, though I hate being called that ... just 'Amanda' will do, or better still, 'Mandy'... pleased to meet you, anyway, Mr Fairclough... Richard did ask if anyone had seen you... there's still plenty of food left, if you're feeling peckish... oh, I think Richard's coming now."

"Hello, Frank... you made it then?" he said, with as much false- bonhomie as he could muster in the presence of his wife.

"Yes, just about," replied Frank, "there was this enormous pile-up on the East-Lancs... I *have* explained to your good lady."

Just at that moment, there was a slight kerfuffle, as the few remaining guests made way for the 'rescue party' entered the hallway with their 'loosened-up' casualty in tow.

"But, more to the point, Mr Nobbs," said Frank, making sure that everyone present could hear, "it seems your main guest has also met with an accident... courtesy of Messrs Blackwell and Titchmarsh here. Apparently, they wanted Mr Riley to 'loosen up... and have a good time'... I think that's what they called it...and it seems they succeeded... well, at least the first part... I doubt very much if Mr Riley had a good time doing his loosening up all over your lawn, though... so mind where you tread, everyone!"

"How are you feeling now, Joe?" inquired Nobbs anxiously. Look, lads, perhaps the garage might be better... it's had the sun on it all afternoon... so it'll be nice and warm in there... and it's got all mod cons... there's a comfy camp bed, if you fancy a lie-down, Joe, to clear your head."

"I'm... feeling... a little better now... Richard... thank you," said Joe, "I think I'll... live! Everyone's been... so kind... and Martha, bless her, has offered... to take me to

302

her place... I'll be all right...tomorrow... you see... my... old stomach... not accustomed to these rich, modern deli...delicacies... but so sorry...to spoil such a grand evening, and putting you all to such trouble. Oh, and thank you, Frank... only for you..."

But there was no sign of Frank, his exit having been as sudden as his entrance.

"Are *you* all right with that, Martha?" asked Nobbs, gratefully, "I'm afraid *I'm* well over the limit, myself... and I suspect Mandy is too."

With great relief, Joe soon found himself safely installed in the front passenger seat of Martha's Mini; and as it pulled away, Nobbs called after it, "Good night, Joe... one of us will pop round in the morning with the presents, okay? Sleep tight. And thanks very much, Martha. Good night and God bless."

JACK HIGGINBOTTOM's designated successor as Chairman of the Governors was his deputy, Martin Shaw, the dentist. Rumour had it that the local authority had tried to expedite events by imposing two county councillors as chairman and deputy. But their ruse had been rumbled at the last moment by Martha, and thwarted in no uncertain terms by Vicar Ramsbottom.

Besides, Martin had always been regarded as Jack's heir-presumptive, not only for his long and valuable service, but also as a highly respected member of the Netherbridge community. He and his wife, Wendy, were noted for their tireless charitable activities, especially the annual Netherbridge Fête in support of the Infirmary. This had been entirely their idea, and what began modestly as a 'one-off' Saturday 'fun afternoon' for families had now become an annual all-day event in August, attracting hundreds of visitors from across the county.

It was partly to accommodate the increased demands on his spare time that Martin had recently relinquished his NHS practice in Netherbridge and set up a private surgery in a spacious property owned by Nobbs in Wigan. The two had been close friends for many years, largely due to their shared interest in classic cars, but it was not generally known that they were now also business partners.

It was Martin, too, who had the thankless task of proposing his friend as a member of the Netherbridge Rotary Club. However, despite all Martin's tact and forbearance, Nobbs managed to become *persona non grata* at the Club within weeks of joining. He might have found this fairly non-judgmental bunch more amenable had *he* been less opinionated and confrontational. But claiming to find their "self-righteousness and false bonhomie arse-achingly irksome", he could not resist continually ruffling their collective feathers, often scandalizing meetings with inappropriate remarks and indecorous language.

Matters came to a head at one business lunch meeting shortly before the annual golf tournament, a prestigious event in the Club's calendar that usually raised more money than all the other activities put together. During a lull in the proceedings, Nobbs saw fit to air some personal thoughts on the subject.

"Mr President, and fellow-Rotarians," he began ponderously, "as most of you know, my golfing credentials are next to zero... although I did play a mean round of *crazy* golf once on the front in Southport!

"But seriously... as a life-long non-participant in this all-absorbing pastime which some people follow with quasi-religious fervour, this Club makes me feel like an infidel in a mosque. Don't get me wrong... I've nothing against golf *per se*, the *game*, that is. For all I know it could be the elixir of ever-lasting life, and should be available free on the NHS. No, fellow-Rotarians, it's not the golf... it's the people... the smug b------- it attracts... and the fuss and palaver that surrounds it. That's what gets my goat. Indeed, this Club might as well be an extension of the Netherbridge Golf Club."

When Nobbs sat down, an uncomfortable silence engulfed the room, broken eventually by the charismatic Monsignor Seamus O'Flaherty. As the Club's chaplain and one of its founder-member, he had always been anxious lest anyone defile its good name, and especially so after the distressing experience during his own presidency when the Club's treasurer helped himself to a substantial portion of the funds.

As a fellow-Dubliner, he had been a close friend of Mrs Davenport, and over the years had consumed many a goodly supper at *Elsinore*. Like many of his compatriots, he was a life-long devotee of Jameson whiskey, (or *spiritus frumenti*, as he preferred to call it) to which he attributed his gloriously stentorian voice. Not surprisingly, he had often tried to initiate "young George" to its "life-enhancing properties", while always insisting that "nothing should ever be added to whiskey, except more whiskey!"

After due observance of this maxim during that memorable lunch meeting, he took it upon himself to round on Nobbs about his discourtesy and inappropriate attitude. By-passing the chair, he began politely in his soft Irish lilt:

"Richard... if I may speak plainly... you have been a member of this Club now for several months... and as you are well aware... one of the cornerstones of the Rotary movement is good fellowship... without it, a club becomes a sterile collection of individuals, without a soul and without *esprit de corps*. Now... and I think I speak for the vast majority of members ... the stultiloquence you continually burden us with... and have done so again today... is not by any stretch of the imagination conducive to good fellowship.

"Furthermore, as a master at the Grammar School, you represent a fine and honourable institution. Your immediate predecessor as the School's representative was not only an incomparable headmaster but also an exemplary Rotarian. Comparisons may be odious, Richard, but the words, 'Hyperion' and 'satyr' spring to mind. But let that be.

"Not to put too fine a point on it, might I suggest that if you cannot desist from your uncivil ways, you do the decent thing, and... feck off back to where you belong."

Nobbs's inappropriate (albeit sometimes amusing) interjections had indeed become an all too regular feature of the meetings, often souring the atmosphere and threatening to poison Martin's year as president. Some members had even taken to casually placing an overcoat or a briefcase on an adjacent chair to avoid having to sit next to him, which in itself contravened the spirit of Rotary fellowship. On one occasion, Nobbs found himself with a table all to himself, and when a sympathetic soul on the next table invited him to join them, two of the other occupants promptly got up and moved away!

Hitherto, Martin had exercised inordinate restraint, as he watched this kind of puerile behaviour from the top table, but this latest gaffe had placed his friend well beyond the pale, although in a way, it had also made things much easier for him. He realised now that he had been deceiving himself all along, and that he should never have agreed to Joe's suggestion in the first place. He should have known that whatever Nobbs was he was not a 'club person', and he should have advised Joe accordingly, but he had always hoped that in time he might have mellowed, or that the other members might have learned to accept his idiosyncrasies.

Now, as Club President and Nobbs's friend, he felt doubly responsible, and knew that urgent action was required. Accordingly, later that afternoon, he called at Nobbs's house on the way home from Wigan, ostensibly to discuss the arrangements for the planned trip to Lake Windermere the following Saturday to try out his new boat. As it happened, Amanda had gone to Chester to visit her parents, so that Martin felt he could talk more freely, and after two or three cans of Heineken, he was sufficiently emboldened to broach the subject of the lunch time incident.

"Look, Rich, you and I have been mates for a very long time... and long may that continue. But I'll get straight to the point... you were right out of order this afternoon... You can smile as much as you like, but I don't think it was at all funny, right... Bloody hell... I was so embarrassed I didn't know where to put myself. In the end

I did nothing, and I felt bad about that too. Thank God for Father O'Flaherty, I say, for stepping in and saving my bacon. And I must say, Rich, I agreed with him every word... he was spot on. Let's be perfectly honest, in the short time you've been with us, I don't think you've really liked the Club, have you, nor what it stands for... and remember, I'm speaking as a mate now, right... your remarks today were totally uncalled for, and they were neither amusing nor constructive... you sounded like a big kid kicking off because he hasn't been picked for the team."

"Yea... yea... yea... Mart, I'm sorry, right... I'm sorry I've been a pain... I'm sorry I've been a disappointing Rotarian... but, most of all, I'm sorry I've let you down...

"Sometimes, I wonder why I come out with these things... but when I feel things aren't right, I just can't stop myself having a go. I *did* mean what I said today, you know... although you're probably right, I should have kept *schtum*.

"But, let's face it, Mart, present company excepted, of course, they're just a bunch of w------. You know that as well as I do, and to be honest, I don't see how *you* can put up with them. But... you're right... I shouldn't have said what I did.

"Huh! I *could* have got back at the b-------, you know, with another quote from *Hamlet*... there's plenty to choose from... but, I thought... well... what's the point...and in view of what you've just said, I'm glad now I didn't.

"I get the message, Mart, and, no doubt, it would be a great relief to everyone... you included... if I took the old fart's advice. Best part of his speech that... our Father tells it how it is. I bet his sermons are a bit lively too! Trouble is, Mandy... the earache... but never mind, eh... I'll knock something together... 'Mr President, owing to the pressure of work... blah... blah... and after much thought and consideration, blah... blah... it is with great... no, deep-felt... regret that I am obliged to resign my membership of this wonderful club. Would that do? Mandy can check it over, and type it up. And I promise you, Mr President, it will be in your hand before the end of the week."

Martin's relief was sullied a little by guilt that Nobbs had been so accommodating. It was out of character, but perhaps a wise reaction under the circumstances. Yes, even as a staunch member of the golfing fraternity, Martin did take his point about the 'clubbiness' and to some extent its 'smugness', although he had not thought of it before. It was the timing and the nature of his remarks that were ill-judged and inappropriate. If only the fellow could learn to keep his trap shut now and again, he mused winsomely, he'd go far.

"So, what time do you want me here on Saturday?" asked Martin, the lunch time gaffe already forgotten.

"Is eight o'clock too early for you? Let's make an early start for once, and beat the weekend rush."

"Fine by me," said Martin, "eight o'clock it is."

Chapter Thirteen

Apart from family and close friends, few would have considered 'Gentleman' Jim Whittaker as 'headmaster material', and especially one that would be overseeing a major building programme during his incumbency. However, his modest and somewhat bookish persona belied that he was as comfortable discussing designs and schedules of works with building contractors as he was evaluating Emperor Constantine's political legacy with his Upper Sixth.

Furthermore, Jim was nobody's fool. Even without Jack Higginbottom's backing, he refused to be "bullied by Preston", insisting that while NGS was NGS, the mandarins' role would be purely advisory. But most surprisingly, he quickly metamorphosed from a seasoned academic into a shrewd manager with a strong sense of fair play and a genuine desire to help others, often at some cost to himself. For these reasons, he soon gained the respect of both his staff and the pupils.

Like his immediate predecessor, he abhorred change for change's sake, meddling for no good reason, as he put it, with something that had served its purpose admirably for generations. In his inaugural address to the parents, he made it clear that if he maintained the School's enviable academic and sporting reputations as Mr Riley had done, he could retire a contented man. Indeed, in normal times his role could well have been largely titular. But these were not normal times. Several of the more experienced masters were expediting retirement, while many of the younger ones were seeking posts in the private sector – "anything to avoid the horrors of the dreaded "c-word". Thus, for the first time in its history, NGS's exalted standards seemed in jeopardy, and would have been doubly so without his firm and sanguine leadership.

Actually, some of the newer governors had advocated appointing a young and enthusiastic outsider with fresh ideas, someone "with vision, who would also be 'in post' ready for the transition from *grammar* to *comprehensive*". But older heads had prevailed. "That might be something for the future," they said, "and why gamble with an unknown outsider when we have an esteemed and experienced insider waiting in the wings?"

Indeed, Jim Whittaker did have impressive credentials, both academically and militarily, although very few knew about the latter. After leaving Cambridge in 1933 with a congratulatory First in history and a rugby half blue, he taught at Wellington School in Somerset until May 1940, when he volunteered for military service with the Somerset Light Infantry, and was commissioned into the 10th Battalion. In 1942 this battalion was converted into the 7th Parachute Regiment, which played key roles in the Normandy Landings, as it did later in the Battle of the Bulge and the Rhine crossings. During the first of these encounters, Jim's platoon came under heavy shell and mortar fire for long periods, but he sustained his men's morale with unceasing cheerfulness, and on more than one occasion rescued wounded comrades while under fire. He was awarded an immediate Military Cross in recognition of his services in this campaign, the citation paying special tribute to "his leadership under extreme duress, his courage and his resolve".

THIRTY YEARS on, Jim's leadership and resolve were called upon again, not least "to put Herr Nobbs back in his box", as he put it one morning to Martha over a cup of coffee! It was not something he relished, he confessed, nor one to shirk. Joe Riley had not made things easy for him, he mused, by giving the fellow too much power and freedom, but things would have to change.

In the first instance, Jim planned to increase his teaching load. That would diminish his status and afford him less time and fewer opportunities to "meddle in matters managerial". Secondly, responsibility for the time-table would revert to the Headmaster. During Joe's final year, apparently, Nobbs had been allowed to award himself as many non-teaching periods as he wished, thereby undermining the morale of other colleagues struggling on almost a full time-table, while also running large departments and organising extra-curricular activities.

However, just as Jim was mentally preparing himself for a heated conversation with his gadfly, events overtook him in the form of a letter from County Hall. Martha had noticed how this might be a neat solution to "Mr Whittaker's problem", and had placed it at the top of the day's mail, lest it found itself hurtling towards the nearest waste-paper basket before being properly read!

It was addressed to the Head teacher [sic] of Netherbridge Grammar School inviting him to nominate "a suitably qualified member of your staff... to take advantage of an innovative County initiative to study for a Master's degree at Manchester University in *Pastoral Care, Guidance and Counselling...* all costs to be borne by the local education authority".

Without so much as a glance at the rest of the mail, Jim rushed across to Martha's office, still clutching the precious letter in both hands. She had never seen him so animated, and with assumed innocence, listened patiently while he explained how he intended to persuade one *very* suitably qualified member of his staff to accept this wonderful, once-in-a-lifetime opportunity. Indeed, he could think of no one else remotely as suitably qualified!

In reality, of course, Jim belonged to the same school of thought as Joe Riley on fashionable educational ideas, especially those emanating from "across the pond", but just for this once he was prepared to sacrifice his principles for an eminently greater good!

"So, Martha, when you have a moment," he concluded, "perhaps you would kindly ask our suitably qualified colleague to come and see me at the end of the day, and we'll take it from there."

"Certainly, Mr Whittaker," she replied, barely able to keep a straight face. "Actually, he's free now, so I expect he'll be in his Stock room. If you like, I could give him the message right away?"

313

"Good thinking, Martha, *sicut et praesens tempus*!"

The much-anticipated meeting at four o'clock turned out to be something of an anti-climax. No sooner than Jim had broached the matter of the secondment, he realised that Nobbs was already fully cognisant of the project, having been briefed by one of his contacts in Preston some days earlier. Nobbs explained to his incredulous headmaster how the local authority was planning to introduce Guidance and School Counselling throughout all its secondary schools, and was looking for one or two forward-looking establishments to become "pilots".

"I appreciate, of course, Jim, that you'll have your own ideas on these matters, and, indeed, may already have someone in mind, but if you find yourself stuck for a volunteer, you know me, I'm always more than happy to help out."

"Well, I haven't given it much thought yet," replied Jim nonchalantly, "I only had the letter this morning and to be quite honest, I'm not sure it's relevant here... we're not that kind of school. But, there again, if *you're* really interested, and prepared to give it a go, I wouldn't stand in your way. You never know, this could well be the future... and to get in on the ground floor could stand you, or anyone else, in good stead!"

"I'll take that as a 'yes' then," replied Nobbs eagerly. As a matter of fact, I have already discussed it with Mandy, in case an offer was made, and, of course, as usual she was very supportive. Bloody 'ell, this is exactly what I've been banging on about. This school is just a results factory... exams and sport... and as long as the monkeys keep performing... and we send a goodly batch up to Oxbridge every year, everything's hunky-dory.

314

Think about it, Jim, even the word *master* suggests mastery of a *subject*... the pupil's well-being is taken for granted. Well, I'm afraid, come the comprehensive revolution, all that's got to change. We never ask these kids if they've got any *personal* problems, anything worrying them... which is just as well, I suppose, because most of these fellows wouldn't have a clue what to do, anyway. As far as they're concerned, that's the parents' job. But then, I thought we were supposed to be *in loco parentis*, and in my book that means the *whole* boy, not just his brain. To coin a phrase, what shall it profit a boy if he gains *fifty* 'O' levels, and loses his *joie-de-vivre*? And anyway, the way I see it... though I know I'll get no thanks for saying it... many of these lads would be better off leaving school at fifteen, and getting apprenticeships. The country's crying out for bright engineers and businessmen. But oh, no... once they're on that academic treadmill, they're never asked if they want to jump off. If you ask me, a lot of it is just parental pride... social climbing... dads ego-tripping on their kids' success. I hear it all the time, 'I left school at fourteen, tha knows, and went down 'pit to help put food on 'table. Well, ma Vinnie won't be doing that... he's going to the uni-*vers*-ity like the doctor's son down t'road' ".

"Yes, very interesting, Mr Nobbs, very interesting," interrupted Jim at last, "Sounds like this pastoral care... initiative... could be just the ticket for you. I may not agree with *everything* you say, but there's something appealing about a man defending his beliefs with passion and conviction. From what I understand, the secondment is scheduled for one year, starting next September. So, if your mind is quite made up, I'll put your name forward, and make the necessary arrangements. Leave it with me, Mr Nobbs... if I hear anything in the meantime, I'll let you know."

NO SOONER than Nobbs had left Jim's office, Martha hurried across to congratulate her boss. Events had undoubtedly played into his hand, but he had obtained an outcome that would displease no one, least of all the *mafiosi* of Preston; and, of course, there would be very few tears shed at NGS. She also imagined Dr Davenport looking down from above with that ironic smile of his, whilst over in the boiler room Alf Newby observed that this would be the first time since WW2 that the School was a "Nobbs-free zone"! Indeed, no one under the age of fifty could remember the place without his intimidating presence.

With Nobbs's secondment now almost a certainty, Jim felt free to concentrate on the things he thought he was paid to do. He was already planning for the following year, and looking forward to devising his very first time-table, ironically on Nobbs's newly-purchased commercial time-table builder; and if he could persuade the Governors to improve the staffing ratio marginally, he was also keen to introduce 'setting' in the third and fourth forms for English and mathematics, in order to refine the crude, 'one-size-fits-all' system of 'streaming' which had prevailed at the School from time immemorial. He also had plans to broaden the curriculum, especially on the technical side. In his view, Dr Davenport had certainly been looking in the right direction, but sadly had not been able to carry things through. If only the 'technical' curriculum had enjoyed parity with the 'academic', Jim

316

believed that NGS would now be a national beacon of excellence, not merely a regional one.

The frenetic coming and going along the M6 had also slowed to a trickle since Joe Riley's departure, to be replaced by the brooding menace of a 'management takeover' registering its presence through a steady flow of 'circular' missives from County Hall. These Martha filed away in a clandestine filing system she called "Rough Beast", and kept them strictly out of Jim's way, unless, of course, there was something he needed to know about, such as the latest on Nobbs's secondment. But much of the correspondence was indeed what they used to refer to at Bletchley as "bumf", and she mischievously categorised it as such in her private system!

One morning towards the end of the Summer Term of 1972, with Jim engrossed in his coloured buttons and grids, Martha brought him an important letter to read over morning coffee. It was a personal invitation from the Director of Education, no less, "to attend a meeting at County Hall together with your Chair of Governors, your designated Area Education Officer, and a member of the County Architects Department to have preliminary discussions on the future enhancement of the fabric at Netherbridge School" (sic). Jim had already heard rumours from Martin Shaw that a major building programme was imminent, and that Phase 1 could well start as early as September 1972. When he considered all the noise and disruption this would entail over many months, he secretly wished it had not happened so soon.

"Hah, that's very kind of them, Martha!" exclaimed Jim, "we've been designated as a future centre of academic excellence. I thought we were that already, and *have* been long before these slick whippersnappers were even a twinkle. *But*, we mustn't be ungracious, or look a gift-horse in the mouth, what! Let's see what they have to say, shall we? Our science labs *do* look a little bit long in the tooth... and some modernisation of the toilets wouldn't come amiss. I'll give Martin a ring this afternoon. Oh, and Martha, when we do go, I'd like *you* to be there as well."

SINCE THE mid-1950s, Jim and his wife had always spent the first three weeks of their summer 'vac' together with his brother and family in a cottage he had bought at Lion-sur-Mer, in Normandy. The little village still held a special place in his heart after all those years, and he had many old friends there. Indeed, Jim had often spoken longingly of living there most of the year when he retired.

But the summer holiday of 1972 was very different. The French sojourn had to be cancelled, and apart from one coach-trip to York, almost every day was spent at school discussing the proposed building plans with some 'important' people from Preston, and negotiating the fine details with a cadre of architects and contractors. But for all the inconvenience, Jim found this novel experience surprisingly stimulating, which was just as well, because for the foreseeable future this was what would be occupying most of his time.

Apologies from on high about "unavoidable disruption" proved grossly understated, as the campus almost overnight was transformed into a noisy building site, and everyone expected to show forbearance and "work around it". At first, there was much muttering and sighing in the Common Room at the 'industrial language' striving to be heard above the perpetual clanking of pile-drivers and the growling of JCBs; but thanks to Jim's mediation skills, disputes were generally resolved without excessive bloodshed.

But there was one matter on which even Jim himself would not compromise. The new buildings would indisputably be a fine thing, but actually, *they* were for the future; for the boys currently intent on their 'O' and 'A' levels, this was *their* time, and on no account would he allow their progress to be jeopardised. Second only to his pupils' welfare, of course, was that of the masters, for Jim had never forgotten his old C.O.'s advice when he took command of his first platoon in early 1944: "Always look after your men, James... then *they* will look after you." His more recent model of this principle, of course, was George Davenport, who had taken it to almost saintly levels. Whilst Jim knew that he was no George Davenport – there would only ever be one *Gaffer* – he also knew from first-hand experience what a difference it makes when a leader puts his troops first.

ONE MORNING during the 1972 October half-term, with Jim engrossed in further time-table adjustments to minimise disruption, there was an unusually heavy knock on his office door. With Martha away in Aberdyfi, nursing her Aunt Hilda after yet another fall, Jim had to attend to the unexpected visitor himself.

As he rose from his chair the door opened, heralded by Taff Jenkins's unmistakable growl, "Anyone at home?"

"Well, I'll be damned," exclaimed Jim, as he reached forward to shake his old friend's hand with both of his, "this *is* a pleasant surprise... *you've* been making yourself scarce!"

"Yes, I know, I know... I've been meaning to pop in, but you know how it is with us retired folk... not enough hours in the day... as you'll find out for yourself one day!"

"Take a pew, Taff... that's right, sit in George's chair. Better late than never, I suppose. Can I offer you a cup of tea?"

"No, I've just had one, Jim... thanks all the same... besides, I'm having a bit of trouble with the waterworks at the moment, and the doc's told me to cut down on the tea! I don't know, no smokes, no tea... it'll be no beer next."

"That's a nuisance for you. Anyway, how's Liz, is she keeping well?"

"Yes, Liz is fine, except for the old ar-thur-itis. She's popped over to Martha's this morning... promised to keep an eye on the house while she's away. Knowing her, she'll probably find some jobs to do while she's there. And how are things with you, Jim?"

"Oh, can't complain, you know. It's a bit lonely here without Martha, and I've been feeling a bit down since we lost poor Monty... his kidneys finally packed in. He would have been 21 this summer... but we didn't want him to suffer. But I must say the vet was very good, and I said to Mary, if *my* life ever became unbearable, that's how I'd like to go too... fading gently away, and leaving all your pains and troubles behind."

"That's a good innings for a cat, Jim... but I know exactly how you feel. Do you know, I cried like a baby the day our Pero died, knowing I'd never hear his little bark again. And that last look he gave me before the needle went in still haunts me. He was a smashing pal...

especially after my accident. Will you get another cat, Jim?"

"Oh, I don't know... not just yet, anyway, though Mary would like one, I think. The thing is, we're both getting older, and the next one might outlive us. And that wouldn't be fair on the little thing."

"Anyway, what it's like trying to run a school on a building site?

"Well, it's different! I don't get much time to myself... but we're winning, I think, and I'm sure it'll all be worth it in the end. And in a funny sort of way, you know, I'm quite enjoying it... makes a nice change, dealing with the real world, for a change."

"I wonder what the Gaffer would have made of it all!"

"Oh, I think he would have been delighted, especially with the new labs."

"I know he would've been chuffed about *one* thing! How the bloody hell did you manage to pull that one off, Jim? I nearly wet myself laughing when Jack announced it one night. Everybody thought he was taking the piss."

"Oh, I can't claim any credit for it, really... it just happened... all I did was oil the wheels. He's on a course in Manchester on pastoral care and counselling, or something. It's all the rage, apparently, and come the brave new world, every school will have to have a School Counsellor'!"

"What's that when it's at home?"

"Oh, don't ask, Taff! But from what little I've read, it's some kind of social worker... to support pupils with emotional problems. Anyway, your former colleague has been given a sabbatical to learn all about it. So I'm not making too many waves!"

321

"Bloody hell, Jim, I've heard it all now! Pastoral care! I thought that was what vicars did. Didn't *we* care for the pupils, then? Sounds like a load of bullsh-t to me. And anyway, even if it is a good idea, like what a *padré* did in the Army, I suppose... someone you could share your problems with in confidence... *he* is the very last person on this earth I'd have doing it. I ask you... the way he used to treat them lads... I could hear it through the wall... bloody disgraceful, it was... I should have intervened, really. Do you know, I think he actually enjoyed humiliating them, especially the really brainy ones who weren't too clever with their hands. And in my experience, leopards do not change their spots. No, for that kind of job you need loads of patience... and someone who actually *likes* kids... not a nasty, foul-mouthed bully."

"Well, as long as he doesn't come back here!" replied Jim wistfully.

"Anyway, I hear you've found a good replacement for him."

"Yes, and that's another stroke of good luck. Things have gone pretty well for me so far, haven't they? The Vicar rang me up one afternoon out of the blue... it was the night before the Cup Final... he said he'd found someone who might be a possibility for the Craft vacancy. Well, it turned out that he was not only a trained draughtsman but had also done shop-fitting with a firm from Halifax. But unfortunately, he'd had a breakdown after a divorce, and was currently out of a job. Well, we interviewed him along with two others, and he was head and shoulders above them. So we gave him a chance, and if he fits the bill, we'll offer it to him permanently."

"Sounds ideal, Jim, and if he only knows how to sharpen a chisel, he'll be improvement on the last one! But seriously it's about time those expensive machines George bought were fired up again. It's been a disgrace them lying idle all them years."

"And another thing I like about him," said Jim, "he never raises his voice, and he's got those boys eating out of his hand... it's a bit like the good old days again! I do hope his health holds up, because he's a most likeable fellow and keen to make a success of things."

JUST AS Taff was leaving, Jim's telephone rang. It was Martha from a public phone box in Aberdyfi, and she sounded distressed.

"What's wrong, Martha?"

"Sorry to disturb you, Mr Whittaker... but... it's... Aunt Hilda," sobbed Martha, "she passed away this morning... I sat up all night with her, and at about six o'clock she said she felt very tired and would like to have a little nap... so I went downstairs to make myself a cup of tea... but when I got back up... I knew... and she never..."

"Oh, I am sorry, Martha... dreadful for you... now, listen, you look after yourself... and don't you worry about the School... we'll manage... you take as long as you need, right?"

"Oh, thank you, Mr Whittaker. The doctor's just been, and... damn, the money's running out... I'll... ring you again this evening."

Jim had been wondering when his good luck would falter. Everything had been falling uncannily into place. First, Nobbs, and his replacement... then, the "most satisfactory" examination results... matched by the equally "satisfactory" results on the playing fields. The First Cricket XI had won the County Championship for the second year running; two members of the Junior Cross-country team had come first and third in the All-England Schools Championships; and the First XV had only lost one game in the '71-72 season, and that very narrowly to a much bigger and heavier Manchester Grammar School side. (Jim still took a keen interest in the rugby teams, and always found time to help out with coaching sessions.) Finally, and most unexpectedly, two members of First Football XI had been selected to represent English Schoolboys during the '72-73 season. Indeed, despite all the menace looming ahead, a strange spirit of optimism permeated the School; and much of this was credited to Jim's gentle but firm leadership.

Nevertheless, even though this was a relatively minor setback, it was something he could have done without. Like his predecessors, he relied heavily, perhaps too heavily, on Martha, and whilst some things, like the university references, could wait, he might have to undertake some of the irksome form-filling himself. But he was determined not to put any pressure on Martha to return, even if it meant asking his Mary to come in and resurrect some of her long-neglected stenographic skills.

MEANWHILE in the School of Education at Manchester University, Nobbs was busy ingratiating himself with anyone who seemed to matter, especially his tutor, Dr Alice Toogood, a visiting professor of Educational Psychology from Wisconsin-Madison University.

Her intense passion for all things 'pastoral', and abhorrence of all things 'selective' were captivating a whole generation of young northern would-be 'educators' into the *a la mode*, pupil-centred style of education, while at the same time offering much-needed hope to a bunch of middle-aged dead-enders.

The neutral observer might have deduced that the chief goal of education in the Toogoodian universe was the promotion of *happiness.*

"When a father asks his child," the good doctor declaimed, looking directly at Nobbs, who was, or seemed to be, listening intently in the front row, 'what did you *learn* in school today?' he is patently asking the wrong question. Children are not just units of humanity to be sorted and slotted into categories. Nor are they raw material to be processed and assembled on a production line before being packaged and marketed like fridges or cars. No, my friends, in case we forget, children are *human beings*, who, like you and me, are equipped with complex emotions, as well as minds and bodies. And you don't need me to tell you that an *unhappy* child will be hard put to learn anything in school.

"And this is where you guys come in. Children's emotions are priceless, that's a given, and they should *never ever* be sacrificed on the altar of academic endeavour, as happens all too often in the English grammar school, with its "stiff upper lip" and "grin and bear it" culture.

"But as School Counsellors, you can be key players in rectifying this imbalance. For instance, students can sometimes feel so bad about a personal issue that they are too embarrassed to tell their tutors, or even their parents. As counsellors, *you* provide the sympathetic and non-judgemental ear into which they can unburden their anxieties in complete and absolute confidence, and help them come to terms with or resolve their issues, so that, hopefully, normal education can be resumed."

Nobbs was quite taken with the blonde and buxom American with more than a passing resemblance to Betty Hutton in *Annie Get Your Gun*, and flattered himself into believing that his feelings were reciprocated, especially when she offered to help him with the reading list for his first dissertation over coffee in the Students' Union.

Having recently celebrated his fiftieth birthday, he seemed to be undergoing what is now often referred to as 'a mid-life crisis'. Among other symptoms, he had begun to experience bouts of despondency that life was passing him by. Certainly, he had much to be pleased about: a comfortable home, a large property portfolio, a stable of prestigious motor-cars, a wardrobe fit for a prince – and, of course, a beautiful wife. Yet, there were two painful gaps in his trophy cabinet, both of which, sadly, seemed to retreat ever further with each anniversary.

But, for now, his morning *tète-a-tètes* with Dr Alice were sufficient unto the day, and, so he fantasised, hers. But in reality, they were mere opportunities for *her* to expatiate on such abstractions as "stratification and mobility in the American high school" to a captive audience, while he contemplated the stratification and mobility of the contents of her blouse.

"So, tell me, Alice," he ventured once, arousing from his reverie, and to drag her briefly away from sociology and education, "where exactly in Wisconsin did you say you came from?"

"I don't recall saying, Mr Nobbs!" she teased, "but since you ask, I was born and reared in Madison, and still live there during the week... I stay with my parents, not far from the airport."

"Are your parents educators too?"

"No! Mom's a nurse, and Dad, well, he's retired now, but before that he worked in the Air Traffic Control at Madison International."

"And at the weekends... where do you live then?"

"Hey! What *is* this? Why do you need to know?   I'm your course tutor, remember? If anything, it is I who should be asking *you* these questions. But, if you must know, I live at Mineral Point... a small mining town, about 50 miles west of Madison."

"Do you live on you own, then? I mean, at the weekends."

After a significant pause, Alice replied, "My partner dropped out of college, and became an antiquarian, specialising in the American Civil War... we have a large emporium in the town centre with an apartment above the shop... it's like an armoury... full of guns and rifles and countless items of military uniforms and equipment... oh, and a bull mastiff. So, I'm well protected at the weekends!"

"Interesting," said Nobbs drily, "must be nice when your work is also your hobby. I must come over there and see it one day."

"Well, Richard, thank you for the coffee. But if you'll excuse me, I've got a lecture to deliver in ten minutes... and *you've* got a dissertation to write... remember? So, there we must leave it, I'm afraid. Enjoy the rest of your day."

"Thank you... and you too, Dr Toogood!" he replied, with more than a *soupçon* of sarcasm.

Chapter Fourteen

As promised, and much to everyone's relief, the noisiest and most disruptive part of the building programme was over by Easter 1973, which meant that public examinations could proceed relatively unhindered during May and June.

On the last Friday before the Whitsun holiday, Jim Whittaker called the last full Staff meeting to be held in the Masters' Room. After thanking everyone for their patience and cooperation during a difficult year, he was still hopeful that that year's crop of candidates would surprise everyone, and much of that would be the masters' reward for their stupendous efforts in the unavoidably trying circumstances. He added that in his experience, adversity, far from dampening the spirit, often brought out the best in people, as they themselves had demonstrated so admirably that year.

The next few months, he went on, would see rapid progress in the building programme, so that some departments could look forward to moving into the new block as early as the Michaelmas half-term break. He himself would miss many features of the old building, not least that very Common Room, which had so many stories of its own to tell, and of course his own little office, but he, like everyone else, would have to guard against the allure of nostalgia.

Finally, while thanking departing colleagues for their hard work and wishing them well in their future careers, he was confident that those who were staying would not regret their decision. He stressed that there were exciting times as well as huge challenges ahead, and there would be opportunities too for those who were prepared to adapt and exploit the changes.

IN THE EVENT, the class of '73 did not disappoint. But like Joe before him, and the *arch*-worrier before that, Jim had also had doubts right up until the envelopes were opened. He knew that there were two or three outstanding scholars in the cohort, but he never expected to find that that year's 'A' level results had only been bettered on some half-dozen occasions since the Second World War!

And so, while he was sitting back in his chair, deservedly luxuriating in a warm glow of pride in the old School, Martha brought in the morning coffee, but this time accompanied by a plateful of her special Welsh cakes, instead of the usual Custard Creams or Chocolate Digestives.

"Oh, thank you, thank you, Martha! My goodness, I'm having my cake and eating it too! They look delicious!"

"Well I had a hunch the results would warrant a little celebration!" she replied.

"And they do, Martha, they do... and what about young Nagy, eh? He certainly pulled out all the stops, what! Look at this, Martha, four A grades: Physics, Chemistry, Biology – and, wait for it, Art. He can certainly take up his place at the Liverpool Vet School now. Or even the Art School, if he so wished, what! Wonderful! I must call on his parents later to congratulate them, because they've been so supportive throughout."

SEVEN YEARS earlier, and barely a week before his tragic death, Dr Davenport had also called on the Nagys, a hard-working family of Hungarian refugee immigrants living temporarily on the notorious Brookdale estate.

Bewildered by his son's failure in the NGS entrance exam that year, Mr Nagy had telephoned the School claiming that the result did not reflect his boy's true abilities, and if someone else could interview him, they would surely see this for themselves. When Martha told Dr Davenport about this unusual request, he decided that it would be best if he interviewed the boy himself, and this time on his home territory.

After the initial pleasantries, it took Dr Davenport only a matter of minutes to establish that the parents' concerns were fully justified. Discounting some difficulties with the English language, Fabio demonstrated high levels of arithmetical skills and logical thinking. He was also blessed with a lively imagination; but what appealed to Dr Davenport most of all was his artistic flair, especially in one so young. When he asked him to make a sketch of a scene or person that had caught his attention recently, he was amazed at both the uncanny likeness and the sly humour the boy managed to capture in a quickly drawn cartoon of a tall, well-dressed gentleman sharing a sofa with a miniscule ragamuffin!

"Yes, Mr Nagy, you were quite right to get in touch with us, and I'm sorry for the anxiety we have caused you. Fabio definitely deserves his place at the Grammar School, and I am sure that one day he will make us all very proud of him. Leave it with me, Mr Nagy."

Sadly, having other, more pressing, things on his mind, Dr Davenport never managed to discuss the interview with anyone, not even Martha, nor did he leave any record of his intention to reverse the selection board's decision. Consequently, when September came, poor Fabio, along with all the other 'failures' in his year, found himself herded into Manchester Road Secondary Modern School, where all too soon he became something of a rebel, wasting his time and talents plastering walls and blackboards with cruelly satirical cartoons of the teachers he disliked, and ingratiating himself with older reprobates from the Brookdale estate.

Towards the end of his first year, when all disciplinary measures had failed to curb his highly original modes of dissent, the Headmaster wrote to the Nagys inviting them to come in "to discuss moving Fabio to another establishment, because clearly he was not making the most of the excellent opportunities available to him at Manchester Road".

Consequently, out of sheer desperation, Mr Nagy summoned enough courage to telephone NGS a second time about his son. On that particular afternoon both the Headmaster and the Senior Master, Jim Whittaker, were attending the funeral of a former First XV captain, who had died suddenly of an unknown heart condition while undergoing intensive training to become an officer in the Royal Marines.

But as luck would have it, who should walk in as the telephone rang but Frank Fairclough, and Martha asked *him* to talk to the gentleman. In broken English, Mr Nagy managed to convey to Frank the gist of Dr Davenport's intentions when he came to their house to interview their boy. He realised he should have done something about it sooner, but wondered if it was not too late to speak to someone now. With his natural sympathy for the underdog, Frank immediately agreed to look into the matter, and discuss it with the Headmaster as soon as he returned.

Being preoccupied with more general matters, Joe asked Frank if he would like to deal with the problem himself, promising his full backing on whatever course of action he decided to take.

Frank, being Frank, visited the Nagys that evening, his growling *Vincent* making a much greater impression on the denizens of Bird Street than Dr Davenport's *Hercules* had done! As he rang the doorbell of No 57, he could hear the closing bars of the *Coronation Street* theme tune, suggesting that his timing at least was well judged; but when he explained who he was, and what he had come about, Mr Nagy had to apologise for his initial wariness, because he had not expected a biker in a T-shirt and leather jacket.

But two or three mugs of Hungarian coffee later, Frank and Fabio *père* were shouting excitedly, re-living the heroic deeds of Ferenk Puskas, Hidegkuti *et al* when the great Hungarian team trounced England 6-3 at Wembley in November 1953 in front of 105,000 spectators, one of whom, strangely enough, happened to be the young Frank Fairclough, then renting a student's flat within earshot of the stadium.

"NEVER MIND the paperwork, Fabio," said Frank at last, a little impatiently, "Dr Davenport was a good friend of mine... and if he gave you his word, that's good enough for me, and I shall make sure it's honoured.

"And as for you, young man," he added, turning to Fabio *fils*, who had been listening intently and staring up at this strange man whose shoulders seem to get broader by the minute, and whose hands were three times as big as his Dad's, "I want you to promise me and your parents that you will work hard and always do your very best at the Grammar School. Do you promise?"

"Yes, sir," said the boy nervously, "I... promise."

"Good... so that's settled, then," replied Frank casually, yet with a solemn finality that defied any future vacillation. "Your Dad tells me you've wasted a whole year at that other school, messing about. Well, there'll be none of that from now on... do you understand? You'll start at the Grammar School in September... but... your *education* starts now... immediately... right?"

"Yes, sir," said the boy, realising that there was definitely no turning back now.

"So, first thing tomorrow, I'll go and see Mr Longworth, your headmaster, to arrange the transfer... and then, if it's all right with your parents, I'll come round and pick you up at eleven o'clock. I'd like you to meet some of *my* friends. But perhaps not the kind of friends you're used to!"

"Yes... sir."

"Well, it's been very nice meeting you both," said Frank, shaking their hands very firmly; and then to the boy, "Tomorrow, at eleven... right?"

"Yes, sir."

When Frank emerged from the house, a bunch of hoodlums had gathered around the *Vincent*, but as he drew nearer, they dissipated one by one sheepishly without a word. From now on, Bird Street would be seeing and hearing a good deal more of Frank Fairclough and his unusual mode of transport, because he too had made a pledge that evening, to take personal responsibility from now on for "Young Nagy's" education – in memory of his dear friend.

The following day, promptly at eleven, Frank called at No 57 again, as promised, and found his charge all scrubbed up and ready for his exciting new beginning. Once the spare helmet was fastened on the boy's head, the 1000 cc engine grunted into life and pulled away, leaving a trail of mothers spying from behind net curtains, and one anxious, but very grateful, lady gazing in disbelief from her doorstep.

Many a time in later years, Fabio recounted his Damascene moment, and how he had lain awake all night wondering what he had meant by, "not the kind of friends you're used to". He never imagined what a close bond he was to form with a succession of these 'friends' as they came and went during his seven glorious years at NGS, nor that it would be such friends as these – the frail, the feeble and the flawed – that would eventually constitute his life's work. Like countless others before and after him, Fabio never missed an opportunity to tell the world how much he owed to his life-long friend, Mr Fairclough.

GOOD A-LEVEL results were not the only good news Jim received that week. Early on the Saturday morning his telephone rang while he was still in his dressing gown.

"Good morning, James, and how are we this fine morning?"

"Oh, hello, Martin... mustn't complain... what can I do for you?"

"Sorry to disturb you so early, but I thought you'd like to know that Richard Nobbs is going to be offered one of these new admin jobs: 'Co-ordinator of Counselling and Pastoral Care for South Lancashire'.

"That sounds like a very big job," said Jim, winking at Mary.

"Yes, they do seem to be expecting a lot of one person: 'with responsibility', it says here, 'for setting up the first of a chain of Strategic In-service Training Centres, and to develop courses for continuing professional development in the field of Pastoral Care.' Anyway, I'm sure he'll tell you all about it when he's got everything in writing."

"Well, thank you for letting me know, Martin. I'm very pleased for him. It's just what he's been hoping for, and I'm sure he will be very good at it," replied Jim, with another wink at his wife.

"Yes, *I'm* pleased for Richard too. He could do with a change. I know he can be an awkward cuss at times, but he means well, and over the years he *has* been a loyal servant of the Grammar School. He tells me they were very impressed with him at Manchester, especially his dissertations... and I know they've got a lot of time for him up in Preston. When you add everything up... his business experience... working with kids, organizational skills, and now this bang up-to-date training and knowledge on top, he's ideally qualified to take on the challenge. And between you and me, looking further ahead, he could be useful for us too... I mean, as a link with Preston, especially during the transition."

As soon as Martin Shaw had finished his eulogy, Jim could not wait to make a couple of phone calls himself.

"Good morning, Martha, how are you today? I think another batch of Welsh cakes is in order!"

"Oh, hello Mr Whittaker... that sounds interesting. I wonder why."

"Well, I'll tell you, Martha... a most welcome piece of news... according to Martin Shaw, our friend won't be coming back in September, after all... he's been offered a 'plumb job' with Lancashire Education Committee... organising pastoral care, or something... right up his street... what!"

"Yes, that certainly is interesting news!" echoed Martha, "I had a feeling we'd seen the last of him... for the time being, at any rate."

"What do you mean, 'for the time being'? I hope you're not going to ruin my weekend with another of your devastating predictions!"

"Well, you never know with the likes of Mr Nobbs!"

"Does that mean we should keep our ammunition dry?

"Something like that!" giggled Martha.

"Well, at least we can block off his retreat by filling the Craft post... soonest."

"I'll see to it first thing Monday morning, Mr Whittaker."

MEANWHILE, Martha had a myriad other things to

attend to, not least getting ready for her friend, Amanda Nobbs.

Ever since Joe Riley's retirement party, she and Amanda had developed a close friendship, and the 'Saturday morning coffee' had become a regular event in their diaries, an opportunity for keeping abreast of the latest tittle-tattle and sharing confidences. Accordingly, when Jim rang Martha about Nobbs's new appointment, she was obliged to feign surprise, because she already knew!

Despite their age difference, the two women had much in common. Both were strong-minded, intelligent and very capable women who had espoused relatively submissive roles in a male dominated world. They were also fairly private people, who felt they could trust each other not to divulge secrets. Amanda was the only person Martha had ever told how intensely she still felt the loss of her beloved Tom; and how when he died, it seemed that her ability to entrust any other man with her feelings had also died. Likewise, only Martha knew about the Nobbses' incipient marital difficulties.

Unless Nobbs was away, these *tête-a-têtes* usually took place at *Elsinore*, because it afforded greater privacy, and besides was a far more agreeable venue. Amanda had fallen in love with it the very first time she set eyes on it – especially the imposing gardens.

At eleven o'clock prompt, she parked her red Mini Cooper as usual under the magnolia tree, behind Martha's almost identical, though much older, model, and jauntily made her way down to the main entrance, where she found Martha on her knees, deadheading geraniums.

"Goodness, Mandy, you're here already... time's just

flown this morning," she said, getting up. "Look, it's too nice to be inside on a day like this. You go and sit by the pond, while I go and make the coffee."

Whenever Amanda sat and watched the fish, she dreamed the same recurrent dream. What if... what if, somehow... she could persuade Martha? What a deal that would be! It wouldn't be easy, of course... well nigh impossible, in fact, because obviously for Martha this was much more than a house. With all her memories, good and bad, it had become a kind of shrine, and even to consider the possibility seemed a betrayal of her best friend, like coveting your older sister's boyfriend. But the dream kept recurring... and, as Rich always reminded her, business is business... and if the price is right, maybe... just maybe... she might do it... for *her*.

The rattle of coffee cups awoke her from her fantasy.

"Oh, let *me* help with those."

"No, I'm all right, thanks."

"You know, Martha, it never ceases to surprise me how quiet this garden is... I could sit here all day doing absolutely nothing, and just let my thoughts wander. It's so peaceful... you'd think you were right out in the country."

"That's what Taff Jenkins always says," replied Martha.

"How is Taff, by the way? Haven't seen him since you took me round to see the cottage... he'd just had that nasty bout of 'flu...

"Oh, Taff never gets a cold... always flu! But he's a lot better now, thanks. Funny, when he was here the other day he was asking after you a lot! I think he must have taken a fancy to you... always was one for the ladies, our

Taff! It's Liz I'm more concerned about... seems to have lost a lot of weight recently."

"Oh, I hope she's all right... I must go round and see them as soon as I get a chance... which isn't *always* easy, as you know!"

"Any more news about Richard's job?" asked Martha, discreetly changing the subject, "you both must be thrilled."

"Yes, we are actually. Obviously, he didn't fancy going back to his old job... no future for him there. And at first he wasn't sure if doing the master's degree would lead to anything either, but things have fallen into place since then. But everyone's been *so* kind and helpful. First, there was Jim Whittaker's recommendation for the course... a bit over the top, if you ask me, but there you go! Then his tutor, that American woman... apparently, she gave him a brilliant reference... probably over the top as well! And Phil Evans, of course, always there when Rich needed him... such a nice man, Phil, and so helpful. *He* deserves promotion when they go comprehensive, if anybody does. And then there's Martin... with all his contacts... he seems to know everybody that matters! Oh, I haven't told you yet... we've put our house on the market... Richard says now is a good time to get rid... before the town is swamped by immigrants... and the traffic on St Helens Road's getting impossible, especially in the mornings and going-home time... sometimes we can barely get out of the drive. He thought it might be a good time to move back to Netherbridge, where eventually he'll be based for the new job. Martin's heard they're going to convert that little building next to the Town Hall as an Educational Centre for him."

"What's the latest on your mother?" asked Martha, deftly changing the subject again.

"Oh, she's supposed to be having another X-ray this coming week. It's a weird thing... apparently her spine bends slightly to the left... and this puts pressure on some nerves, or something... which causes the pains in her legs... she's all right sitting down, but she can't stand for more than a minute or two, and creeps round the house bent over like an old woman. Dad says it's a ruse to get out of washing up... or to get him to buy a dish-washer! And now she won't even leave the house except in the car... in case someone sees her. Nothing wrong with her tongue, though! She started off about grandchildren again yesterday... says we can't be doing it right, and if we don't get a move on, she'll come over and show us... honestly! And then, have I been to the doctor yet... to which I reply, no, Mum, we haven't been to the doctor yet, and so it goes on, until I see Dad's eyes rolling, when I remember, all of a sudden, I'm late for that appointment with the bank manager. Of course, Rich never has to put up with any of this nonsense. But I've a feeling that he'd be on her side, anyway, and assumes it's the 'woman's responsibility'. Oh, but listen to this... I never told you... when we went out for that meal in Southport a couple of weeks back... I don't know if he was trying to tell me something, but we *happened* to park right outside one of those new 'fertility clinics'. And as we were making our way towards the restaurant... it was quite bizarre, really... he suddenly stopped, turned and cupped my face in his hands, ruined my lipstick, and then quoted... or tried to quote... that bit out of... I think, *Twelfth Night*...something about not leaving the world a copy... do you know the one I mean?"

340

"'Lady, you are the cruel'st she alive, if you will lead these graces to the grave, *and leave the world no copy',*" enunciated Martha, in her seductive Salopian tones, "*Twelfth Night*, Act 1, Scene 5. Viola to Olivia."

"You're a flipping genius, you are... how do you remember all that? You must have a photographic memory!"

"No, Mandy, not a genius... School Cert. 1935! But, in fairness, I *was* also Viola in the school play that year!"

THANKS LARGELY to Jim's continual cajoling and exhortations, and his good-humoured working relationship with the Architect and the Site Manager, Phase I of the building programme was completed a good fortnight ahead of schedule, and apart from a few minor titivations, the 'New Block', by which name it became known thereafter, was ready for occupation well before the start of the 1973 Michaelmas Term.

Meanwhile, he had also arranged a so-called "experimental, pre-season strengthening programme" for the First Rugby XV! Needless to say, they were all present to a man, and for two full days the erstwhile building-site was transformed into a gigantic 'ant colony'; and by Wednesday teatime all items of furniture or equipment that needed shifting – favourite arm chairs, bookcases, display cabinets, epidiascopes, overhead projectors, cupboards, desks, blackboards, easels, wall charts, an upright piano, and much else besides – had taken up their specified places in the new building.

As expected, the most challenging cargo of all was the occupants of Frank's 'menagerie', but he had spent some time during the summer break at school planning and preparing, so that the animals would suffer minimal distress. When everything was ready, he had arranged for his team of trusty weight-lifters to put the fruits of their labours to some practical use. Indeed, Frank was so pleased with the smoothness of the operation that he treated them all to a fish and chip supper at *Fred Challinor's* later that evening.

Unlike Jim, Frank was also very pleased with his new workplace, his very own 'Skylab', as he called it, on the third floor overlooking the playing fields and the parkland beyond. With his knowledge of best industrial practice, the Science Advisers had given him virtually *carte blanche* to design and equip the three new science laboratories as he saw fit. However, unbeknown to Frank, as part of Preston's plan to make Netherbridge a "centre of scientific excellence", an unexpected bonus had been added in the form of a roof-top weather station and observatory, surreptitiously equipped by Martha with the instruments from Dr Davenport's observatory in *Elsinore*.

On the first morning of the new term the School was abuzz with anticipation as everyone filed into the cavernous New Hall for its very first assembly. According to the Architects' blurb, this was to be "the jewel in the crown... a well-equipped, multi-purpose space at the heart of the building serving both the school and the community". There were indeed many apologists, and necks often craned in admiration of the dizzyingly high ceiling and the impressive array of theatre lights and sound equipment. But apparently it was not to everyone's taste, especially one cynical Old Netherbridgian, who said it reminded him of the concourse at Manchester

Airport, all function and no soul, and so unlike the beloved Old Hall with its centuries-rich ambience.

After delivering one of his customary pithy and thought-provoking orations in this spacious, and allegedly soulless Hall, Jim sought a little respite in the privacy of his new 'executive office', which he found just as spacious and soulless, and so unlike his old 'study', which radiated 'soul' aplenty, as well as time-honoured warmth and cosiness. But at least he still had George Davenport's armchair and desk, albeit, like himself, looking a little forlorn in their new 1970s setting.

But even Jim had to admit that some features of the new 'admin suite' were an improvement on the old, especially his private bathroom facilities, and the large south-facing window looking out onto the playing fields. But putting Martha in a separate office on the other side of the foyer was in his opinion a mistake, and if Martha had not been so pleased with her own private space, he would have objected a little more robustly!

This was not the only time that Jim had had to accept decisions that flew in the face of common sense. Shortly after Christmas, the arch-planners of Preston suddenly offered to provide the then much-lauded Tannoy 'intercom' system at the School in order "to facilitate and enhance intra-institutional communications in keeping with best industrial and commercial practice". However, Jim was so incensed with this proposition that he wrote to Preston to register his strongest disapproval: "Speaking as someone who has devoted his professional life to facilitating and enhancing communication," he said, "I very much doubt that putting loud-speakers in every corridor and classroom is either desirable or sensible". He also raised the matter at a Governors' Meeting, predicting that it would prove so irritatingly intrusive that some masters might be driven to silence the infernal contraptions with a judicious application of a pocket screw-driver! But when the matter was put to the vote, Jim found himself in a minority of two (Vicar Ramsbottom being the other); and during the February half-term of 1974, the system was duly installed.

WHILE JIM was quietly reflecting on what he had just said in assembly about life resembling a river, constantly changing while seeming to stay the same, he was almost catapulted out of his chair.

Formerly, the one and only, black office telephone had always been located at a safe distance on Martha's desk. But now, a brand-new, red telephone had infiltrated his space and sat impertinently within reach. He picked it up, wondering who the devil it might be that early in the day.

"An outside call for you, Mr Whittaker," trilled Martha's disembodied voice mischievously, "You're through now."

"Whittaker speaking," growled Jim.

"Good morning, Jim, Richard Nobbs here. How are things with you?"

"Oh, hello... I was wondering how you were getting on," said Jim, blurting out the first thing that came into his head.

"Missing me already?" teased Nobbs in his treacly, telephone voice.

"Not really," parried Jim, "we've decided to offer the Craft post to the gentleman who stood in for you last year."

"I thought you might," countered Nobbs, "He sounded like a good man."

"Yes, he is, and he's fitted in very well, and doing a fine job. Anyway, what can I do for you?

"Well, it's just a courtesy call, really," said Nobbs a bit limply," "to fill you in on how things stand this end. They'll be contacting you from Preston any day now. I expect you'll have received my letter of resignation?"

"Yes... thank you... it came on Friday. Oh, and congratulations, by the way. Things are looking up for you."

"Well, yes, they *are* actually. Mandy and I are very pleased. If you ever want to get in touch, ask for the Education Department, extension 372."

"Thank you, I'll let Martha know."

"Oh, before I forget, I've heard on the bush radio that I'm going to be based in Preston until Christmas... at least until they sort something more permanent for me... could be in Netherbridge itself, so I've heard. It would be nice to keep up the links with the old place. Anyway, nice talking to you, Jim, and remember, if you need anything, you know where I am. I'll call and see you when I'm in the area."

"Thank you," replied Jim, absentmindedly, and immediately wondered why on earth he *had* thanked him! He sat there for a few moments settling his nerves, before standing up suddenly and making his way to Martha's office.

"What is it with that fellow, Martha? I hope we're not going to get too many of his damn "courtesy calls". I thought we were rid of him, but clearly not, especially if he's heading back to Netherbridge."

"'What rough beast'", quoted Martha with a playful frown, 'its hour come round at last/ Slouches towards Bethlehem to be born?' "

Chapter Fifteen

As C-Day loomed, there was much speculation on both sides of Manchester Road about Joe Riley's "winners and losers"; and while the respective staffrooms reverberated with raised voices and hopes, one or two opportunists were quietly plotting glorious summers for themselves after long winters of discontent.

Those to the south of the road presumed that senior posts and 'special responsibility allowances' would be theirs by almost divine right, and feelings frequently ran high in the Staff Room,

"With all the good will in the world," declared a dyspeptic mathematician, "how can *college-trained* teachers extend the minds of future physicists or... classical scholars?"

"Quite!" concurred his colleague, "And conversely, none of *us* ever came into education to teach dunderheads... any more than a neurosurgeon went into medicine to empty bedpans."

"If you ask me," exclaimed a third, "the whole thing's a political stunt, and sadly one with grievous unintended consequences. Nobody said the 'eleven-plus' was perfect, but what does abolishing it achieve?

"Nothing," replied a fourth, furiously, "except ruin the life chances of bright, working-class boys."

"Well, gentlemen," counselled an old war-horse from behind his *Times* crossword, "since political opinion has prevailed, it will be up to the likes of us to try to uphold standards, and limit the damage."

Even the fair-minded Frank Fairclough, who had always questioned NGS's selection procedures, predicted that both academic and sporting standards would decline, and most manifestly as soon as the last 'grammar' cohort had worked itself through the system.

Jim Whittaker, however, was more optimistic, but he too shared his staff's mindset on the future management hierarchy. If there had been a straight choice for the headship of the combined schools between him and Dave Longworth, his opposite number at 'Manchester Road', he would have been dumbfounded if the governors had chosen Dave; and very likely, he thought, so would Dave. But after twenty tranquil years in charge of his so-called "happy school", he felt seeking to improve his golf handicap appealed far more than negotiating the minefields of the brave new comprehensive world, and had decided to "call it a day" at the end of the Christmas term.

But the situation among the 'rank and file', especially at Manchester Road, was far less straightforward, with much in-fighting and jockeying for position in preparation for the new order. Feelings also ran high

348

because since eighty per cent of the pupils would be coming from the 'secondary modern' sector, the cake should be cut proportionally. Those so-called 'masters', they argued, might be very clever in their own fields, but it was only 'book-learning'. Cocooned in their artificial little ivory towers, what did they know about *ordinary* boys and girls? Yes, and *girls*! Indeed, most of them wouldn't last five minutes in a secondary modern classroom, especially now after ROSLA[1]. 5C would eat them alive! Being good at your subject was no doubt a fine thing, but sadly for them, soon that would no longer be the flavour of the month. In future, education was to be for everyone, and not just for the chosen few. The Sixties and 'rock'n'roll' had broken the mould, and the 'comp kid' would be very different from the 'hot-house' variety they'd been used to nurturing. Furthermore, it would be about the 'whole person', not just about brains; and with one or two exceptions *they* would find themselves hopelessly out of their depth.

And the war of words was not confined to the schools. The coming of the 'Comp' seemed to be in everyone's thoughts, if not on everyone's lips, in the town as well, and it polarised opinion alarmingly, often splitting families and neighbourhoods. It was as if centuries of passive acceptance of the old order had suddenly been vexed into a wild nightmare of questioning, likened variously to Enoch Powell's "rivers of blood" speech and the miners' strike in 1970. Disputes often erupted on street corners, in cafés, or indeed wherever two or three were gathered together, whilst those with more time on

---

[1] Raising of the School Leaving Age from 15 to 16 (Sept 1972)

their hands wrote letters to the *Netherbridge Chronicle*.

One genial old-timer from 'Manchester Road' was moved to open his heart one evening in the *Boar's Head*: "It's like dog eat dog up there, Jack, you wouldn't want to know. And it used to be such a nice place to work. But for the last few months it's been nothing but mud-slinging, and back-biting... and (pardon my French) arse-licking. If only people knew what goes on... I would never have believed that so-called professionals could stoop to such shenanigans... and I don't mind telling you, I can't wait to go now. If this is what 'comprehensive' does to you, you can shove it where the sun don't shine... give me the old 'Sec Mod' any day... with one boss, and everyone else getting on with it best they could, pulling together, without all this scrabbling after 'special allowances' and the like. But, to me, the worst of all are those creeps who spend half their time across the road trying to wheedle their way in by currying favour with anyone who looks important. It's obvious what *they're* after. And, bloody 'ell, Jack, there's over a year to go yet!"

Of course, Jack Higginbottom's own disillusionment with education was now happily behind him, but he, along with Taff Jenkins and one or two of the other regulars, still loved hearing tales from both sides of the academic divide confirming their prejudices from a safe distance.

MEANWHILE, heedless of the trials affecting ordinary men and women, Richard Nobbs was intent on a glorious summer of his own, and by all accounts had already taken Preston by storm. Boosted by his master's degree and a celebratory new Jaguar, his ego, never miniscule, had suddenly assumed cosmic proportions. His 'little learning', far from being a 'dangerous thing', impressed and confounded in equal measure, and his gift for repartee had acquired a new potency, courtesy of a liberal sprinkling of half-understood sociological terms and allusions. Like the proverbial one-eyed man in the country of the blind, he passed for a king, so that "Has Richard seen this?" or "Let's see what Richard thinks, shall we?" or "I think this is Richard's call, don't you?" became common currency in the corridors of power.

Being well over six feet, even without his shoe lifts, Nobbs had always stood out in company, and albeit now in his sixth decade, with his luxurious halo of golden hair, and a nigh-perfect set of preternaturally white teeth, most men (and some women too) found merely standing next to him at once intimidating and exhilarating. Even his one physical flaw had been carefully concealed by the 'vanity girdle' that Amanda had bought him, partly tongue-in-cheek, for his fiftieth birthday!

His colleagues at County Hall had never met anyone so confident, so articulate, and so dominant, and although he did not seem to have any close friends, there were plenty who would hang on to his every word and do his least bidding. He seemed like the living embodiment of a comic-book hero, and, as many thought, the *Ubermensch* to lead them into the promised land of "a grammar school education for all".

When he eventually moved into his own little "Education Centre" next door to Netherbridge Town Hall on 4th February 1974, he felt he had reached Everest Base Camp. "Yes," he hissed, "this is *mine*, my very own, and no one else's." Then peering up through his office

351

window at the massive, Victorian edifice towering above him, he recalled the countless mind-numbing evenings of speechifying and mutual congratulation he had had to endure inside that building. Not to put too fine a point on it, he thought, the whole malarkey was nothing more than a glorification of the f------- *grammar school,* and he had had enough of that with Harry Shaw at Oldham Hulme, a man, some said, who loved his C.C.F almost as much as he loved himself. Indeed, Nobbs once overheard an elderly mistress from the adjoining Girls School likening it to a corps of the *Hitlerjugend!*

By way of release, he flung open his office window, disturbing some pigeons in the process; and then staring upwards beyond the topmost spire, he yelled, perhaps more loudly than he had intended, "Listen, *Doctor* D... *if* you're up there, listen to the wise words of *Mister* D: '*For the loser now/ Will be later to win/ For* the *times they are a-changin'*. And they f------- well are an' all, mate... and, do you know what, *I'm* having a piece of it!"

And so, all in all, Nobbs was not altogether displeased with his new lot in life: whether ensconced in his own little citadel, or cruising around in his majestic limousine, it was infinitely better than being cooped up in a dusty workshop with a bunch of pimply adolescents, who, he knew, would have much preferred an extra Physics lesson with "f------ Fairclough".

Secretly, he also relished the status and the symbolism of being a '*bona fide* county council officer', doing proper, grown-up things, dealing with adults, and having a private 'hotline to the Director'. And the Jaguar too: what had once languished ignominiously between a tradesmen's entrance and a cookhouse, now enjoyed universal acclaim, whether gliding through the myriad towns and villages of North West England or waiting patiently for its master in a designated parking space.

In addition to his role of "Pastoral Care Co-ordinator for South Lancashire", Nobbs had also contrived to be Preston's "eyes and ears on the ground to monitor schools as they prepared for the comprehensive changeover". His official role was "to observe and offer advice on setting up pastoral structures within schools, and to arrange short in-service training courses at his Education Centre, in order to 'de-skill' and re-train suitable candidates in readiness for a career switch from the academic to the pastoral". But it also gave him licence to visit any school in his area – grammar or secondary modern – ostensibly "to keep the Director of Education abreast of developments".

NOBBS WAS never noted for his patience or long attention span, and, whenever he grew tired of his own company, he would instinctively pick up the telephone and randomly pick a school and arrange 'a courtesy visit'. He defended this impromptu approach, because it gave him a truer picture of "the institution's state of play and organisational health". However, he himself would never leave his Centre without a rigorous inspection of his appearance.

This process began with the Chindits regimental tie, which he had recently acquired, boxed and in pristine condition, for a few pence at the Longsight flea market. If he adjudged the Windsor knot too large or too small, or not forming a proportional rhombus within the angle of his shirt collar, the tie would be removed forthwith and a new knot tied, this time with slide-rule precision.

Next, his critical gaze would veer upwards to his magnificent mane, wave upon golden wave cascading in 1970s splendour onto dandruff-free shoulders. But, perish the thought, should a single strand or ringlet have dared to stray from its correct trajectory, be it ever so little, a pair of silver-encrusted ivory hair brushes – a fifteenth birthday present from his doting mother – would be brought to bear on to the entire coiffure until its effulgent glory was restored.

Finally, his bespoke shoes: since Nobbs believed that shoes revealed as much about a person's character as any other article of clothing, he inspected his own regularly and scrupulously; and should the slightest scuff mark mar their high-gloss perfection, vigorous corrective procedures would be applied.

Thus, it was only when he deemed his whole person to be sartorially irreproachable, would he venture out into the world, confident that his appearance, from head to toe, was nothing less than the envy of everyone he encountered.

Interestingly, Martha herself had noticed Nobbs's recent preoccupation with his appearance, even remarking on it once to Amanda during one of their coffee get-togethers. "Men as physically well-endowed as he", she said, "often affect an air of abandon about their appearance, but Richard looks as if he's striving to grace the covers of *Vanity Fair*!"

"Exactly," said Amanda, "*vanity* being the operative word. Every time we go out, he spends aeons in the bathroom, preening and primping like a prize peacock. It's usually us ladies who get blamed for that."

"Dr Davenport, too, was meticulous about his appearance," replied Martha, adding, "as, of course, he was about everything. He wouldn't even let his mother iron his shirts! Attention to detail was an obsession with him. In fact, I'm pretty sure that's what killed him... that constant striving after impossibly high standards. He never really recovered after "failing to save the Grammar School", as he put it. He saw it all as *his* fault... he had let the side down, the masters, the parents, the boys... even the old boys. No matter how much everyone tried to reassure him otherwise, as far as he was concerned, he had 'let everybody down'."

"That's terribly sad. And it must have been dreadful for you too, Martha, being so close to him, and working with him for all those years?"

"Yes, thirty, actually... well, bar a couple of months."

"Gosh! That *is* a long time... that's almost as long as I've lived! And longer than many a marriage! Unfortunately, I only met him a couple of times – I don't think he and Richard got on very well! The first time was at the 1962 Speech Night, and I remember thinking then no wonder people call this man 'GOD'! It wasn't just his physical appearance... I remember he had a special presence or aura about him as well. But what *really* struck me (apart from those gorgeous eyes, of course!) was how polite he was... and how humble... a real gentleman... and nothing like how Richard had described him. During refreshments afterwards, he came over and sat with us for a good ten minutes and took a real interest in us, and how we were settling down in our new home in Leigh, and things like that.... and when I said we lived right by the cricket ground, he said he remembered playing in a charity match there once in 1928, when he was a young master at Manchester Grammar School. But he said it wasn't a very happy memory for him, because he was out for a duck! What a lovely man!"

"Now, that's just typical," said Martha, with a wry smile... he spent his whole life dwelling on his failures. From what I remember, it was usually fifties and sixties, and often not out!"

"*ACHTUNG*, Mr Whittaker!" announced Martha on her intercom telephone, "ETA 1400 hrs... en route to Preston... ten minutes for an update."

"*Mein got*! I see more of that fellow now than when he worked here. Martha, think diversionary tactic... quick... I really can't do with him today." He could have added "or any time before Christmas."

"I'll make him a cup of tea when he arrives," said Martha, "and I'll keep him talking."

"Good thinking, Martha, you do that; I just can't do with his palaver today. Besides, I've promised my Upper Sixth an extra class, and this afternoon seems as good a time as any. You can have him all to yourself, Martha! If you manage to get a word in, ask him if he knows anything more about the new library... or indeed ask him anything at all... just keep him out of my way!"

The proximity of Nobbs's Education Centre to NGS meant that he often called in on some official pretext, but it was mainly to glean snippets of 'inside information' or gossip about former colleagues and recent appointees. He had long learnt that knowledge, even trivial knowledge sometimes, is power, and that knowledge about people is often the most empowering of all. Of late, he had made a point of paying regular visits to the Secondary Modern School 'across the road', because this school came directly under local authority control. He made it his business to find out everything he could about the school's organisation and the individuals working there – the cleaners, the cooks, the caretaker and the teaching staff – and was especially interested in the 'plotting and manoeuvring' that had recently come to his notice. Not unexpectedly, the welcome he received was no less frosty there than at NGS.

While Martha was still on the phone to Mr Whittaker, she watched the great white Jaguar carefully negotiate the final narrow bend of the drive, and then turn adroitly into one of the visitors' parking bays beneath her office window. Eventually, its impeccably attired occupant emerged, stretching himself up to his full height. Then after carefully retrieving his jacket from the rear compartment of the limousine, he stood a good half-minute surveying all around him, before finally making his way slowly and deliberately towards the new main entrance and foyer. He stood there too for a while inspecting the decor, and taking in the general ambience. At last, he knocked on Martha's door with his 'signature' rat – tat – tat-tat – tat, and waited for it to open.

"And how's my lovely Martha today? I'm sorry it's such short notice, but is Jim available? I was hoping to pick his brains about one or two things... I've got this bloody questionnaire to finish by the end of the month."

"Come in, Mr Nobbs," said Martha politely, "When you rang, Mr Whittaker had nothing in his diary for this afternoon, but he'd forgotten to tell me about the extra lesson with his Scholarship class. Would you like a cup of tea?"

"Oh, yes, thank you... that would be lovely. You know how I like it... one and a *soupçon*. Bloody hell, Martha, he's not still doing that teaching malarkey, is he? He should know by now that modern heads don't *do* teaching. You could get away with it in the old days, but this is 1974, for God's sake. And besides, I would have thought running a school like this is a full-time job. 'Okay, helping out in an emergency, maybe, but it's about time Jim said good-bye, Mr Chips, and hello, CEO."

"Maybe Mr Whittaker takes being 'head *master*' literally," countered Martha, "and, as you know, he's always been one to lead from the front."

Nobbs was one of the few people who knew about Jim Whittaker's distinguished war service, and had long suspected that Martha knew about his own less than distinguished one.

"Ah well, I suppose you can't teach an old dog new tricks," retorted Nobbs the best way he could, realising that it was as pointless arguing with Martha as it was with his Amanda. "And talking of new tricks, Martha, don't you think it's about time we dropped this 'Mr Nobbs' bullsh-t, especially now I don't even work here? We're supposed to be friends! I would much prefer 'Richard'. 'Mr Nobbs' sounds so bloody formal."

"Well, I've always addressed the masters by their titles and surnames. I find that works very well, and I believe the masters by and large prefer it too. Some of the older ones even call me 'Miss Wolf', which I find rather sweet! Using first names in the workplace presumes a degree of familiarity, and we all know what familiarity breeds. Besides, old habits die hard! I remember my Aunt

Hilda once suggesting I drop the 'Aunt' bit, but I could never bring myself to do that either... just 'Hilda' sounded wrong... as if I presumed to be her equal. She had always been my 'Aunt Hilda'. It would have been like calling one's parents by their first names, although even that's becoming more commonplace nowadays, as if modern parents want to be their children's best friends, instead of... well... parents. And so, I'm afraid, 'Aunt Hilda' she remained!"

"Well, have it your own way," replied Nobbs, a little crest-fallen, and suddenly with an ostentatious flourish of the Rolex-encrusted wrist, he got up, and made for the door. "I must be off, Martha. Thanks for the cuppa. Give my regards to Jim. Tell him I'll try and catch him next week. I wonder if you could help me out, Martha... if I left this questionnaire with you, could *you* possibly have a 'decko'? But don't worry if you haven't got time... thanks... must dash... 'bye for now, God bless!"

HAVING NOT had a proper holiday in three years, Jim and Mary decided to spend the first three weeks of the 1974 summer holidays at their little cottage in Lion-sur-Mer. On the eve of their return, they were sitting in their front garden enjoying the evening sun and a pre-prandial glass or two of *Chateau Latour*, when Mary said, "You're very quiet tonight, Jim, anything bothering you?"

"Well, there is, and there isn't," replied Jim unhelpfully, and after another pregnant pause added, "Do you know... I wouldn't mind doing this sort of thing full-time."

"What do you mean?"

"Well, it just occurred to me that this is the first time

in months I've managed to forget about the School. I'm 63 in October, Mary, I've given good service, and counting war service, I've got my full 40 years in. I could retire tomorrow... well, not tomorrow exactly... I'd have to give a term's notice. But, let's say Christmas... and then, *Vive la France!* What do you say, Mary?"

"This is sudden, isn't it? What about Phase Two? All that work, and then some Johnny-come-lately gets all the credit. But... this is *your* decision, love... all I would say is, don't rush into *anything*... take your time... think hard. As for me... well... of course, I'd be delighted. You've given more to the School than most, and much of it above and beyond the call of duty... and thankless. Besides, it won't be there for much longer... well, the building maybe, but not the School. It could end up like that monster in Liverpool... what's it called?"

"Ruffwood... yes, and that's in Harold Wilson's neck of the woods! Purpose-built, no expense spared, and a brilliant young headmaster head-hunted to prove that *big* is beautiful! What could go wrong? Well, for one thing, even with 2000 pupils, I'm told, they can only manage a Sixth form of 150. And when one of our chaps (I think it was Joe) took an Under15s side there one Saturday morning not so long ago, only nine of their players had turned up, so our two reserves had to play for *them*, to make a game!" It must be very demoralising working under those conditions. I don't know what the answer is, but I don't think it's that.

"'Ruffwood' reminds me of that film with Glenn Ford!"

"*Blackboard Jungle!*"

"Yes, and tell me who in his right mind would want to

be in charge of a thing like that?"

"Well, I can think of one or two!" replied Jim. "But seriously, Mary, what would *you* do if you were me?"

"Honestly?"

"Yes... honestly!"

"Quit while you're ahead, Jim boy... while you've still got your health. Yes, I suppose you'd have a bigger pension pot... but bigger headaches too! And we're not exactly paupers, are we?"

"Well said, Mary! My thoughts exactly... let's drink to it!"

After which he started singing the WW1 marching song, *Mademoiselle of Armentiere, Parlez-vous*, discreetly humming the rude bits!

MEANWHILE, Amanda, too, was feeling pleased with herself, because, despite her husband's cynicism, she had managed to sell the 'big house' even before it was officially on the market, and moreover to a cash customer, an Indian doctor who had just moved into the area and was desperate for a spacious house right away to accommodate his large family. However, there was one difficulty: the cash sale was dependent on a very rapid exchange of contracts.

As luck would have it, the house attached to Nobbs's first home in Netherbridge had recently become vacant, and Amanda thought that moving in there would give them time to find a more suitable home. Meanwhile, their 'good' furniture would have to go into storage, and some renovations carried out to make their temporary home "habitable".

At times like this, there were two things about his old

job that Nobbs really missed: the free use of his workshop and facilities to carry out maintenance work on his properties; and secondly, the long school holidays during which to do the work. But from now on he would have the extra cost of engaging tradesmen, or at least Amanda would, now that she was "the person responsible for the day-to-day running of Shaw Enterprises". Clearly, if this cash customer was to have early access to the Leigh house, there would be a great deal to be done in a short time, and Nobbs offered to take a week's leave to help out; but unfortunately, a letter from the Deputy Director of Education thwarted his plans.

THROUGHOUT much of the 1970s, it was *de rigueur* for followers of the new-styled "Pastoral Curriculum" to make at least one pilgrimage to Woodberry Down High School in North East London. They flocked in coachloads – believers, converts, opportunists, or plain classroom-dodgers – to break bread with the great Michael Marland, their 'philosopher king', whose book, *Pastoral Care* (published 1st April, 1974), acquired almost biblical standing during the comprehensive revolution.

However, Nobbs, despite his professed enthusiasm for the new orthodoxy, did not take kindly to his 'invitation' to attend a week's course in Pastoral Care and Counselling at Woodberry Down.

"Listen, Mand, I'm not going, and that's that... we've got too much on. I'll ring him now and tell him I've got a previous engagement, or something."

"Do you think that's wise?" replied Amanda, "Why blot your copy book? Look, if it's this sale that's bothering you, I'm quite capable of handling it, right? Or don't you trust me?"

"Oh, Mand... don't be like that... you know I trust you... if I can't trust you, who *can* I trust? It's just... well, I don't like leaving you with everything to do... that's all. And anyway, I need to keep my hand in with the business, or else I'll end up like a spare part... redundant... surplus to requirements."

"What, you a spare part? I like that! Look, Rich, I can manage. If I'm to be a full partner, you must let me make decisions. Anyway, you've got a career to think of now, remember? And even if this course *is* a waste of time, the fact that you've put yourself out to go on it won't do you any harm with the powers that be. So, chop-chop! Get packed, and just go. I'm telling you, everything will be all right this end."

Apart from wanting a free hand to prove her worth, Amanda was also secretly glad to have her husband out of the way for a while, just to have some time to clear her head... and perhaps dream a little too. And if truth be told, Nobbs too, for all his protestations, was not altogether averse to a little time to himself... a whole week of self-indulgence and swagger down in the big, bad city at the local authority's expense.

As soon as the Jaguar was safely off the premises, Amanda was on the phone to Martha, who, naturally, invited her down for a light lunch. Amanda never refused invitations to *Elsinore*, and within half an hour she too was on her way.

After lunch, the two women drove over to Fishwick and Hall's, the local builders in Netherbridge whom Nobbs had employed previously, most recently for the big extension at the rear of Martin Shaw's dental surgery.

363

Amanda explained the urgency of the job, and combining a little of her husband's guile with her own allure, she was assured that the work would begin the following Monday, and to expedite matters was advised to call in at their new show-room next to the bus station that afternoon to choose from the latest range of kitchen and bathroom units. Since this house would soon revert to being a rental property, Amanda allowed good value to trump quality in her choice of units, whereas Martha, who initially had gone along merely to lend moral support, appeared to be taking an inordinate interest in some of the more expensive brands, even making notes and picking up leaflets and price lists.

On their way back to *Elsinore*, Amanda could not contain her curiosity any longer and asked, "What's up, Martha? *You're* not thinking of moving as well, are you?"

"Oh no, well, not immediately, anyway," replied Martha, with Bletchleyan obliqueness! Then after a short pause she added, "Listen, Mandy, do you really have to go back tonight... because you could stay over with me. A few days, if you like... I mean, while you're on your own."

"Oh, that would be lovely, Martha, as long as it wouldn't be too much trouble. Thank you very much. I've got a few things to see to at home first... a few phone calls, and I promised to pop in at the estate agent's before they close. Tell you what, what if I drop you off... and then I'll go straight back to Leigh. I should still be back here by, say, seven-thirty... complete with an overnight bag!"

"Perfect!" said Martha, "by which time I'll have your bed made up and have rustled something up for dinner."

AFTER A FRANTIC few hours, Amanda eventually arrived back at *Elsinore*, a little later than anticipated, and as excited as a schoolgirl being invited to dinner with her headmistress. She could not quite fathom why she was so excited, except that she had a strange feeling that something special was about to happen.

She parked her car in its usual place under the magnolia tree, and half skipped down the path to the front door, as she had done dozens of times before. She rang the doorbell and waited. Eventually, the door opened with Martha standing there in her trade-mark red and green apron, looking a good ten years younger than her fifty-four years. Amanda was transfixed and speechless until at last she could not hide her excitement at the thought of spending four whole days with her special friend. She lunged forward, tripping over the brass threshold in the process, and held Martha in a tight embrace for a full ten seconds, and would have kissed her on the mouth had Martha not instinctively turned her head at the last moment.

Martha had grown up in an age when displaying emotions was not encouraged: such unbridled affection, therefore, especially from a woman, took her by surprise. But then, this was no ordinary woman, this was Amanda, *she who ought to be loved...* and with whom Martha, if she were brutally honest with herself, *was* indeed more than a little in love already; not so much for her physical beauty, which was self-evident, but for her energy and *joie-de-vivre*, her kindness, humility, sincerity, forthrightness... oh, the list was endless. Indeed, it had often crossed Martha's mind how in another age, another life, or indeed on another planet, this demigoddess would have been a fitting consort even for Dr Davenport.

"Come through," said Martha, by way of restoring some equilibrium to her emotional state. "Here, give me your coat... supper won't be long... what would you like to drink?"

"Oh, just a glass of water for me, please," replied Amanda, as her eyes swivelled upwards in child-like wonder at the glorious atrium above her, and then down again along the renowned winding banisters.

"Please come through, Mandy... we might as well sit in the kitchen... then we can chat and keep an eye on the stove."

"This house really does you credit," said Amanda.

"Well, the credit's hardly mine."

"But *you've* kept it in this pristine condition, and I'm sure he's up there looking down on you and thinking, this is my beloved Martha, in whom I am well pleased!"

"Oh, I doubt that very much," chuckled Martha, "he set himself (and me!) *very* high standards. Hanging on the wall facing you as you go into the coach house, there's a large wooden replica he'd made himself of the Everton Football Club coat-of-arms, with the motto, *Nil Satis Nisi Optimum*... nothing but the best is good enough. That was *his* life motto... but, sadly, it also proved his undoing."

Amanda reached across the table and took hold of Martha's hand, stroking it gently with her thumb, and gazed into her moist eyes, neither saying a word for a good half-minute.

"Right!" said Martha, getting up, "I think that pie should be about ready... and, as the guest, you can have the honour of sitting in Dr Davenport's chair."

"Oh no, only *you* should sit in *his* chair... and I'm quite

366

all right here,

"Well, anyway, *bon appétit...* I hope it's done enough."

"*Nil satis nisi optimum*?" teased Amanda.

"Could have done with a couple more minutes... and a smidgeon more salt?" said Martha.

"Don't let perfect be the enemy of good!" replied Amanda, "It's delicious."

"Thank you!"

"Where did you find the recipe?"

"It was one of Mrs D's Irish specials. We often had it on Fridays when Father O'Flaherty came to supper, and Dr Davenport continued making it most Fridays after his mother died. But, of course, *he* made it with scientific precision, weighing every ingredient to the last milligram, and timing every procedure to the nearest millisecond!"

"I can just imagine!"

"Now, I'm afraid I haven't got much for 'afters', Mandy... there's fresh fruit, if you like, or plain ice cream?"

"I think I'll skip dessert, if you don't mind. That pie was very filling, and besides his lordship says I must watch the calories!"

"Nonsense... anyway, people in glasshouses..." rebuked Martha, with a quizzical smile.

"Quite! With him, it's always do as I say, but not as I do! But maybe I should heed his warnings a little at this stage in my life. How do *you* manage to keep so slim? Or are you one of those lucky ones?"

"Don't you believe it... it's always been a battle. Dr Davenport once gave me a very good tip: you should always get up from the table feeling a little bit hungry, and I've tried to practise that all my life, though not always successfully, mind! Coffee?

"Oh yes, please, Martha, but with no sugar, and just a teeny drop of milk!"

"We'll take it through to the study, shall we, just as Dr Davenport and his mother used to do after dinner. He worried a lot that his mother spent too much time on her own in the house. Apart from Mrs McAllister next door, she might see no one for several days when he was away. Yes, that worried him a lot. So, when he *was* at home that half-hour after dinner was sacrosanct."

"God, Martha, I do envy you, you know... one day you should sit down at that desk and write that man's story... he was such a special person... a one-off. Knowing him so well, you'd be the ideal person... and do you know what, it would be a best-seller!"

"Except I don't have the writing skills... besides I could never do him justice. But I agree, it's a story that should be told. Perhaps we could give it a go together one day!

"That's a thought!"

AFTER CLEARING the dinner things, Martha took her friend on a conducted tour of *Elsinore*, something she had been planning to do for some time, but had never had a proper opportunity until now.

"First of all, about the name, *Elsinore*... was it Dr Davenport's choice?" asked Amanda, as they began to climb the grand, oak stairway.

"*I* wondered about that too. No, *he* didn't choose it. The house was built in 1906 for a mill owner as a wedding present for his son, a Mr Alfred Peacock. In the title deeds it's simply called 'Plot 7 Lancaster Avenue'. Mr Peacock's wife was a native of Elsinore in Denmark, so that probably explains it. Interestingly, some of its architectural features, like the tower with the green copper roof, and the dormer windows, are copies of the ones on the Kronburg Castle in Elsinore. Anyway, in 1934 Mr Peacock died in a motoring accident on the East Lancashire Road. Soon after, Mrs Peacock put the house on the market, and moved with her two teenage sons back to Denmark to be near her family. Then, of course, in 1936 Dr Davenport bought the house, and although he didn't much like the name *Elsinore*, he never got round to changing it."

"That *is* interesting."

"All the bedrooms are on this first floor... this one was Mrs Davenport's, facing south and overlooking the pond. This is where Aunt Hilda slept as well when she came to stay, and it's where you'll be sleeping tonight. I'll show you the other bedrooms later. But I want to take you up to the 'observation tower' now, and you'll see how cleverly designed it is with all-round visibility... ideal for star-gazing or, if you're so inclined, spying on the neighbours! I learned so much about astronomy up here... and climatology too... he was such a brilliant teacher... he had that gift of making learning so interesting that you remembered it effortlessly. We even got to see the early satellites through this telescope... but sometimes, like tonight, we just enjoyed the views in all directions... celestial and terrestrial."

"I can't believe how tidy and spotless you keep the place, Martha! All the rooms are immaculate. I'm afraid mine aren't anywhere near this standard. How do you find the time, and the energy, on top of your work at school? You must be at it day and night."

"No, not really; but I suppose it *is* a bit like the Forth Bridge. I start at the top and systematically work my way down, until I've been round everywhere, and then start all over again, though I must admit of late I've been concentrating mainly on the actual living quarters. But Liz Jenkins helps a lot. I really couldn't manage without her help, and when I go away, she and Taff come and stay here, which works very well."

"Ooh, look at how the sun casts the colours onto that wall...it's just like the east window in Chester cathedral."

"Yes, and it's even more striking at dawn, and then moves round with the sun... a lot of thought must have gone into the original design, and though I've lived here for eight years, I keep finding new things. Anyway, we'll go down now, and have a look at the coach-house."

"Are we taking the express route, or the scenic one?" asked Amanda."

"You're younger than me, Mandy... but don't blame me if you break your neck!"

In the event, they descended slowly and elegantly together, Amanda instinctively holding on to her friend's hand.

"I do like this hall and stairway... and it's so tastefully decorated with all the intricate plaster mouldings... and the details of the grape vines on the pillars are unbelievable... the trouble they went to... and then, all the paintings and photographs... it's like being in an art gallery. By the way, who is that lady?"

"Oh, that's his grandmother, Mrs D's mother."

"She's beautiful!"

"Yes, she is... and, if you don't mind me saying so, you bear a striking resemblance to her!"

"Oh, I don't know... well, maybe a teeny bit... but she's got far better cheek bones... and a straighter nose than me."

"Apparently, she was an actress with a repertory company, and according to Mrs D, this was one of her promotional portraits. Sadly, she died of consumption when poor Mrs D was only 15."

When they stepped outside, the air was heavy with the scent of phlox. They stood together for a moment in silent reverence, savouring being alive on such a perfect evening, and both lost in their respective thoughts. While Martha recalled the summer evenings of her childhood helping her father in the vegetable plot on Underdale Road, Amanda fantasized about one day being 'Mistress of *Elsinore*'!

They looked at each other and smiled, and as they did so, a lone blackbird alighted on the topmost twig of Mrs McAllister's linden tree, rudely interrupting their reveries with a lungful of the here and now, his paean to the joy of being alive.

"You've never been in the coach house, have you?" said Martha, as she opened the heavy side-door, "Dr Davenport always used this side door... I don't think he ever opened the main doors."

"Had no cause to, I suppose," replied Amanda matter-of-factly, "with just a bicycle. And this is where he..?"

Martha nodded slowly, but walked straight past it, towards the antique bicycle leaning against the far wall, exactly where it had been left on that fateful evening nine years ago. It still looked clean and well cared for.

"Mind the step, Mandy... the lighting isn't brilliant."

"Yes, I see what you mean!"

"This was *his* place. Apart from Mrs D, I think I was the only person allowed in here. This is where he came when he wanted to be alone, to think... or to experiment with his inventions... he was so ahead of his time... he could have been a brilliant engineer... he was so creative and so skilled. As you can see, everything pretty well has been left exactly as it was."

"But why is it called 'the coach house', and not 'garage'?"

"I don't know for certain. But that's how it appears on the plans. Perhaps they thought 'garage' didn't sound grand enough! And, of course, very few people had cars in 1906. Horse-drawn vehicles were still the normal means of transport for the well-heeled."

"And this is *the* bike?" said Amanda, "Blimey, I wouldn't want to go far on that... it must weigh a ton!"

"Well, *he* thought the world of it. I did suggest to him to get a nice modern one, but to no avail. I think, for him it would be like deserting an old friend, just because he's getting a bit old!"

"He never had a car?"

"I'm afraid Dr Davenport was *not* a car enthusiast!" said Martha with a smile.

"What about Mr Peacock, then? What did he use the coach house for?"

"Now, he *was* a car enthusiast... Bentleys, I believe, and, apparently, he used to do all the repairs on them himself in here... hence, the lifting contraption."

"And what's all this weight-lifting equipment over here?"

372

"Oh, that was Dr Davenport's. As I said, I've left everything exactly as it was when he died. Apparently, he was a *very* good amateur boxer in his day, and he kept up the physical training regime all through his life.

"Was this generally known in the School? I mean, Rich never mentioned anything to me."

"Oh, yes. The boys were in awe of him, and most of the masters were too! He was a great believer in *Mens sana in corpore sano*, and tried to instil that into school life as well. Anyway, before we go... let's have a look at the Everton crest I mentioned."

"Gosh, I like that... *nil satis... nisi... optimum...* yes, and one might add, in both word, and deed!"

"Yes, I think even *he* wa*s satis*-fied with that!"

The coach house was not Martha's favourite place, and she was glad to get out into the fresh evening air again. The blackbird had moved on, and so had the sun, but the garden was still awash with birdsong and the sweet aromas of summer.

"'A garden is a lovesome thing, God wot!'", declaimed Amanda.

"Especially 'when the eve is cool'", concurred Martha. "That was one of my dad's favourite poems... I think he must have learned it in primary school... he certainly loved *his* garden... found great solace in it. I don't know about you, Mandy, but I feel it's getting more chilly than cool now! Do you fancy a cup of coffee... or something stronger, if you prefer?"

"Coffee would be lovely, Martha, thank you. It's been quite a busy afternoon between everything."

"I hope I haven't tired you out."

"Good heavens, no. It's such a beautiful house, with

so many fascinating features... thank you for showing me around."

"I'm glad you enjoyed it."

Both women were more tired than they cared to admit, and retired early to their separate bedrooms, each with quite a different take on the evening's deliberations: Martha pondered on when exactly to broach the subject foremost in her mind, whilst, unbeknown to her, her friend fell asleep delving for auspicious hints about the very same subject.

AMANDA awoke from a deep sleep with a mock-peremptory "Wakey, wakey, rise and shine!" from the landing.

"Gosh, what time is it?"

"Only nine o'clock!" said Martha, putting her head round the door.

"I'd no idea... why didn't you wake me earlier?" said Amanda, checking her watch.

"I didn't have the heart... you were sleeping like a baby! You were quite tired last night, weren't you? I could tell."

"Yes, I did sleep very soundly, but it also helped being in a snore-free zone for a change!"

Martha had always regarded herself as a 'morning person', and had already been up two hours, during which time she had fed the fish, re-stocked all the bird-feeders, picked the odd errant weed from the flower-beds, and laid up for breakfast. She had also had time to ponder, and ponder again, before finally deciding that there was nothing to be gained by further delay. "*Carpe diem*, Martha," as Dr Davenport used to say, and so she should, indeed would... today... nay, this morning... in fact, why not over breakfast!

"So, while you're getting up, I'll get cracking with the breakfast. Are you all right with bacon and egg?"

"O, yes, please, but it's a lot of extra work for you, Martha."

"It's no trouble at all... your bathroom's the first on the left."

"Thanks, Martha... I won't be long."

Amanda got up slowly, thinking that another half-hour in bed would not have been amiss. She padded across to the open window, and was mesmerised by the sheer perfection of everything around her: the crisp morning air, the view across the Cheshire plain, the pristine sky, and even the goldfish glinting in their pond below. The scene evoked that Victorian hymn, *For the beauty of the Earth,* which she had sung so often and so lustily at school without ever fully understanding the words as she did at that particular moment.

The refreshing aroma of coffee and bacon wafted up from the kitchen, and never being one to waste too much time on ablutions and getting dressed, Amanda suddenly found herself poised on the top step of the grand staircase debating whether to "risk her neck" on the doctor's descent, or to act her age. In the event, wiser counsel prevailed.

"My goodness, Martha, this is like the Chester Grosvenor."

"The pleasure is mine; and besides, this is a special occasion, and a very special guest."

"Well, you've certainly made me feel special. Ever since I arrived yesterday afternoon, everything's felt so...

I can't think of the word... anyway, you're a wonderful hostess, Martha, and when we eventually find our new home, I shall definitely return the compliment... I mean, just the two of us, of course!"

Martha gazed at her lovely friend and smiled broadly.

"Why are you smiling?"

"After a pause, she replied, "Let me tell you... it's after what you just said... you see, I've been thinking... well, I've been thinking for a long time actually... about this house. It is a bit of an extravagance for one person... well, for me anyway... so, with mixed feelings... I've decided to... sell up."

"What!" spluttered Amanda, spilling coffee all over her dress, "You're actually putting *Elsinore* on the market?"

"Yes, after a lot of heart-searching, I've decided to do just that... and, more to the point, I'm offering *you* first refusal."

"I don't know what to say!"

"Well, are you interested?"

"*Interested*? Of course I'm interested. I can't believe what I'm hearing. Things are happening so quickly... it's like a dream... and I hope I won't wake up and find it *is* only a dream. While you were thinking, Martha, I was dreaming that one day I would be hearing those very words you've just uttered. But are you sure you're doing the right thing? Where will *you* go?"

"O, don't you worry about me... I've got two or three options in mind. But I was thinking if you moved directly in here, it would save you a lot of bother. But, of course, you'll have to talk it over with your husband first, before we can go into the details."

"I assure you, Martha, *Mr Nobbs* won't take much persuading... he's had his eye on *Elsinore* for a very long time."

"Yes, I suspected as much! But there's no great hurry... have a good think about it. It's a big decision."

"Have you got a price in mind, I mean, a reserve price?" asked Amanda, knowing that that would be her husband's prime concern.

"Well, I've had two independent valuations, but since, I assume, it'll be a cash sale, and with no agents' fees, no mortgages and no chains, I'm sure we can come to some agreement fairly quickly.

The word 'mortgages' reminded Amanda of how different things were for her fifteen years earlier when buying her first little property in Leigh. She was also very aware that she had Richard to thank for her changed circumstances, and was determined to do all she could for him now.

Chapter Sixteen

For all Nobbs's cavilling at Amanda's overgenerous offer on *Elsinore,* he was the proudest man in all England when he carried her over the threshold on 11th October 1974.

Amanda shared her husband's euphoria, but not his sense of entitlement, nor his complacency. Indeed, if anything, she felt guilty about adding to her best friend's litany of life-long losses by depriving her not only of her magnificent home, but a tangible link with her late, beloved friend and mentor.

But Martha soon disabused her of this guilt: "Look, Mandy, it's a 'win-win' situation: you get your 'dream house', and I'm relieved of an enormous responsibility. Furthermore, I know *Elsinore* will be in safe hands, and that you'll cherish it, as I did, though probably for different reasons. Besides, you're in a far better position financially to maintain it than I could ever be. As for myself...well... I've got to think of *my* future now. But don't you worry about that, I'll soon find something... and with 'demob' beckoning, I want to spend more time in Aberdyfi from now on, and maybe settle there eventually, who knows? Think of that, Mandy, on the river every day... rain or shine... waving to Ellis... can't wait!"

In the end, rather than waste time looking for alternative accommodation, Martha accepted Taff and Liz's invitation to move in with them until she found somewhere suitable of her own, but after only a few weeks she found their company so congenial and mutually beneficial that she felt no urgency to uproot.

WHEN JIM WHITTAKER submitted his notice of retirement on 1st September 1974, the governors were astounded. They had assumed that after overseeing the building works so ably and enthusiastically, he would have wanted to stay in post at least until the comprehensive changeover. But Jim's mind was irreversibly made up.

After much heated discussion about what to do next, the governors reluctantly accepted Vicar Ramsbottom's suggestion of inviting Dr Hendricks, the Senior Master, to serve as a "temporary, acting Headmaster" until a permanent appointment could be made. Many of the new governors rejected this as a retrograde step, but Martin Shaw, the Chairman, saw it as an opportunity to make a virtue out of necessity.   He proposed that if they could persuade the Head of Manchester Road School to delay his retirement, say, for twelve months and share the headship of both schools with Dr Hendricks, the partnership might facilitate the unification process.

Accordingly, an unprecedented joint meeting of

governors was held in the Men's staffroom at Manchester Road School, specifically to discuss Martin Shaw's proposal, and surprisingly, apart from some concern about both men's ages, it was warmly received as a sensible solution under the circumstances.

However, the following day it suffered a major setback when Dave Longworth let it be known that he had no more stomach for "comprehensiveness" than Jim Whittaker, and regardless of any financial inducements, he would not be changing his mind.

Later that week, Martin Shaw arranged to meet Nobbs at Leigh Cricket Club for "a noggin and a chat" about the latest developments.

"So, how's Mandy? I haven't seen her about for some time."

"Yes, Mandy's fine, thanks... at least she was when I spoke to her on Monday night. She's staying with Martha Wolf at the moment... they're like sisters, them two."

"So, when are you actually moving, then?"

"Oh, not long now... 11th of October, I think she said, if everything goes to plan. And it can't come soon enough either, with all the furniture in storage. I'm like a night watchman, sleeping rough in the garage!"

"Oh dear, my heart bleeds for you! Anyway, just to fill you in, you'll be glad to know that my 'double-header' idea's still alive... but not exactly kicking."

"Why so?"

"Oh, don't ask... Dave Longworth... he's refusing to play ball."

"What's up with the daft bugger? He'd be quids in."

"I know, I know, but there you go... no pleasing some folk."

"So, what's the score now, then?"

"Well, everything's to play for... we'll have to advertise, of course... if only to make it look *kosher*."
Nobbs gazed thoughtfully into his fast disappearing pint. "Hey, are you thinking what I'm thinking?"

"I've no idea what *you're* thinking, Mr Nobbs," replied Martin, "but what *I'm* thinking is you should be spending more time with that lovely missus of yours! Anyway, I must push off... I'll give you a ring in a couple of days."

THE FOLLOWING evening, Martin called an unofficial meeting of some half-dozen NGS governors at Netherbridge Vicarage for a further airing of the 'shared headship' idea, which proved far more controversial than he had hoped.

As the elder statesman of the group, the Vicar as always urged caution. "The idea may be commendable in principle," he said, "but I fear problems might arise in its implementation. In my experience, when in doubt, there is much to be said for staying with the tried and tested."

"Maybe, Vicar," replied one of the newer governors, "but, let's face it... Hendricks *is* getting a bit long in the tooth."

"And more to the point," echoed his friend, "could he cope with the stress?"

"But it would be a nice reward after forty years of loyal and highly professional service," countered a third, "as well as a substantial enhancement to his pension."

"Provided the job didn't kill him first!" quipped a fourth.

"Look," said Martin, a little impatiently, "let's not get

carried away, shall we? We're talking twelve months here, tops? And remember, as Jim's current number two, Dr Kendricks will be up to speed with most things from day one... which you must admit is a big plus."

This last point seemed to settle the matter, until Dr Winstanley hurled a huge boulder into the pond.

"In my humble opinion... we've had too much of this 'dead men's shoes' business since George died. I accept, it's worked out very well up to now, but, to coin a phrase, times they are a-changin', and this could be *our* time to change tack too. Don't get me wrong... in principle, I've nothing against keeping things in the family, but since this is a temporary post anyway, it *could* be used as a proving ground for a younger chap, like, say, John Halliday, before he moves on to greater things."

"Oh!" said the Vicar, suddenly taking a renewed interest, "if we're going down that road, I'd like to propose Frank Fairclough."

"I don't think Frank would be the slightest bit interested, Vicar," interjected Martin.

"How can you be so sure? Frank's a good man... he's given sterling service... and is very highly regarded both in the School and the town. Indeed, were it not for Dr Kendricks, he'd be my number one choice."

"Yes, I know, I know, Vicar... Frank is, as you say, very highly regarded, but, he's... how can I put? He's a bit too... traditional... and he's not an 'organisation man', not a 'team player'. Besides, I don't think he'd take kindly to job-sharing!"

Eventually, Dr Kendricks re-emerged, though not unanimously, as the default safe pair of hands, and would be recommended as such at the full Governors' meeting in October. It would then be up to Manchester Road to choose his "opposite number" from among their ranks. But, of course, being a local authority school, such matters as advertising vacancies and job specifications had always been left to local education officers.

Since county boundaries changed with the reorganisation of local government in April 1974, Netherbridge came under the jurisdiction of Cheshire County Council. Consequently, Tony Whittingham, their former local Education Officer, was replaced by his equivalent from Chester, one Andy Goody, whom Nobbs incidentally had managed to befriend while on the Pastoral Care course at Woodberry Down School in July.

WHEN NEWS OF the joint headship first broke at Manchester Road School, a palpable wave of optimism swept through the staffrooms, with two or three of the older teachers openly declaring a keen interest. Comprehensive education would eradicate the invidious scholastic *apartheid* that had always limited their career opportunities.

As it happened, this was also Mr Andy Goody's first important appointment, and, as an ardent convert to the new doctrine of pastoral care, he was determined to accord it its proper status. Thus, if Dr Hendricks was to be given full charge of the "academic curriculum" of both schools, as seemed likely, it seemed only fair and right to him that Dr Hendricks's compeer at Manchester Road should be granted parity of esteem with overall responsibility for the "pastoral curriculum".

Perhaps the strongest and most popular candidate for the post was Dennis Peterson, the former Sports Master at the School, who, now in his mid-fifties and nursing a troublesome back condition, had been reduced to filling in with English, geography and R.E. During WW2 he had served as a sergeant with the Lancashire Fusiliers in North Africa and Italy, and had retained much of the military in his bearing and manner thereafter. Despite being an acknowledged disciplinarian in the School, he was very popular with the pupils, and was always the person they gravitated towards when they had a problem. He was also highly respected in the town for his work with the Samaritans.

Equally suitable for the role was Miss Barbara Pearce, the *de facto* (unpaid) Deputy Head when Dave Longworth was away. A tall and well-proportioned woman, also in her mid-fifties, she had spent most of her career at Manchester Road, teaching the basics to generations of 'Remedial' pupils. Like her good friend, Dennis, she too was universally liked and respected, and for many years, together with her live-in woman-friend and colleague, the Music teacher, she had written and co-produced the annual Christmas pantomime, a highlight in the School's, and indeed the town's, calendar. Furthermore, perhaps appointing a woman to a senior position would have had many advocates, if only to challenge the age-old presumption that men made better bosses.

But sadly, when the job description appeared on the notice-boards, the optimism was short-lived. Couched in 1970s socio-educational parlance, the document drew a variety of responses, mostly less than charitable, and some unrepeatable.

Whilst the opening paragraph explaining how "this

unique and challenging opportunity" had arisen seemed harmless enough, the remainder meant little to anyone unfamiliar with the jargon of the day. Phrases such as "behaviour support strategies", "resource-based and pupil-centred pedagogies", "spectrum of ongoing responsibilities", "philosophical melding of the pastoral and academic", "the hidden curriculum", and so forth, far from clarifying the nature and requirements of the post, engendered profound cynicism among those who had already devoted half their working lives to toiling, often thanklessly and in under-resourced classrooms. One wag could not resist pinning a copy underneath the dart-board at the *Boar's Head* lest an 'old contemptible' like Taff Jenkins should miss out on the "unique and challenging opportunity". While Dave Longworth considered the position custom-made for the Archangel Gabriel, Phil Evans likened the job description to "a spoof cobbled together by a couple of his irreverent sixth-formers".

But what really did it for the 'mere mortals' of Manchester Road was not the pretentious language, nor even the extravagant expectations, but the deadly sting in the tail:

Finally, the successful candidate will not only have had practical experience in the field of pastoral care, but will also possess a thorough knowledge and understanding of the principles underpinning its philosophy. To this end, it would be advantageous if he (or she) had studied the discipline at least to first degree level.

And so, while the chief aspirants for the post settled into a stoical silence, the 'foot-soldiers', with little to lose, vented their frustration volubly, if not always coherently.

"Typical!"

"Stitch up!"

"Blatant fix!"

As the expletives exploded, one thing became clear: "the successful candidate", whoever it might be, would require more than a degree in pastoral care to keep that particular flock within the fold.

ON THE FIRST Saturday in November 1974, the Nobbses hosted the most lavish reception ever witnessed in Netherbridge, eclipsing even Joe Riley's 'farewell do' in 1971. Clearly, the cost had been the least of their concerns: Taylors of Leigh did the catering again; a specialist firm from Manchester set up a superb public address system; and with its being so near Guy Fawkes Night, a pyrotechnics company from Stoke-on-Trent brought the evening to a climax with a spectacular fireworks display at the stroke of midnight.

Although ostensibly a house-warming party, the invitations specified a black tie, and for good measure Nobbs designated it as a charity event, "to give it a bit of tone". After consulting several directories in the town library, he eventually settled on *Barnardo's*, although neither he nor Amanda had ever had any dealings with that organization.

As expected, everything was organised with military precision, and thanks to Amanda's persistence and charm on the telephone, the final guest-list would have graced a lord mayor's banquet. In addition to several local dignitaries, she had persuaded two or three *names* from the worlds of sport and television to put in an appearance, "to add some oomph", as she put it, but perhaps more importantly, to impress the *ex officio* guests: businessmen, local authority officials, and of course school governors.

Lavishly flood-lit for the occasion, and with light classical music wafting through the evening air, *Elsinore* looked distinctly palatial, and its glamorous new owners cut a dash as they welcomed each guest into the imposing entrance hall of their grand residence. A fanciful bystander might have bethought him of a medieval prince and his beautiful princess welcoming the nobility of North Cheshire across their drawbridge to join in the festivities at their castle.

Several members of staff and ancillary workers at Manchester Road had accepted their invitations, but apart from one or two stalwarts like Phil Evans and Titchener, there were very few guests from NGS. Martha had given her apologies beforehand to Amanda, and also by letter, because of a pre-arranged visit to Aberdyfi to look at a sailing cruiser that Ellis had suggested for her.

Despite all the ungallant mutterings beforehand about the host, the function itself was deemed an unmitigated success. Everyone had exercised their taste buds amply, some excessively, but Nobbs had ensured that there would be no repeat of the Joe Riley debacle on this occasion.

Thanks to another judicious phone call by Amanda, the event was given front page coverage in the *Chronicle* under the banner headline "A Right Royal Welcome at *Elsinore*" accompanied by a skilfully taken photograph of the host and hostess looking for all the world like a real royal couple mingling graciously among their adoring

387

subjects. As usual, clichés abounded and hyperboles rocketed across the page while Nobbs was adjudged a thoroughly good egg and the toast of Netherbridge.

But, for all that, it could well have rained on his parade. While everyone was waiting anxiously for the opening volley of fireworks, Nobbs, feeling enormously pleased with himself, strolled across the manicured lawns to join Phil and Shirley Evans sitting on the bench overlooking the fish pond. After gazing for a moment into the middle distance, he declared with a mixture of triumphalism and contempt, "A question for you, Phil... tell me, if Georgie Porgie were to return from the dead, what, do you reckon, he'd say about all this wassailing and carousing in the grounds of his precious *Elsinore*?"

Fortified by the alcohol, Phil was ready with an equally facetious retort, but it was strangled at birth by the considerable weight of his wife's left boot on his right instep, so that their host's rhetorical question prompted only a foolish, insincere smile.

But reflecting on the way home on what Phil's stifled response might have been, Shirley ventured, "Was it 'the time is out of joint' by any chance?"

Phil nodded, 'Yes, either that, or, 'something is rotten in the State of Denmark'".

"Or what about ''tis an unweeded garden that grows to seed," giggled Shirley.

"Things rank and gross in nature possess it merely," added Phil, warming to the game.

"But, changing tack a little, what about 'that one may smile and smile and be a villain'?"

"Spot on, Shirl!" said Phil. "And there was me, smiling and smiling with all the other grovelling toads."

"'Fie on't! Ah fie!' But never mind, dear, one day you'll thank me."

"Do you reckon?"

THE INTERVIEWS for the shared headship were held at Manchester Road School on Tuesday, 10th December. Andy Goody met the candidates personally at the main entrance at a quarter past two, so that interviewing could begin promptly at three o'clock. After the usual courtesies, they were asked to wait in the Headmaster's office until called.

During the next quarter of an hour several important-looking men put their faces round the door and then disappeared without so much as an apology. But by twenty to three all was quiet, and nerves were beginning to jangle. There appeared to be only three candidates in the race after all: Dennis, Barbara, and a surprising outsider, Geoff Rawlinson, the Headmaster of Queen's Street C of E Junior School. The two 'insiders' suspected that he was in possession of the "magic piece of paper", or that he might be part of some covert scheme known only to the great and the good at County Hall.

As the school clock crept towards 3.45 pm, both Dennis and Barbara were growing in confidence. Perhaps their new Area Officer was not as prejudiced as they had thought, or maybe no graduates had applied. Whilst being keen rivals for the position, they had agreed that whoever lost would accept defeat graciously and be fully supportive of the other. Neither worried over-much about Mr Rawlinson, even though he was a headmaster already, because he only had primary school experience, and besides, it had always been understood that the

389

appointment would be internal.

Then, just as the clock's big hand jumped to a quarter to three, the door opened again, to admit none other than the ubiquitous Area Education Officer, Mr Richard Nobbs, who promptly drew himself up to his full height, as if claiming ownership of the room and the situation. Then, with a perfunctory nod to the others, he sat down in the chair opposite and crossed his legs.

He did this, not in the usual, relaxed manner of casually resting one knee on top of the other, but rather as *young* men often do when subconsciously, or otherwise, 'displaying their credentials' in mixed company, but alas *without* their sublime aplomb. Defying gravity and an incipient hip problem, Nobbs was obliged to grip the outside of his left ankle with both hands, then tug it upwards before lowering it again gingerly on to his right knee, the right hand always at the ready lest the ankle slip off! Finally, as if to affirm that neither age nor any other adversity could ever curb his effortless supremacy, he assumed an expression of Zen-like calm and insouciance.

But after barely half a minute, he stood up again and proclaimed, "God, it's like a f------ morgue in here... I'm going for a leak!"

The others looked at each other in amused bewilderment, and indeed wondered why Nobbs was there at all, unless perhaps in some professional capacity, like talking to the candidates beforehand to put them at their ease, or conduct some preliminary assessment.

When Nobbs returned to the room, he did not sit down, preferring to move around, looking at the various team photographs and pictures adorning the office walls. To their right, masking a disused fire place stood a large glass cabinet full of trophies and memorabilia, including an England Schoolboys football cap belonging to one Stanley Osgood, an ex-pupil killed in action, aged 20, while on National Service with the Duke of Wellington's Regiment in Korea.

"Look at these things," said Nobbs, picking up one item after another from the cabinet, "junk from a bygone era soon to be flushed down the sewers of history, along with much else in this, and that *other* place."

As it happened, Dennis Peterson was especially fond of that cabinet, because he had been largely instrumental in raising the money to purchase it, and also because much of the contents represented the fruits of his labours as a young man straight out of the forces in 1946. He had given freely of his time coaching generations of boys, including young Stanley, and that cap was a constant reminder for him of happier days working outside in all weathers striving to build decent teams before they left at 15 to start work in the mills or the coal pits. More importantly, it also illustrated what ordinary youngsters can accomplish when given encouragement and support. In different circumstances, he would have confronted Nobbs, but this was hardly the time or the place, and somehow, he managed to restrain himself.

But, while Dennis could barely hide his disdain for such brash and contemptible behaviour, Barbara could only think what a magnificent figure its perpetrator cut in his bespoke suit – more like a 1950s film star, she thought, than a county council official. Barbara had always had a weakness for waistcoats, and she found Nobbs's irresistible, with its interminable row of mother-of-pearl buttons, and the bottom one, of course, undone.

And that wife of his, she romanced, was a bit of all right too... why do some people get all the luck?

Suddenly, her delightful daydream was broken by the appearance of another, though less arrestingly attired gentleman, who introduced himself as John Unsworth, a colleague of Mr Goody. He then proceeded to read out the following statement from a type-written piece of paper:

(1) Candidates will be called for interview in alphabetical order of surname.

(2) Each interview will take approximately 30 minutes, during which time candidates will be asked to (a) give a summary of the last five years of their careers (b) explain what personal qualities and knowledge they could bring to the role and (c) describe how they would see the role developing during the next five years.

(3) Candidates are advised to leave the premises after their interview, and not confer with each other or with other colleagues until such time as they have been officially informed of the governors' decision.

"I believe, Mr Nobbs, you are the first on the list... if you would like to follow me, please, sir."

As soon as the two had left the room, Geoff Rawlinson, who hitherto had observed proceedings silently and impassively, remarked, "Bloody hell, anybody would think they were choosing a Pope!"

"So, now you know, Barbara," said Dennis, who could smell a rat as well as anyone, "why our friend has been hanging around the School so much of late!"

AFTER THEIR interviews, candidates were invited to attend a 'feedback session' the following morning with Martin Shaw, Ted Hoyle (Chairman of Governors at Manchester Road), Dr Kendricks, and Andy Goody, when the appointment would also be announced. All were present except for Nobbs, who apparently had been called away to an important meeting in Chester with the Deputy Director of Education.

Speaking on behalf of the panel, Mr Goody said he was very impressed by the candidates' experience and professionalism. "All three of you," he said, "came over as having a genuine interest in the role, and indeed being more than capable of fulfilling its practical requirements. However, unfortunately, you were all, to coin a phrase, a little light on theory, and as the old adage goes, practice without theory is as bad as theory without practice. And so, the governors have come to the difficult but, I must stress, unanimous decision to ask one of our own officers, Mr Richard Nobbs, who has both the experience and the required qualifications, to take on the role in the interim.

"However," he continued, barely stopping for breath, "in view of the exceptionally high level of the candidature, I have been asked to make the following announcement. As you may have heard, our Deputy Director is very keen for Netherbridge to become a standard bearer for comprehensive education within the Authority, which explains in part why these two schools have been selected as pioneers, if you will, in the reorganisation. The Deputy Director also regards pastoral care as the *sine qua non* of the comprehensive system, and with that in mind he has this week authorised an exciting new initiative, which may well be of interest to you. Put simply, the L.E.A has agreed to finance twelve-month secondments on full salary and expenses for suitable teachers wishing to study for a Master's degree in this particular field at Manchester University.

"Now, as it's December, and places for these particular courses are filling up rapidly everywhere, time is of the essence. But thanks largely to Mr Nobbs's connexions with the Education Department at Manchester, we have been given priority on fifteen places there. Now, if any of you are interested, I urge you to move quickly and give me a ring first thing tomorrow morning on my office number. Well, thank you all for your time. I hope you found the experience interesting and instructive... and good luck to you all with everything."

Chapter Seventeen

Never one to procrastinate, Nobbs spent most of that Christmas holiday transforming Dave Longworth's "Dickensian" office into "something befitting the twentieth century". Aided and abetted by Fred "the Fixer" Broadbent, the School's capable and versatile caretaker, he set about eradicating all traces of the room's previous occupier and anything else suggestive of "that most invidious of constructs, the secondary modern school".

The 'cleansing' process began with the sign on the door, which read simply, "Headmaster". It had been *in situ* since 1952, Dave's first year at the School, and he was especially fond of it because it had been hand-carved for him by a second-year pupil, called Brian Edge, on a piece of pitch pine taken from a broken desk. Despite being confined to a wheelchair after contracting polio in the 1947 epidemic, Brian became an accomplished woodworker, and went on to study Furniture Design at

Bolton Technical College. After two further years' industrial experience at Parker Knoll in High Wycombe, his father set him up as a bespoke furniture-maker in Netherbridge.

Be that as it may, Brian's time-honoured handiwork had no place in the 'Nobbsian' world order, and the sign on the office door was summarily removed and replaced with a factory-made, brass and mahogany name-plate, emblazoned with the words, "Mr Richard C. Nobbs, M Ed, Head Master".

The next casualty of the grand purge was the display cabinet which had aroused such heightened emotions on the day of the interviews. After emptying its contents into a large cardboard box expropriated from the cleaners' store-room, Fred was instructed to trundle it off to a storage hut next door to the girls' toilets. Then, warming to his novel, iconoclastic role, he proceeded to strip the walls of all photographs and pictures, which, like the other memorabilia, were stuffed into cardboard boxes and taken away. Finally, every item of furniture, apart from the green leather-topped mahogany desk, was to be disposed of as Fred pleased.

On New Year's Eve, after Dave's office had been thoroughly "expurgated and deterged", Nobbs took Fred to the *Duke of Argyle* for a "Christmas pint". Naturally, Fred was extremely flattered by this unexpected and kind-hearted gesture, little knowing, of course, that its main purpose was not so much to express gratitude or friendship, as to winkle out a little more of what *really* went on behind the scenes at Manchester Road School, especially if any of the teachers had "little secrets" or vulnerabilities that might be exploited. Meanwhile, Fred in all innocence was relieved that his new boss, for all his funny ways, was at heart "a genuine, down-to-earth bloke who understood people like him, someone you could get along with." And yet, sadly, on the last Friday of the holiday, when Fred rang him excitedly to say that his "throne" had arrived, he received a four-lettered rebuke for presumptuousness bordering on *lèse-majesté*, even though the chair was indeed so extravagant in style and proportion that to call it a mere *chair* was an affront to its resplendence.

THIS WAS the second time in a matter of weeks that Nobbs had carried out these 'cleansing' operations. All creatures do it to some extent when establishing new territory, but with Nobbs it was an obsession: the old order, however laudable, must be annihilated, and a new one established according to his own *desiderata*.

He had barely moved into *Elsinore* before he began "expurgating and deterging" the coach-house, eradicating everything associated with George Davenport. Even the name, "coach-house", with its overtones of a former, golden era, to which Nobbs had not belonged, had to be changed to something more functional like "annexe", although Amanda, much to his annoyance, often 'forgot'! Martha had managed to salvage as many mementoes as she could fit into Taff's shed, but everything else related to "Davenport" or "the f------ grammar school" that Nobbs could not sell he burned or took to the rubbish dump – barring the Hercules bicycle, which he thought might "fetch a bob or two someday as a collectable".

As soon as the annexe had been cleared, the "re-creative" process could begin, and he set about that with the same crazed sense of urgency, engaging professional help when the tasks proved beyond his own and Fred's capabilities. The wiring was up-graded, the original lighting was replaced with bright, fluorescent tubes, and the 'inter-com' system, which he had brought from the Leigh house, was reinstalled and extended into the annexe. Then, to lighten the austere ambience, he painted the walls white, and then covered them with posters of scantily clad female film stars and famous car models from the 1930s onwards.

With winter approaching, and Leigh 1963 still fresh in his memory, he had several radiators installed, and for good measure, an "office", or "inner sanctum" as Amanda called it, built into the corner on the right of the side-entrance. Fully equipped with a kitchenette and a refrigerator, this afforded a snug space away from the main house where he could meet friends for a beer and a game of darts on cold winter nights; and it was also large enough for a television set and his beloved *chaise-longue*. Since the annexe's main purpose was to garage the motor cars, he also had a large work bench built and several tool cupboards affixed to the wall opposite the main doors. However, very much against Amanda's wishes, he decided to retain the notorious hoist, arguing that it preceded Davenport, and, besides, might one day resume its original function.

Nobbs's need to stamp his authority on the annexe was matched only by his need to rid himself of George Davenport's ghost. For some years, if ever he had been thwarted at work or in his private life, he had often been troubled at night by a recurring nightmare. This invariably took the form of being trapped in a room with a class of unruly pupils over whom he had no control, and just as matters were reaching crisis point, "this thing", as he called it, would appear, at the door, like Hamlet's father's ghost, attired *cap-à-pie*, so to speak, in mortarboard and gown, shaking his head and smiling sadly.

The details were so vivid and so disturbing that he would sometimes lie awake all night afraid of going to sleep again. He had never told Amanda about it until one night a few weeks after moving into *Elsinore*, when he had another, even more disturbing, experience. He dreamed that he was looking down from his bedroom window onto the moonlit gardens below, and looking up at him from the other side of the fish pond was his smiling, ghostly nemesis again, dressed in his usual academic garb, and beckoning him to come down into the garden. Feeling irresistibly drawn, he obeyed, until both were facing each other across the pond. Then when he began to walk round the pond to join the spectre, it moved slowly away towards the front of the house, periodically half-turning and beckoning before finally disappearing through the side-entrance into the annexe.

Waking suddenly, Nobbs rushed into Amanda's room shouting, "MA... MA... MANDY... where... where are you? Oh, I'm sorry, Mand... I must have been... dreaming."

Suspecting that he had had a nightmare, Amanda tried to keep calm, and humoured him as she might a small child. "Come into bed, sweetheart... everything's all right now... nothing to worry about... there... you come into bed with Mandy," she said, adding with a faint smile, "You're safe with your Ma-Mandy!"

The following morning he got up first as usual, going

through all his complex morning routines, as if nothing untoward had happened, even bringing Amanda her morning cup of tea, but this time sitting down on the bed beside her. Clearly, he was not his usual self.

"I'm sorry about last night, love... it was really weird... I just can't get that bugger out of my head."

"What do you mean, 'bugger'?"

"*Davenport*, of course... who do you think?"

Amanda had difficulty in hiding her amusement.

"It's not funny, Amanda. "It feels like the sod's still here... haunting the place. I always thought the name, *Elsinore*, sounded cold and spooky... perhaps we should have changed it to something more... you know... welcoming. It feels like this thing's telling me something. And it's damned annoying because this was always my dream house, and you did great getting it. But these effing dreams, Mand, they're getting to me."

"You mean you've had more than one?"

Nobbs nodded, and eyed Amanda nervously.

"Well, you could have mentioned it."

"I know, I know... but I thought they'd blow over... and anyway, I didn't want to bother you."

"Look, they probably *will* blow over... there's always a perfectly good explanation for these things. You probably had too much to do during the house move. They do say moving house is a very stressful thing, second only to bereavement, I believe."

"And then there's Martha..."

"Martha? What's wrong with Martha'?"

"Nothing *wrong* with her... it's just... well... you know... she's always hanging around, isn't she?"

"Martha is my *friend*, Rich... and a damned good one

too. Are you saying she mustn't come here?"

"Of course I'm not saying that. I know she's your... best mate an' that, but... I might as well be honest... she makes me feel... uncomfortable. In fact, if you must know, she always has done... ever since I've known her. Mind you, I don't suppose she likes me very much either... I don't know why, because I've always tried to be nice to her. There's just something weird about her. When she's here, she makes me feel like it's still *her* house... well, hers and Davenport's... and we've stolen it off 'em... like, what's that word in *Hamlet*?"

"Usurped?"

"Yes, that's right, *usurped*, that's what it feels like, Mand, we're *usurpers*... and it's doing me 'ead in."

Amanda barely stifled another chuckle, almost spilling the tea on the counterpane as she put her cup down on the bedside table.

"I'm glad somebody thinks it's funny," he said.

She reached up and slid her left arm round his neck and gently pulled him down beside her. They lay there quietly for a good minute, she caressing his hair and admiring his perfect profile. Then she suddenly leaned over, she kissed him firmly on the mouth, and whispered in his ear words she had not uttered for some time, "I *love* you, Rich."

Still feeling perturbed by the night's events, and not a little abashed at his wife's sudden show of affection, Nobbs sprang to his feet, and said, "I wonder if Shakespeare was haunted by effing ghosts."

"What do you mean?"

"...and he managed to exorcise them by putting them into his plays?"

"Look, Rich... that was four hundred years ago... back

401

then, people actually believed in ghosts. And anyway, ghost stories have always been popular. So, Shakespeare probably used them just to put bums on seats. Trouble with you, Rich, you've got a hyper-active imagination. You watch, this is just a phase you're going through, and if you were a woman we'd probably put it down to the *change* or something. We've both been over-working, especially you, and what we could do with is a week away somewhere nice, like Lake Garda."

"How does that quotation go?" continued Nobbs, regardless, "Something like I could call myself the king of all space if I didn't have bad dreams."

"'I could be bounded in a nutshell and count myself a king of infinite space were it not that I have bad dreams'," corrected Amanda a little impatiently, showing off her A-level English. "Look, would you like me to make an appointment for you with Dr Winstanley?" suggested Amanda after a slight pause.

"Winstanley? What does he know about dreams? 'There are more things in heaven and earth...'"

"'...than are dreamt of in your philosophy, Horatio'. Yes, I know, I know, science can't explain everything, but at least the doctor could give you something to help you sleep. And if that doesn't work, then perhaps he could recommend a good psychotherapist?"

"So you think I need a shrink, now? Thank you very much. Shrinks are for loonies, Mandy, and I'm not a loony... well, not yet, anyway."

"Look, it probably won't happen again... but if it does, promise me you'll go to and see the doctor?"

"Yes... if you say so. Do you fancy kippers for a change?"

"Oh yes, please... that's the sanest thing you've said this morning!"

Amanda knew there was no love lost between her husband and Martha, but she had not realised how strong and how long-standing his feelings were. Martha, the ultimate diplomat, had never given an inkling that things were anything but cordial between her and Rich, and in fairness neither had he, until now. But how was this dilemma to be resolved? Clearly, in the short term, or at least until her husband's "night terrors" had subsided, certain adjustments would be needed: Martha's visits would have to be curtailed; and she herself would have to curb those hasty and waspish ripostes of hers. Already, her dismissal of his "improvements" to the coach-house as "just a mid-life crisis vanity project" had sent him into a deep sulk, whereupon she had retaliated by taking herself off to her mother's for the day to "clear the air" in the hope that things would be back to normal by the time she returned.

ON HIS FIRST morning as Head Master, Nobbs had set his alarm clock an hour earlier than usual, to give himself ample time to perform his elaborate morning ablutions, and to ensure that every fibre of his attire caressed his frame to absolute perfection. After countless inspections from every angle in his bathroom mirrors, he finally took Amanda's cup of tea and biscuit up to her bedroom. She was fast asleep, or feigned to be, and half-opened one eye when he kissed her lightly on the forehead.

"Well... I'm off, love. Be good!"

"Ooh! I don't know about that!" she said, yawning. "Enjoy your first day. I hope everything goes to plan."

"By God, it had better," he hissed with a cynical grin. "I've left some porridge for you on the hob. See you later."

"'Bye, sweetheart."

As the white Jaguar crept up past the magnolia tree and turned into Lancaster Avenue, Nobbs recalled setting off for the Grammar School on that first morning in 1947, and noted with a mixture of disdain and imperiousness how his fortunes had changed. He glanced at his new Rolex 'work' watch, and was gratified to see that it was synchronised precisely with the seven o-clock time signal on his car radio. The leading news item that morning was the shipping disaster in Australia: a large container ship colliding with the Tasman Bridge in Hobart, and sinking within minutes with the loss of a dozen lives.

At last, the all too familiar school gates, and after twenty-five years of turning right into the *grammar* school entrance, where he never felt truly accepted, it felt strange to be turning left into his *own* school. As he did so, he was also very conscious of the enormous sign, "Manchester Road Secondary Modern School" towering above the gates, very different from the Grammar School's unpretentious sign, half-hidden by over-grown laurel bushes. Another job for Fred, he hissed to himself, that f------ sign has to go... or at least those two vile words in the middle.

Meanwhile, he could see Fred in the distance unlocking the main doors, and it struck him how shabby he looked in that dreadful brown boiler suit. He would have to organise something smarter than that for him... this was a *school*, not a factory.

"Good morning, Fred," he called out cheerily, as he

404

hoisted himself awkwardly out of the deep leather seat of the Jaguar, "everything under control?"

"Oh, good morning, Mr Nobbs... yes, everything's under control. I painted the lines... hope they're wide enough... a bit of a monster, this, Mr Nobbs!"

"I think we'll manage, Fred. Good work. Come to my office when you're done."

Dave Longworth apparently used to park his rusty, old Ford Cortina wherever there was room, and when the staff car-park was full, on a side-street nearby. That might have been all right for Dave, thought Nobbs, but I'm not Dave, and a Cortina is not a Jaguar... which deserves its own parking spot, incontrovertibly marked, "Head Master", and situated immediately next to the front entrance. Dave was too familiar by half, which, as Martha said, breeds contempt.

As he made his way along the dark corridor towards his office, the glint of the brass name-plate caught his eye. That's what I call classy, he thought, and Mandy was right, plain Mister does have an understated *cachet*. He opened the door, and stood still in the doorway for a full half-minute inhaling the aroma of fresh paint and new furniture. This was all his own doing, and he was well pleased with it. He hung his new black trench coat carefully behind the office door, and looked slowly around him with an air of absolute and unassailable authority. He stretched up to his full height, looking every inch the headmaster in yet another bespoke suit, before lowering his considerable bulk carefully into the vast executive chair. He bared his teeth into something between a grin and a grimace – the alpha-male supreme had reported for duty.

He felt inside his leather attaché case for the matching leather desk diary that Amanda had given him as a 'first day' present. He positioned it dead-centre on his desk pad, which he had already placed dead-centre on the desk. Then he picked up the diary and sniffed the new leather deeply before opening its covers. Inside the front cover he had affixed a card with the renowned quotation from Machiavelli's *The Prince*:

Secure yourself against your enemies, conquer by force or by fraud, make yourself feared and loved by your people... destroy those who can or are likely to injure you.

Although he knew the words by heart, he read, and re-read, them aloud with grim satisfaction until interrupted by a clumsy knock on his office door.

"Come!" he barked in the manner of a fearsome quartermaster he remembered from Donnington Camp in 1942. When the command was repeated, the door opened an inch or two.

"Oh, it's you... come on in, Fred... close the door. Listen, I'll come straight to the point... I've called you in for a special reason. Now, tell me, how long have you had those overalls?"

"*These* overalls, Mr Nobbs?

"Yes, *those* overalls, Fred... I can't see any others!"

"Now, let me see... you've got me there... yes, if I remember rightly, the wife got them on Netherbridge market... let me see..."

"I asked how long, Fred, not where."

"Oh... I reckons... about three year since, Mr Nobbs."

"Three years, you say. Have you got any others?"

"Oh yes, I do have some others, Mr Nobbs... the ones I wear on coke deliveries... but I wear these mostly."

Nobbs shuddered at the thought of Fred's *other* overalls.

"Now... listen, Fred. I don't know what went on before... and I don't want to know... but, as far as I'm concerned, you are a key member of my staff, right? The School couldn't function without you. But, not only that, you are often the first person any visitor to the School comes across. First impressions count, Fred. Do you get my drift? The apparel oft proclaims the man."

"What's that, Mr Nobbs?"

"It means that what you wear says a lot about what kind of person you are, Fred, and what kind of institution you represent."

"Oh...right." (Bloody 'ell, thought Fred, Mr Longworth never used big words like that) "Yes, Mr Nobbs, yes, of course... thank you... thank you... I'll try and smarten myself up a bit, like."

"Good. Now, at 11 o'clock report to me again. We'll go down to Fishwick and Hall and get you fixed up with some decent work clothes. Trust me, Fred, by the time I've finished with you, you'll be the smartest caretaker in the North West!"

"Yes, of course, Mr Nobbs, 11 o'clock it is," he replied with a broad smile, and almost clicking his heels as he left the room.

Nobbs glanced down at the glistening Rolex, and thought, f--- me, Fred Karno's mob will be drifting in shortly, and I expect I'll have to have the same conversation with some of them. The trouble is, Dave had let things slide... some of them dress like f------ beach bums. What sort of example is that for the kids?

Another, slightly more circumspect, knock on the door interrupted his thoughts a second time.

"Come!" he bellowed again in an outrageously pompous voice.

"All right, love, all right!" purred Mrs Bagshaw, the School Secretary, "it's only me."

"Oh, it's you, Peg... take a pew."

"My, this looks different! What happened to all Mr Longworth's stuff?"

"All sorted and taken care of, Peg."

"Well, it certainly looks different, especially that chair. Will it be tea or coffee, Mr Nobbs? Mr Longworth always had coffee, black and no sugar... I don't know how he could drink it."

"Well, I'm more of a tea person, myself, Peg... milk and two spoons, if you don't mind... and if you've got any biscuits... that would be even better."

"See what I can dig out from my little cupboard, Mr Nobbs... we always try to please... any announcements for the Tannoy?"

"Yes, we'll have a slightly extended lunch break today for a short staff meeting. Just announce that... will you, Peg?"

"Very good, Mr Nobbs... will do."

Nobbs winked his approval.

Salt of the earth, that one, he thought, someone I can relate to... and I wouldn't kick her out of bed in a hurry either!

ONE OF Nobbs's more appealing attributes was his ability to make conversation, even with complete strangers. Moreover, he could also be an attentive listener, for he had long learnt that by maintaining eye-contact and listening intently to what people had to say he could take them into his confidence, inducing them to reveal more about themselves, and others, than they had intended. On his previous visits to the School he had often sat down and talked with individual teachers, often assuming a semi-recumbent posture in order to come across as someone friendly and unthreatening. By this means, he had already amassed a fund of personal information about his new Staff, and one of his chief objectives now was to build on this, and identify potential allies and adversaries, especially the latter.

He felt that his first morning at the School had been "quite constructive", especially organising Fred's three sets of work clothes, "one on, one in the wash, and one in the wardrobe", as he had explained to Fred. Perhaps less "constructive" was entrusting his finely honed taste buds to Norah the Cook's Lancashire hotpot and jam roly-poly. However, a mitigating diversion was having the dishes delivered to his office, not by Norah herself, nor even by Peg, but by a pair of nubile fourth-formers who had patently outgrown their gym-slips in every department. This was a novel, and to some extent discomfiting, experience for Nobbs, but for the moment it provided a welcome distraction from the staff meeting he was to hold shortly.

IN A BRIEF inaugural speech, Nobbs stressed how "humbled" he was to be taking over "such a fine ship and crew to set sail on such an exciting voyage of discovery". As they all knew, turbulent seas lay ahead in order to put right centuries of injustice, and they all had to "put their shoulders to the wheel" and get ready for whatever changes that came their way. But during his period of office he promised not to make any unnecessary changes, and certainly none before consulting the people affected.

He then reminded them that he had been appointed first and foremost to oversee the pastoral dimension of the curriculum, and during his time at the helm he would not be interfering unconscionably in their day-to-day teaching as such. Finally, if anyone needed to talk to him about work or anything at all, personal or professional, his door would always be open.

He did not invite questions, nor wait for any feedback, before retreating quickly to the safe haven of his office. He knew from experience that none of *his* fine words would butter many parsnips with this "crew"; all they wanted was an easy life, as they had had in Dave Longworth's "happy school". They certainly would not welcome change of any kind. "Wall-to-wall teaching" of recalcitrant teenagers, desperate to leave school and earn money was hard enough: being obliged to forgo decades of coping strategies in favour of some perceived and relatively unproven alternative demanded faith, hope and charity aplenty.

At first, Nobbs felt that his speech had been better received than he had expected, even if the analogy of the skipper and his crew caused a few eyes to roll. But he had not expected his audience's cynicism when he went on to describe his role as "*primus inter pares*, a facilitator whose chief function would be to provide the necessary tools and support for his superb team of proven educators."

However, after the dust had settled, a significant number of them, depending largely on their specific individual circumstances, were willing at least to be charitable, in the hope, perhaps, that faith might follow.

"He's not as bad as I thought."

"Give the devil his due... that's what my old man always said."

"I think he might be all right, you know."

"He strikes me like a straight-talking bloke."

"He'll certainly shake things up a bit."

"Yes, Dave was a smashing bloke, but he just wouldn't move with the times."

"And too easy-going an' all, if you ask me."

"This bloke sounds as if he's got his finger on the button."

"As long as it's not the nuclear button..."

"Oh, I don't know, some of this lot could do with a bomb under them!"

"Any roads, I, for one, am prepared to give him a chance."

"Well, we'll have to rub along with him, whether we like it or not.

"No point doing otherwise!"

Whilst the majority stood somewhere in the middle, caring little whether their new "skipper" was a "facilitator" or an "out-and-out bastard", and holding few delusions about "voyages of discovery", another significant number, too set in their ways, or too old to curry favour with their new boss, adopted a less hopeful and less charitable stance.

"He were only a woodwork teacher... and from all reports not a very good one at that."

"You should hear what Taff Jenkins had to say about him... and he should know, working with him all them years."

"Some say he caused Taff's accident."

"Aye, and why wasn't there a proper inquiry? You tell me that."

"I bet that suit cost him a bob or two."

"Too well dressed for a woodwork teacher..."

"Might have done better as a male model..."

"Aye, he does look a bit of a faggot an' all..."

"Got a nice missus, though... spit image of Sophia Loren."

"They haven't got kids, though, have they?"

"Perhaps he doesn't want kids!"

"I heard he were very nasty to the kids over there, especially the small, sensitive types."

"Doesn't exactly fit in with this pastoral care thing, does it?"

"If you ask me, he's just an out-and-out fraud."

"What do you mean?"

"Well, for a start, all that about being an officer in the War... I heard it were a pack of lies."

"Well, he's a bloody clever liar then, that's all I can say."

Clearly, judging by the perceptiveness of some of these comments, securing oneself against the enemy would not be a one-way street.

WHETHER it was a reaction to his first staff meeting, or the aftershocks from Norah's Jam roly-poly, Nobbs's afternoon was not as "constructive" as the morning. He was also having problems deciding which picture should go on which wall in his office, especially the Turner he had picked up at an auction just before Christmas. Amanda had suggested the wall behind his desk, but he felt it deserved a more prominent, eye-catching position, and where he himself could see it without having to swivel round in his chair. While thus engrossed in his picture-hanging, he heard a soft, nervous tap on his office door.

"Come!" he called out a little impatiently, but slightly less bombastically than before. The door opened slowly to reveal two well-dressed young men looking like two naughty boys who had been sent to the Headmaster for a telling off.

"When two or three are gathered together..." enunciated Nobbs like a Vicar at Evensong.

"Oh, good afternoon, Mr Nobbs," said the taller of the two in an oily public school accent, "we should like to... introduce ourselves, if we may. I'm Smiley, Brian Smiley, and this is my friend, John Shufflebottom."

"Don't tell me," said Nobbs, "*you* smile... and *he*... ha ha!"

"We were thinking," said Smiley, quite unfazed by Nobbs's schoolboy humour.

"With you being new, and tha'," interjected Shufflebottom.

"We just wanted you to know," continued Smiley, "that if you ever require assistance with anything..."

"We'd be very glad to help, Mr Nobbs," added Shufflebottom eagerly.

"As you can see, my hands are full at the moment... ha ha! But I'll bear it in mind," replied Nobbs, not quite sure what to make of them, or their offer of help. Never look a gift horse, he thought, but on the other hand, beware of Greeks.

"Thank you, Mr Nobbs, thank you," said Smiley, "we'll call again when you're less busy."

As they turned to leave, they almost collided with Peg who was on her way in with the tea tray. "Oh, come in, Peg... just what the doctor ordered... yes, just put it down there. Now, since you're here, I want your advice... stick your bum down on that chair for a minute, and tell me honestly where, do you reckon, this picture should go?"

"That's a nice picture, Mr Nobbs... what is it, exactly?"

"*This*, Peg, is one of the finest pictures ever painted... so atmospheric. It shows a magnificent battleship being towed up the Thames to its final resting place."

"Aw...what's it called?"

The Fighting Temeraire, Peg, by Joseph Mallord William Turner... and I wish I was rich enough to buy the original."

"What about there, above the fireplace?" said Peg.

"Now, that's exactly what I was thinking. My wife says it should go on this wall, behind me, but I agree with you, Peg, above the fireplace, that's its place. You haven't got anything for indigestion, have you? It's been bothering me all afternoon."

"I'll go and have a look."

"But just before you go, tell me, Peg, what do you make of Tweedledum and Tweedledee?

"Oh, you mean Brian and John?"

"Yes...or Smiley and 'Bottom!"

"Brian Smiley teaches Careers," explained Peg, trying to suppress a giggle... and John, he does Science and

Gardening. I must say, I've always found them both very helpful and polite. They tend to keep themselves to themselves... but there's no law against that."

Then after a slight pause she added, "I don't know if I should tell you this, Mr Nobbs..."

"Listen, Peg... as my private secretary, you are my eyes and ears on the ground. You can tell me anything, absolutely anything, in complete confidence."

"Well, all right then... but strictly between you and I. People say... they're... erm... you know..."

"They're what?"

"Well, you know... I don't like saying it."

"Queers, you mean... poofs?"

"Well... yes... but aren't we supposed to call them... 'gay' or something now?"

"Gays, queers, poofs... what difference does it make? It amounts to the same thing. Can't say I'm keen on them, whatever you call them. Saw too much of that out in the Far East during the War. It's not natural, Peg."

"They've not been here long, about two or three years. I think Brian's from Bournemouth originally, and John's local, from Newton. I believe they met in college somewhere. Anyway, they always go around together... even live together, in Newton. But, whatever anybody says, they're both lovely people... kind, and well-mannered... what you might call real, old-fashioned gentlemen. They even look a bit old-fashioned, don't they, for teachers, I mean, in their dark grey suits! They got on really well with Mr Longworth, but since last summer they've started spending a lot of time across the road... they're big friends with the new Headmaster."

"Kendricks, you mean?"

"Yes, Dr Kendricks... now, there's another proper gentleman for you... so kind and helpful... and so funny... he could have been a comedian... and with him having had such a bad time in the War an' all... but I expect you know all about that. I do hope he'll cope all right with this reorganisation, I mean with the two schools being so different an' that, and him not being very strong. He used to lodge with Mrs Wilkins on Agnes Street for years, and when she died he bought a nice house in Newton... so all three travel to school together now in Mr Smiley's car."

"Now, that *is* interesting, Peg, very interesting. You're a mine of information, aren't you... and so observant. Remember, I meant what I said... you can trust me one hundred per cent. Anything you say to me stays with me. And I expect the same of you, right?"

"Of course, Mr Nobbs, of course... oh, I've just remembered, there's a packet of Rennies in the medicine chest after Mr Longworth."

"Excellent. Oh, and Peg, I hope you don't mind me saying, but you look absolutely stunning in that dress... shows off your... erm... figure to a tee!"

"Oh, thank you, Mr Nobbs," replied Peg, blushing, "I'll go and get the Rennies."

By the time she returned, another visitor had taken advantage of Nobbs's open-door policy. She could tell even through the closed door that feelings were already running high, and decided the Rennies would have to wait.

"LISTEN, Den, I had no idea you were so attached to the f------ thing. Obviously, if I'd known..."

"With respect, Mr Nobbs," interrupted Dennis

416

Peterson... and by the way, no one else calls me 'Den', not even my family."

"Oh, for f--- sake, let's not get hung up on names. As I said in my spiel, I'm just a *primus inter pares*. So, let's ditch the 'Mr Nobbs' crap, shall we? So, 'Richard', please... and 'Dennis', if that's all right with you"

"With respect then, *Richard*... my attachment, or otherwise, to an inanimate object is not the issue here. What *is* at issue, though, is that a well-qualified and experienced teacher like yourself failed to grasp the significance of what the contents of that inanimate object represented –years of dedicated application by a succession of colleagues and pupils who had given their all with whatever sporting talents they'd been born with... or put another way, unremarkable people achieving remarkable things by dint of determination and hard work."

"Well, let me say first of all how pleased I am that you feel so strongly about these matters. And do you know what... you're a man after my own heart. I admire someone who speaks his mind honestly and passionately. Like you, I believe in telling it how it is... no flannel... no bullsh-t. And you're absolutely right, of course... these things do matter... a lot. That's why you can rest assured that the glass cabinet and its contents are all perfectly safe. I gave Fred Broadbent strict instructions to pack the items individually and store them securely until an alternative location had been identified. I felt the Headmaster's office was not suitable... that's all... didn't do them justice. As it says in the Good Book, let your light shine before men, so that they may see your good works... don't hide your light under a bushel, and all that. So, when you've decided on a new location, just let Fred know, okay? Now, if you'll excuse me, Dennis, I'm afraid I've got a meeting with the education officer in Chester at seven o'clock... but remember, my door is always open, and if I can ever help you, all you have to do is ask."

"Well, thank you for hearing me out. Yes, I *do* believe in getting things off my chest... no use letting them rankle. Just one more thing, and then I'll leave you in peace. As it happens, I've also got a meeting at seven o'clock tonight. I'm picking Stuart Ashworth's parents up and taking them to the Infirmary. Stuart's one of our fifth-year lads... a promising actor... always stars in the Christmas panto. However, last Tuesday... on New Year's Eve... he tried to do away with himself."

"Bloody hell... I *am* sorry to hear that, Dennis... thanks for letting me know. Anyway, good luck with it... and you *will* keep me posted, won't you?"

After a half-hearted handshake, the two men parted civilly, Dennis feeling completely vindicated after obliging his new boss to execute a nifty, though blatant, *volte-face*. To some extent, he regretted not pursuing the matter more vigorously, perhaps even exacting an apology, but by the time he had reached his car, any lingering hard feelings were forgotten, as his mind now focused on the more difficult encounter at seven o'clock.

Nobbs, on the other hand, was consumed with self-pity and resentment that his first day had been ruined by a "balding, washed-up ex-PE teacher with a gigantic chip on his shoulder because he didn't get the job he thought he should have got". After parking the Mark X beneath the magnolia tree, he remained seated for several minutes, his eyes closed. What would Fred make of having to retrieve Dennis Peterson's "junk"? He'd have to catch him first thing in the morning and give him an alternative version of events before the captain became the laughing-stock of the ship. But there was little he could do about it now... except hope that Peterson with his other problem would just forget about it. Meanwhile, Machiavelli's prophetic words kept repeating themselves in his head: *Secure yourself against your enemies... destroy those who can or are likely to injure you.*

While he was dwelling on these matters, there was a gentle tap on his window. "Aren't you coming in, love? You're later than you said. Are you all right?"

"I've got this effing indigestion again, Mand... have we got any of that Magnesia stuff left?"

"Yes, I think so... but we've got this dinner at the Goodys at seven, remember?"

"Yea... I hadn't forgotten."

"Anyway, how *did* your day go?"

"Oh, pretty good... on the whole! I'll tell you about it later. I'll feel better after I've had a shower."

Chapter Eighteen

Appointing Dr Herbert William Kendricks as Headmaster of Netherbridge Grammar School had much to commend it. Apart from having an outstanding mind, he was enormously well-liked and respected, and despite his quaint and donnish manner, he had never found controlling his classes difficult, largely because of his infectious enthusiasm and his captivating lessons. Like many a born teacher, he was also renowned for his digressions, examples of which were often recounted at Old Boys' Association dinners. Some no doubt were apocryphal, but most were authentic, albeit occasionally 'engineered' by a wayward scamp with his mind on the after-school rugby match, or out of sheer devilment. But with 'Doc Kenny's' remarkable capacity for finding connections between disparate subjects, the memorable ones were invariably his own, such as when a lesson on the Greek genitive absolute famously evolved into an erudite account of the great crested newt's mating rituals! In short, Dr Kendricks was one of those rare individuals who could "rise to faults that critics dare not mend", and be adored all the more for doing so.

After his expected Double First in Classics at Oxford in 1932, followed by a DPhil three years later, he spent the next eighteen months travelling on a scholarship, mainly in Greece and Italy. But when the money began to run out, he returned to the family home in Haslemere, Surrey, and was minded to take a teaching job as a stop-gap measure before settling down to a 'proper' career. Despite being over-qualified, he hastily accepted the first post offered, as a Classics master at an unheard-of grammar school in one of those northern towns he had only glimpsed before through the paintings of L.S. Lowry.

This also happened to be Harry Whitworth's last appointment before retiring, and, seeking, as always, to raise the School's academic profile, he dismissed the governors' misgivings, and followed his own judgement. Some wondered why a young fellow as well qualified as "this Dr Kendricks" would want to be a schoolmaster at all, let alone in an establishment like theirs, and especially in that part of the world. Surely, one of the top public schools in the south would have bitten his hand off – unless of course he had something to hide. On another tack, one or two felt that Classics was already adequately provided for, and that the money would have been better spent on a modern linguist or a chemist. However, albeit thanks to the Chairman's casting vote, Harry's powers of persuasion prevailed, so that on April 20th 1936 Dr Kendricks's tentative teaching career began – on the same day, incidentally, as Dr Davenport's began as a headmaster. Although the two appeared to have little in common, they formed a firm friendship from the outset, both perhaps feeling a little apprehensive about what their respective futures held in store.

But under the careful tutelage of the Senior Classics Master, Joe Riley, Dr Kendricks grew in confidence, which was further boosted when Dr Davenport suggested he start an after-school Sixth form Arts Society to broaden the pupils' horizons. This initiative, which began modestly in January 1937 with a series of weekly talks on Greek mythology proved very popular, and by the following September Dr Davenport had managed to persuade Ian Hutchinson, the Music Master, to widen the scope of the society with illustrated talks on classical music, which were also very well received. Despite the dire economic times people were living through, Dr Davenport felt strongly that education should always aim to be more than a preparation for a career.

Then, one Saturday morning, towards the end of Dr Kendricks's second year at the School, a couple of parents approached him in Tiplady's, saying how much their boys, both studying physics and mathematics, had enjoyed the talks, and wondered whether something similar could be arranged for the parents either at the School or possibly somewhere in the town. Naturally, Dr Kendricks was delighted that his efforts were appreciated, and despite being heavily committed with examination classes, this was an invitation he could not resist. But he could never have guessed how successful this venture would become: what again began modestly with a series of talks and amusing anecdotes attracted a wide audience from far beyond Netherbridge, eventually growing many years later into the Netherbridge Arts Society. And so, Harry's hunch had been well and truly vindicated, for far from being the fish out of water the cynics had warned against, Dr Kendricks soon found himself lionised by 'town and gown'.

Netherbridge Grammar School was still not three years into its new regime, and Dr Davenport feeling his way. Unlike his predecessor, who was essentially a businessman with an uncompromising, 'results-driven' style of management, he worked through people, effecting changes not by *diktat* but through charismatic and inspirational leadership. Schoolmasters, as a breed, were never noted for their willingness to embrace change: indeed, for many of them there would have been no call for it during their careers, handing on, as they often did (sometimes verbatim and even incorporating the same jokes and anecdotes) the same body of knowledge that *their* mentors had bequeathed to them.

But under Dr Davenport things seemed altogether different: his natural, undemonstrative authority found even the most entrenched recusant suddenly 'in agreement', sometimes even claiming what was proposed as *his* idea! Likewise, the governors, a reactionary bunch, especially where money was concerned, surprised themselves by agreeing unanimously (a rarity that) to his request for massive investment into making physical education and the arts into central pillars of the School's curriculum and its life generally. Hitherto, these had been deemed peripheral pursuits, of little 'market value' and at best light relief from 'proper' studies, or embellishments to a university application. When a very able boy famously asked Harry Whitworth if he could take music as one of his Higher School Certificate subjects, the reply was predictably unequivocal: "Music, boy! What do you think this is... a girls' school!"

Be that as it may, within a very short period of time, NGS had changed noticeably into a gentler, more humane, but no less demanding institution that could look forward confidently to a successful future, and young Dr Kendricks was proud to be part of it. He had almost forgotten that the 'teaching job' was only meant to be a 'stop-gap' measure!

Not unexpectedly, his mother had hoped for something nearer home, and something perhaps more in keeping with his qualifications... maybe the Civil Service, or if it had to be teaching, a university lectureship, or *faute de mieux* "a nice little private school on the south coast". But for reasons beyond his ken, and certainly his mother's, he had been smitten with Netherbridge from the start, not only the School, but the town and its people. He could never have imagined the joy, the privilege, the deep sense of fulfilment, and yes, the pathos, he had felt on that first day, sharing Keats's "pure serene" with a 3A comprising mostly under-privileged, but for all that, gifted and receptive thirteen-year-olds.

WHEN THE School re-convened for the Michaelmas term of 1938 after a mostly sunny summer vacation, alarming noises were emanating from central Europe. There was talk of little else in the Common Room except Nazi Germany's expansionist and anti-Semitic policies; and as in the country at large, the word *appeasement* was on everyone's lips.

Many of the masters, especially those who had served

424

in the Great War, found the idea of 'negotiating' with a Fascist dictator repugnant. The Sixth form concurred unanimously: "Churchill's right," declared young Jimmy Ravenscroft, the Head Prefect, "Give the buggers an inch, and they'll take Czechoslovakia!"

But there were several in favour of appeasement, Dr Kendricks being among them. "Maybe it's time to cut him a bit of slack," he reasoned, "and besides, anything's better than another war," little suspecting that, far from placating the beast, appeasement would only feed the flames of his ambitions, and render Chamberlain's triumphal piece of paper signed by Herr Hitler a mere sales-slip for a monstrous confidence trick. But Dr Kendricks also had a very personal reason for loathing war.

MONDAY, 15th October, 1917, was young Billy Kendricks's seventh birthday. It was also the first day of his autumn half-term holiday, but most importantly, his father and hero, Capt Hugh Kendricks of the *Queen's (West Surrey) Regiment*, was coming home on short leave from fighting in the Battle of Passchendaele. All in all, therefore, despite the incessant thrashing of rain against his bedroom window, life felt pretty good for our birthday boy.

Opening birthday and Christmas presents at the Kendrickses was a strictly observed ritual, which could never begin until everybody was "present and correct". However, on this occasion, even though young Billy, with remarkable forbearance, had agreed to wait until his father arrived in the afternoon, Mrs Kendricks broke with tradition and after mid-morning cocoa, took him and his little sister through to the dining room, where all the presents were laid out neatly on the sideboard.

After a hearty rendering of "Happy Birthday, dear Billy", the frenetic parcel unwrapping process began, while Mama made a list of who had given what, ready for writing thank you letters. First, there were the miscellaneous small gifts from his friends at school; then, the large jigsaw puzzle of the map of Europe from Uncle Pete and Auntie Tessie from Kidderminster. This being wartime, some presents were not always available, but much to Billy's delight, Uncle John had managed to find the promised fretsaw set. Last but not least was quite a heavy parcel from Mama, Dada and Alice. Billy was already an avid reader, and Dada had gone up to London especially during his last leave to buy a set of Jules Verne's five *Voyages extraordinaires* novels. What more could a happy seven-year-old wish for?

Alice seemed almost as excited as her brother, but when at the end Billy handed his present to *her*, she did not know whether to laugh or cry, whereupon Billy glanced up at his mother and shook his head in world-weary bemusement. However, he had wrapped his sister's present as if he had never intended it to be unwrapped, but when she did manage to remove the final layer, her body tensed with delight. She was speechless, as she held in her hand the tiniest golden teddy-bear imaginable, barely three inches tall, but perfectly formed. It was evidently a case of love at first sight, and from that moment onwards little Ted became her constant companion: wherever Alice went, Ted went too, always there for her whenever she needed comforting.

When all the wrapping paper and string had been tidied

426

away, Mrs Kendricks withdrew discreetly into the kitchen, where she tried to occupy herself with practical things like putting the final touches to the birthday cake, or thinking about what they could have for lunch. All of a sudden, she felt a gentle tug on her apron.

"Mama, you're crying," said Alice, looking up at her mother anxiously, while holding on tightly to little Ted.

"No, I'm not darling," replied her mother with a forced smile, "I've got some soap in my eyes... I'll pop to the bathroom to wash it out. You go back to Billy, sweetheart... I'll come to you in a minute."

After washing her face thoroughly and reapplying her lipstick, she steeled herself to rejoin the children in the dining room. "My goodness, Billy, you *are* doing well with that jigsaw... you've done half of Scotland already."

After helping him with an awkward piece around the Shetland Isles, she sat down on the sofa next to Alice. She had waited anxiously since Saturday morning for 'the right moment', but had finally concluded that there never would be a *right* moment, and now was no worse a time than any other. Cradling Alice with her left arm, she said, "Billy, could you stop doing the jigsaw for a moment, please... Mama's got something very important to tell you both." She took a deep breath before continuing. "I've had a telegram... saying... Dada won't be able to come... to the party after all."

Billy froze, and stared hard at his mother. "Is that why we opened the presents early?"

"Why not, Mama?" interrupted Alice innocently.
Desperately trying to hold back her tears, and pressing her daughter to her, Mrs Kendricks replied, "I'm afraid, darling... Dada won't be coming back to us... ever again."

On hearing those last two words, Billy rushed out of the room.

"What's the matter with Billy, Mama?"

"He's very upset, sweetheart. But we've all got to be very brave now, without Dada... all of us... you, Billy, and me."

"What's brave, Mama?"

"Brave means keeping going when terrible things happen to you."

"Dada's brave, isn't he, Mama?"

Mrs Kendricks lifted Alice on to her lap and held her tightly to her bosom before attempting an answer.

"Yes, sweetheart, very brave."

The finality of death is difficult for anyone to grasp, let alone a three-year-old, but after a moment's silence, Alice said, "I want to be brave, Mama. I'll go and tell Billy."

Billy had been listening just outside the door, and at this point dashed back into the room. He leapt into his mother's outstretched arms and hugging her tightly said, "I will be brave too, Mama... and we'll put an extra candle on the cake for Dada, shall we?"

Then after a slight pause he added, "Why do we have to have wars?"

"Yes, why indeed, darling," replied Mrs Kendricks.

DR KENDRICKS had always tried to spend his birthdays at home in Haslemere, although the occasion was always marred by the memory of that little boy hugging his mother in their mutual distress. Sometimes, he would re-live every detail of that day, and grapple with a plethora of emotions: loss (of a wonderful and caring father); regret (for what might have been, had he lived); gratitude (for an intelligent and loving mother, who had brought her two children up to be honest, happy and selfless adults); hatred of all violence, (especially the violence of warfare); and more.

But on his 28th birthday, in 1938, he had been obliged to stay in Netherbridge because his mother had had to go to Norwich to help while Alice was in hospital having her third child. Accordingly, he had decided to have a quiet time to reminisce – and ponder with increasing alarm how history was threatening to repeat itself.

Knowing that he was on his own, Dr Davenport had invited him for lunch at *Elsinore* on the Monday, and he knowing from experience the Irish hospitality awaiting him, had eaten only a rudimentary breakfast before setting off on a long walk along the canal, waving cheerily at every passing bargee along the way. A thin, cold wind whistled across the moss, but clearly not too cold for one intrepid, old man perched on a rickety stool waiting patiently for hope to triumph over experience. After some pleasantries about the weather and the fishing, the conversation turned inevitably to that other ubiquitous subject – what to do about Mr Hitler. Like most ordinary folk, the old man had no stomach for another war – he was still grieving the death of his brother in the last one. "But fair do's," he said, "Mr Chamberlain has tried to sort things... well, for now, any roads... 'cos you never know with them Germans".

Dr Kendricks had enjoyed his little chat immensely, and as he went on his way, he reflected on how the old man's thoughts chimed with his own, even to the doubts about the Munich Agreement. Indeed, as October slid into November, and reports of escalating violence against

Jews in Germany dominated the daily newspapers, it was becoming clearer by the day that sweet reasonableness and diplomacy would cut no ice with this dictator.

BY JANUARY 1939, Dr Kendricks had lost much of his ebullience, preferring to remain in his classroom during break-times reading *The Times*, or chatting with one or two of the more thoughtful senior boys. Interestingly, with conscription looming, a tacit camaraderie burgeoned between Sixth form pupils and some of the younger masters, with Dr Kendricks often finding himself playing the reassuring father-figure. Then, when news broke about Czechoslovakia in March, a palpable gloom descended on the whole School, and although the pupils in the main were as intent as ever on their studies, lessons often veered, inadvertently or otherwise, towards the 'elephant in the room'.

During the summer term of 1939, people noticed that Dr Davenport was spending several days at a time away from the School, which led to speculation that he might be involved in some top-secret operation at the War Office, or, as one cynical old Oxonian would have it, "working for the Russians"! However, when he was not away, he invariably took morning assembly himself, which usually included up-dates on the rapidly changing international situation, not only in Europe, but also in Japan, China and Russia. Occasionally, he would remind his young audience how these conflicts had arisen in the first place and the likely consequences if they were not resolved diplomatically. Furthermore, with the help of his Radio Club enthusiasts, he rigged up a wireless public address system in the main assembly hall, which was tuned into the BBC National Programme every lunch hour. When historic speeches or announcements were to be broadcast, the whole School would assemble in the hall to listen in solemn silence. This was especially appreciated by the boys who had no wireless set at home, and it also helped to foster a strong School spirit to confront whatever dangers lay in wait.

DR KENDRICKS spent most of the 1939 summer vacation at home with his mother in Haslemere. It was a nervous time for both of them, with Europe teetering on the brink of war, and when Poland was invaded, the die seemed irredeemably cast: clearly, negotiation had never been part of the Hitler's plan.

At 11 o'clock on Sunday morning, 3rd September when Chamberlain's declaration of war speech was broadcast, the two had coffee side by side on the familiar old sofa in the dining room, expecting the worst, and when the speech was over, he turned to his mother and said mournfully, "It feels like my seventh birthday again, Mama... and Dada died in vain."

His twenty-ninth birthday was fast approaching, and although no longer a *young* man, he had kept himself reasonably fit and healthy. Accordingly, with the upper age-limit for conscription for men now extended to 41, and school mastering not being a 'reserved' occupation, there was little likelihood of his avoiding military service. Unlike his father, he did not relish the idea of being a soldier, but he did have a strong urge now to do something to prevent the Fascist pandemic from spreading to his country.

Accordingly, when he returned to school the following

Tuesday, he resolved to face up to reality, and to do his duty stoically whatever form it took. Meanwhile, like many of his colleagues, he was living in a state of limbo, unable to focus properly on the task at hand for wondering about his call-up date. At first he thought of enlisting in order to end the tension of waiting, but during the Christmas break of 1939 his mother and Alice between them implored him to wait his turn, which would come soon enough. Alice's husband, Robert, was more fortunate: as a family doctor in his late thirties, he would very likely be exempt.

The 1939-40 'Higher' Latin and Greek class was Dr Kendricks's very first. At Dr Davenport's suggestion, Joe Riley had kindly entrusted him with an especially bright 3A when he first arrived in 1936, and having shown what a high standard he could achieve at School Certificate level in 1938, he was determined to repeat the feat at Higher Certificate level. He had imbued the dozen or so boys with such a love of the subject, and trained them to such a high standard, that they all passed with Distinction, almost as a matter of course. Fortuitously, he had also given the lie to the notion that Classics was too esoteric for a grammar school.

Those boys were indeed an exceptional bunch and would have shone in any discipline. Interestingly, they also came from a diverse background, mainly manual, with a sprinkling of 'professional', but what they all shared was a thirst for knowledge, so much so that while in their company Dr Kendricks found little time to worry about his call-up or indeed anything else! In later life, he always looked back on those four years with that group of boys as the most enjoyable of his career. Sadly, several of *them* never had a career at all.

On Friday, 10th May 1940, the day Churchill became Prime Minister, Dr Kendricks was sitting at his desk in front of his current 3A class as they were finishing their mid-term Greek test. It was the last lesson of the week and only a few moments before the end-of-school bell, when there was a gentle tap on the door. As Dr Kendricks turned to see who it might be, the class stood up as they always did for a visitor – especially this visitor. Barely recognisable in a classically trimmed beard and resplendent uniform, Lt James Ravenscroft R.N. looked even more heroic now than when he graced the cricket square with his elegant cover drives. He had shone throughout his School career and, no doubt, wherever he went in future years the world would surely beat a path to his door. After one year at Clare College, Cambridge reading Modern Languages, he had felt compelled to enlist in the Royal Navy.

"Just paying my respects, Dr Kendricks."

"Well, thank you, James, I'm honoured."

After 3A had been dismissed, the two sat and chatted for a good half an hour, whilst skirting deftly around what was at the forefront of both their minds.

"At least we've got someone to stand up to them now," ventured James at last, "poor Chamberlain didn't stand a chance. But what I'd like to know is how they managed to build up their armaments so quickly... I thought that was one of the conditions of Versailles... I mean they weren't supposed to, were they?"

"We'll find out one day, James, but I suspect the Americans had something to do with it."

"If only they'd listened to Churchill... let's hope it's

not too late, that's all," said James.

As they shook hands and bade each other Godspeed, Dr Kendricks recalled how confident his own father had looked when he set off that last time to defend his king and country, and now with Europe hurtling towards a vortex of mass-destruction for a second time, he sincerely hoped young James would not be sacrificed on Bellona's altar, like his own father.

While the Class of 1940, his Classicists amongst them, were getting to grips with their Higher and Scholarship papers throughout May and June, boys barely two years older were doing battle of a different order in the skies above them, in the North Sea and on battlefields of Europe. Could Sophocles or Tacitus inform this twentieth century tragedy? The *Blitzkrieg*, the Surrender of France, Dunkirk, and The Battle of Britain all happened so quickly that it was difficult to grasp their significance until Churchill "spoke out loud and bold" only five days into his premiership, especially the last two words, *never surrender.*

THE DAY after the School closed for the summer vacation, Dr Kendricks travelled down to his mother's in Haslemere, which was still his official home address, and where his call-up papers would eventually be sent. Indeed, seeing James Ravenscroft in his splendid uniform had aroused a strange feeling of bellicosity in him too: who did this loud-mouthed ideologue think he was?

The long-awaited documents finally arrived on the last Saturday in August, which meant that he would not need to return to Netherbridge. He had already paid a brief visit earlier to see the examination results, and settle up with his landlady. Much to his delight, all seven of his Classics 'geniuses' had passed with top grades, two gaining places at Cambridge and one at Oxford.

During his short stay he also discovered with sad forebodings that several boys from the 1937 and 1938 Sixth forms had already enlisted in the RAF, and that three of his closest colleagues had also been called up that week. There would probably be more masters eventually, which would cause considerable staffing difficulties for Dr Davenport. But through his network of contacts he had anticipated the likelihood of a staffing crisis and made contingency arrangements. Of course, they were not ideal, but when resources are scarce, ingenuity and compromise are called for to make the best use of the means at one's disposal.

Since this would be his last visit to Netherbridge for some time, Dr Davenport invited him to *Elsinore* for supper, and as usual Mrs Davenport's culinary arts all but defeated him, especially the apple pie. During the evening, Dr Davenport took the opportunity to reassure him that his post at the School would be kept open for him when he returned after war service, provided, of course, he wanted it. The two men had a special affinity, holding a similar view of the world, and as well as being blessed with superbly trained minds, they also shared another bonding quality: the trauma of losing fathers at a very tender age. On parting, they shook hands firmly and looked each other in the eye for several seconds, as if to be asking the same question, would they ever see each other again?

ON THE 23rd April 1941 Lt H. W. Kendricks bade his

mother a tearful farewell on the gangway of his troopship bound for Singapore. After six months at Mons OCTU in Aldershot he had been commissioned into the Royal Artillery, for which he felt more suited than his father's beloved *Queen's*.

With more pressing matters nearer home, Britain had neglected Japan's expansionism in East Asia, and Dr Kendricks's Artillery regiment was one of many reinforcement units belatedly dispatched to protect the so-called impregnable "Gibraltar of the Far East". Unfortunately, by the time these reinforcements had been fully deployed, the Japanese Army had made huge advances southwards through Malaya, forcing the Allied troops into an ignominious retreat, until by January 1942 they were back in Singapore where they eventually surrendered on 15th February, much to Churchill's disbelief and consternation.

Until then, Dr Kendricks had managed to send weekly airmails to his mother, those much anticipated and long cherished blue letters comprising detailed accounts of the Malayan fauna and flora and the extreme weather conditions. Occasionally, there were fleeting references to his fellow officers and mess life such as it was, but he always glossed over the reality of life under fire and the disastrous retreat. She, of course, had replied religiously to each of his letters with gossip and anecdotes about Alice and the children, the W.I. meetings, and the sales-of-work for the Red Cross. But after he was taken prisoner, Mrs Kendricks heard nothing from him for three and a half years, except for an official telegram informing her that he had been taken prisoner of war. Nevertheless, throughout that time, she had sent her weekly missives unfailingly, not knowing, of course, whether they ever reached him.

At first, the British officers were separated off, and treated tolerably well, because the Japanese had hoped to subvert them to their cause. But after about a year, things changed dramatically, when they were taken by ship in appalling conditions to mainland Japan, to labour in various factories and mines. Dr Kendricks was allocated to a cement factory in Kamiiso on the northern island of Hokkaido, his work consisting mainly of carrying heavy sacks of sand from delivery trucks into the storage bays inside the building. Clearly, his slight build was not suited to such exhausting work, eight hours a day, six days a week on a daily ration of a cup of rice, a small bowl of soup, and a little bread. It was no surprise, therefore, that the ordeal, compounded by the gratuitous beatings, took its toll on his health, and the wonder was that he survived at all when so many of his younger and physically stronger fellow-officers perished.

Japanese companies were partial to employing Korean guards to supervise their POW workers, because of their reputation for ruthlessness. Among their most brutal was one Dae-Jung (meaning honest and righteous) who prided himself on his capacity for striking fear into the bravest, and delighted in inflicting pain on the defenceless. Being of a short and stocky build, he seemed to take a dislike to Dr Kendricks's tall and slender physique from the outset, for he needed only the flimsiest excuse to make him kneel before him and then bring his stout cane down hard on his fleshless shoulder-blades three times. This happened at least once a day, depending on Dae-Jung's mood. Small wonder, after two and a half years of bracing himself against such brutal maltreatment, Dr Kendricks's shoulders had become permanently hunched. The Japanese military authorities sanctioned, indeed encouraged, such callous behaviour because soldiers who *surrender* were deemed *ipso facto* to be less than human, and should therefore expect nothing better.

COULD THOSE sad figures shuffling wearily down the ship's gangway be the same self-assured young warriors who had climbed aboard in 1941? And could that matchstick man, bent double beneath his heavy kit bag, be the same Artillery officer of whom his father would have been justly proud? Now emaciated and demoralised, he could barely stand up, let alone acknowledge the jubilant crowd waving and cheering on the quayside below. His time as a POW had all but destroyed him, and envisaging such a reception as this, he had asked his mother not to meet him in Southampton and be "part of that insufferable charade". If only their landing had been less public, stealing instead into some nameless harbour farther along the coast, and melting into a dark and protective obscurity.

When they finally stepped ashore, even the officers in their newly fitted uniforms had the resigned look of 'rescue' dogs. But it was not so much the inglorious defeat that troubled them, nor the institutional abuse that followed, nor even the gnawing guilt about having survived, when so many of their friends had not, but the shame of having been party to one of the most deplorable acts of corporate cowardice in British history. He, along with 80,000 others, had *surrendered* to a patently inferior enemy: *Malo mori quam foedori* – could he ever look his pupils in the eye again?

DR KENDRICKS eventually arrived home on Friday 7th June 1946, on what would also have been his father's sixty-fourth birthday. This coincidence gave a poignant ring to the occasion, which in his mind's eye could and should have been very different. Sadly, it was not the home-coming his mother had envisaged either, although his father would have been very proud of him, regardless: his son had gone through hell, and had kept going. As far as his mother was concerned, well, her boy had come home... that was all that mattered now, and she had baked an enormous cake with *two* candles on it to celebrate the fact, which brought a tear to Billy's eye. A few weeks of home-cooking, she thought, he'd be as right as rain. The home-cooking would certainly do wonders for his ribcage, and some pampering would palliate his residual pains, but whether the mental scars would ever heal was an open question.

Towards the end of August Dr Davenport paid him a surprise visit. They had been in touch by letter and telephone already, but the two or three hours chatting together proved an enormous boost to his flagging morale. Dr Davenport carefully avoided any mention of the war, except in general terms, concentrating mainly on what had happened at the School during his absence, and how he had been missed. He did not mention Jimmy Ravenscroft, or the other six: he would find out soon enough. Looking to the future, he advised him to take as long as he needed to recuperate, but perhaps he might consider returning, say, at the beginning of the Lent term, if necessary, on a part-time basis to begin with; but in any case, he should be guided by how he felt. Dr Davenport assured him that he was held in such high esteem that his position was probably more secure than his own!

As they walked back to the station, Dr Davenport also revealed, a little coyly, that he had persuaded the governors to appoint a full-time secretary. Indeed, after only a year she was proving so efficient that he himself was in danger of becoming 'surplus to requirements'!

DR DAVENPORT'S visit had not only lifted his friend's spirits, but it had a long-term healing effect as well, for that very evening he resolved to make an effort to slough off the millstone of *victimhood*, and pick up his life again. Obviously, it would be difficult to forgive and probably impossible to forget Dae-Jung, but equally there would be no point in nursing a corrosive bitterness for the rest of his days. Somehow, he would have to try to learn from the experience, and use it constructively: maybe, he could even be a better person for having experienced the purgatory of Kamiiso. Time would tell.

That very evening he also made a conscious effort to straighten his shoulders and pull himself up to his full height, as the drill sergeant-major had trained them to do at Mons, but it caused him considerable pain. X-rays revealed three historic fractured thoracic vertebrae, which at the time triggered his anger afresh, but he was determined not to let even that overwhelm him: *mens omnia vincit!*

An old Oxford friend suggested that it might help if he wrote his experiences down, but he found re-living the atrocities gave him nightmares. *In extremis* even the most morally upright of us resort to conduct unbecoming, as

440

happened frequently in the POW camp at Kamiiso. On this occasion, it was Dr Kendricks's turn to 'misappropriate' something from the cookhouse. However, not being the most accomplished thief in the camp, he was caught red-handed with a tin of evaporated milk under his shirt.

If anyone challenged Dae-Jung's authority, he usually flew into a frenzied rage, but on this occasion, he maintained an ominous silence and sat on a nearby log staring impassively into the middle distance as if consulting some higher authority. After about an hour's wait, when everyone was beginning to think that maybe their tyrannical taskmaster was not utterly devoid of compassion, he called the miscreant over, opened the can of milk, drank some of it, and poured the remainder onto the ground. As Dr Kendricks was preparing himself mentally for the usual punishment, for some reason it was not forthcoming. Instead, Dae-Jung disappeared into the nearest hut, reappearing a few minutes later with another, much thinner, cane which he placed carefully on the ground about a foot away from the milk puddle. He then ordered Dr Kendricks to kneel on the stick and keep his hands firmly behind his back. After about three hours, he ordered him to stand up, which, of course, he could not do owing to the numbness in his legs. For some reason, Dae-Jung found this hilarious and for good measure gave Dr Kendricks a 'playful' kick in the ribs, causing him to fall over sideways. He remained lying on the floor until one of his friends risked the same punishment by helping him to his feet.

Dr Kendricks spent the autumn of 1946 convalescing and reading widely, though he found concentrating difficult. Throughout this time, there was one thing continually on his mind, the callous mindset of the Japanese military. He could not understand why for instance they put their own soldiers on half-rations when wounded, on the grounds that they were no longer fighting men. Small wonder, then, they treated prisoners so badly, especially if they had also done the unthinkable – surrendered. Like the Spartans, the Japanese deplored surrender.

By Christmas, thanks to his mother's cooking, his skeletal frame had reclaimed some semblance of its pre-war configuration. Unfortunately, however, his upper spine retained a distinctive hump, which, together with an accompanying low-level pain made him look older than his thirty-eight years. He had hoped to return to school towards the end of January, but decided to wait until the bitterly cold weather had passed. Shortly before the end of the Lent term, Dr Davenport invited him to come to stay for a few days at *Elsinore*, so that he could reacquaint himself with the town and, if he felt like it, visit the School. On the second day, he walked into the town, calling at several of his old haunts, including Tiplady's, where he stayed for much of the morning drinking coffee and chatting with one or two old acquaintances. Netherbridge had not changed much, except the buildings looked a little run down after the war, and he was pleased to see that most of the little shops and pubs were still trading and the townspeople were just as friendly as they always were. On the second day, he reprised the walk he had taken along the canal in 1938, half hoping to meet the old man again, and talk about the weather – and Mr Hitler. But he was disappointed: apart from one bargee and an

442

off-duty miner with his dog, he had the canal all to himself. As he strode back towards the town, he reflected on all that had happened to him since he last walked that way, and whether the pains and indignities of his incarceration could ever be expunged from his memory. Then he remembered with an ironic smile that he had spent three whole years at Oxford studying the Stoics for his doctorate, and perhaps it was a good time to re-think his own life in accordance with some of their tenets.

On the third day, Dr Davenport persuaded him to visit the School to meet his glamorous secretary, who had conveniently arranged tea and cakes for the occasion. The two took an instant liking to each other and became good friends, a friendship that would be fostered over many years by the regular Friday night dinners at *Elsinore*.

DR KENDRICKS thought there was no point in further delay, and resumed work at the beginning of the Summer term, 1947, mainly sharing classes with Joe Riley. Having been away since 1940, he knew none of the pupils and *vice versa*, although one or two of the Upper Sixth remembered him vaguely as "that master who used to laugh a lot". Accordingly, with a whole generation of pupils having come and gone, he would have to establish himself all over again, only this time as an older, wiser and more sober version, but still a touch eccentric, he hoped, and with a ready laugh.

Meanwhile, adding to his woes, he learnt about Jimmy Ravenscroft, and the other five – Frank Woolham, David Lowe, Will Shawcross, Paul Saunders, and Chris Gallimore (another Head Prefect) – all cut off in their prime: future doctors, barristers, research scientists,

443

entrepreneurs, captains of industry – and of course, husbands, and fathers of children who now would never be. The waste was obscene, and he found it deeply distressing.

Yes, *he* had suffered too, but at least he was still here, although he often wondered why, bearing in mind Dae-Jung's assiduous ministrations. Martha was the only person he had ever told about the brutal beatings. He established a special rapport with her, and could tell her anything, knowing that it would go no further. She was such an attentive and sympathetic listener that confiding in her had helped enormously in his restoration.

By the end of the Summer term, he had managed to reunite with one of his former friends in the town, and together they set about resurrecting the Netherbridge Arts Society, but they suffered an early setback: the Council's refusal to renew their former grant. Apparently, the harsh winter of 1946-47 had taken its toll on their finances. However, thanks to a timely intervention from a newly-demobbed young dentist who had just become a governor of NGS, and also knew that year's Mayor well, the grant was reinstated the following year, together with the use of the Town Hall free of charge on Tuesday evenings as a token of good will!

As the months passed, Dr Kendricks's self-confidence in the classroom strengthened, as did his old gift for story-telling and the sense of humour that could lighten even the most abstruse point of Greek grammar. By the late 1950s, his former reputation as an inspired, but demanding, schoolmaster was fully restored, and it was largely thanks to him that Classics acquired a *cachet*, rivalling mathematics and physics, as the subject of choice for very able pupils. This harmless rivalry appealed very much to Dr Davenport, not only for his friend's sake, but also because of his long-held belief in broadening the curriculum without sacrificing standards. Besides, he argued, the high-calibre pupils who had chosen NGS deserved no less.

With hindsight, many regretted that Dr Kendricks had not been appointed Headmaster while he was still at the peak of his powers, and not now when it seemed more like a token gesture to rectify an injustice. He may not have possessed Dr Davenport's grasp of the 'big picture' and his forward-planning abilities, nor Jim Whittaker's organising skills, but what he did have was presence, allied to unbounded enthusiasm and an ability to bring people together to get things done, as demonstrated by the way the embryonic Netherbridge Arts Society grew into the two-day Netherbridge Arts Festival. On the other hand, had his promotion come earlier, his pupils would have been deprived of an exceptional teacher: his genius belonged in the classroom, not in an office.

His first assembly was reminiscent of Dr Davenport's last. He entered the Hall to a deafening standing ovation, and when he reached the platform to face his audience, there was instant and total silence. It was a mystery to his junior colleagues how such a gentle, unimposing, hunched old man could command such authority, but his older colleagues knew, as did the pupils: it was their privilege to have worked with not only an outstanding professional but with an exceptional human being who, like Abu Ben Adhem, loved his fellow-men, and they irresistibly him.

Chapter Nineteen

Martha had not been looking forward to the Lent term. After an exceptionally busy end to the 1974 Michaelmas term, she had spent the first three days of the Christmas holiday helping Mr Pickering tie up loose ends and clear his office ready for its new incumbent. Then, when she thought she could have a little time to herself, fate decreed otherwise. Three days before Christmas, Taff suffered a major stroke resulting in right side paralysis. Consequently, she spent much of the holiday ferrying Liz to and from the Infirmary, or sitting with Taff herself.

But above and beyond all this, 1975 was the "year of the rough beast", and in her darker moments she wished she could retire to Aberdyfi, and escape what she called the "mindless vandalism", not to mention the elation of those who had craved it. But maybe fifty-four *was* a tad early to call it a day; and perhaps things might not be as disagreeable as she feared... well, not for a while, anyway.

Amanda had also helped to disabuse her of the "silly idea"; and of course, the Jenkinses would need her more than ever now.

But in the event, as soon as the great NGS machine sprang into life on January 6th, she soon found herself immersed in the bustle and excitement of the first day of term, albeit without Mr Pickering's acerbic wit, and the company of several masters, who had left for the private sector at the eleventh hour.

But for all her angst, Martha had one very good reason for optimism. During her thirty years at NGS she had worked for three headmasters, forming close, albeit very different, working relationships with them. Now, a fourth was about to make his debut, and she knew that whatever the future held for her, working with him would be an unqualified joy. Whilst she had adored Dr Davenport, looked after Mr Riley like an elderly uncle, admired Mr Whittaker, she *loved* Dr Kendricks like that older brother who (annoyingly) seems to know everything, and for whom even the most intractable problem solves itself!

For all his sixty-three years and visibly declining health, Dr Kendricks still had enormous reserves of energy and endless good humour, and it was generally thought that if there was one person capable of bringing the two schools together into one happy, working partnership, it was he.

He had certainly thought hard about how things might look after the two schools had been unified. In particular, whilst not forgetting that a *comprehensive* curriculum caters for a wide range of abilities, he was also anxious lest academic standards be compromised. To this end, he had persuaded the Governors to make two or three urgent appointments to replace the invaluable colleagues who had left precipitately, and even asked Joe Riley to pay a visit to his old college in Durham to see if he could recruit a bright young Classics graduate to help carry the torch forward into the comprehensive era.

Accordingly, by the February half-term, with Martha's devoted help, and after consulting widely with both sets of staff, Dr Kendricks had set out in some detail how he proposed to organise and time-table the classes for the following year; and to be certain that his plans were viable and acceptable, he had arranged a meeting with Nobbs, Andy Goody, and a curriculum specialist from the Chester College of Education on Wednesday of the half-term week. Unfortunately, Nobbs was unable to attend because of a "long-standing sailing arrangement", but the meeting went ahead regardless, and the proposals were warmly received, especially for their clarity and flexibility.

Although a capable administrator, Dr Kendricks's *forte* was people, and for that reason, he rarely used his office, except as a depository for his hat and coat, and for teaching his Classics Scholarship class. He said that sitting in an office all day, moving bits of paper around, appalled him. Accordingly, when not perambulating the School, chatting to whomsoever he happened to meet, he could usually be found in Martha's office, dealing with matters of the day, and, increasingly now, Martha's 'rough beast'.

Although morning assemblies were outside Dr Kendricks's remit, he was keen for them to continue after the merger. The New Hall was certainly large enough to accommodate both schools, but the hazards of bringing a large number of pupils across Manchester Road during rush hour made a combined assembly impracticable. However, he was pleasantly surprised when Nobbs agreed that having NGS staff taking assemblies at Manchester Road, and vice versa, would help bring the two schools together.

Dave Longworth's assemblies had been uninspiring affairs, consisting mainly of announcements, or warnings about smoking and latterly drugs: they were rarely seen as educational opportunities. Dr Kendricks, on the other hand, saw educational opportunities in everything, and with his gift for story-telling and his infectious sense of humour, he could capture the imagination of even the most disenchanted teenager.

Accordingly, undeterred by Martha's wry asides, and to some extent his own doubts, he spent the remainder of the Lent term trying to secure some form of *entente cordiale* with Nobbs, and building bridges between the two institutions, whose cultures were manifestly poles apart. As in any partnership, he thought, this is something that will need working at for many years. If it was easy, why did both Dave Longworth and the masterly Jim Whittaker balk at the challenge? And for sure, unless proper structures are put in place, and capable people appointed to lead the venture, it will sink into a quicksand of envy, animosity and bitterness. Unless the two parties respect one another, work together and for each other, it will remain a union in name only – a sham.

ALL IN ALL, Dr Kendricks was quietly pleased with his first term as Headmaster, even though he knew it had taken a great deal out of him. On the last afternoon of term, Jim Pickering called to see him, and was shocked to see how emaciated he looked. Clearly, something was amiss: either he was over-working, or he was ill and needed to see a doctor. Seeing him every day, Martha had not noticed the decline so much, and his constant joviality and enthusiasm had teased her into believing that his loss of weight was due simply to over-work, allied possibly to an unsatisfactory diet. But a brief exchange with her former boss convinced her that perhaps she should take matters into her own hands.

Accordingly, on Martha's insistence, Dr Kendricks was to take a proper holiday that Easter, and forgo all work connected with school and his beloved Netherbridge Festival. He had never known Martha being so adamant, and decided that perhaps under the circumstances it would be prudent to comply with her instructions!

The School closed on Friday 21st March, and at nine o'clock on Monday 24th he found himself sitting in a first class compartment with a copy of *The Times*, waiting for the train to pull out of Manchester Piccadilly on its four and a half hour journey to Norwich.

Whilst not close, he and Alice were always pleased to see each other, and she was especially pleased this time, because it was his first visit for over two years and his first as a headmaster. But when the train arrived, and he stepped on to the platform, her excitement was quelled somewhat by his gaunt look and less than upright bearing, reminding her of the broken brother who had returned to them after his incarceration in Japan.

After a much anticipated embrace and caress, Alice began, "Well, Billy, you got here then, and how's life treating you?"

"It's treating me very well, Alice... and thank you for having me at such short notice."

"We love having you... you know that. Fasten your seat belt."

Alice kept glancing across at her brother.

"Are you eating properly, Billy?"

"You're beginning to sound like Mama now! Besides, I'm in the fashion... thin is the new beautiful... and healthy too?"

"Yes, but there's thin... and thin, Billy, and you're in the second category. I'll have to feed you up a bit, while you're here."

"How's Bob?

"He's very well, thank you... semi-retired now, of course... doing a bit of locum work, and playing a lot of golf, to keep out from under my feet, I think."

"And the children?"

"Oh, they're also fine, thank you... all living with partners, but no wedding in sight. I suppose we all have to get used to that sort of thing in this day and age."

After a sumptuous dinner, he and Bob had a brandy and a cigar in the conservatory, as they always did when he came to stay.

"Your garden's looking good, Bob, and it's only March. Do you do it all yourself?"

"Well, I mow the lawn, and that's about it. We have a man in to trim the hedges. Alice is the head gardener. By the way, Bill, Alice is a little concerned about your weight-loss. Are you eating proper meals?"

"If I'm honest, Bob, probably not... but then I rarely feel properly hungry, although I did enjoy that dinner."

"When did you have your last MOT?"

"Well, the trouble is, I hate bothering my doctor, when he's so busy dealing with really sick people. And I don't want to get a reputation as a fuss-pot!"

"You *should* bother him. That's what he's there for."

"Now you mention it, I *have* been having these funny little pains down in the tummy area of late, but they don't last long, so I put them down to wind."

"Listen, while you're down with us, would you like me to arrange a 'once-over' for you? It won't cost you anything, and it won't do any harm."

"If you insist... but honestly, I feel perfectly all right, and, as they say, if it ain't broke, why fix it?"

"I could ring him now, if you like."

The following morning Bob took his brother-in-law to a nearby private clinic where he was submitted to a thorough examination and a battery of tests, all of which proved inconclusive. However, to make sure, he was then asked to return the following day for a barium enema X-ray examination, which also proved inconclusive, and vindicated our impatient patient's scepticism!

On Good Friday, Dr Kendrick's "little pains" grew more persistent, and more severe, and on Easter Saturday he agreed to being admitted as an in-patient at the private clinic until after the Easter weekend, when he could be examined by a specialist.

On the Wednesday after Easter a specialist carried out an exploratory operation for suspected bowel cancer. Alice held his hand while he was being anaesthetised, and was there again when he awoke about an hour later. Sadly, the operation confirmed their worst fears, and it had spread too far to warrant further surgery. Alice knew that her brother would want to know the truth, that nothing more could be done for him except to administer end-of-life care, which she willingly undertook, and he accepted stoically.

"Count your blessings, Billy boy!" he said with a chuckle, "what more could a man want... a beautiful, kind nurse dancing attendance, and a good doctor on call in the house!"

Indeed, after the diagnosis, he developed a very close relationship with Alice, something he regretted not having enjoyed throughout his life, but he was determined now to make the most of what time he had left, which the specialist had optimistically put at three months.

He wanted to break the news to Martha himself, which he did wonderfully, sounding as if he had won the pools and was retiring to the Bahamas! They talked for a good half-hour, and there were so many jokes that poor Martha did not know whether to laugh or cry, and ended up crying with laughter, which was exactly what Dr Kendricks wanted.

He assured Alice that all his affairs were in order, and that his papers, including his will, insurance documents and so forth could be found in his desk at his home in Newton-le-Willows. Furthermore, he had decided long ago to be cremated, and for his ashes to be scattered on his mother's grave at St Batholemew's Church in Haslemere: "no fuss, no solemnity, just a short reading by the graveside... something funny if you like, or whatever you fancy, but nothing too serious... and Bob's your uncle!"

Dr Kendricks died in his sister's arms on Tuesday morning, 1st April 1975, and his ashes were scattered according to his instructions.

AS SOON AS Martha had regained her composure after receiving the devastating news, she set about the equally distressing task of informing the relevant people: Martin Shaw, Ted Hoyle, Andy Goody and, of course, Nobbs, who was yet again unavailable, but she managed to catch Amanda as she was setting off to a business meeting.

Nobbs was so excited by the news that he found it difficult concentrating on anything. Was this really happening, he thought. I have waited thirty years, and then, like buses, two come along at once... first, the house, and then the job. I must be doing something right.

At ten o'clock the following morning, Martin Shaw rang him to say that he had had telephone conversations with one or two 'key' governors, and they had agreed that representatives of both sets of governors should meet Andy Goody urgently to discuss the future of the headship. In fact, such a meeting had already been 'pencilled in' for late May or early June, but events had overtaken them. Accordingly, Martin Shaw had gone ahead and arranged a meeting at NGS on Monday 7th April, the last day of the Easter holiday.

Martha, still feeling numb from her sudden loss, was appalled at the callous and indecent haste of events. If this was a glimpse of the future, then she was right to have had misgivings, and perhaps she did not belong in that future. She had always kept a copy of Dr Davenport's last letter to her in her desk, and had recently made a point of taking it out and reading it carefully, especially one prescient sentence:

Beware, in particular, of certain self-seeking, treacherous iconoclasts in your midst, and their lackeys, an equally treacherous bunch of time-serving bootlickers.

Clearly, it's time to heed his advice, she thought, as she steeled herself for the hurriedly arranged meeting on the 7th April, to which Martin Shaw had invited her to take the minutes. It was obvious from the start to Martha that the decision had already been taken, and the meeting was a mere formality. Mr Nobbs was to be offered the headship of both schools for the remainder of the school year, and meanwhile he was to invite a competent person (or persons) to be responsible for the day-to-day running of the Manchester Road site. It also suddenly occurred to Martha that this would be the first time during her whole career at the School that she would have no close colleague with whom to share her thoughts and worries, and she could have done with someone at that very moment.

When the Schools re-opened the following day, the pupils and the staff at NGS were still in a state of shock at the news of Dr Kendricks's passing. Boys, as a rule, do not feel the death of an unrelated, elderly person too intensely, being more exercised by how any resultant changes might affect them. But Martha was not alone in noticing palpable grief hanging in the air at NGS that morning. They had all lost a true friend – and the community was about to lose an ancient and revered institution. She herself had never felt so demoralised, and there was little about her new situation to which she could relate, but then she remembered the hell Dr Kendricks had endured in Japan, and felt a corrective pang of shame.

She had spent the previous afternoon at *Elsinore* with Amanda, seeking some comfort when all about her seemed to be falling apart. The conversation had eventually turned to Nobbs's sudden promotion.

"He's wanted this for so long, Martha," she said, "and I do want him to make a success of it. I know the two of you have not always seen eye to eye, but with your support, he'll stand a better chance of creating a good impression and getting the job permanently. It may come as a surprise to you, but for all his outward confidence, deep down Rich is quite a nervous, sensitive person, and he'll certainly need your guiding hand until he finds his feet."

"Oh, Mandy, you don't have to worry about your husband. I'm sure he'll manage very well without my help," replied Martha. "After all, I'm there to carry out *his* instructions, which I promise to do to the very best of my ability, as I have always done."

Amanda hugged her tightly, and whispered "thank you," in her ear.

On her way home Martha wondered whether in reality she could ever establish a working relationship with Nobbs, when they had so little in common, but since she had given her plighted word, somehow, she would have to work round the obstacles and develop an amicable *modus operandi*.

NOBBS ARRIVED at school very early on Tuesday, 8th April, like a man on a mission. After parking the Jaguar carefully in its usual place, he went straight to his office, and waited impatiently for the expected knock on the door.

"Good morning, Fred... everything all right?"

"Yes, as far as I can tell, Mr Nobbs... I had a bit of trouble with..."

"Listen, Fred, we're upping sticks."

"Beg pardon, Mr Nobbs?"

"We're on the move, Fred. In case you haven't heard, old Kendricks died suddenly last week.

"Oh, I'm sorry to hear that, Mr Nobbs..."

"... and the governors have asked me to take charge of both schools. So, I've got a nice little removal job for you."

"Does that mean I'll be 'avin' a new boss over here, Mr Nobbs?"

"No, it means you'll be moving across the road with me."

"Oh, right," said Fred, wondering if this might mean more money in his wage packet.

"So, you can make a start straightaway... these pictures, the bookcase, coffee table... everything except the desk and the chair. I've had another name-plate made for my new office, and you can screw that on when you're over there. And this afternoon, I want you to start marking some new parking spaces near their main entrance like you did here... and make sure my space is wide enough".

"Righty-o, Mr Nobbs."

"Oh, and if anybody asks you what you're doing, tell 'em you're carrying out the Headmaster's instructions."

"Yes, of course, Mr Nobbs." (Bloody hell, thought Fred, he doesn't hang about, does he?)

Nobbs felt a surge of authority welling through his veins as he drove his Jaguar the few yards across the road and parked it right next to the new main door of the Grammar School. "Rich, lad," he snarled to himself. "You can do anything you f------ want now."

Just as he was heaving himself out of the driver's seat, Martha's red Mini arrived, which she parked in its usual place on the far side of the car park. He walked across to meet her.

"Good morning, Martha, and a good morning it is too. They say the sun shines on the righteous! You couldn't spare me a couple of minutes before the hordes arrive?"

"Yes, of course, Mr Nobbs."

Alf Newby, the Caretaker, had already unlocked the front door, and they went straight into Martha's office, which was not as tidy as usual because she had had to rush home after the governors' meeting the previous day to take Taff for his physiotherapy appointment at the Infirmary.

"First of all, Martha, could you announce on the Tannoy that there will be no morning assembly here this morning... and pupils are to remain in their form rooms until the start of the first lesson."

Martha was taken aback, and said, "Do you think that's wise, Mr Nobbs? Dr Kendricks had been at the School a very long time, and was very highly thought of... I know that some of his colleagues, and maybe one or two of the senior boys too, would want to say a few words."

"Good thinking, Martha. Yes, all right then... I suppose this *is* a special occasion, but looking ahead, I'm planning to down-grade school assemblies altogether... they've had their day, and I want to allocate the time more usefully for form-teachers to get to know their form groups better pastorally, and hold counselling and guidance sessions with individuals or groups. But what I really wanted to talk to you about was *you*. I want to change your title, Martha. "School Secretary" sounds so old-fashioned, and I thought something like "Senior Administrative Officer" would be more in keeping with a modern educational establishment, don't you think?"

"To be honest, Mr Nobbs, I'm not fussed about titles, but if that's what you want, it's fine by me... but why "Senior"? There's only one of me, and I'm not that old, even though I feel it sometimes!"

"Ah, I'm thinking ahead, Martha... when the two schools merge in September, I plan to make Peggy Bagshaw your number two, and see how we can dove-tail your respective roles. Oh, and I've been looking into the pay-scales too. In view of the increased work-load you'll have, I'll see what I can do about a pay rise for you, but of course I'll have to clear that with Chester first."

"Thank you," said Martha, wondering what exactly the increased work-load would involve, but feeling grateful even for small mercies. (She also wondered if Amanda was behind all this sweet-talking!)

"And by the way, Martha, so that you're fully up to speed, Fred Broadbent will be moving some of my stuff across this morning... no point in shilly-shallying. Right, I'd better get back. I'll leave the car here. See you anon."

Martha felt exhausted even before her day had begun. She made herself a cup of coffee and sat at her desk for a few minutes to gather her thoughts, when there was a heavy knock on her door.

"Come in," she called, barely hiding her weariness.

"Martha, what the hell's goin' on? Nobody tells me nowt... just seen Fred Broadbent humping stuff into the

Headmaster's office. Who gave him the key? And then he says he's going to re-paint the white lines in the car park this afternoon. This is my patch, Martha, and I should be told what's goin' on."

"I agree, Mr Newby, I agree," said Martha, "but we're living in strange times, and I expect we'll all have to get used to sudden changes, myself included. I've been told nothing about white lines."

BY THE following Monday, Nobbs was fully installed in his new, palatial office. Ensconced in his magnificent chair, behind an equally imposing desk, he thought, yes, Richard, this is an office worthy of the headmaster destined to break the mould, the headmaster who will establish comprehensive education in Netherbridge... in this very room you will formulate your policies to decommission two old, dysfunctional institutions and build in their place one glorious, vibrant entity, where all children, regardless of their ability or background, will be treated as equals... and all teachers will be valued, whether they went to Oxford or Ormskirk.

A gentle knock on his door suspended his train of thought.

"Your tea, Mr Nobbs," said Martha, "only plain biscuits today, I'm afraid."

"Oh, thank you, Martha, they'll be fine. By the way, Andy Goody, and his assistant, John Unsworth, will be paying us a visit on Wednesday morning. I think they just want to see how I'm settling in, and how I see the way forward. He said an officer from another part of the county might be coming along as well, just to observe... so, if you could remind whoever's on yard duty to keep the front of the School and the foyer clear during morning break... oh, and can you get a message to Alf Newby to come and see me at 12 o'clock today?"

"Will do, Mr Nobbs," said Martha, wondering how he would cope with his first confrontation!

At 12 o'clock prompt, a heavy, not to say disrespectful, knock on Nobbs's door heralded an aggrieved Alf Newby.

"Come!" yelled Nobbs. "No need to knock the f------ door in. Take a seat, Alf."

"I prefer to stand, thank you."

"Please yourself. Look, I haven't got much time, so I'll come straight to the point... there's going to be some changes around here, right? The truth is, you and your ilk have had it too easy for too long, and, as you're about to find out, there's more to caretaking than carrying a bunch of keys around all day. *I'm* the Headmaster now, you lazy turd, and you'll do as I f------- well say."

"Huh, *you* a headmaster!" said Alf, "For a start, proper headmasters don't use language like that... and, I'm telling you... if you ever swear at me again, you'll be hearing from my Union."

"Ooh, I'm quaking in my boots! As I was about to explain... before I was rudely interrupted... as from next Monday you and Fred Broadbent will be working together, looking after *both* sites. But *you* will be based at Manchester Road, and Fred will be over here."

"But you can't..."

"That will be all for now, Alf... Fred will fill you in on all the details. Any appointment with me in future must be made through Martha.

Alf had barely left the room before Nobbs was on the

phone to Chester. To his annoyance, the legal people were all at lunch, and for want of official advice, he asked Martha to call for Fred to come to the Headmaster's office urgently.

When Fred eventually arrived, breathless and believing there was a major emergency, Nobbs launched into how he had had to reprimand Alf Newby for his discourteous attitude that morning, and in doing so, he may have used, well, some strong language. He, in return, had threatened to report Nobbs to his Union, and Nobbs needed to know if he was bluffing or not. As a former local branch official, who had known Alf for more years than he could remember, Fred did not think he was bluffing, and if the Headmaster had indeed sworn at Alf, he *was* within his rights to report the matter to his Union.

After Fred had gone, Nobbs slumped in his chair feeling forlorn and dejected. My day started so well, he thought, and then that scumbag had to piss on my parade. But, never mind, as the saying goes, revenge is a dish best served cold.

It was now the first period of the afternoon, and to clear his head he thought he would stroll across to his other office. As he was making his way up the main drive of the Manchester Road School, he heard mindless sniggering coming from behind a nearby bush, and just as he was turning the corner towards the main entrance, he heard further laughter, followed by two shouts of "Knob'ead". Having had one confrontation that day already, he pretended not to have heard, and hurried towards the safety of his old office, where he sat for a good half-hour considering whether to ring Chester again about the Alf Newby business. In the end, he decided

462

against it, in case he came over as weak and naive; he also hoped and prayed that Alf would do the decent thing and let sleeping dogs lie.

As soon as the second lesson of the afternoon was under way at Manchester Road, he made a swift return to his new office, and just as he was about to fall asleep in his chair, his phone rang.

"Yes, who is it?"

"I hope I'm not disturbing you, Mr Nobbs," said Martha, "I've got a file here that might be of interest to you. Would you like me to bring it across, or shall I keep it until later?"

"I'll take a gander at it now, Martha," he said grudgingly.

The quite substantial file was the product of Dr Kendricks's planning for the incipient Netherbridge High School. This was what the Area Education Officer and the curriculum expert had discussed and extolled at the meeting which Nobbs had seen fit to miss. It was, as one might have expected, a professionally produced collection of documents, with tables and diagrams – in short, a ready-made curriculum *schema* tailored for their comprehensive school.

When the file arrived, Nobbs pulled a face like a little boy being asked to tidy his toys, "Bloody hell, Martha, have I got to read all this. Anyway, leave it with me... I'll have a look when I get a spare moment."

As soon as Martha had gone, Nobbs could not resist opening the black file with its intriguing title, "Taming of the Beast!", and he suspected straightaway who the author might be. As he riffled through its pages, he took a liking to it, not only for its obvious usefulness, but how, with a few judicious changes, he could pass it off as his own work. Unusually for him, it had slipped his mind that this was the very document which had been discussed during the meeting he had missed.

NOBBS WAS desperate to create a good impression on Wednesday, 16th April, his first official visit from LEA officers. Martha had kindly prepared her usual plateful of mouth-watering Welsh cakes, and the whole place smelled strongly of freshly-brewed coffee.

The three men arrived promptly, and having paid their respects to Martha, proceeded to Nobbs's office.

"Come in, gentlemen," said Nobbs, "come in... make yourself at home."

"You've met John before, haven't you?" said Andy Goody, "and this is Derek Pratt, my colleague from the other side of the county who has come to observe, if that's okay?"

"Pleased to meet you," said Nobbs.

As he was pouring the coffee, his guests could not help noticing how lavishly appointed his office was... clearly not County Council furnishings.

"My, this is some office, Richard!" said Andy Goody, "it's grander than the Director's!"

"We like to set the bar high," said Nobbs.

"Didn't the desk used to be on the other side?"

"Yes, but the light's better on this side, and it provides a better vantage point when people come through that door," he added, tapping his nose, "you can take the boy out of the jungle, but not the jungle out of the boy!"

Andy Goody glanced quizzically at the other two, but they seemed equally mystified.

464

"Anyway, hard for you losing Dr Kendricks like that so suddenly."

"These things happen... life goes on... one door closes, another opens. It's early days yet, of course, but... put it this way, my mission is to knock this grammar' /'modern' divide on the head. That's key, and I'm already on the case. As from next Monday, instead of looking after the two sites separately, the two caretakers will share the duties for both sites, and to reinforce this, I've swapped their work-bases around. A small change I know, but from little acorns... and, you wait, I'll be making similar exchanges for the teaching staff."

"Interesting," said Andy Goody. "So, now *you're* based over here, who'll be overseeing the Manchester Road site?"

"I'm still mulling over that one, but I think in the end it will boil down to the either Dennis Peterson or Barbara Pearce... there'd be hell to pay if I appointed anyone else!"

"Have you thought of giving them a half-term each, before making the appointment?"

"Yes, that's a possibility too."

"How about pastoral care?" said John Unsworth at last, knowing that that was Nobbs's special interest.

"Well yes, of course, that's constantly on my mind... that too will be part of my strategy to stamp out this whole "grammar school" thing. And I thought I'd start with school assemblies.

"Assemblies?" said John Unsworth.

"God, I've sat through thousands of the f------ things, and you can take it from me they're a waste of time. They're just an opportunity for certain opinionated individuals with inflated egos to sound off in front of a captive audience. No, the time would be far better spent letting form-teachers get to know their pupils better, and conducting counselling sessions. Of course, some of the staff, especially this lot over here, will need training, but I can lay on Inset courses for them."

"I know your expertise is in pastoral care, Richard," said Andy Goody, "and, of course, when Dr Kendricks was here, you could concentrate on that, but now you're on your tod, you'll soon have to start thinking about next year's curriculum and timetable."

"Well... I haven't exactly been just sitting on my arse, you know, Andy," said Nobbs with that broad, toothy grin of his. "Let me show you."

He reached down to the bottom drawer of his desk and lifted out a bright red box file, marked, "Netherbridge High School – Academic Curriculum" (1975-76)". He then handed it triumphantly to Andy Goody, who, after making some appropriate complimentary noises, soon recognised it as Dr Kendricks's *schema* in disguise!

Not wishing to let on that he knew, he passed the file to John Unsworth, and said, "An ambitious programme, Richard, and aiming to action it this coming September would be very ambitious... even for you! If you wanted, the two schools could continue as they are for the first year... under the new name, of course, and with any changes you care to make... then you'd have more time to work out the logistics of this impressive programme of yours for the following year. It would also give you more time, should you wish, to appoint a curriculum coordinator to help with heavy lifting."

"That's exactly what I was thinking, Andy, I'm glad

you agree."

"God, is that the time!" said Andy Goody, "we'll have to leave you now, I'm afraid. Impressive, Richard, you've hit the ground running. I'll be seeing the Deputy Director tomorrow morning, and I'll see what I can do about getting some extra funding. Good luck."

Nobbs spent the afternoon going over every detail of the meeting in his head, and when Martha brought his cup of tea, he began enthusing like a little boy telling his mother that the teacher had given him three stars for effort. "I think they liked what they saw, Martha, and were impressed with how quickly things were moving. They were especially interested in this file of yours."

The red file had now been restored to its original black livery, and had been placed casually on the desk for Martha to see.

"I hoped it might be of some use," said Martha insouciantly, knowing full well that Andy Goody would have recognised it immediately.

"Changing the subject, Martha, from next Monday Fred Broadbent will be based over here, and Alf Newby across the road. But they'll be sharing the responsibilities for both sites between them. Oh, and while I remember, can you ask Fred to report to me at the end of the afternoon? Thank you, Martha."

"Yes, Mr Nobbs," replied Martha. For Amanda's sake and her own sanity she would have to get used to this policy-making on the hoof, and much else, no doubt.

Encouraged by the morning's meeting, Nobbs wondered what next he could do to debunk the grammar school myth. The most obvious was the school names: the Manchester Road site could become Block A (for Arts) and the 'grammar' site, Block S (for Science). Then the uniform, those stupid red and green caps and blazers with the school crest... then the house system, copycatting the public schools... and prefects with their poncy little badges... he had spent half his time at Oldham Hulme picking fights with them! And those pretentious black gowns, they'll have to go. Yes, Richard lad, you're going to have fun. Revenge is sweet! Let battle begin!

"Come in, Fred, sit down a moment... I've got another little job for you... I want all the silver cups in the glass cabinet taken over to the junk room next to the old library. Then, tomorrow you can give the cabinet a good clean, inside and out, right?"

"Will do, Mr Nobbs..."

"Has Alf Newby mentioned anything to you about the other day?"

"No, not a word, Mr Nobbs."

"Well, let me know if he does."

"Yes, course, Mr Nobbs."

Two days later, Nobbs called Dennis Peterson and Barbara Pearce to his office during the lunch hour.

"Look, guys... I won't keep you... I know you're busy... the governors have asked me to appoint someone to oversee the Manchester Road site. Obviously, either of you would fit the bill admirably... so, after a lot of thought, what I've decided to do is to give you both a half-term each and decide at the end of term... that is, if you're both agreeable. By the way, I've also decided to make this post one of the three Scale 6 posts the School has been allocated. The remit is broadly to oversee the day-to-day running of the site in all its aspects, and to keep me fully informed with weekly reports. Now, since 'Pearce' has the edge on Peterson alphabetically... I suggest Barbara does the first stint up to half-term, and then Dennis follows till the end of term, okay? If you've got any questions, give me a ring."

Apart from the Alf Newby incident, Nobbs's week had gone pretty well. Indeed, he was so pleased that he rang Amanda to book dinner for two that evening in a quiet country pub of her choosing, which she was pleased to do if only to avoid cooking after a strenuous day's work. As soon as he arrived home, he began rhapsodizing about how well things were going, especially how well his Staff was responding to his innovations. "Even Martha," he said, "couldn't be more helpful."

"Why '*even* Martha'?"

"Well, I thought she'd be more bolshie, that's all... but no, fair do's, so far she's been great... I think we'll get along fine when she gets to know me better."

Amanda had her doubts about that, but said nothing.

The quiet dinner out on a Friday night became a regular feature in the Nobbses' schedule; indeed, it was about the only time they could sit down and talk to each other, although the talk consisted mainly of his "reporting back to base", little knowing that Amanda knew a great deal of it already! But even she marvelled at her husband's capacity for embellishing or even misrepresenting facts, and wondered why he did it.

The Summer Term came and went, with much despondency on both sides of Manchester Road, but whilst many hankered after a golden age long gone, a few wasted no time in ingratiating themselves with the new regime.

Meanwhile, Nobbs had appointed Dennis Peterson as

469

the Senior Teacher in charge of the newly-named 'A' Block. Knowing what a formidable 'enemy' Dennis could be, he had thought it wiser to "secure (himself) against" him by *buying* his loyalty. Furthermore, he had appeased Barbara with promises of "something better later on", which she had taken to mean a deputy headship. Barbara thought he was the most handsome and most self-assured headmaster in all England, with splendid waistcoats to boot!

The following day, Nobbs asked Phil Evans to call in his office when it was convenient. Thinking that there might be something amiss, Phil called during the mid-morning break, and was pleasantly surprised by Nobbs's genial welcome.

"Oh, come in, Phil... sit down... coffee? Help yourself to biscuits." Then, after pouring the coffee, he said, "We go back a long way, Phil, and I've been thinking how I could reward you for all you've done for the School over the years. So, I decided to create a new position especially for you. That lot in Chester told me to advertise the post externally, but I said why go looking elsewhere when there's a pot of gold sitting in your own back yard. I think Head of Sixth Form would suit you right down to the ground, Phil... you know, university applications, academic references and such like. I've made it a Scale 6, and there'll be a reduced teaching load. Anyway, think about it."

Phil did think about it for several days, consulting friends, and colleagues past and present, all of whom warned about the snake in the grass, but in the end he decided, against his better judgement, to follow Shirley's advice and take the king's shilling.

"Good decision, Phil... you'll enjoy the challenge," said Nobbs and thought, that's two of the buggers sorted, one to go!

And he wondered if he could dispose of Barbara in similar fashion: buying her silence, and shackling her to a busy role. He was half-listening to the six o'clock news on his way home that evening when it came to him: 'Pastoral Care of Years One to Four... that should keep the silly cow happy.

The next morning he called Barbara into his office. "Come in, Babs... sit down. F------ hell, you look younger every time I see you! I do like your new hair-style... really suits you..."

All Barbara could do was blush and giggle like a schoolgirl.

"Where was I? Oh, yes... remember when Dennis Peterson pipped you for the Manchester Road job, I promised you 'something later on'? Well, I know I'm not perfect, Barbara, but I am a man of my word. 'Pastoral Care Coordinator for Years One and Two, and liaising with feeder primaries'... Scale 6 and a reduced teaching load. How does that grab you?"

"Gosh, I don't know what to say, Mr Nobbs."

"Sleep on it, Babs, and let me know what you think. Don't hang about, though... I've got one or two others who fancy it, especially on that grade, but you are my number one choice."

"Well, thank you, Mr Nobbs, that's very kind of you."

The following morning, Barbara was waiting for him in the foyer, her mind made up.

"I've decided to accept, Mr Nobbs," she said.

"Good decision, Barbara... I think it will be right up

your street. Like me, you're a *people* person... we understand kids and what makes them tick. Look, I've got a couple of phone calls to make. But you can come and see me any time you want."

"Oh, thank you, Mr Nobbs."

Chapter Twenty

NETHERBRIDGE High School was formally opened on Monday, 8th September, 1975 with much glitz, but little actual change.

"In keeping with the Government's thinking," proclaimed the Town Mayor, "we are proud to present the good people of Netherbridge with a comprehensive school worthy of the town's long and glorious educational tradition; and we are equally proud to have one of our own adopted and highly respected sons, Mr Richard Nobbs, as its first headmaster. Under his experienced and pioneering leadership, I am confident that Netherbridge High will uphold that glorious tradition..."

Amanda had persuaded the *Chronicle* to give the event full publicity with the headline, "First Comprehensive in the County". She had also arranged afternoon tea on the lawn at *Elsinore* for the governors, the dignitaries of

Netherbridge and members of School's staff. Absentees were duly recorded in Nobbs's preternatural memory.

As expected, many of the masters were more interested in their 'A' and 'O' level results, checking whether their Upper Sixth pupils had gained the grades they needed, and which fifth year pupils would be choosing *their* subjects in the Lower Sixth. In fact, the results that year at both levels were surprisingly good, considering all the disruptions, not that Nobbs took much notice. Ever since his schooldays, he had loathed formal examinations, sitting in rows for hours in silence, relieving the boredom by drawing rude cartoons on the back of his question paper, or trying to catch a fellow-sufferer's eye, while desperately avoiding the invigilator's. And forty years on, he felt no urge to change his opinion, especially now, having planted the problem fairly and squarely in Phil Evans's lap.

The following Saturday, Martin Shaw called at *Elsinore* for mid-morning coffee. "Well done, Mandy," he said, giving her a peck on the cheek, which she neatly converted into one on her mouth, "everything went like clockwork... nice coverage in the *Chronicle* too... and the tea on the lawn was a masterstroke!"

"Well, thank you, kind sir!" said Amanda, looking archly at her husband.

"Listen, Mart," said Nobbs, "since you're here, can we talk shop for a moment? As you know, I've got to appoint these two deputies soon. Andy Goody says we should advertise nationally, and I agree. I want, preferably a man, to look after the curriculum and the time-table, and a good strong woman to oversee the girls."

"But you've already got a good woman," said

Amanda. "Barbara Pearce has done the job for years... and was also Dave Longworth's deputy. And then there's Phil Evans... he'd be ideal for the timetable and things... meticulous organiser, hard-working... and, like Barbara, highly respected... what more do you want?"

"Yes, I know... Barbara's got a lot going for her," said Nobbs, "trouble is, she's too 'familiar' for the role I have in mind... too matey with the girls. And Phil's okay too, except he's so... dyed in the wool grammar school... so exam-orientated. All that stuff he does... you know, the school magazine, theatre trips and things, it's all so... middle class... of no interest to your average kid. No, Phil's just a traditional, subject teacher, not an educationalist, and he'll be fine in that job I've given him... and Barbara likewise. Anyway, even if we did appoint them, I'd still have to find two others to replace them. So, we'd be back to square one."

"I still don't think you should write off two excellent people you *know*," said Amanda, "in favour of two absolute strangers."

"Mandy's got a point, you know, Rich," said Martin. "They both deserve an interview at least. But of course, at the end of the day, it's you who has to work with them."

In reality, Nobbs's real objection to Barbara had nothing to do with her imputed "closeness" to the girls. As he had recently discovered, teenage girls can be fiendishly difficult to deal with, and he needed someone who could "put the fear of God into those stroppy, pubescent wenches". Likewise, it was not Phil's reactionary attitudes or his indifference to current educational thinking that troubled Nobbs, but the fact that Phil knew too much about *him* personally, having spent countless evenings at his house in Leigh helping him with his M.Ed. assignments, and more recently, writing his letter of application for the headship of Manchester Road. But most of all, he feared Phil's intellect, and being eclipsed by him. He preferred to surround himself with his intellectual inferiors.

THE TWO DEPUTIES were duly appointed during the last week of October, 1975, to begin duties the following January. Several of the governors had expressed deep concern about the quality of the field, and wanted to re-advertise. Indeed, both appointments were decided on narrow majorities, the male deputy's even requiring the Chairman's casting vote. "Why hadn't Dennis Peterson or Barbara Pearson applied? And where were Phil Evans and Frank Fairclough?" Actually, Frank had ruled himself out because he was planning to retire in three years' time – that is, after his current fourth years had passed through the School.

Dr Winstanley could barely contain his rage: "With respect, Mr Chairman, I believe these appointments are both a travesty and deeply insulting to the excellent people we still have at the School. There's John Halliday, for instance, a headmaster in waiting if ever there was one... and likewise Dr Morrison, who in the old days would have been an automatic choice for number two. And there's Charlie Aldridge, who could treble his salary in industry. I could go on... but there we are... what's done is done, and I suppose we shall all have to move with the times."

"Thank you, Dr Winstanley, for that observation," replied the Chairman, "of course, you're right, we are

476

indeed blessed with an abundance of talented people, including the three you mention, but unfortunately, as you know, we did not receive a single internal application."

"I wonder why!" muttered the good doctor, voicing what many of the others were thinking, judging by their knowing nods.

"If I may add a word here, Mr Chairman," said Andy Goody. "Let us be quite clear, ladies and gentleman, the two candidates appointed today were not chosen for their academic qualifications, or indeed for their teaching abilities, but because they satisfied the requirements of their respective job specifications, and projected themselves well in their interviews. Incidentally, from what I remember as a teacher, highly qualified people do not necessarily make good teachers, or indeed good leaders, but I am confident that the two young people you have appointed today will more than fulfil their obligations, and they deserve your full support."

In fact, neither of the two was a graduate, and had barely a dozen years of classroom experience between them, but they were both outgoing and very confident, and had the specified skills and qualifications, including diplomas in counselling.

The young man, one Edward Payne, was the only son of a clergyman from Chessington in Surrey, with the self-regard of someone who had never known anything but praise. He addressed the governors about pastoral care like a parish priest explaining a theological nicety to his uninformed but deferential flock.

Having refused to join his father's profession, he had agreed to train as a teacher, attending the Sarum St Michael's College in Salisbury, one of the Church of

England's several teachers' training establishments. His classroom experience was limited to teaching Religious Education in a small private boys' school run by a close friend of his father; and when the demand for his subject declined, he had cannily switched to the burgeoning field of Guidance, believing that to provide a surer route to promotion. However, as insurance, he had also attended courses in time-tabling, and latterly helped his headmaster with that task.

The female deputy was older and had a far more varied *curriculum vitae*. Raised by a single mother in Invergordon, Ross and Cromarty, Margaret McGregor had left school at fifteen without any qualifications, but possessing a strong work ethic and a desire to improve her lot in life. During her teenage years she had earned her keep variously, in department stores, hotels, and once on a cruise ship, before joining the Women's Royal Army Corps, rising to the rank of acting sergeant. After six years in the armed forces, she had left to train as a secondary school teacher, specialising in 'remedial' education. After a few years' teaching, first in Aberdeen and then as a head of her department in Dundee, she spotted an advertisement in the *Times Educational Supplement* for a female deputy head teacher at a newly established comprehensive school 300 miles south in a small industrial town called Netherbridge in north Cheshire, and applied largely out of a sense of adventure.

Four others had applied, but she stood out as the most likely prospect. Six feet tall, with a compelling personality and a laugh that could start an avalanche, she seemed the living embodiment of what Nobbs had envisaged. But he knew immediately that, if she was not to steal his thunder, he would have to deploy her very firmly, as one might, say, an excitable, partially-trained Rhodesian Ridgeback.

WITH HIS senior management team now complete, Nobbs turned his mind to his first full staff-meeting, to be held on Tuesday, 4th November in the new Staff Room. Fred and Alf had spent the afternoon arranging the chairs in a semi-circle around a portable platform, from which Nobbs would deliver his inaugural address.

After checking his appearance many times in his bathroom mirrors, he finally made his entrance, and made his way slowly onto the platform; but before starting the speech he stood for several moments looking for any revealing behaviour patterns, such as who sat where and next to whom. He noticed straightaway how they had segregated themselves into 'masters' and 'teachers', except for a handful from Manchester Road, foremost among them being the ubiquitous Messrs Shufflebottom and Smiley. Equally noticeable were those who had occupied the rear seats, notably Frank Fairclough and his fellow motor-cyclist, Peter Halliwell. As expected, Barbara Pearce had positioned herself in the centre of the front row, together with her friend, Dennis Peterson, while Phil Evans, being the last to arrive, had taken the only seat left, on the end of the front row.

For the occasion, Nobbs had ingeniously recorded some notes onto his Dictaphone, and asked Martha if she could transcribe them into a reasonably coherent speech, a procedure she did not find easy because the notes were disjointed and often unclear. However, he seemed pleased with what she did eventually produce, and proceeded to read it out slowly into his Dictaphone. Then one evening when Amanda was out at a business meeting, he retired to his 'office' in the annexe and listened to the tape many times until he knew it by heart. In this way, he believed, he could trick his audience into thinking that he was speaking spontaneously, and without notes.

"Good afternoon, friends, thank you for your time... and welcome to our very first full staff meeting at Netherbridge High School.
    "As most of you know, I was never a great fan of the grammar school."

He paused here for the words to sink in, a spiteful smirk playing around his mouth.

"Writing off four-fifths of our children at the arbitrary age of eleven was never a good idea, and it took thirty long years for politicians of all colours, yes, all colours, to see sense and get rid of it. Imagine how many youngsters were damaged in the meantime. Personally, I would get rid of public schools as well. All *they* do is provide an education for a bygone age – the age of empire – and charge parents a fortune to keep their precious little darlings safe from the hoi polloi. But, of course, public schools will never be got rid of because, as you know so many of our MPs, including some so-called socialists, send *their* children to them. Even the right honourable Harold Wilson, that great champion of the comprehensive school sends his boys there!

"Which brings me to my second point... the sooner we get rid of this 'grammar-modern' divide here in

480

Netherbridge, the sooner we can start building the new vibrant institution the town deserves, where all children, regardless of their ability or background, will be treated as equals... and all teachers will be valued, whether they went to Oxford or Ormskirk.

"Thirdly, in order to facilitate this development, I propose changing some things immediately, and other things as soon as practically possible. For instance, the school uniform... personally, I would get rid of it altogether, and replace it with a simple dress code as they have in American high schools... but after consulting with parents and colleagues there is a strong feeling in favour of some kind of new basic uniform for Netherbridge High School. As I say, I would prefer the first option, but I'm open to suggestions. And then there's the house system... do we really need that? Or should we have a completely new house system? And prefects... there's another example of the grammar school trying to be the poor man's Winchester... and they have no place in a school where all youngsters are treated equally. And what's more, I don't believe being made a prefect *does* develop a sense of responsibility, as they would have you believe, it merely provides opportunities for authorised bullying.

"Which brings me to my fourth point: I'm sure we can all agree that bullying in all its forms is unacceptable... it certainly won't be tolerated in this school while I'm the Headmaster. On the same theme, I know teenage boys and girls can be trying at times, but to use physical violence against them does not make them less trying: it simply makes them sullen and resentful. Besides, it is morally wrong and will soon become illegal. Therefore, I must remind you that the only person with the authority to carry out corporal punishment is the Headmaster.

"For my fifth and final point, I want to stress the importance of educating the *whole* child, not just his or her brain. Secondary school children are at a very delicate stage in their lives, and we have an enormous responsibility to care for their emotional needs. We must also make sure that everything we say or do is in the child's best interest. I remember from personal experience how even a casual remark or act can have a devastating and long-term effect. So, as professionals, we must all be vigilant that these children, whose parents have entrusted their care to us, are not hampered in their learning with personal or any other problems. This is why I shall be promoting the role of the form teacher into more than just calling the register and collecting dinner money. As from next September, they will be called form *tutors*, and they will be responsible for the pastoral welfare of the pupils in their designated forms throughout their first five years at the School. They will undergo in-service training in Guidance, and as from next September form tutoring will replace morning assemblies. But at the end of the day, all teachers are pastoral carers, including me, and we must all be proactive, but tactfully of course, in winkling out any personal problems a child under our care might have. It's no use waiting for problems to erupt, or saying, I'm a history teacher not a social worker. We've got to ask these kids, for instance, if everything's all right at home. They won't volunteer the information because they're usually too ashamed.

"Well, my friends, I'm very conscious of the time... but I would like to leave you with this one thought: a parent said to me the other day that education must be very different now from what it was when *he* was in school. And I had to tell him, tragically, that it was not... because we're still educating children for the past, instead of the future.

"If anyone would like to discuss any of the points I've raised today, they're welcome to come and see me in my office; but to make sure I'm available, it's best if you book an appointment through Martha first. Thank you."

Throughout the speech, Nobbs had scanned the room to see his audience's reactions, especially negative ones. As he expected, there was enthusiastic nodding among the Manchester Road contingent, especially when he decried the grammar school and the "grammar-modern divide", whereas most of the 'masters' had either wriggled in their seats, looked across tellingly at fellow-wincers, or rolled their eyes. The 'old guard' on the back row had sat with arms folded and expressionless throughout, looking like a bunch of recalcitrant third-formers pretending to be good in the hope that the teacher might let them out early at home-time.

Dennis Peterson was more interested in Nobbs's body language than his words: his dramatic but ineffectual entrance, his continually shifting his weight from one leg to the other, his avoidance of eye-contact, and then his rushing off at the end without an opportunity for questions or discussion, all confirmed what he already suspected, that here was someone to be pitied rather than feared. Barbara, on the other hand, was beside herself with adulation, simpering and hanging on to his every word. Phil Evans, an inveterate people-watcher, took a very different view. The more he saw of Nobbs the more he reminded him of Milton's Satan: the unhealthy thirst for revenge, a demented belief in his own lies, a sinister mixture of charm and menace, and "his words, replete with guile". As he once said to Shirley, "I've never met anyone who could lie so convincingly, be so blind to his own hypocrisy, and yet, when it suited him, could charm the birds out of the trees."

THE MORNING after the Staff meeting, Nobbs arrived in school very early and tannoyed for Fred to meet him outside the 'junk' room straightaway. He had had the locks changed during the October half-term, so that only he had access to it.

"Listen Fred, would you like some over-time tomorrow night?"

Nobbs never refused over-time.

"What time do you want me, Mr Nobbs?"

"Let's make it six, shall we? And bring your little van."

"Righty-o, Mr Nobbs."

"No one goes in here, Fred, except me and thee, right? And I mean no one. Here's your new key."

Fred was quite mystified by Nobbs's secrecy about the 'junk' room, but thought he had better do as he was told.

"Right," said Nobbs, "see those items with green stickers?

Fred nodded, and thought his boss must be up to one of his clearing out crazes again.

"I want them packed and brought over to my house...they're only gathering dust in here... I'm going to keep them in my annexe for the time being. But this is just between us, right?"

"Certainly, Mr Nobbs."

By ten o'clock on the Thursday evening, Fred had made three trips from the School to *Elsinore*, and stacked several boxes full of the *objets d'art* and memorabilia neatly in the far corner of the annexe. When he had finished, Nobbs invited him into the 'office' for a can of lager as a thank you, but as usual his motives were far less benign. First of all, he needed to know if Alf Newby had mentioned "that business" since, and whether he was pulling his weight now... and what Mr Peterson had said about re-instating the trophy cabinet. Then much to Fred's embarrassment, the questions became more personal and also more demanding in tone. What could Fred tell him about Mr Smiley and Mr Shufflebottom? Was there anything "going on" between Mr Peterson and Miss Pearce? And the last straw, was Mr Longworth "having it off" with Mrs Bagshaw?

Like many before him, Fred had fallen victim to Nobbs's seductive 'friendliness', and felt obliged to repay him with any inside information he possessed. Yes, he *had* walked into Mr Longworth's unlit office one night when locking up, and to his horror had found the pair "at it".

Poor Fred was in a cleft stick. He had known Mr Longworth as a kind, considerate boss for many years... what he did in his private life was none of his business... and certainly not something for him to blab about. Consequently, he had never told anyone, not even his wife. But Mr Nobbs was his boss now, and he was eager to remain on good terms with him. He had only a second or two to make up his mind, and he did something that went very much against his nature.

"No, Mr Nobbs... she were often helping him in his

office, like... but no, I never saw nothing like that. And, as far as I know, the same with Miss Pearce and Mr Dennison... they're good friends, I grant you, and work together a lot... but no, I never seen nothing."

Nobbs looked him straight in the eye for a full ten seconds before replying, "Thank you, Fred... thank you for being honest with me."

This backhanded compliment hurt Fred to the quick, for he sensed Nobbs knew the truth already, and he sensed correctly, because Messrs Smiley and Shufflebottom had revealed all to Nobbs over dinner at their house in Newton soon after he became the Headmaster of Manchester Road. According to his informants, the Longworth-Bagshaw relationship was far from platonic, and Mr Peterson had been spotted with Miss Pearce late one Saturday night in Southport. But the piece of intelligence that had surprised even Nobbs was that John Higson, the Games teacher, had once been caught stealing a set of screwdrivers from Woolworths, and according to some had only escaped dismissal because his father was a freemason.

As soon as Amanda saw Fred's van disappear onto Manchester Road, she wandered over to the annexe to see what was going on.

"What are all these boxes?"

"I'm clearing out that room next to the old library to make it into an extra classroom. I've brought anything of value over here for safe keeping, in case some bugger nicks it. It's only old stuff connected with the Grammar School, but I thought I might get a bob or two for it as a job lot from an antiques dealer.

"But never mind all that, listen to this, Mand. I thought

it would be a good idea if the School had its own bus... not a crappy little mini-bus, but a proper forty-five-seater, to take whole classes out on field trips and things, instead of hiring expensive coaches all the time. They're very low maintenance, and if we could set up one big fund-raising effort, we could pay for it outright in twelve months. We could also get sponsors. And I thought I'd put your friend, Barbara, in charge of the fund-raising! What do you think?"

"Yes, the bus sounds a great idea... I'm sure Barbara would be excellent, and *I* could help with sponsors, if you like. But think hard before selling off the memorabilia. Some of those paintings must be worth quite a bit... and remember, they were given in good faith to the Grammar School, which no longer exists, and the donors' descendants could ask for them back one day. No, better get legal advice on that one. I would hate to see you embroiled in some dodgy business. You don't need it, Rich."

"Fair point, Mand... what would I do without you, eh? Come here." And he pulled her down onto his *chaise longue*, hugging her tightly, something he had not done for some time.

THE DAY before the School broke up for Christmas, Nobbs asked Barbara to call in his office after school, ostensibly to congratulate and thank her for another magnificent Christmas pantomime.

"It's wonderful how you get those kids to perform like that, Barbara... they're so enthusiastic... you can tell they love their Auntie Babs! It took me right back to when I was a little boy in Oldham. My mother used to take me to see the panto at the Coliseum every Christmas... *Aladdin* was my favourite... but your production of it was just as good, if not better."

Poor Barbara was speechless, and only for the fear of seeming too familiar, would have kissed him there and then. Instead, she funnelled her rush of emotion into a deep blush and a grossly inadequate "Oh, Mr Nobbs, thank you!"

"Not at all, you deserve our warmest congratulations, Babs... fantastic show. Oh, before I forget, I happened to be talking to Amanda a couple of nights ago, and she agreed with me it would be great if the School had its own bus... I mean a proper full-size bus to take kids out on field trips, and such like. But of course, we'd need to raise some funds first, and a little bird tells me you've been involved in fund-raising projects before."

"Of course, Mr Nobbs... I'd love to. I'll jot down some ideas over Christmas."

"Great! I tell you what, why don't you come over to our house for coffee some morning during the holiday. I'm sure Amanda would be glad to help as well. You two would make a great team."

WHEN SCHOOL re-opened for the 1976 Easter term (names like Michaelmas and Lent were among the first victims of the Nobbsian axe), Martha felt pleased with how she had adapted to the new regime. With discreet interventions and frequent biting of the tongue, she had somehow managed to maintain a delicate balance between performing her duties as the "Senior Administrative Officer" (a title that never ceased to amuse her) and her own principles and values. In fairness,

Nobbs had played a part too, if for no other reason than he needed Martha's quiet dignity and restraint to leaven his impulsive and domineering style of management.

As soon as the first lessons were under way, Nobbs introduced Miss McGregor and Mr Payne formally to "Miss Martha Wolf, the Senior Administrative Officer". Of course, Martha had met them briefly on the day they were appointed, and although her first impressions had not been favourable, she was reserving judgement until she knew them better.

"Martha has been here longer than any of us, and what she doesn't know about the place isn't worth knowing. She and I were appointed within a couple of years of each other, the only difference being she doesn't look a day older. Ha, ha! Anyway, if you need any help with anything, just ask Martha."

The two were to share the old Headmaster's office, Mr Payne occupying the Headmaster's section, and Miss McGregor, Martha's. For such an unlikely pair, they seemed to get along quite well, which was just as well because they would soon need each other's support when the Nobbsian whip began to crack.

During morning break that day, Nobbs ventured to perambulate the playground, making a great show of talking to some first year pupils, mainly to impress the two deputies. Much to his consternation, however, whenever his back was turned, he could here faint, two-tone cries of "Knob-'ead" echoing around the playground. He manfully pretended not to hear, and carried on talking to the children, hoping that they did not link it with his name.

That was the last time Nobbs ventured outside his

office during break-times for some time. He cursed his father for choosing such a "stupid name". Why had he not chosen something sensible like 'Smith' or 'Johnson'? But to be fair, no pupil had ever made fun of his name before, neither at Oldham Hulme, nor during all his time at NGS. This sudden turn of events was a novel and unnerving experience for him. It was all the more annoying because it was not something he could discuss with anyone, not even Amanda, because he knew she would have dismissed it with some gentle ribbing of her own! Accordingly, he decided to lie low for a while, and run the School entirely from his office, in the hope that the taunting would eventually cease.

Unfortunately, he was not safe from it there either. Some weeks later, a young lad, who had left Manchester Road School some two years previously, returned to see some of his old teachers. Now an eighteen- year-old mineworker, he took great pride in lighting a cigarette, and indeed offering one to Mr John Higson, his old PE teacher, who happened to be on yard duty that lunchtime, and who had slippered him many a time for smoking on school premises!

Encouraged by his temerity, the leader of the current bunch of rapscallions, a certain Darren Gentle, dared him to crouch beneath the new Headmaster's window and call out his nick-name in the prescribed sing-song way. Compared with the hazards he faced daily in his work, this barely registered on his radar. Besides, even if the Headmaster did take him to task, could he not deny all knowledge of it with a mouthful of industrial expletives! In the event, this was not necessary because, fearing loss of face, Nobbs had made a strategic retreat to his

490

washroom, and remained there until the end of the school day. Keep you powder dry, Richard lad, he said to himself, the better part of valour is discretion. But, for all that, the bystanders' raucous laughter outside the main entrance hurt his pride more than he would ever admit.

Martha had witnessed the incident through her office window, and knew that Nobbs must have heard it too. She had never experienced this kind of behaviour before, and felt slightly uncomfortable that Nobbs, with his size and razor-sharp repartee, had not dealt with it summarily. However, she gave him the benefit of the doubt, for a reaction might have been just what the miscreants had hoped for, and it was more sensible for him to dismiss it as a silly prank beneath his notice.

But alas, it was very much not beneath his notice, and the nick-name began to play on his mind, resulting in sleepless nights, and arriving at school even before the caretakers, "to have some peace and quiet to work before the great unwashed arrived", as he told Amanda. His office became both his citadel and his prison cell where he sat all day in splendid isolation, barking out orders either in person or over the telephone. He reckoned that if he could weather the storm until after Easter, when many of "the current bunch of delinquents" had left school to start work, or indeed found other targets for their bullying, he could rest easy in his bed again.

He knew from his own schooldays how devastating a cruel nick-name can be. Once, during his third year, a new boy had joined his form. Like Nobbs, he was tall for his age and handsome, except for a disfiguring cyst on his forehead. But unlike Nobbs, he was also an able scholar, and soon became popular with the masters and his classmates. Perceiving him as a threat to his supremacy, Nobbs thought he would "teach this bumptious Johnny-come-lately a lesson". Accordingly, one morning before the form-master had arrived he called out to him, "Hey, Lumpy, tha flies are undone!"

Unfortunately, the nick-name stuck, as they often do, causing so much misery to the boy that eventually his parents had to withdraw him from school, and arrange private tuition until the cyst could be removed.

Two terms later, when the wound had healed, the boy returned to school in much better spirit, until, that is, Nobbs saw fit to re-dub him "Scarface".

ONE DAY towards the end of the Summer term, Phil Evans and Ian Moore, the Head of PE, called at Nobbs's office together during the lunch break to voice their grievances.

"And to what do I owe this pleasure, gentlemen?" began Nobbs with his ingratiating grin.

As an ex-Royal Marine, Ian Moore feared neither man nor beast.

"Never mind the bullsh-t... why did you send 'Little Eddie' round to tell me about the account? Couldn't you have told me yourself? In case you haven't noticed, I keep that little reserve of money for a specific reason, to buy bits of equipment not covered by the requisition. Martha keeps an up-to-date record of all the ingoings and outgoings, as she's always done. So, what's the f----- problem?

"Now listen here, mate, don't you swear at me," said Nobbs.

"Don't you call me "mate". I'm no mate of *yours*.

492

"All right, then, Mr Moore, let me explain. The local authority has asked all heads to review their financial practices. They recommend that internal accounts, such as yours and Phil's and several others too, are amalgamated into one central account, with the Headmaster as a co-signatory of every cheque issued. It's as simple as that... that way, everything is transparent and no one is exposed to accusations of fraud."

"Fraud?" said Ian, "You must be joking... that account stays, whether you like it or not."

"In that case, I'll have to report you to the Director."

"You can report me to the f------ Pope, if you like. Anyway, I'm off. I've got a football practice in five minutes."

"You're very quiet, Phil."

"I'm speechless, that's why... you should stand up to these little mandarins from County Hall. We're being run by petty bureaucrats. You know as well as I do the amount of effort and time people like Ian put in outside school hours, and it all relies on goodwill, and trust that professionals conduct themselves with integrity."

(In fact, the local authority had never requested a review of financial practices. As Phil had suspected, it was another of Nobbs's little ruses to prevent departmental heads from making decisions outside his control).

"Edward Payne also said something about stopping the annual school play. You're not serious, are you? Or has that come from County Hall too? Look, I've got kids clamouring for parts in the next one already."

"What will that be, then?"

"Thank you for asking. It's *The Playboy of the*

Western World, actually...do you know it?"

"The only playboy I know, Phil, is the *Playboy* magazine... ha ha! Anyway, how many kids will there be in it?"

"Does it really matter? Anyway, if you must know, about a dozen actors, plus understudies, plus all the others involved in the production... stage managers, prompters, lighting, sound effects, costume-making, make-up...oh, I don't know, about thirty or forty altogether, I suppose."

"Look, Phil, all this sounds fine and dandy for your clever-clogs kids. But the majority of our kids aren't interested in plays... nor are their parents. They'd rather watch *Coronation Street* or go and see *One Flew Over the Cuckoo's Nest* at the Odeon. It's that grammar school thing, isn't? And you just can't shake it off."

There was a time when Phil would have fought his corner, and overwhelmed Nobbs with cogent arguments, but he thought this fellow's becoming more asinine by the day, so what was the point. From now on he would do exactly what he was paid to do, much as that grated with him.

"Well, you're the boss now, and if that's what you want, so be it. Let me know if you change your mind. I'll apologise to the kids. And now, if you'll excuse me, I'll see if there's anything left in the canteen. I've got a lesson in twenty minutes."

No sooner than Phil had left the room, Nobbs's hand was on his intercom telephone. "Listen, Barbara, Phil Evans has just been in, and he's quite agreeable to not doing the play this year. To be honest, I think it's getting a bit much for him, anyway. So, since the Hall won't now be needed for rehearsals and things, you can have it every lunch time for discos. How does that sound?"

"Brilliant, Mr Nobbs. You're a genius!"

Later that afternoon, Martha walked across to his office, to report that an elderly man from the nearby council estate had rung up to complain that some boys were smoking and swearing behind the bushes adjacent to his garden.

Being more bothered about the old man's complaint than the boys' misbehaviour, and to show Martha that he could take decisive action when needed, he picked up his internal telephone and dialled the deputies' office.

"Listen, Maggie, you're not teaching, are you? So, get your fat a--- over to Block 'A' *now*. Some miserable old fart from the estate has rung up to complain about a smoking party going on behind the mulberry bushes.

"There you are, Martha, sorted... never a dull moment, eh?"

ENCOURAGED by the success of his first staff meeting held the previous autumn, Nobbs thought he would use the same format to address the parents of the September intake. As before, he handed Martha some rough notes, from which she managed to construct a reasonably fluent and coherent speech, which he, as before, committed to memory.

Like every other evening during the longest hot spell of the twentieth century, Tuesday 6th July was not an ideal time to hold a meeting. Even with the windows and doors wide open, there was little relief from the oppressive heat for the young and enthusiastic parents gathered to hear what the new headmaster had to say.

After his usual primping and preening, Nobbs

eventually made his grand entrance through one of the rear doors, and processed slowly down the central aisle smiling graciously to the left and right as he did so. As he mounted the platform, and turned to face his capacity audience, the noisy chatter faded into an expectant silence, which filled him with a surge of pride.

"Good evening, ladies and gentlemen, welcome to Netherbridge High School... if only all our children were as well-behaved as you! Ha, ha! No, seriously, I have a feeling that you and I are going to get along just fine, and I am as excited about September as you are, getting to know your children, and making sure they're happy as they settle into their brand new school. I can tell you now, they couldn't have had a more caring and able person to look after their needs than our very own Miss Barbara Pearce, who's here with us this evening... let them see you, Babs. Your children have already met her, and if you want to discuss how your son or daughter's settling in, she's the one to ask for. *Your* children are our future, and as Headmaster I shall be especially interested in their welfare and progress, each and every one of them.

"Before I begin my short address, let me also introduce my two deputies to you, Miss Margaret McGregor who hails from wildest Ross and Cromarty, in Scotland ... and Mr Edward Payne from leafy Surrey. We already had an Irishwoman on the Staff... all we need now is a Welshman, and we'd have the full set! Ha, ha! Both Margaret and Edward joined the School in January and have already made a great impression on everyone.

"Now, my main aim this evening is to tell you something about my educational beliefs, and how I want our school to develop. By the way, I shall never refer to

496

this school as *my* school, because it is not *my* school, it is *our* school. We own it jointly, and we're all partners in pioneering comprehensive education in Netherbridge. It's a privilege, but it's also a huge responsibility, for you as parents and for us as teachers to provide the very best education possible for each and every one of your children.

"But some people ask me what was wrong with the old system. Well, I'll tell you. First, as everybody knows, children mature at different ages, and grading them like eggs at the arbitrary age of eleven... especially using dodgy tests devised by some fraudulent boffin down in London out to make a name for himself... is just plain stupid, but it's also immoral – immoral, because it branded seventy five per cent of our children as failures. And what made it worse, this grading was more or less final... it made no allowance for a child having a bad cold on test day, or having a difficult time at home. That was it, and to make matters worse, if you didn't fit in at the grammar school, you were slung out, but... you rarely heard of pupils from the Secondary Modern being promoted to the grammar school. How fair is that?"

(When Martha had typed this, she recalled her own anguish when her Tom had failed to get into grammar school, and he was just as clever as she was, cleverer in some ways.)

"And if that, my friends, wasn't bad enough, the lucky twenty five per cent were then further sub-divided into boys and girls and educated in different schools, boys taught by men, and girls by women. How bizarre is that! It's like sons being brought up by their father, and daughters by their mother, in different houses!

"Secondly, despite all the propaganda you hear about how wonderful a grammar school education is, take it from me it's not as wonderful as it's cracked up to be. It is certainly no preparation for the real world, which consists of men, women, boys and girls of *all* abilities working and playing together, as they do, of course, in a normal family.

And that, ladies and gentlemen, is how I see our school, as one big family, where all the children are loved, whatever their abilities. We're not simply in the business of getting children through examinations... although that is important too... we want to give every child the opportunity to grow into a sensible, honest and caring human being.

And so, there will be no selection by ability during the first two years. Instead, all pupils will be taught in their form groups so that they can discover which courses suit their specific talents best. Whether your child eventually wants to go to university or take a craft apprenticeship, start a business or train for one of the professions, you can rest assured that he or she will get the best start in life here at Netherbridge High.

Much to Nobbs's gratification, he heard several "Hear, hears" after that last sentence, although not everything he had said received unanimous approval, as attested by a scattering of slow head-shakes and eye-rolls. But by and large, the parents seemed more than satisfied with Mr Nobbs. He looked like a headmaster, tall, authoritative and well-groomed; he spoke like a headmaster, in a loud, clear voice; and he must be very clever too, they thought, how else could he remember all those things without any papers or anything? He also sounded like a man who knew what he wanted and was determined to get it. In short, he seemed like the kind of headmaster they wished they had had when they were in school, sympathetic but not weak, strict but not heartless.

"Thirdly, it is often said that grammar schools were excellent for clever children. Yes, their exam results were good but that was only because the children were clever, and didn't *need* much teaching. The *masters* with their silly, black gowns weren't necessarily any better than teachers in any other school. And I should know, because I worked with them for 25 years... there were some, I can tell you... well, perhaps I'd better say no more.

"I myself had the so-called privilege of attending such a grammar school, and I can tell you now, it did nothing for me... indeed, I couldn't wait to leave. It was a typical grammar school, all boys, and all men teachers, mostly old, who had no interest at all in us as kids, only as vehicles for promoting their subjects. Examinations were the be-all and end-all. You could be the most miserable kid in the school, but as long you got your 'As' at A level or your scholarship to Oxford... that was all that mattered. The Headmaster didn't help either... he *claimed* he'd been an officer in the First World War... but there had been doubts about that. Anyway, he loved the military so much that he started a cadet force in the School, which seemed to take over his life, and, some said, the School. He took a dislike to me because I didn't want to join it. The truth was I was a timid little soul... all I needed was someone to put his arm round my shoulder and find out what my problems were. But no, it was, 'Forgot your kit, Nobbs... you'd forget your head if it wasn't stuck on to you. Put those on, you'll look nice in pink.' That may sound funny in retrospect, but it's not funny when you're a shy little 13-year-old. But I can promise you now, ladies and gentlemen, *your* children will never have to suffer that kind of humiliation at Netherbridge High School... not as long as I'm Headmaster.

He paused after the phrase, "not as long as I'm Headmaster" for dramatic effect, his eyes swivelling to and fro across the room. A born salesman, he knew how to manipulate an audience, and that evening even the "comprehensive sceptics" could not but admire his eloquence and passion. He commanded his audience like a true professional, and they in turn gazed up at him in rapt silence.

But then, as he was about to resume his oration, something happened – a distracting 'noise off'. If it had been scripted, the timing could not have been better, and Nobbs was mortified, cut off as he was about to mount his triumphant finale.

Wafting in through the rear doors came the sing-song cries of "Knob...'ead, Knob...'ead" followed by muffled giggling from the perpetrator's fellow-conspirators. This was then repeated from a side-door, and again from the opposite side-door, the giggling becoming louder each time. More seriously for Nobbs, these were evidently not fourth-form hoodlums bearing a grudge, but first- or second-year children "having a laugh" – and at *his* expense. Even more distressing, he suspected that the dreaded nick-name was now known to some of the parents, judging by the amused faces and sniggers all around the Hall.

Several middle-aged parents with older children at the School looked at each other in dismay, thinking that this sort of thing never happened in the Grammar School.

A signal from Nobbs sent Miss McGregor striding down the central aisle, hell-bent on catching the culprits, but by the time she appeared outside the door, they had all retreated to a safe distance, except for one tiny boy whose shirt tail she managed to grab as he too was trying to make his escape.

But she had only caught one of the accomplices, a little brother perhaps, aged no more than six or seven. Yet, since he was an accessory after the fact, Nobbs's enforcer felt he merited at least a gentle rebuke.

"What do think *you're* playing at, you cheeky little monkey?" she yelled in his ear, "don't your parents teach you manners?"

"Get your paws off me, you f------ bitch," screeched the boy, whose head barely reached the top of her legs.

At this juncture she was joined by her colleague, Edward Payne, who whispered that every word could be heard inside the Hall.

"Right," she said quietly to the boy, "I'm needed back in the Hall. If I catch you doing this sort of thing again, you're in big trouble. And you can tell your friends that as well, or they'll end up in front of the Headmaster."

But as soon as her back was turned, distant chanting of "Knob...'ead, Knob...'ead" could be heard coming from those waiting by the main gate.

In order to drown out the altercation taking place outside, Nobbs had tried to resume his talk, but in a much louder voice, but as soon as he realised that his audience were now only waiting politely for a signal to leave, he decided to cut his losses.

"Every family has a black sheep, ha, ha! Well, it's

been a delight seeing you all... I hope you go away with a better understanding of what we're about at Netherbridge High. You're welcome to come and see me any time, but to make sure I'm available, it's best to make an appointment through my Senior Admin Officer, Miss Martha Wolf. You've been a wonderful audience. Thank you for your time on this hot, sticky evening, and for listening so intently. Have a safe journey home.... Good night and God bless."

Sadly, for Nobbs, despite his valiant attempt at salvaging some dignity, once the magic spell had been broken, there was nothing he could do or say to save the situation. When he eventually arrived home, Amanda was already in bed, reading.

"How did it go, love?" she asked.

"Great, Mand! I think they liked me... I had them eating out of my hand."

That night, partly because of the heat, but mainly because of the name-calling, he could not sleep, and at the first hint of dawn he crept downstairs, got into the Jaguar and drove at break-neck speed up the M6 as far as the Charnock Richard Services, where he stopped for a pot of tea and a muffin. Sitting alone sipping his tea, he watched enviously some lorry drivers laughing and joking as they devoured their early morning "full English". They reminded him of happier times when he and Joe Riley used to stop there on their way back from Preston. Poor Old Joe, he thought, and yet for some reason *he* never got troubled by name-callers... so, why should these f------ guttersnipes from the Brookdale estate do it to him? The very kids he was trying to help.

502

NOBBS ARRIVED at school early despite his disturbed night, and on the stroke of nine Martha informed him that a parent was waiting to see him as a matter of urgency. Nobbs was in no mood to see anyone, let alone someone called Annabel Makin-Taylor, but he reluctantly agreed.

"Good morning and thank you, Mr Nobbs. I think we've met before... my two boys were pupils here when Dr Davenport was Headmaster, and I must say the schooling they had was first rate, both getting to Oxford, one to read history and the other PPE..."

"Yes, yes, very good, I'm sure," said Nobbs, "look, I was up all night preparing a paper for the Director of Education... please get to the point."

"Oh, I am sorry, Mr Nobbs, my point is this... Madeline, my youngest, is down to come here in September, and I didn't like the way you decried the grammar schools in your talk last night."

"Really? Can you be more specific?"

"Well, Maddie wants to be a doctor like her father and hopes to follow her brothers into Oxford... or possibly Cambridge, and to put it bluntly, I sincerely hope that academic standards under the comprehensive system won't be allowed to drop."

"Why should they?

"Well, for a start, I hear Latin is being phased out."

"Tell me, Mrs Taylor, what's the point of learning a dead language?

"Well, for a start, certain careers, like medicine and law, require it, and besides it's good for you."

"Good for what, for Christ's sake?"

"Well, good for the brain... it teaches you to think and express yourself clearly."

503

"Where's your evidence? Winston Churchill never did it and he learned to express himself pretty clearly. Unfortunately, I *had* to do it. I loathed it, and it never did my brain any good either. No, take it from me, this is just another myth handed down from the Middle Ages through the public schools (which the grammar schools mimic) and I'd be surprised if you found another comprehensive in the area persisting with that myth. Most Latin teachers I know are now re-training to teach living languages, like Russian or Mandarin."

"Well, it looks like I'll have to reconsider my options for Maddie, then. Maybe a comprehensive school is not for her after all. I'm no great fan of private education, but if needs must."

"You'd be wasting your money, Mrs T, all she'd learn there is how to lower her knickers elegantly... oh, and maybe a little Latin... ha, ha!"

LATER THAT morning, Frank Fairclough was taking his 4A for a double lesson of Physics.

"Now then, 4A," he began in his usual no-nonsense manner, "before we start today... I want to talk to you about something else."

The class was agog, wondering if Mr Fairclough was going to share some interesting, private information with them. Was he going to break that promise to them, and retire early? They could sense he was not as happy as he used to be.

"Now we're a comprehensive school," he continued, "we... the masters, that is... we're required to find out if any of our pupils have any problems, and would like to talk to someone about them."

The pupils looked at each other, not quite sure what he meant, most believing that he probably meant problems with their work. He too wondered if he was making any sense, and was beginning to wish he had never even raised the matter, but help came from an unlikely source.

"Yes, Ashworth?" said Frank.

"Ashworth hasn't *got* a problem, sir," quipped a wag on the back row, "he just *is* one!"

Yes, Ashworth?" repeated Frank, with a severe glance at the would-be comedian.

"Well, there *is* something I have a problem with, sir."

"Listen, Ashworth, before you go any further, you're not meant to go public on this sort of thing... come and see me during the lunch break".

"No, it's nothing like that, sir... it's just that, you know... when we went metric in 1971, yeah, why didn't they change *all* the units at the same time? It's just a mess as it is, isn't it, sir?"

"Thank you for that, Ashworth, although that's not quite the sort of problem I had in mind! But if any of you do have something that's bothering you of a more personal nature, you are welcome to come and see me, or your form master, at any time."

NOBBS WAS feeling so pleased with himself that as soon as school broke up for the summer holiday, he treated himself to a brand new white Jaguar XJC, and during the sweltering heat of the first fortnight of August he took Amanda on a surprise tour of Devon and Cornwall, a reprise of their honeymoon tour.

He had promised Amanda not to mention school at all, but by the third day, he could restrain himself no longer.

"Mand", he said, assuming that his wife was thinking along similar lines, "my priorities for next year are to get rid of the 'grammar' clique, right, and convert those reactionary b------- on the governing body."

"How will you get rid of the 'grammar clique'?"

"Well, it's Ed's pigeon, really... but, there *are* ways. Some of them are approaching retirement... so, we could hurry them along a bit by making life a bit uncomfortable for them, like, moving them across the road... they'd hate that... or giving them some rubbish classes, ha, ha!"

"Isn't that a bit mean?"

"No, Mand, it's what's called *realpolitik*? And as for the slightly younger ones, Andy tells me the local authority's giving generous pension enhancement... up to ten years in some cases. Then, there's always re-deployment... if you've got too many teachers for a particular subject, then you can re-deploy them to schools where there are shortages. We'll weed the buggers out one way or another!"

They eventually got back to Netherbridge just in time for the 'A' level results, which, like the previous year's, were remarkably good, and which Nobbs again claimed as proof that the jeremiahs were demonstrably wrong.

Refreshed by his stay in Cornwall, and emboldened by the gleaming new limousine gracing his parking space, Nobbs was back to his old, overweening self, and on Thursday 9th September he held his first staff meeting of the year, which this time was to be a discussion rather than a monologue. After a brief self-congratulatory introduction, which included reading out a letter from the Director saying what a good start the School had made, and how it could become "a model on how to implement change", Nobbs invited questions or suggestions on how the School could do even better.

"I wonder, Headmaster, if I could make a suggestion?" said the young Classics teacher, little imagining how soon he would be receiving his redundancy notice, "many of us find Tannoy announcements during lessons very distracting, and I wondered if they could be limited to real emergencies at those times."

Nobbs stared at him in disbelief, and construing his point as a personal criticism, he dismissed it coldly with, "Good administration is just as important as good teaching. You need both."

Peter Halliwell, irked by Nobbs's glib reply to his colleague's perfectly sensible suggestion, raised a point of contention of his own, "Could the substitute cover be made more equitable, that is, more proportional to the number of free periods? It's not good administration, Headmaster, to take someone's only free of the day, when others with far lighter time-tables are keeping the staffroom cushions warm."

"Let's get one thing straight," replied Nobbs, his nostrils flaring, "there's no such thing as a free period, right... only a *non-teaching* period, and the Headmaster has to deploy his staff's teaching time as he thinks fit.

"For my sins," said Phil Evans, equally riled by Nobbs's replies and bumptious manner, "as you know, one of my briefs is to implement *The Bullock Report*, whose main purport is to teach English across the curriculum, not just in English lessons. One of its suggestions is that we sit in on each other's lessons to see if we could learn good practice from each other. How do you all feel about all this?"

"Well, I wouldn't want anyone sitting in on my lessons," said Brian Smiley, "it would cramp my style."

"Quite agree, Bri," said Nobbs, "I wouldn't want someone sitting in on my lessons either!

"If I may make a more general point, Headmaster," said Charlie Aldridge, "whilst conceding that in the past perhaps we did take our pupils' personal development largely for granted, in our efforts to rectify the situation, we should not over-compensate so as to neglect their *intellectual* development. In particular, we have lost several highly qualified and experienced teachers of late and unless they are replaced soon with similarly qualified people rumour has it that we risk losing some of our most able pupils too.

Nobbs paused a little before replying.

"Some of you will recall the scathing HMI report not so many years ago that lambasted the School, as it was then, for its extreme selection procedures and the ridiculous demands it made on those 'most able pupils' you are so concerned about. My prime concern is not for them but for the other seventy-five per cent, and especially for the poor sods that haven't got much going for them either at home or in school. Your *crème de la crème* will succeed regardless of, and sometimes in spite of, their teachers. Give them the books and they could probably teach themselves.

"Well, I'm very conscious of the time, ladies and gentlemen, and I'd like to push off early, if you don't mind... I'm meeting the Chairman of the Governors at 7.30. Just one announcement before we go... I've decided to hold a whole school assembly next Monday morning. It will take a little organising, but I'm confident Maggie will have everything under control! Thank you for your time... enjoy the rest of your evening."

IN FACT, the idea of a 'whole school' assembly had been entirely Margaret Macgregor's. Nobbs had resisted it until he remembered that Dr Kendricks had "wimped-out" of it.

Margaret organised the event with military precision, even arranging for two local 'lollipop ladies' to assist with the road crossing. By 9 am all pupils were seated in their ascribed places, and the new Hall was brimful and absolutely quiet. Immaculately groomed and towering over the whole assembly like an Amazonian queen, there were very few among the staff, let alone the pupils, who would have dared to defy her intimidating authority.

The Hall clock was now creeping towards 9.05, and the tension of waiting for the Headmaster in total silence was becoming unbearable for the staff as well as the pupils. Dan Carrington, who was standing near the rear entrance, went to investigate, and almost collided with him as he was leaving his office in some hurry, having spent the previous twenty minutes carrying out the usual checks on his appearance and rehearsing his lines.

At last he arrived, and as he was making his way along the main aisle towards the podium, a series of farting noises erupted from the ranks of the fourth years, followed by thunderous laughter, and to compound the disorder, when the laughter had subsided, and Nobbs had changed places with Margaret on the podium, a forlorn cry of "Knob-'ead" went up from somewhere on the back row.

Margaret was in a quandary, should she intervene and

add to her headmaster's humiliation, or remain silent? She decided on the latter, much as it irritated her that the pupils' lack of respect for the Headmaster reflected on her too. Had she been asked to take the assembly, as well as organise it, she was sure all would have been well, and she felt so frustrated having to restrain herself that she was tempted to join in the laughter!

Nobbs realised that any hope of restoring dignity to the occasion was lost, and he wished he had not acceded to holding the assembly in the first place. Clearly, it was a bad decision, and one he would never repeat.

He made one or two announcements and then withdrew, leaving Margaret to take control once more. There was immediate silence, and as soon as she felt that Nobbs was out of ear-shot, she proceeded to explain quietly but eloquently the importance of showing respect to one's superiors, drawing examples from her military training and experience.

After collecting his coat and briefcase from his office, Nobbs informed Martha that he would be working from home for the rest of the day, and the two deputies would be in charge of the School. The Jaguar had joined the traffic on Manchester Road long before the pupils had begun filing out of the Hall.

When he arrived home, Amanda was busy ironing.

"What's wrong?" she asked.

"Nothing... except I've got that pain again."

"Look, you *must* see someone about it. Shall I ring the surgery now?"

"No, stop fussing... once I've had a hot bath... and a lie down, I'll be all right."

"How did the assembly go?"

510

"Don't ask... I *told* Maggie it wasn't a good idea bringing those kids across the main road during rush hour. But other than that, it was fine. I made it short and sweet... and with all this paperwork to do for Andy, I thought I'd have more peace at home."

"Do you mind if we have lunch a bit early?" said Amanda, "I've got a viewing at two o'clock."

Chapter Twenty-One

When Amanda heard about Frank Fairclough's *contretemps* with the Gentles, she was shocked. She had no idea that that kind of thing went on in schools; and of course, 'Murphy's Law', it had to happen on Rich's watch. When she asked him about it, his reply was masterfully evasive, "Oh, that! Mr Five by Five flexing his muscles again! If it weren't so sad, it would be funny... poor chap, that gammy leg has a lot to answer for.

"Listen, Mand... in my very first staff meeting I made it perfectly clear that only the Headmaster is permitted to administer corporal punishment. He was well out of order, and I was on the point of calling him in and issuing a formal warning, but then I thought, I'd also have to mention that scuffle he had with the father, which would open a whole new can of worms. But if it happens again, I'm telling you, I'll have no choice but to initiate disciplinary proceedings... I won't have a member of my staff committing common assault on County Council premises. For one thing, what does that say about the institution? Let's hope the *Chronicle* doesn't get wind of it.

"Anyway, I've apologised to Darren, and to make it up to him, I thought it would be in everyone's interest if instead of attending R.E. lessons with that McCarthy woman Kendricks appointed, he helps Fred with jobs around the School. I've cleared it with Chester. Oh, and while I was at it, I asked him if he'd like to earn a few quid in the summer painting our fences. You don't mind, do you, Mand?"

"No, that's fine by me," she said drily, but thought, it would have been nice to have been consulted. "Trouble is, doesn't helping the Caretaker look like rewarding bad behaviour? What sort of signal does that give out... to the other pupils, and the staff?"

"Oh, I wouldn't worry about that. The way I see it, he'll be doing something useful, instead of disrupting lessons... and he'll probably learn more about real life with Fred than messing around in R.E. lessons. Anyway, in six months he'll be sixteen, and no longer my problem."

"What sort of boy is this Darren, anyway? He sounds a bit of a handful!"

"Darren? Oh, he's not a *bad* lad... just a little bit lively, that's all. Funnily enough, I see a lot of me in him... a bit too quick with his tongue sometimes... ha ha! All he needs is to be shown a bit of respect, and not to be treated like a little kid. But with the likes of Fairclough and his effing grammar school attitudes, what hope have we got?"

During the last week in July, Nobbs was due to attend

an NAHT meeting in Milton Keynes, and he thought it might be convenient if Darren came to do the painting then. Amanda said that then was as good a time as any, but it would be nice if they could have a few days away together first, in case something cropped up later. Nobbs said that it was a brilliant idea, and suggested *she* arrange it as a surprise for him, which she quickly spotted as a ruse for scoring brownie points without having to lift a finger!

AMANDA had last visited her parents on the 26th March, the day after her sixteenth wedding anniversary, and Nobbs's fifty-fifth birthday. She had been surprised when her mother by-passed the usual list of her ailments and launched into her other jeremiad of choice.

"So that's it, then, is it? No patter of tiny feet – ever! It's a crying shame, Amanda... with you being such a fine-looking lass... and *he* sort of scrubs up okay, too."

Mr Green shot a quizzical glance at his wife over his newspaper, "You know what they say, dear... never judge a book by its cover... my guess is he's been firing blanks!"

"Da-ad!" exclaimed Amanda.

That possibility had occurred to both women, but neither had actually mentioned it, and certainly did not expect to hear it being articulated so succinctly and matter-of-factly by her father. If truth be told, he had never liked Nobbs, and in his eyes he could do no right – why, oh, why did his Amanda, who could have had anybody, have to take up with a loud-mouthed know-all nearly twice her age!

Naturally, he was also very conscious and proud of having such a beautiful daughter, and over the years had

had to put up with quite a bit of ribbing from his workmates: "How come an ugly bugger like you, Ted Green, fathered such a stunner!" Someone even started a rumour that his wife must have had a 'one-night stand' with an Italian from Ancoats!

Strange as it may seem, it is not uncommon for exceptionally beautiful girls to find it difficult to attract suitable boyfriends, presumably because they are perceived as unattainable, if not intimidating. Indeed, until Amanda met Nobbs, her friends had been exclusively girls, and it was little wonder, therefore, that her father had been anxious lest she threw herself at the first fellow who showed any interest.

He had warned her repeatedly that an age-gap of eighteen years, whilst feasible now, could become a real problem ten years down the line; and furthermore, if something looks too good to be true, it probably is. But his words of wisdom, far from being heeded, had hardened her resolve: apparently, she was in love with Nobbs, and he with her, although, as Mr Green once remarked, if it had been a choice between Amanda and the Jaguar, it might have been a different story. Nevertheless, what was done was done, and they had given her away in good faith: the least they could expect now was "a return on their investment", as he put it; and it gave him no satisfaction seeing his forewarnings vindicated.

"Have you considered adopting?" asked her mother, helpfully.

"Mu-um, we've been through all that... we're both very busy people... we never have time to consider anything as complicated and time-consuming as that."

"I know, love, I know. Only what I meant was... sometimes, just the decision to adopt can trigger something in a woman's body that enables her to get pregnant... don't ask me why... hormones, I suppose. But, of course, the trouble with that is you could be letting someone down the last minute. It happened to someone I knew once. She couldn't... so she and her husband decided to adopt her sister's love-child... she'd been badly let down by, wait for it, 'a man of the cloth', and she wouldn't have been able to look after the child on her own, because she was the headmistress of the local church school. Anyway, everything had been arranged for the adoption when lo and behold, she got pregnant herself, and had to leave her sister in the lurch. Fortunately, the baby was fostered by a local well-to-do couple, and I believe the boy did very well, ending up as a barrister... and he's got a family of his own now!"

"Aw, that's a lovely story! Thank you, Mum, I'll bear it in mind! But the thing is, I don't think Rich would ever accept someone else's child. He's too proud. It's his or nothing with him, I'm afraid."

Amanda usually put up with her mother's *cris de coeur* good- humouredly, but on this occasion, they had struck a chord deep within her, and on her journey home she pondered hard on what her mother had said. She had also noticed recently one or two grey hairs lurking in her glossy dark mane, and whilst the incipient crow's feet added a hint of sultriness to her flawless face, they also reminded her that sixteen years had passed since that chance meeting at the estate agent's in Leigh. It also occurred to her that had they "got cracking" straightaway, as her mother had suggested, their child would now be about this Darren's age, and, who knows, could even be his friend – or girlfriend! (Rich had always said that no child of his would have to suffer as he had done in a grammar or independent school; but maybe that was just a political rant.)

As she was approaching the big roundabout outside Netherbridge, a madcap idea entered her head; but it was so bizarre that she dismissed it out of hand, just as she had dismissed those irrational impulses she used to have as a child to jump from a railway bridge on to a passing train, or step into the path of an oncoming car. But unlike those childhood impulses, this 'idea' refused to be dismissed. "Have you lost your mind?" she kept asking herself defiantly, "Don't you realise the consequences? You're still in love with your husband, for heaven's sake."

Neither she nor Rich had much time for conversation, he with his endless meetings, and she with business commitments far and wide. And even when they did manage a precious half-hour to themselves, the topic of "starting a family" never appeared on the agenda, not even as "any other business". However, even as recently as the previous summer, when he had taken her out to dinner at that new Italian restaurant in Warrington, he had suddenly said to her with a toothy smile, "Sweetheart, (he very rarely called her that these days) I was just thinking... somebody up there must like me. I've got the perfect wife... a beautiful home... a bob or two in the bank... and now my own school. Not bad, is it? But there's one aspiration still remaining. You've managed everything else for me, Mand... and knowing you, if it's meant to be, you'll manage that for me too... if we keep on doing... what comes naturally."

That was just over a year ago, and she had dissected that speech so often that she knew the words by heart. The speech sounded too much like a list of things *he* had wanted to achieve, so many boxes for *him* to tick... she herself being one of them, and the last one, a little matter of her producing an heir to inherit the benefits of all his other achievements. And if she failed, well, she would be nothing more than an ornament for him to show off on special occasions. His choice of the word 'aspiration' sounded a bit weird too in that context, unless, of course, it was the wine talking, which often made him sound pompous. She had looked the word "aspiration" up, and it said "hope or ambition of achieving something". There was something too impersonal about that for her: "hope" sounded vague and unemotional, and 'ambition", well, that was something you'd worked out in your head. The words she wanted to hear were "long for" or "love"... "I'd *love* to have a child"... not "aspire" to have one! And another thing, he could not even bring himself to say it in so many words: "if *it's* meant to happen". It was as if he wanted *it* to happen, but in the third person, as it were! And worst of all, he might only have said all this because of the pressures of expectation: (1) duty to his wife; (2) her mother's continual hints, albeit partly in jest; (3) convention; (4) fear of ridicule: soon, he would look more like a grandfather than a father pushing a pram around Netherbridge; (5) the greatest pressure of all: people might think (if they had not done so already) that he was – *incapable*. (6) Martin's teasing after a few cans of lager on the boat. Men!

AMANDA felt thoroughly refreshed after the surprise

sojourn she had arranged, and was pleased that Nobbs had enjoyed the change as much as she had, including her choice of venue, *The Old Bulls Head Inn* in Beaumaris, Anglesey. To please her, he had even agreed to go in the SS100, which he was reluctant to use these days because it had become more of an investment than a mode of transport. Of course, it was not as comfortable as the big Jaguar, but being red and noisy, she said it was more "sexy", and more in keeping with the destination and the occasion! Wherever they parked, a crowd of admirers would gather round, and when Amanda appeared, they clamoured for snap shots of her posing in it like some latter-day Elsa Martinelli on the Italian Riviera with her latest beau.

Nobbs had been unusually attentive day and night, and more unusually, had been quite happy to fit in with any of her wishes, even if it meant simply sitting near the little pier, gazing out over Traeth Lafan towards the hills behind Abergwyngregyn, with the soft swish of breaking wavelets and seagulls' plaintive cries as 'mood music'. One day, they did venture as far as Penmon to see the lighthouse and hear its famous bell, and on another explored the town itself, the Castle, the Old Court House and the Old Jail. Otherwise, they spent the whole time consciously doing nothing. As her father often said, "A lot to be said for doing nothing, my girl... all this rushing about isn't good for you." And Amanda was beginning to agree.

During breakfast on their last morning, the waiter asked them for their autographs, because it was rumoured that a film was to be made in the town, and two of the 'stars' were staying at *The Bull*!

Amanda would have loved a few days longer, but unfortunately, Nobbs had "things to do at school" before his trip to Milton Keynes. To avoid the early morning traffic, they had left Beaumaris early, but were only minutes into the journey when their idyllic holiday very nearly took a dramatic turn for the worse. Warming to the husky growl of his three and a half litre engine, and showing off his double-declutching and bend-straightening skills, Nobbs began to treat the narrow, twisting stretch of road just beyond Gallows Point like a race track, and was crossing the central white lines with careless abandon. Suddenly, a huge green tractor appeared, eliciting an ear-piercing scream from Amanda as Nobbs struggled to bring the powerful sports car back onto the correct side of the road. Fortunately, the tractor driver had anticipated the danger, and stopped his behemoth safely on his side of the white line. Alas, not so Nobbs. The SS100 eventually came to a screeching halt athwart the line, narrowly missing both the tractor's front wheel and the nearside stone wall.

Notwithstanding Amanda's protests and restraining arm, Nobbs leaped out of the car, and stood with his usual foul-mouthed tirade at the ready against all things Welsh, especially "subsidised Welsh farmers clogging up our beautiful country roads". Dreading an embarrassing scene, she tried to dissociate herself from the situation, but was pleasantly surprised to see a heroic-looking 'Cynddylan' climbing down from the elevated cab of his John Deere. He was even taller than Nobbs, about half his age, and sporting a lustrous mop of blond curls bouncing on massive, sun-kissed shoulders. As he got nearer, she could barely hide her amusement at the caption on his immaculate white T-shirt – *Twll din pob Sais*. Thanks to Martha, she knew exactly what that meant, and looked away when she sensed that he had twigged that she knew!

"You both okay there?" he said, "Dangerous road this, especially with the visitors. Anyway, nobody's hurt... that's the main thing. Take care now, and enjoy the rest of your journey. Nice motor, sir."

The young man spoke in such calm, mellifluous tones that Nobbs was utterly nonplussed, and did not open his mouth once. Indeed, he never said another word until they were approaching Llanfairfechan, which he tried to pronounce mockingly two or three times.

"Bloody hell, why they want to preserve this effing stupid lingo beats me. What use is it? Hardly anybody speaks it outside Wales. If they want tourists to come, they should make them feel welcome, and they could start by getting rid of all these stupid signs and names. Some of them don't even have vowels. Look at that one... *D-w-y-g-y-f-y-l-c-h-i* ...I ask you! How can any civilised person get his tongue round that? And when you hear the locals talking in a pub, they sound as if they're about to puke over each other... ha ha! It must be the ugliest sounding language ever invented. But what really gets my goat is they don't have the good manners to change into English when an Englishman enters the pub. When I first started coming here with my parents in the thirties, things were very different... they showed respect... even offered to carry your bag and such like. But they think they're as good as you are now. You'd have thought that living in such a pretty part of the country they wouldn't have become such an ill-mannered and mean little people.

"Martha wouldn't agree with you," replied Amanda

with remarkable restraint, "about the people, or the language,"

"Yea, well, she wouldn't, would she?" he said sarcastically. "Anyway, what did it say on that fellow's T-shirt?"

After that last remark she nearly told him, but then thought, what was the point?

"Wales for the Welsh," she lied tactfully.

"Typical! What *is* the matter with the buggers? They're all so bloody inward-looking. That's why they're backward. That Thomas poet was spot on."

"Dylan?"

"No, not the piss artist... the other one."

"R S?"

"Yes, that's the one... the vicar... ha ha. Can't be much of a vicar... they say he spends most of his time bird-watching... the feathered variety, I presume... though you never know with them vicars... ha ha. And the rest of the time, he's taking the piss out of the Welsh... let's see if I can remember that good line... yes, 'an impotent people, sick with inbreeding'... that about sums them up, Mand... and the funny thing, *he* was one of them... ha ha!"

"That tractor driver didn't look impotent!" said Amanda with a sly smile.

THE LANKY youth who turned up at *Elsinore* the following Monday, was just as Amanda had imagined: surly-looking, and clad *à la mode* in Motörhead T-shirt, Wrangler jeans, and Doc Marten boots. That he also bore a passing resemblance to the American actor, James Dean, her teenage idol, was a pleasant surprise.

"Oh, hello, Darren... bear with me a moment, while I

get the keys for the annexe."

If *she* was 'pleasantly surprised', poor Darren was dumbstruck. He had heard that Nobbs's missus was "a bit of alright, like", but he never expected this! Like most boys of his age, he spent hours drooling over enhanced pictures of Raquel Welsh or Joan Collins in *Playboy* magazine, but coming face to face with reality in all its splendour totally overwhelmed him, and she could sense his discomfiture. The circumstances did not help: with its being warm and muggy, and "his lordship" not around to make snide remarks, Amanda had taken a chance on one of her old, 1967 'summer of love' dresses. Darren looked at her open-mouthed, his eyes feasting on every visible (and invisible) inch of her... the face, the bosom, the well-proportioned thighs and calves. Gone in an instant his cheeky grin and haughty jut of the jaw; just a pitiable man-child now gazing helplessly at this indomitable force of nature. F------'ell, he thought, fancy waking up to that every morning!

"This way, Darren, please."

He came to with a start... that sultry voice again.

"The painting things are over there. I believe he's left you some overalls as well. He's told you what to do, hasn't he? But let's have some coffee first, shall we?"

Darren felt his heart miss a beat as he sat down on Nobbs's beloved *chaise longue*. He watched her every move, mesmerised... filling the kettle, reaching across for the coffee jar, one and half spoonfuls in each mug, and then reaching down for the milk from the fridge, revealing more than she had intended in the process.

"You couldn't get the biscuit tin down for me, please, sweetheart? I think Mr Nobbs keeps putting them up high to stop me getting fat!"

When he turned round, she was standing right up against him, and he was obliged to put his hand on her shoulder not to fall over as he sat down again. She loved the feel of his strong grip.

She smiled at him, and he returned the smile shyly.

She handed him his coffee, and sat down next to him, a little too close for comfort, he thought, her knee accidentally brushing his.

"Help yourself to sugar, Darren... and biscuits... plenty more in the cupboard."

Darren nodded, and shifted awkwardly in his seat.

Eventually, he plucked up courage to say something, but immediately wished he hadn't, because it didn't "come out right"... like a child trying to act grown-up, and sounding absurd.

"Nice little room, this, Mrs Nobbs."

She hadn't thought about what he should call her, but maybe "Mrs Nobbs" would do for now.

"Yes, it is very useful, especially when we've been gardening. The bathroom is through there... so, after you've finished, if you want, you can have a shower before going home."

He nodded seriously, striving to seem grown-up, despite feeling uncomfortably gauche, but the knee, which had mysteriously come to rest touching his, felt strangely reassuring now.

"It's good of you to come and do the fences, Darren," she said, patting him on the arm, "it's a great help, because we're very busy people. They need doing badly, and Mr Nobbs hasn't got the time any more."

Amanda could sense his embarrassment, recalling

524

when grown-ups tried to engage her in conversation when she was his age, and patronising her in the process. The last thing she wanted to do was to patronise him. But she felt she had to say something.

"Mr Nobbs tells me you'll be leaving school soon."

He nodded.

"And then you'll be looking for a job, I suppose. Any plans?"

"No, not really, no... I'd like to learn to drive... and then get my HGV licence. Me Dad wants me to join the Army. But me Mam says over her dead body, cos they send you straight to Northern Ireland, she says."

"I can tell who's boss in your house... and quite right too! Same here!

He smiled.

God, he's good-looking when he smiles, she thought, and nice teeth too. I'd better scarper soon before I say (or do) something I shouldn't!

"You'll be all right now, won't you, my love? I've got to pop to town this morning. You help yourself to more coffee and biscuits. I should be back by half-twelve, and then I'll make us something quick for lunch. Nice jeans... you mustn't get paint on them... so don't forget the overalls."

They smiled at each other again.

Darren was relieved to be left to his own devices for a while. He was confident "messing around" with girls of his own age, but this was completely different, and he hated himself for feeling so ill at ease. He noticed his hands were still shaking after she had left. It was more than he could bear, and he went at the painting straightaway with frenzied enthusiasm.

When she returned, it was nearly one o'clock, and she apologised for being late. Instead of cooking lunch, she had brought fish and chips and lemonade back from Fred Challinor's, and they sat by the fishpond to eat them, neither saying very much, only smiling at each other occasionally. It had occurred to her that the age-gap between Darren and her was not much greater than between her and Rich.

"Bloody 'ell, that's a big one!" exclaimed Darren.

"That reminds me... I didn't feed them this morning. Mr Nobbs usually does that."

"He's massive!"

"Moby? Yes, he *is* a big boy, isn't he?

"What kind is he?"

"I'm told he's a *koi carp*... but I know nothing about fish. Well, Darren, I'm afraid I've got to love and leave you again... another meeting... but I should be back by 4.30. Don't work too hard now... you've done a tremendous amount already."

As it turned out, she might as well have cancelled her meeting with the Planning Officer, because her mind was now preoccupied with a 'plan' of a different order, conceived on the M6 some four months earlier, and now developing into something of an *idée fixe*. The more she railed against its utter implausibility, the more persistent its pleas became. Phrases like "the cruel'st she alive", "leave the world no copy" and "barren as a brick" kept recurring, along with depressing images of middle-aged, unmarried schoolmistresses, making the best of things by forming 'couples' or jolly gaggles, as if to tell the world that they would have it no other way. Fancy being one of them! And how sad too for people like Taff and Liz

Jenkins... what wonderful parents they would have been. What if *she* became like them, past child-bearing age, and Rich hobbling into his sixth age, "his youthful hose / A world too wide for his shrunk shank". Didn't bear thinking about! In truth, Amanda was not thinking about anything very clearly, perhaps not thinking at all, as her heart did battle with her head, her primordial urges warring with her moral compass and common sense.

While driving back from the Planning meeting in Warrington, another image entered her head evoked by an event she had witnessed as a youngster. Despite her father's misgivings, her mother had given her full support. "It's a fact of life," she had said, "and she'll learn more about it there in five minutes than she'd ever learn from a book."

As it happened, Amanda did find the experience instructive, and exhilarating too, so much so that she wrote a story based on it for her next English homework at school.

A Memorable Event

I shall never forget the day when my best my friend, Marianne, invited me to witness something very special, something very beautiful even, although in some people's eyes something unsuitable for a girl of thirteen. But I am fortunate in having broad-minded parents.

Marianne had a ten-year old pony, called Anna, and her father had decided it would be good if she had a foal before she was too old. Accordingly, on the first Saturday in June, she was taken by horse-box to a neighbouring farm to meet the father-to-be of her foal, or as Marianne knowledgeably put it, "to be covered by Black Prince, a three-year-old Connemara stallion". I had no idea what to expect, but I would describe what I saw more like a short three-act dumb show than a commonplace event on a farm.

First of all, the leading lady, Anna, was ushered into what Marianne called the "breeding shed". Meanwhile outside, impatient snorting and neighing noises could be heard, growing louder and louder until at last the lead actor appeared, the Prince himself, imperious-looking and much larger than Anna. Arch-necked and haughty, he continued his barnstorming entrance, prancing to and fro and sideways, as if playing to the gallery.

After much grunting and sniffing of the air, his mood changed as he began to focus on the object of his attentions – Anna. He sidled up to her, rubbed heads with her, and nuzzled her affectionately for several seconds. She seemed to welcome his attentiveness and nuzzled him in return. Then, for some reason, he walked away as if having lost interest, until suddenly he turned and swished his tail vigorously, as if bracing himself for the next phase of the drama. He sniffed the air again, and adopted a more assertive stance. Without further ado, he approached Anna from behind and mounted her, performing, almost brutally, what Anna seemed to accept submissively.

After the intensity of this main act, the conclusion was an anti-climax: poor Prince dismounted lethargically, looking more like a deflated nag than the patriarch of a famous bloodline. As he was led out of the breeding shed, oblivious to all the plaudits showered on him, he looked almost crest-fallen, his exit markedly less

528

spirited than his entrance. Anna on the other hand
seemed to have a spring in her step!

I looked at Marianne, who had gone red in the face,
and we smiled at each other, somehow feeling we had
shared a life-enhancing experience, almost a rite of
passage, that would remain with us always, and cement
our friendship even more firmly.

When Amanda's English teacher returned essays, she usually spent a whole lesson highlighting their main features, good and bad, but on that occasion, she handed them back without any comment. However, much to Amanda's relief, she had been given her a creditable A-, with the accompanying comment, *Interesting approach to an unusual subject!* Not unexpectedly, Amanda valued the exclamation mark as much as the grade.

BY THE time Amanda arrived back at *Elsinore*, her head still reeling, it was fast approaching five o'clock, and as she got out of her car, she could see Darren still busy painting at the far end of the garden.

She waved to him, and beckoned him to come in.

"You've done enough for today, Darren... all work and no play makes Jack a dull boy! I'll make us something quick in the microwave, while you get yourself you cleaned up. You know where the bathroom is. If you need anything, give me a shout on the intercom.

Amanda disappeared into the main house while Darren removed his sweaty overall and disappeared into the Nobbs's "inner sanctum". He had indeed worked very hard, and had been looking forward to a shower and something to eat for some time.

When the intercom buzzer sounded, Amanda wondered if there was a problem, and went to investigate. Meanwhile, she had freshened herself up a little, and made herself presentable, as she called reapplying her lipstick.

"Everything okay in there?" she called.

"Yes, ta, Mrs Nobbs... except there's no towel!"

"Oh, I am sorry... I must have forgotten... wait a sec. There you are, sweetheart."

As she passed him the towel, she accidentally touched his back.

"Let *me* dry you," she said, and did not wait for an answer. She had never seen a young naked man before. She could feel his ribs through the towel, and loved his gaunt physique. Rich was never this thin, she thought. Enjoy your thinness, my boy, before time and life's excesses take their toll.

She handed him the towel again, and could not resist sliding her arms underneath his armpits, and drawing him towards her, with her head nestling between his shoulder blades. When he had finished drying his front half and secured the towel firmly around his waist, he turned to face her, and kissed her gently on her forehead. Flattered and enthralled by her prepossessing charms and seductiveness, he cupped her face in his big, bony hands, as if to savour every finely chiselled feature of it. Then, stroking her glossy tresses gently with the back of his hand, he gazed into her riveting hazel eyes, and said, "God, you're *beautiful*!" Those three simple words from this shy boy, unschooled in the dark arts of disingenuous compliments, about *her*, a woman old enough to be his mother, rendered her speechless. Never before had she heard them uttered with such sincerity, intensity and – heaven forbid – *love*. Who could resist him? She responded the only way she knew how, with a passionate kiss on his mouth and a rib-crushing hug. Then, still clinging on to him, she led him out of the shower compartment towards the *chaise longue*, and they collapsed on to it in a tight embrace.

Having now wilfully triggered an inexorable chain reaction, Amanda was obliged to let Nature take its course, and submit, like Anna all those years ago, to the unbridled exertions of a novice. In the event, what Darren lacked in *savoir-faire* and adroitness, he compensated for with vigour and earnestness. Like the Connemara stallion, he was quick and efficient – whether he was effective too, she thought, only time would tell. The deed itself was just as she had wanted it to be, a necessary biological procedure with a handsome youth, almost a 'lie back and think of England' affair. She did not allow herself to become emotionally involved in the *act*, merely infatuated with the *actor*, nothing more; not so much making love, therefore, as making a "copy".

When he had finished, Darren stood up and started dressing, struggling to avert his eyes from Amanda's semi-nudity.

"You're not going already? I was going to make us something to eat."

"No, I'd... I'd better go, Mrs Nobbs. You see... me Mam... she'll be wondering where I am."

"You can phone her, if you like, and tell her you're having your tea here!" said Amanda with a smile.

"You don't know my Mam... she'd *kill* me if she knew... about this."

"I don't think she'd be very pleased with me either!"

"What about Mr Nobbs?"

"Don't *you* worry about Mr Nobbs."

"No, I mean, what if he finds out."

"Why, are you going to tell him?"

At last he managed a weak smile, but said, "I think I'd better push off now, any roads, Mrs Nobbs... thanks all the same."

"Well, it's up to you."

"I'll come and finish the fence tomorrow morning, then."

"Yes, please... and I've got no meetings tomorrow. Take care, love. See you in the morning."

He picked up his bike, straddling it as he did so, and pedalled up the drive as if his life did depend on it, although he managed a backwards glance and a cursory wave before entering the road.

AMANDA returned to the annexe feeling a little disappointed, and began tidying up and removing all traces of the afternoon's activities in case the cleaner found anything suspicious in the morning – or worse, Nobbs returned unexpectedly. Unlikely though that was, she could not resist dallying with the idea, and even imagined being caught *in flagrante*, before quickly chiding herself for harbouring such crazy thoughts.

Be that as it may, after tea, she began mulling over the day's events, her mood darkening as the evening wore on. If only Martha were here, she thought. But she was in Aberdyfi seeing to her boat, and that being so, Amanda did what she often did when she had things on her mind, she went to bed early with a book in the hope that a good night's sleep would remedy most of her concerns.

As usual, when the big clock in the hall struck eleven, she marked her page and switched off her bedside light, trusting that Morpheus would do the honours and whisk her off to oblivion quickly. Alas, it was not to be. All too soon, the clock struck midnight... and then one o'clock, with still no sign of sleep. In desperation, she got up, looked out of the window, went to the bathroom, and returned to bed, but although physically tired, her brain was more active than ever. Having now abandoned the idea of sleep, she involuntarily began going over the previous day's events in her head like an episode in a novel, except that any self-respecting novelist would have dismissed it as too far-fetched. But far-fetched or not, it assuredly did happen, and both Darren's life and *hers* would never be the same again.

Whilst the act itself, she thought, had been largely functional for both of them, its consequences would be far-reaching. By having his way with her, Darren had crossed a developmental Rubicon, and perforce been catapulted into the world of adults, where responsibilities are meant to trump privileges. Thus, arguably, she had only accelerated his emotional development, and indeed one day he might thank her for having done so!

She, too, had entered new territory, albeit one of her own making, but she felt partly vindicated, because at last she had done something about her abiding dread of childlessness, although her actions, whatever the result, might well have created more problems than they sought to solve. Apart from satisfying her need to procreate (and test her father's theory!) she might also give her parents their long-awaited "return on their investment". But ironically, she chuckled to herself, perhaps the most grateful beneficiary might be Rich himself, who was desperate for an heir to his burgeoning fortune, to say nothing of tangible 'proof' that he was still – capable!

But as the 'witching hour' drew near, the elation of a possible 'happy outcome' became shrouded by an awareness of her guilt and moral responsibilities. After all, had she not been the prime mover in a sordid act of betrayal – arguably the ultimate betrayal? Furthermore, and perhaps more reprehensibly, had she not compounded her transgression by engaging in an illicit act with an underage boy? On the other hand, however, she thought, it was not done purely out of self-interest, and certainly not for physical gratification. Yes, she had seduced him... but he had been a willing collaborator. At no stage had she coerced him... merely set the process in motion, encouraged him perhaps, and smoothed the way.

But the potential implications were sobering and needed careful consideration. There was no telling, for instance, what psychological or other effects the experience might have on the boy. Yet, he seemed resilient enough – unlikely to be 'damaged', as social workers would have you believe. On the contrary, he might even have been enriched by it: what doesn't kill you makes you stronger!

By the same token, she could feasibly find herself a victim of blackmail. He (or his parents), knowing her financial circumstances, could demand money or other favours. She would have to have her answers ready, and at the very worst, especially if the parents were involved, she could counteract with an accusation of rape. But that scenario was unlikely and barely worth thinking about.

Of course, the poor boy could succumb to the psychological pressure of his situation, and inadvertently divulge their secret, or even confide in a friend, or even his School Counsellor. What effect might that have on her, her husband, her parents, and her friends? Well, her 'catch-all' defence would have to be a categorical denial, and trust that all parties, including the courts, would prefer the respectable headmaster's wife's version of events to "the preposterous fantasy of an impressionable adolescent". And should her "madcap plan" turn out well, it would be accredited to the romantic properties of *Ye old Bulls Head Inn* and the bracing air from the Menai Straits!

There were many other considerations, of course, not least the legal aspects of the situation. But it had been a long and busy day, and matters like divorce, custody, access, paternity could wait until Martha returned.

After such an intense period of self-questioning and speculation, she took another quick look out of her bedroom window. She was rarely awake at that hour and was surprised how exotic her garden looked at dawn. It reminded her of her English teacher telling the class the reason Shakespeare depicted the muted shades of daybreak so vividly in the first scene of *Hamlet* was that his audience would very likely have been bathed in afternoon sunlight, or pouring rain: "But look, the morn, in russet mantle clad / Walks o'er the dew of yon high eastward hill," she enunciated, and thought, happily there's no ghost in *Elsinore* tonight! She also noticed, with a little pang of pathos, where Darren had left off painting, which suddenly reminded her that he would be back before she had turned round. Eventually, Morpheus did grant her request, and remained with her until the unnatural bleep of the digital watch, which Rich had bought her for her thirty-fifth birthday, woke her at 7.45 am.

The restless night notwithstanding, the new day brought her fresh hope bordering on euphoria. She felt physically good too. She could not quite put her finger on it, except that she felt pleasantly relaxed and could readily have slept till midday.

She missed her early morning cup of tea when Nobbs was away, but strangely this morning the mere thought of it, let alone its taste and smell, turned her stomach. Strangely too, she found herself reaching for the milk bottle in the fridge and pouring a large glassful, and would have drunk a second had the doorbell not rung.

"Oh, come in, Darren, you've caught me on the hop... didn't sleep very well last night. How are you?"

"I'm okay, thank you, Mrs Nobbs. I'll crack on, if you don't mind, and get it finished. I've got to help me Dad this avvy"

"Yes, yes, of course. I'll get the keys for you."

Darren had not slept very much either, which explained why he was so early.

"You sure you won't have a coffee first?"

"No, you're all right, thank you, Mrs Nobbs."

"Perhaps later, then... my friend keeps telling me *I* should cut down too. So, I've decided to try drinking milk instead for a bit."

Darren wrinkled his nose, and smiled sympathetically.

God, she thought, that one will have all the ladies of Netherbridge chasing after him before the year is out.

EPILOGUE

15 March 1978 Taff Jenkins passed away peacefully in his sleep.

1 May 1978 Amanda gave birth to a baby boy weighing 8lbs 10 oz. Nobbs was thrilled that she had finally provided him with his long-awaited son, and arranged a reception at *Elsinore* for his staff and the governors. During the evening, after two or three glasses of champagne, Phil plucked up courage to approach the proud father.

"Congratulations," said Phil, shaking Nobbs's hand, "you must be very proud."

"Certainly am, Phil," replied Nobbs, "we've waited a long time, but there you go, all things come to them as wait. And time's not on your side either, mate... do you want your kids to remember you with hair or without? Ha ha! Take her away for a little holiday somewhere nice and quiet... you never know your luck. There's nothing like reproducing your own flesh and blood, Phil... believe you me."

"Anyway, I'm very pleased for you both," replied Phil, "I've already had a chat with Amanda. She's looking very well. Unfortunately, Shirley couldn't make it this evening... she's working late, but she sends her love, and will call to see the baby soon."

August 1978 Dennis Peterson retired, and John Shufflebottom replaced him as head of the 'A' Block.

September 1978 Ellis Williams (Aberdyfi) passed away, the last of the six important men in Martha's life. Unfortunately, she was unable to attend the funeral because she had to take Liz to see an oncologist at Christies Hospital in Manchester.

December 1978 Nobbs took delivery of his much-heralded bus, and appointed Brian Smiley as its official driver on a head of department Scale 4, the highest-paid bus-driver in the north-west, as one cynical wag remarked. Apparently, before training to be a teacher, he had been a coach-driver for Bournemouth Corporation Buses.

August 1980 Martha retired, and continued living with Liz Jenkins, but made frequent trips to Aberdyfi, occasionally accompanied by Liz.

August 1980 Frank Fairclough retired, having accepted Nobbs's 'magnanimous' offer of ten years' pension enhancement! The following month he married his lovely long-term girl-friend, and emigrated to New Zealand, settling in Omahuru, a small seaside town on the southern tip of South Island. Thereafter, they spent their time exploring the natural beauty of New Zealand on his new Honda Goldwing, and also went on trips across the Americas and parts of Asia. Every summer he returned home to Leigh to see his elderly mother, and a few friends, especially Martha and Phil Evans; but he never set foot in the School again.

NOBBS'S LIFE was now complete: "the perfect wife, the top job, a few bob in the bank, the dream house", and now the son and heir on whom he doted. As soon as he arrived home from school, before taking his coat off, he would rush up to the nursery and pick up the baby even if he was asleep. Of course, Amanda was delighted, and not a little surprised at what a devoted father he had turned out to be. Furthermore, it was not just a father's infatuation with his firstborn either; his devotion never wavered as the baby grew into a demanding and troublesome toddler. Amanda could not believe her good fortune, and felt more confident with each passing day that her husband, the world, and even she herself truly believed in the invigorating effects of the breezes off the Menai Straits!

1 May 1981 was Edward's third birthday, and as Nobbs drove to school that Friday morning, he felt truly blessed, and was so looking forward to the three of them going to Chester Zoo the next day. When Peg (now the Senior Administrative Officer) brought in the mail, he was in such high spirits that he gave her a good hug and a kiss. Among the official letters, there was a personal one with just "MR NOBBS" scrawled in block capitals on the envelope. Inside he found a cheap birthday card with a mysterious message, "YOURE FENSES NEED DOING AGAIN". He put the card in his pocket, and tried to concentrate on the business of the day, but kept taking it out to see if he could deduce what the message meant.

At 11 o' clock he went across to Peg's office and told her that he was going home early because he could concentrate better there, and besides it was his son's birthday and he wanted to help Amanda with the party.

Later that evening when all the children had gone home and their son was asleep, he took the card nervously out of his pocket and showed it to Amanda. At first, she was as mystified as he was, until she sensed its potential significance.

"Oh, I expect it is some unemployed lad wanting to earn some extra pocket money, and noticed our fences needed doing. I should ignore it unless it happens again, then you must go to the police."

"Yes, you're probably right, Mand," said Nobbs, although not altogether convinced.

The Chester Zoo trip was a delight, with Nobbs re-living his own third birthday trip there, which he could barely remember except for a baby elephant urinating profusely in front of a crowd of shrieking children. By Monday morning he had forgotten about the mysterious fence-painter, and after hugging his firstborn tightly, he set off for school feeling very pleased with his world. He arrived at the same time as Fred, and as he approached his office door, he noticed that someone had written the letters "COOKOLE" on his name plate. At first, this made as much sense to him as the message about the fences, and he asked Fred to clean it off immediately.

When he had a spare moment he looked up the word "cookole" in a dictionary to find that no such word existed, unless of course it was a misspelling of "cuckold" – the husband of an unfaithful wife.

WHEN AMANDA had consulted Martha originally about the possibility of being confronted by her husband, Martha had advised her to adhere to her original version of events, that it was simply a schoolboy's fantasy, and that nothing had happened between her and Darren that day. That way, it would be kinder to the child, to her husband, and perhaps most of all to Darren, whose life otherwise might well be blighted.

For three happy years, she had had no cause to articulate this lie, but on the Monday after the Chester Zoo trip, Nobbs arrived home in an agitated state, so agitated that he only gave his little boy a perfunctory caress.

"I've had another effing message today, Mand," he said, "the b-----d who wrote the note about the fences has now written a misspelt word on my office door, 'c-o-o-k-o-l-e'…it's the same felt pen and the same handwriting. It must be somebody who's got it in for me. I think what he meant to write was 'cuckold', which means the husband of an unfaithful wife. What do you make of it?"

"I agree, it must be some malicious individual bearing a grudge… probably because you told them off or something several years ago and wants to get his revenge."

Amanda had long believed that this situation would never happen. And Darren did not seem the kind of boy who would bear a grudge, and anyway he had had a good relationship with her husband, and apparently was doing well now as a long-distance lorry driver. But the combination of 'fences' and 'cuckold' did sound ominous.

"Well, if you're the cuckold, I'm the unfaithful wife… and I am telling you now, Rich, I've never been unfaithful."

"That's a relief, anyway…not that I had any doubts, of course, ha ha!"

"No, it's just malicious gossip, Rich, there are lots of jealous people about, and they see us, living in this grand house, as having it all. I'm surprised it hasn't happened before, to be honest."

For all Amanda's reassurance, Nobbs did not sleep that night. Yes, he certainly had made enemies during his time, and yes, there were plenty of people in Netherbridge who were jealous of his success, especially so now that in his late fifties he had been blessed with a beautiful son. But was Mandy just saying all this to spare his feelings? What if she had been unfaithful? Could he forgive her? But, of course, she hadn't been unfaithful, because she told him so… and everyone, including Martha, said how much the boy looked like him.

Amanda had not slept much either having wrestled all night with her dilemma, should she persist in the lie, albeit with good intentions – or confess.

Nobbs got up at about 7 o' clock and rang Peg to say that he was working at home for the rest of the week. He brought Amanda's cup of tea up as usual and then went to the nursery to see Edward, who had woken early and was playing happily with the wooden car garage that Martha had given him for his birthday.

Nobbs then returned to Amanda's room and complained that he had been awake all night and was in no fit state to go to work.

"These effing messages, Mand, they're getting to me. There must be a link, 'painting fences' and 'cuckold'…I assume it's a misspelling…and I need some answers."

Amanda's heart sank. Lying had never been her forte. When as a little girl she had tried to deceive her mother about some minor misdoing, her facial expression had always let her down and she had long learnt that lying was not only wrong but unwise. Besides, one day Edward would need to know who he was, and would also need answers.

Nobbs cooked Amanda's favourite breakfast, kippers, and they ate quietly together until Amanda broke the silence. "Sweetheart, you know I love you very much, don't you, always have done, always will. I've tried hard to provide us with a child, and I thought a change of air might do the trick... hence the Anglesey trip...and indeed quite possibly did".

"What do you mean 'possibly'?"

"Well, that day you sent Darren Gentle round to do the fences..."

"Yes, yes, I get the message...spare me the details. I can imagine one thing leading to another. But that doesn't mean little Edward isn't mine, does it?"

"No, of course not," said Amanda, and burst into tears. "I'm sorry", she said through her sobs,

"I'm so sorry." Amanda was so relieved at her husband's response that she walked round the table and put her arms round his neck and rested her cheek on his head.

"Thank you, sweetheart, thank you for giving us such a beautiful son."

At this point, little Edward rushed into the kitchen demanding to be picked, which Nobbs did willingly. "You're Daddy's boy, aren't you?"

The boy giggled and put his arms round his father's neck.

"Listen, Mand we'll have to move...we can't stay in Netherbridge. If this gets out, it will be intolerable. For all

I know, it may be out already. I'll hand in my notice, put *Elsinore* on the market, and we'll move to… Kyle of Lochalsh! I'll go to see Martin this morning and tell him I'm retiring to make room for a younger man. I've got enough years in, counting my war service."

After washing and shaving, he dressed quickly and rushed off in the Jaguar, with no particular destination in mind. First, he drove up the M6 as far as Preston, then across country to Balderstone, Salesbury and Whalley. Shortly after passing Whalley, he was caught behind a slow-moving furniture removal van. Losing patience, he took a chance and overtook on what looked like a straight stretch of road, but he had not seen the car in front of the furniture van, and was unable to avoid a head on collision with an oil tanker coming in the opposite direction. Two ambulances and three police cars arrived quickly, but Nobbs was pronounced dead at the scene.

7 June 1982 Liz Jenkins passed away after a long illness. Martha had nursed her diligently throughout and was at her bedside when she died at home.

Martha continued living in her little cottage, but spent most of the summer months in Aunt Hilda's house in Aberdyfi, which she had converted into three flats, two of which she rented out.

August 1996 Amanda had remained in *Elsinore* after her husband's death, and watched Edward grow into a tall and handsome young man, "like a Greek God", as Martha put it.

After he had done his 'A' Levels at Netherbridge High School, he decided to settle the question of his paternity which had troubled him ever since he had heard rumours at school. His mother was very apprehensive, but the boy was eighteen and did not need permission. In the event, the result provided "extremely strong support in favour" of Nobbs's paternity.

Amanda had appointed a full-time manager to run the business until Edward had completed his law degree, after which he took over. They both continued living in *Elsinore*, although Amanda spent more and more time with Martha in Aberdyfi.

BY THE SAME AUTHOR

A Montgomeryshire Youth
Compton Books, 2000

Llanbrynmair in the Twentieth Century, Llanbrynmair
Local History Society, 2005
(Editor: Marian Rees; Translator:
Alun D W Owen)

Printed in Great Britain
by Amazon

79172143R10318